Ilona Bannister was a dual qualified US attorney
and UK immigration solicitor before she started
writing fiction. Her first novel, *When I Ran Away*,
was developed on Faber Academy's Work in
Progress course. Ilona's experiences as a mother,
lawyer, and an American transplant in Britain
are reflected in her novels. Although she will
always be a New Yorker at heart, Ilona's home is
in London with her husband and young sons.

Ilona Bannister

Little Prisons

First published in Great Britain in 2022 by Two Roads
An imprint of John Murray Press
An Hachette UK company

This paperback edition published in 2023

1

A CIP catalogue record for this title is available from the British Library

B format ISBN 9781529353921
eBook ISBN 9781529353938

Typeset in Sabon MT by Hewer Text UK Ltd, Edinburgh
Printed and bound in Great Britain by Clays Ltd, Elcograf S.p.A.

John Murray policy is to use papers that are natural, renewable
and recyclable products and made from wood grown in sustainable
forests. The logging and manufacturing processes are expected to
conform to the environmental regulations of the country of origin.

Two Roads
Carmelite House
50 Victoria Embankment
London EC4Y 0DZ

www.tworoadsbooks.com

For those who did not survive. And for those who did.

PROLOGUE

2017

On one side of Bedford Road, an empty lot borders the pillar of the disused railway bridge which Overground trains no longer traverse. It is an undisturbed patch of wild in the London landscape, where the weeds and lone sapling that grow out of the concrete collect the kind of human detritus that suggests middle-of-the-night violence and tawdry under-the-train-tracks activity: a single football shoe; an overturned traffic cone; a soggy notebook; a child's sock; one half of a broken scissor; an empty bottle of supermarket gin. An invisible space that most people do not see when they walk by, consumed with their phones and getting to work on time. Although once in a while, if they drop their keys or need to tie a shoelace and they stop on the pavement bordering the lot, they look up and wonder what kind of personal calamity could have caused one sleeve of a red leather jacket to end up here, wrapped around a crushed plastic bottle of bleach.

When the building next to the lot is gutted in the fire, no one is hurt, except for the lady who dies. The new owner of the empty lot and the burnt-out building learns of her death as he twists the gold band on the ring finger of his left hand in a way that is the opposite of nervous. He understands that death is often the collateral damage of business. But despite the ease with violence that he wears under his Savile Row tailoring, he is not without compassion. He offers the dead woman's sister, with whom she had lived for many years, a studio flat on the third floor of the new building that he erects next to the railway bridge. Through his agent he offers a very reduced rent, astonishingly low for the area and the quality of the new flats, and the old woman accepts it, despite having to climb an additional flight of stairs to reach her new home, where she will now live alone.

The building is hurriedly built and shabbily constructed, but inside the flats are clean, functional and modern, fitted with cheap but nice-looking stainless steel appliances, bathrooms with glass shower doors that do not quite meet each other when closed, and shiny, plastic, granite-effect countertops. Three floors, three flats per floor. Two flats, A and B, on one side of a central corridor. They each have windows overlooking the old railway tracks along one wall. Each A is a two-bed flat, with a window in the kitchen that looks out on a small patch of struggling grass at the back of the building. Next door to each A is B, a studio flat, with a window facing Bedford Road. Across the corridor from the two-beds and studios there are larger flats, the Cs. The Cs have three bedrooms. The master bedroom in each has an en suite bathroom, and there is a large family bathroom across from the modern, open-plan kitchen/dining/living room. The absence of walls is meant to convey a sense of space, but, somehow, does not.

Lives are lived in buildings like this one, but no one notices. The tenants go to work. They come home. They do not ask questions about their neighbours. They do not want to get involved. They do not inquire about the jobs, the children, the tragedies or the triumphs of the people in the flat next door. They see each other only in passing in the corridor. They do not look at one another. It is not polite to meet each other's eyes.

And so, the tenants do not realise that the owner of the building lives with his family on the second floor, in flats 2A and 2B. He knocked down the walls between the flats to make a large apartment. The tenants do not notice that different people come in and out of flat 2C and that there is no regular occupant there. The people in this building do not visit the second floor because they do not live there, so they do not see anything unusual, and even if they did, they would pretend not to. When something breaks, they call the property manager and he deals with it. That is all the tenants know about the building – the mobile number of the property manager – and that is enough.

The lift is the first thing to malfunction in the new building. When it does work, it is the sort of lift that takes so long to arrive at its destined floor that the tenants opt to take the stairs instead. And so, the wide concrete and metal staircase with open railings, connecting the floors to each other at the end of every corridor, becomes a hub of tenant activity, where the echoes of their footsteps and voices reverberate loudly against the walls. Although everyone can hear everything that happens on the staircase, they pretend not to. The tenants use the lift when it works. They use the stairs when it does not. They use the stairs so much they become used to them and forget there is a lift.

The walls are painted magnolia, new and unstained by the decades of damp and hardship and dirt and acrid air of the Big Smoke that were baked into the old walls of the building that stood here before. The new walls are thin, and corners were cut on the insulation. The tenants do not enjoy the privacy that many layers of paint and wallpaper, solid wood and brick and mortar, asbestos batting to deter the draughts and steel wool stuffed in the cracks to deter the mice, had provided the people who had lived in the old building, before it turned to ash. But the fact of people living here is only incidental. It is not the new building's main purpose. Rent collection is not the owner's main intention.

As the new building goes up, clean and gleaming, a strong but inaudible wave of fear and discontent ripples through the other buildings and their inhabitants on Bedford Road. The fear is of change. And the discontent is with the dirty windows and fading canopies and general shabbiness that the shopkeepers and flat dwellers had not noticed in their shops and flats until the new building – with its steel and glass and yellow brick and rounded box hedges in planters – makes them feel resentful and embarrassed and poor all at once. But the residents agree, implicitly, that they are happy to be rid of the empty lot, at least, which used to make them feel all the same feelings that the new building does.

An old man stands in front of the empty Bedford Road playground across the street from the new building. It is home to a giant dome climbing frame and other ageing equipment painted the municipal green of hospital corridors and police stations. The old man surveys the street looking for the empty lot. He liked to have a poke around in it sometimes. He once found a five-pound note there that was torn in the middle which he traded in at the bank for a new one.

But the lot is gone.

He leans on his walking stick and notes the disappearance of Diamond's Wash and Dry, the old laundrette, and its replacement with First Premier Dry Cleaner and Laundry on the ground floor of the new building. He looks at the three storeys of flats that rise above it. He is positive he has taken a wrong turn and that this cannot be Bedford Road, except that Baxter's, the Black men's barber shop next door to Diamond's, is still there, the top right corner of its sign slightly melted from the fire. All the other buildings are still there, with their sagging, crooked two storeys of flats above their shops.

Adjacent to Baxter's is the newsagent, shelves heaving from floor to ceiling, the one run by those Indians or Muslims or whatever they were that he didn't like. Then there is the Poland Association, a building that no one seems to ever enter or leave but which always features colourful flyers advertising Polish events in the window. Next to this is Justin's Noodle Place, an aged café that serves instant coffee and full English breakfast any time of day, in addition to any kind of noodle you could want, although the old man doesn't mess about with foreign food and only orders the Nescafé. Finally, on the

4

corner, there is Dirty Betty's, a restaurant furnished with old wooden desk chairs and church pews that charges six pound fifty for toasted sourdough because it is baked in Brixton. He went in there once for a cup of tea when Justin's was closed. It was served to him on chipped crockery printed with the gold emblem of an old hotel. 'The Excelsior', the faded gold script on the saucer proclaimed. The old man left without drinking the tea or paying for it. 'Excelsior, my arse,' he'd said. The cheek of it.

He knows he's been ill, and then there was the stretch of bad weather, and then Lavinia, his downstairs neighbour, was taken to a home, and there were new tenants who moved into her place whom he had to watch carefully until he was sure they could be trusted. So he hasn't been to Bedford Road for quite some time, but has it been *that* long? He looks at the new building while he decides whether to go to Justin's to have a coffee and think about how things never stay the same, or to go to the Sainsbury's car park to have a look-see at the overflowing Oxfam donation bins.

He notices a woman in a dressing gown in a first-floor window of the new building, looking out at the street. When she sees him she lowers her blind abruptly. Then a red-faced, stout woman with wet, curly hair hurries out of the heavy glass and steel door, an open, drooping bag hanging off one shoulder, pulling her blouse and jacket askew, as she barks into a mobile phone, two sullen children reluctantly following her. He wonders at the state of women today and remembers his Doris. And his mother. They were proper women, not like this lot.

He decides he'll go to the café after all; maybe that foreign lady, Justin's wife, can tell him about what happened here and when the building went up. He crosses the road to go to the café and have a quick look in the window of the new laundry and dry cleaner that's replaced Diamond's. A young woman sweeps the floor inside and is startled by the old man's face as he presses it up against the window, peering at her, as he does most mornings. He knocks his cane against the window like he always does. She looks down and goes back to her sweeping. She is thinking about the red-faced woman and her children who had passed by the window a moment before. They live on the floor below the young woman and the family she works for and her red-faced voice is familiar. She thinks about how her voice yelling into the phone had penetrated the shop window. The young woman wishes she had such a voice. She thinks that if she could speak with such a voice, her life would be different.

The woman in flat 1B on the first floor of the new building, still in her dressing gown, peers around the side of her blind to see if the old man has finally crossed the road before she raises it again. He is there almost every morning, in front of the playground leaning on his cane. If he's gone then it must be half past eight. She opens her window and leans out and confirms that the red-faced woman, her neighbour, from flat 1C across the hall, has just gone into Justin's. The woman pulls her dressing gown tighter about her waist. She clips one side of her hair back with a child's barrette, white metal with a red plastic heart. She begins her day. As she prepares breakfast, she hears a clanging in the hall. She puts her ear to her door but does not open it. The clanging stops. She exhales.

She sits down to eat a plain Warburton's thin bagel, thin so that it can fit in a toaster and provide fewer calories while still giving the consumer a bagel-like experience. She sips her tea. She exhales. She hears the rolling, tartan shopping trolley belonging to the old woman from the third-floor studio flat, 3B, bump down the stairs twelve times as she reaches the first floor, and then twelve more times down to the lobby. She listens for evenness in all twenty-four bumps to make sure that the old lady hasn't fallen or lost her cart down the stairs. She can hear everything in this building.

6

At the café, Mali, Justin's wife, gives the red-faced woman her large takeaway coffee, three sugars, extra milk, and two bacon baps for her children. Then she brings the old man his hot drink and tells him again, as she does a few times a week, that the building has been up for about a year, and yes, it was very fast, and yes, nothing ever does stay the same. The old Black lady in her lavender church hat with her rolling tartan shopping trolley comes in and asks whether she can leave some literature about the Good News and Jehovah's Kingdom on the ledge by the door. Mali does not have the heart to say no. Since Justin died she hasn't had the heart for many things. When the old man is ready to leave, she helps him count out his change. She only charges him thirty pence. It is the sort of thing Justin would have done.

The old man leaves Justin's and makes his way back down Bedford Road. The young woman in the laundrette has finished sweeping and is now pressing shirts in the back of the shop. The woman in the dressing gown moves a small table to the window and begins to write on her laptop. The old man walks to the corner of the new building, near the tenants' steel and glass entrance, and looks for the empty lot that used to be there.

Justin's is empty, rush hour now over. Mali clears the tables, collects the newspapers, puts the Jehovah's Witness brochures in the bin. She thinks about how the rhythm of your life is other people. People you live with side by side, whose lavender hats and coffee preferences and walking sticks become the intimate details of your life, mundane markers of every hour. She thinks about how your life is just a part of someone else's habit, and yours of theirs. Just a step in someone else's routine. A series of little shuffles, they move around you and you around them. They exhale and you inhale their air. They inhale the air you exhale. It can't be helped. All the air's already been breathed.

Part One

January 2020

I

Friday

Penny
Flat 1B

'Jamie, I left the baby on the train. You had better go and find her. She must be nearly at Camden by now.' That's what I said to Jamie the day I came home without the baby.

'Oh, I see, I'd better go find her then,' he said, with mock disbelief and a half-smile as he walked past me into the foyer, thinking I had left her there in the buggy, her little chubby hands over her eyes, hiding from him. She was still small enough to believe that if she covered her own eyes that no one else could see her. It was a game we played. They played. I was never any good at the games.

'Penny?' His voice changed when he saw that she wasn't hiding. When he saw that she wasn't there at all. 'Penny? Where's the buggy? Where's Olivia?'

'She's on the Tube, Jamie. I left her on the train.'

That was the start of all this, and the end of us.

Carla
Flat 1A

'. . . *and the end of us*.'

I look at the wall. Jesus Christ, what a wackadoo. Talking to her imaginary friends again. I wrap my hands around my hot coffee cup, feel the burn on my palms.

Deep breath in and, 'Daniel, Mary Rose? You gotta get up!' I shout over my shoulder, but it's useless. In a minute I'll leave this table and my coffee, and go to their rooms, and knock on the doors, and ruffle the covers, and plead, and request, and cajole, and then that won't work, so I'll shout and yell, and then we'll all be in bad moods, and then we'll all be late. Like every morning, of every day. And now here goes her kettle. That's the third time since six this morning. *Whistle, whistle, whistle.*

I sip the coffee. It scalds my tongue. Who needs a kettle that whistles? Her apartment is, like, eight feet by eight feet, and she needs to be alerted that the water is boiling by whistle? What, because it's the Industrial Revolution and the fucking whistle was just invented? I swear to God, as soon as I can get us out of this building, as soon as I work this shit out with Tom, I am getting us the fuck out of here.

Deep breath in. 'Daniel, Mary Rose! You gotta go to school. GET UP!' I shout, my eyes still half closed, my palms burning and then—

'Mary Rose!' I jump, coffee spills, she flies across the room, whirlwind of hair and oversized T-shirt. She gets up on the table and pounds on the wall, *boom-boom-boom.*

The whistling stops.

She looks at me, breathless, fists resting on the wallpaper.

'Couldn't you hear that? Why don't you ever do anything? You *never* do *anything* for us,' she says, her accent clipping her words, sharpening them to hurt me. She rages back to her room and slams the door. She doesn't realise she sounds like me, just with a British accent. She doesn't hear how our voices are the same. Or maybe she does. And she hates that too.

Woman
Flat 2A–2B

The pounding of a fist three times. I jump. Then stay very still. Blood rushing in my ears. A moment to be sure that it was not in this flat. That it was not Sir or Master. I hold my breath and listen. It was the people below. The woman below and her daughter who shout and pound their fists.

With shaking hands, I press the buttons on the phone, too afraid to remember the numbers in the right order. The first time I'm wrong, there is only a tone, then a recording in a language I do not know. I look over my shoulder. I am still alone. I do not have time for mistakes. I try again. It rings, my heart in my mouth, and then, her voice.

I say, 'Mother, is it you?'

'Where are you? Are you all right?' Mother asks with tears in her words. We have not heard each other's voices for many months. A year. More.

'Mother, listen, and do not speak. I do not have much time. I am in London. I am a housekeeper in a rich man's flat, he owns the building. They look after me. I am safe. I have not sent money yet because I have not been paid, but soon I will be. They said they will pay me all my money at once, at the end of my service, and soon I will send you everything. Do not worry. Tell Beauty I love her, I have not forgotten her, will you tell her that? Tell her every day.'

I cannot control the trembling in my voice. I clear my throat so the lies will come out more easily. Mother says nothing. I hear her quiet sobs, see her nodding, dishrag clenched in her fist, held up to her face, sitting on the stool in the kitchen. I see her rocking on the stool to keep herself from crying aloud, so that Beauty, my girl, will not hear her.

'Mother, I have not called because I am busy with work, but very soon, they will pay me, and I will have my own mobile phone and we will talk every day. And I will come home to see you. Very soon. God protect you, Mother.'

I hear her breath jar and shudder in her chest. Then the silence when I end the call before she can answer.

I slide the phone back into the pocket of Master's jeans, the ones he left on the pile of washing. This is a dangerous thing he has done. That I have done.

Penny
Flat 1B

Boom-boom-boom.

I jump at the sound, look away from my laptop. Oh dear, they must be having quite an argument next door if there's already wall pounding. Carla, poor thing, alone with two adolescents. Well, Daniel's only just turned twelve, but children are much older than they used to be. I know it's not easy but I do wish they didn't carry on so, they'll wake Susannah. I check on her in her Moses basket. Still asleep, thankfully. I don't know how, between that whistling kettle that's been going all morning in someone's flat and now this. But Susannah's always been easy.

Olivia was a terrible sleeper when she was small, not like Susannah who loves her sleep. I'm lucky that she sleeps, because it would be all the more challenging being on my own if she was a bad sleeper.

It was the sleep that was our undoing. Olivia still woke twice in the night at fifteen months and she was up most mornings at five. I often logged back in after we put her to bed at night and worked until eleven. Jamie always tried to get me to bed earlier but there were emails to catch up on, so many emails, and the diary to schedule, and laundry, always laundry. I slept very little.

The exhaustion unravelled me gradually, slowly, an incremental daily torture of dry eyes, forgotten words, caffeine jitters, blurred thoughts. They never showed that on the news or the online clips of the CCTV footage of the Tube platform where you can see me get off the train at Balham without Olivia. People rushing and crowding in, jostling me to get to the doors of the carriage. And then me standing on the platform with my back to the train as it pulls away with my daughter. But you can't see how tired I was. They never explained on the news that she never slept. That she woke twice in the night and was up by five and that I often worked until eleven.

'*You're so useless!*' comes through the wall; a door slams. Mary Rose and Carla at it again.

Ah, and now Susannah is awake. And so, the day begins.

Carla
Flat 1A

'You're so useless!' Mary Rose screams at Daniel. He left the seat up again. He did it on purpose because it pisses her off. He did it because he heard her yelling at me. He doesn't know I know he does these things for me. These kids are gonna kill me, either with their love or their hate. I don't know which will do it first.

I fold the sofa bed up from last night. We've only got two bedrooms, so it's where I sleep since I gave Daniel my room. It's important for the kids to have their own rooms. For them to feel like we can afford that.

I open the cabinet. I bypass the oat cakes and the natural peanut butter and I shove two Oreos in my mouth instead. I eat them hiding behind the open cabinet door, facing the shelves so the kids don't see. I think about putting that peanut butter on the next one and then my phone buzzes.

Oh fuck.

'Hello . . . I know. I'm sorry . . . I didn't know . . . well, can you just . . . but then I have to . . . Tom . . . I'm sorry . . . the kids are here, I can't say that . . . don't make me say that in front of them . . . no, I didn't call the lawyer about the visa; I promise, please . . .' Click and he's gone.

I turn back to the cabinet, stare at the shelves, try to breathe, and then her voice, 'What *are* you doing?' Mary Rose says, furious, reaching her arm over my shoulder to get the cornflakes. I can hear her eyes rolling.

'Gimme a break, all right? I had a long shift at the front desk last night. Asshole tourists,' I say, turning around. I watch her pour cereal into a bowl. She's wearing bright red lipstick. She has his face. His nose, his lips. She's rolled up her uniform skirt to make it inappropriately short. I should say something but it's not worth the argument.

'Was that Dad?' she asks, raising her eyes from her bowl. She has great eyebrows. The kind I never had.

'Yeah,' I say, sipping my coffee, cold now, sitting down across from her. Some Oreo crumbs fall from the lapel of my robe to the table. I see her see them.

'When are you going to stand up for yourself, Mum?'

When she says things like this, her accent makes it so much worse. She can sound like a real bitch when she wants to.

'Eat your breakfast, Mary Rose,' I say, regretting that we gave her that name while I finish my coffee. I wanted Roxane. Roxy for short. Roxy would have had a sense of humour. Roxy would have been my girlfriend. We'd get our nails done together and she'd be my confidante. But he made me give her his Irish Catholic mother's name. He made me do so many things.

'Well, it's your life. I'm never going to ask permission from a man for anything,' she says, flipping her hair and sprinkling sugar and her fourteen-year-old wisdom on her cornflakes.

I look at my daughter. She wants to hurt me. She doesn't know how well she's doing it. I close my eyes, put my cold cup to my lips, and pray that she's right. I pray she grows up and her life is nothing like mine.

I get up from the table, pull my robe around me, and say, 'Don't be so angry all the time. It'll give you wrinkles, Mary Rosie.'

She hates when I call her that. She hates when she's laid the bait and I don't fight with her. I walk past her and brush my hand along her shoulder on my way to make another coffee. I'm still her mother, no matter what she says to me.

16

While my back is turned, she gets up and leaves for school without a word, slamming the door behind her in goodbye.

'Daniel, you'd better go,' I call, standing at the kitchen counter, staring at the cabinet door. When he emerges I put a five-pound note in his pocket and run my hand through his hair.

'Get breakfast at Justin's so you won't be late.'

'Okay, Mum, love you,' he says.

And when the door shuts behind him, I reach into the cabinet and eat every Oreo in the pack, until all of them are gone.

Woman
Flat 2A–2B

Another slam, muffled, from below. I know it is the people below but still it makes me jump. I check the hallway between the bedrooms. I have only seconds to think.

If I bring the jeans to Madame and show her I found Master's phone, she will accuse me of stealing it and beat me. If I bring the jeans with the phone to Master, he will taunt me, he will make me do things to keep him from telling Madame that I stole his phone, even though he will know that I did no such thing. Even though he will know that he left it in his pocket because he is a careless boy. If I put the jeans back in Master's bedroom, leave them on the floor, as though he just dropped them there, I will be punished for not tidying properly. If I keep the phone and they find it on me later, they will kill me. If I break it into a million pieces and throw it in the rubbish, Master will think he lost it, but he will accuse me of stealing it so that his parents do not beat him, and they will turn the house upside down looking for where they think I have hidden it, and then they will kill me. But first they will make me clean up the mess and put the flat right before my execution.

The only answer is to put it under My Lady's mattress. My Lady often pilfers things – pens, chocolate bars, Madame's earrings – and hides them under her pillow or in her pink handbag with the sparkly horse or under the sofa or behind the coffee tin in the kitchen. She is punished for these transgressions if she is found out, and for hiding her brother's mobile, the penalty will be severe. I have saved her many times from Madame, her mother. Many times I have found her stolen things in places where they should not be, have put the watches and keys and television control in my apron pockets when I have found them in the oven or in a shoe and replaced them so that My Lady would feel her mother's hand across her face one less time in the day. But today is not such a day.

I put the washing in the machine, fold a pile of clothes, put the phone in the pocket of Master's jeans, and carry them on top of the pile to My Lady's room.

2

Mable, Carla
Flat 1A

'Hi Mable, you here to tell me Jesus loves me?' Carla asks flatly as she answers the door, groggy, having just woken up at five in the afternoon, recovering from her night shift at the hotel. Carla is wearing her navy, satin shorty robe with the white lapels, the one she always seems to be wearing whenever Mable knocks every third Friday of the month. On this occasion, Carla does not realise that the left bottom hem of the robe has tucked itself into her underpants, exposing her pink and fleshy left thigh, which is perhaps not her best physical attribute.

Mable, accustomed to her neighbour's semi-nudity, adjusts her lavender ministry hat, checking with her fingertips that the frayed bits of the polyester flowers are facing the back where they won't be noticed.

'Good afternoon, Carla, dear. I have some Good News to share with you ...' she says, with her slight Jamaican lilt, smiling, averting her gaze from the crisis unfolding at Carla's waist.

Carla bought the robe in La Perla on Sloane Street in the heady, early days of her relationship with Tom, in preparation for the weekend she thought he would propose. She chose the shop because her mother had always bought La Perla, the finest there was, and because when she felt the silk, it had transported her to her future with Tom. To the honeymoon she'd hoped they'd have, on a cruise ship, where she'd stand on the private balcony, holding a Martini glass, watching the sunset over the sea, her hair cascading down her silk-satin back, Tom, stopping still in his tracks at the sight of her, hand resting on the doorknob, overcome, in lustful awe of her womanly shape under the lustrous fabric. She saw him sweeping her hair over her shoulder without a word, gently kissing her lovely neck, loving her completely.

Of course, she'd never had the sort of hair that cascaded, and there never was a cruise ship. And Tom left her. But at least Carla still had the robe.

Now, with its tattered cuffs and lopsided hem, the shiny navy struggling in its efforts to contain Carla's ample assets, it looks more like the shabby cloak of a woman defeated than the elegant lingerie of a lady of leisure. Carla knows the robe is ageing, like she is, but she wears it for the La Perla label on the inside, still intact, a reminder of a time when she had nice things. When she was worth dressing in silk. When she was worth something, anything, at all.

Carla's phone rings. Mable sees the change in her face, suddenly alert. Afraid. 'My phone,' she says, and Carla lets go of the door to find her mobile, hoping Mable will get the hint, but the old woman catches the door with her foot, holding it open. Despite her age, her reflexes are quick, especially when she senses that she, and Jehovah, may soon be needed. She inclines her head to get a better view of Carla's flat through the door and she sees – and immediately wishes that she did not see – that the hem of Carla's robe is actually tucked into a pair of men's large, white, cotton briefs.

Mable tries not to look at the sad cotton drooping between Carla's thighs from under the robe and thinks, 'Whose underpants is she wearing?' and covers her mouth to muffle her gasp. But she quickly self-corrects and remembers that this was why one of the top tips for urban ministry was to minister in pairs so that there would be a witness to refute any suggestion of impropriety in case someone came to the door inappropriately dressed. But Mable has always preferred to minister alone, even though the elders discouraged it, and today she is glad to have insisted on it. It is a blessing, a small mercy, that no one else is with her to witness the droopy gusset of Carla's life.

'Everything all right, darlin'?' Mable asks when Carla returns to the door.

'I'm fine, everything's fine, I gotta go, Mable,' Carla says, her American accent flattening and widening all of her words. Carla tries to close her door, but Mable puts her hand on it, stops it with surprising strength, and says, 'You sure, now?' noticing the drip, drip, drip of a dried coffee stain on Carla's right lapel.

It's been there for months and months. Evidence that Carla has not washed the robe since the morning that she brought her too full cup too close to her chest as Tom explained his plan for leaving her and her hands shook, spilling the hot coffee. Her body had numbed itself to insulate her from the reality of her life with him and the disastrous consequences of her decisions, and so she didn't feel the searing heat of the hot coffee on her skin when it dripped on to her robe and soaked through the satin. There is still a tiny red scar on her chest that only she knows is there.

Mable happened to call on Carla that day, in the early afternoon, before the children were home from school and several hours after Tom's exit. Enough time for Carla to have become properly inebriated. In the absence of anyone else who would listen, drunk and alone, Carla told Mable the story of her tumultuous marriage. Of infidelities, deceits, misunderstandings, the temptations that led her husband astray, and the ecstasies of forgiveness.

Mable stood in the doorway, listening, never allowing her face to betray the fact that she and Jehovah both could have done without the descriptions of the ecstasies. She did not show Carla that she understood that she was using romance and passion to disguise and justify Tom's cruelties. Mable knew that the wounds he'd left her with were the kind that weep and never heal.

When Carla was finished, Mable took her hands in hers and prayed: 'Almighty Jehovah, please take Carla into the warmth of Your perpetual grace, guide her on the road to righteousness, soothe her with the healing light of Your love so that she can feel Your strength and bring it into her so that she may be strong for her children, in Jesus' name.' Carla held Mable's gaze for a moment then, before she closed the door.

But it is many months later now and Carla still has not laundered her robe. She is sighing and rolling her eyes and dismissing Mable as just an old woman, a doddering annoyance to be tolerated politely, though she knows that Mable is one of the only people who has ever truly seen her.

'Thanks for stopping by, Mable. I'll see you around,' Carla says. But as she gently tries to push her door closed, Mable falters, loses her balance, and knocks over her rolling shopping trolley. Her magazines spill out all over the corridor floor.

'Oh no, I'm sorry, dear, don' you mind me, I'll just be getting on my way,' Mable says, acting as though her old lady confidence has been dented by this bout of unsteadiness, as she slowly starts bending down to gather her literature. It is a charade, of course, a little test Mable uses to check on the state of Carla's heart.

With a whispered '*Jesus Christ*' under her breath, Carla stoops down to gather the magazines for the old woman and then says, 'I mean, honestly, should you really still be dragging that grandma cart around with all those magazines? I'm sure Jesus doesn't want ladies your age breaking a hip over him, you know what I mean?'

Carla helps, reluctantly, but she does help. Mable is thus satisfied that her spirit is still intact, prickly and tired, but not hardened. And if the spirit is still there, then there is reason for her to return.

'Carla, thank you for your concern. But I'm confident that my Almighty Father is with me, protecting me and guiding me as I spread the Good News,' Mable answers her.

On her hands and knees, Carla gathers up the scattered *Watchtowers*, too tired to notice that her bosom is alarmingly close to breaking free of her robe. Mable, hearing other tenants approaching on the staircase and concerned about Carla's imminent nudity, silently prays, *Jehovah, please help Carla in her time of need, and spare us all the embarrassment of her impending indiscretion in this hallway, in Jesus' name. Amen.*

And at just that moment, Carla rises from the floor, tightens the belt of her robe, and pulls the straying hem out of her men's briefs. *Thank you*, Mable silently says to Jehovah, as she takes a deep breath and lifts her eyes back to Carla.

'Thank you for that, dear, now, can I interest you in some reading material?' Mable says, holding out a magazine.

Carla looks at Mable, and wants to say, 'Are you kidding me, old lady?' but she finds the will to say instead, 'Sure,' and accepts the pamphlet.

'You know—' Carla is about to continue, to tell Mable she can just push the magazines under her door in future, when she catches her reflection in the mirror at the end of the hallway. It's a full-length mirror left behind by previous tenants that has stayed propped against the wall since they moved away. It is the sort of lost property that accumulates in the communal spaces of buildings, the kind of forgotten object no one will ever claim.

At this angle, under the glow of the fluorescent lights, Carla sees that her décolletage is very red, her thighs covered in dimples. She looks down to dismiss her reflection, only to see the yellowing, jagged toenails of her bare feet, remnants of old polish worn to tiny circles at the centre of each toe. She feels worn and threadbare, like her robe. Like the shredded

23

edges of the ancient, artificial flowers Mable tries to hide on her hat.

Mable waits for Carla to finish her thought, but she sees something pass over her neighbour's face, and instead she says, 'Well, I'm happy to go away knowing you have held in your hands words of peace and inspiration and an invitation to be saved.'

'Okay,' Carla says, 'whatever, thanks,' and closes her door.

Mable, reassured that Carla is not in need of more intervention today, continues her pilgrimage down the corridor to Penny's flat. But as she turns away, she hears, '*Friggin' wackadoo*' from behind Carla's door.

Many doors remain closed to Mable as she spreads the Good News through her territory, and she wishes – deeply, secretly – that Carla's was one of them. But every time she knocks, Carla answers. And every time she tolerates Mable, just barely, through their conversation, and ends each interaction with an insult like this one, which Carla does not realise can be heard in the hallway if she says it close enough to her door. But still, she answers her door and Mable knows this means that there is something missing in Carla's life that her presence provides. And so, every third Friday, she knocks on the door of 1A, waiting for the day when Carla might answer fully clothed, ask her in for a cup of tea and listen attentively to the Good News.

But when she hears 'friggin' wackadoo', Mable also knows that Carla will probably not be one of the Anointed joining her in the Kingdom of Heaven when the end finally comes.

And Mable is all right with that.

Mable, Penny
Flat 1B

Mable arrives at the door of 1B, sighing deeply. She looks forward to the quiet encounter she knows awaits her here after the challenge of 1A. Penny Danford is the tenant's name. Mable discovered this when Penny's post was accidentally placed in her letter box downstairs, as they both have Bs in their flat numbers.

Mable sees her rarely and knows little about her neighbour, other than she's very polite. And that it's her habit to take her laundry to the laundrette on the ground floor of the building on a Tuesday morning. Mable knows this because she gives herself Tuesday mornings off and treats herself to tea and toast at Justin's. She sits by the window of the café, looks out over the goings-on of the street and observes humanity's godlessness in all its shapes and forms. On her way back to the building, she often encounters Penny going to the laundrette.

Penny is a tall, overweight, ghostly pale white woman. Mable thinks she looks unwell and fragile despite her heft, but she assumes it's the unceasing chill and damp and sunless sky of the London winter that make all the white English look this way – peaked, sickly, their whiteness almost fluorescent under Great Britain's perpetually grey clouds. And Mable doesn't understand why Penny goes to the laundrette rather than using the washing machine in her flat. But she appreciates that Penny is quiet, and keeps to herself, a quality in short supply these days among the general population.

'Hello? Mable here, just coming to share the Good News . . .'

After waiting a few beats Mable carefully does a sideways bend, to check the shadows dancing under the door jamb. She knows Penny is there. She knows that Penny knows that Mable checks the slivers of light under the doors when she knocks to see if the inhabitants are in, but still choosing to ignore her. Mable appreciates that Penny, once she learned Mable's trick, began silently bringing a chair over to the door to stand on when Mable knocked. Penny stands on the chair so Mable can't watch for movement, and in this way Penny thinks she

25

makes it seem that she isn't answering because she truly is not at home, and not because she is avoiding Mable, thus sparing the old woman's feelings. In a world where most people disregard Mable openly, she appreciates Penny's effort at covert avoidance.

Penny is now indeed standing on a chair on the other side of the door, looking through the peephole at the distorted lavender form of Mable and her hat, politely pretending not to be there so that Mable won't wake Susannah.

But Mable knows every trick in the book. It is no accident that the Service Overseer of the congregation often cites her work as an Auxiliary Pioneer to encourage other brothers and sisters in their field ministry. Even the Circuit Overseer lauded her consistent sixty hours of ministry per month during his last visit. Sixty-two hours last month, to be exact. Her monthly field service reports are exemplary, and Mable knows they would have been the envy of many Publishers in the congregation, if envy were permissible.

'Penny, darlin', just Mable here, come to give you the Good News.'

No answer. Mable adjusts her hat. Three years they have played this game through the door, but she doesn't have the patience for pretence today. She waits several beats.

'Penny, shall I just leave a magazine here for you? It's a good one this time . . .'

No answer. Mable stands her ground, hand on the handle of the rolling cart, and she stares straight into the peephole, daring Penny to keep ignoring her.

Penny is no good at playing chicken, and she cannot take the pressure of Mable's gaze through the fisheye lens for long, even though she knows it is a one-way system and Mable can't actually see her. Finally, a whisper so quiet that Mable must put her ear to the door to hear it.

'Hello, Mable, I didn't realise it was you,' Penny lies from behind the door.

'Yes, darlin', it's me, just come to bring you some Good News,' Mable replies, going along with Penny's prevarication.

'Well, it's just not a good time right now, but thank you ever so much for your visit. I would love one of your very interesting magazines, if it's no trouble?' Penny whispers, nervously checking that Susannah is still napping. Last night was horrible, Susannah's reflux causing them both great distress and broken sleep.

'No trouble at all. Would you like to have a little chat about this month's issue? There's a very interesting article about how to manage our stress in times of great consternation and anxiety such as we are now living in . . .'

'Oh,' Penny continues, 'that is ever so kind, but I'm afraid I'm indisposed at the moment. Susannah is asleep and I don't want to disturb her; I'm sure you understand. If you would just slide it through, I shall read it and next time perhaps you can give me your thoughts . . .'

'All right, darlin', that would be nice,' Mable says. She slides the magazine under the door and prepares to roll her cart away. It's not much, this conversation with Penny, but it's something. Penny at least has an open heart, and perhaps a word or two of the Message might reach her. But then again, Mable knows it might not.

Mable, Woman
Flat 2A–2B

Mable rests at the top of the stairs and finds her breath. Someone brushes past her, a blur of headphones and fruity shampoo, yoga mat and youth. It's one of the three white girls that live across the hall from her in 3C, all of them interchangeable with their purple highlights and tattoos and eco coffee cups. Like most city dwellers, they do not notice their neighbours, especially not neighbours like Mable.

Perhaps Carla is right. Her bunions are throbbing against her shoes and her compression stockings are cutting into the creases behind her knees. Her left hip aches. The rolling cart is heavier than it used to be. She could change her ministry. She could sit outside the Tube station with a literature stand, allow passers-by to take what they need, and pray with those who request it, instead of repeating this exhausting journey of doors left unanswered or opened and then slammed shut before she can say, 'Good afternoon.'

Slowly dragging her cart behind her, Mable knocks at 2B. 'Hello? This is Mable, visiting with my neighbours to share the Good News, the wonder of everlasting life.'

It is the businessman's flat, and Mable does not expect an answer because she knows that he and his family usually aren't home. She suspects that others live there besides just the businessman and his wife and teenage son. She thinks she has heard young children, but she can't be sure. Mable has knocked on enough doors in her time to know when there is life behind one and when there isn't. She feels people on the other side of closed doors holding their breath waiting for her to walk away. She feels their eye-rolls, the rumble of their aggravated mumblings about her. People think locked doors are impenetrable, but no lock can keep a soul from reaching out to her even when its bodily vessel objects. And no man-made door can keep Jehovah from going where He's needed.

Despite the silence at 2B, Mable feels the heat of life behind the door. She knocks and waits for an answer. A dying fluorescent bulb in the ceiling, grey on one end but still flickering on the other, casts a dim light in the hall.

Mable sighs, but as she turns to leave she sees the slightest darkening of light just under the door. Someone's there, perhaps looking at her through the fisheye of the peephole. Mable, seasoned in her ministry, steps back and centres herself in the view of the door. *Always stand back from apartment doors so that occupants can have a full view of you through the peephole and therefore not feel threatened by your presence.*

'Hello? It's Mable here, your neighbour. I wonder if I might have just a moment of your time . . . to share the Good News?'

The light doesn't shift under the door. Someone is there who has not yet rejected her. Who can hear her. Who may need her. Who may need the promise of Paradise. She puts her hand to the door, closes her eyes, and bows her head. She senses the brush of eyelashes against the peephole, the tension of held breath, the thudding of a heartbeat.

She prays, in a whisper: 'Almighty Jehovah, protect this occupant of 2B, wrap Your arms around this child and hold them close to You. For You taught us to give the hungry sustenance, to give the thirsty drink, to receive strangers hospitably, to clothe the naked, to look after the sick and to visit those in prison, for when we do this, in Jesus' name, for the least of our brothers, we do it unto You. And those who have been blessed by the Father will reach the Kingdom of Heaven.'

With a heavy heart she slides a magazine under the door and hopes that it will reach the soul she knows is watching her through the fisheye lens.

Mable stands back from the door a moment, just in case, then gathers herself for her journey upstairs to her flat. 'Give me strength,' she asks Jehovah, straightening her hat, unconsciously checking its flowers and the frayed edges. She shuffles towards the stairs, but then a large, heavy-set, black-haired, olive-skinned man dressed in black – who she hasn't seen in the building before – comes out of flat 2C. He locks the door behind him. He walks down the corridor towards her.

Mable is overcome with fear, feeling vulnerable and in the presence of danger. Unable to run or to protect herself, she does the only thing she can, and prays. The man moves past her to the stairs, and she is flooded with relief until he stops and turns. She leans back against the wall for support, heart thumping, and wordlessly she watches as he lifts her shopping cart and gestures to the stairs. In his hands it is as small and light as a child's toy.

Realising that he is offering to help her, Mable exhales. 'Thank you, that's very kind,' she whispers, grasping the bannister to steady her trembling hands. As usual, there is nothing to fear. Her prayer was answered.

3

Penny
Flat 1B

What a relief. Mable has shuffled away now, and she didn't wake Susannah, thank goodness. We had an *awful* night last night with her reflux which is why she's still asleep even though it's almost teatime now. I wait at the door and listen to Mable clunking along with her cart on her way upstairs. I do worry about her on those stairs, but daren't leave Susannah alone in the flat. I wait to make sure she's got to the top. Twelve clunks, twelve steps. Take care, Mable.

I make myself a cup of tea, put Olivia's barrette in my hair, and sit down to check emails while I have a moment's peace. A message from @1mum2boys on the mumyougotthis.co.uk forum pops up. I read it quickly:

> @solomama367, *I'm writing to say THANK YOU. There are no words! Your advice over this past week was a life-saver!!! I was really at my wits' end with DS but after your post, I just pulled myself together, held fast to that routine, did his meals at exact times with a top-up banana before bed, and let him cry it out (not to a point of actual distress, before you all get at me) and we actually SLEPT THROUGH THE NIGHT for the first time in months! I feel amazing! OMG I am so ecstatic that I bought a bottle of champers for tonight for me and hubby. Not even prosecco – real champagne! Thank you so much for your*

31

help – you can't imagine how much it means to this tired
mama. xxx

What a lovely message! Oh, I'm so glad. But I must be quick in my response. I have to get supper sorted. Carla and I are joining forces tonight. I do hope she's all right after her difficult morning with the children, all that banging and arguing. Like every other mum I know, she just needs some support. That's why this twice-weekly supper that we do together is so important. Her children are older – Mary Rose, fourteen, and Daniel, only just twelve – but still, we're both single mums, so it helps to share the burden, to weather the witching hour together. And Susannah distracts her children, makes them smile. Anyhow, I think it's pasta tonight so I'd better find some bits to contribute.

I check the basket. Susannah's still asleep. We are completely off routine and it's far too late for a nap, but I'll just put her to bed at a later time tonight and hopefully we'll get back on track tomorrow. I'm a big advocate of routine but I also recognise, better than anyone, that sometimes it all falls to pieces, even with the best of intentions. The key is to get up the next day, clean slate, and try again.

I gather bread rolls, grated parmesan – Carla never has little extras like that – and, of course the wine. I reckon I have five minutes before Susannah is up, enough time to respond quickly to that lovely message. I type:

@1mum2boys, you are sooooo very welcome. I am
thrilled for you and humbled by the opportunity to help
another mum. We must stick together! It's like I always
say, the only remedy for when life has got on top of you is
to get back on top of life and do it like a boss! Because
you ARE the boss, Mama! Enjoy your bubbly with the
hubbly! Lol xx

I know a lot about routine. Routine is essential. Especially when you have a baby, especially for first-time mums. Routine and connection. Even virtual connection is so important for new mothers. And I feel, very strongly, that when you're an experienced mother it's important to pass on your knowledge whenever you can and to connect with mums who are struggling.

Now with Olivia, we'd tried everything under the sun to get her to sleep. And then I realised that we were too haphazard in our days, not regimented enough in how we did things, and it had confused her little internal clock. So, I worked very, very hard on the routine. But Olivia was not a compliant child, and I gave in instead of standing my ground. And that's where I went wrong.

If I had just stuck to it, found the inner strength to withstand the tantrums and the crying, things would have improved, and she would have been a happier baby. We would have been a happier family. Unfortunately, things didn't work out that way. However, it's an important takeaway, not just for child-rearing but for life – the key to success is perseverance.

I can't let the knowledge gained from all of that hard work go to waste, so I contribute to chats on all the sites – Mumsnet, Netmums, NappyValley – but I like the camaraderie on this one best. I've even become a little sought after. Every time I post on someone's thread it inevitably leads to a bit of a Q and A session. Because all that mums need, especially new mums, is connection. Reassurance, connection, and routine. That's what I do for new mums and look – it works!

It keeps me busy too. It occupies that space that work used to take up. Well, you know, it's the same story for a lot of women. Stay home for a bit, for the good of the children, and you don't regret it, but you do get restless. Sometimes.

Susannah is stirring. Now, just because our afternoon routine went haywire today doesn't mean that we won't follow through on the bedtime routine. In fact, it's essential that we do. So, we're going to have supper with Carla and the children, and then sort ourselves out properly for the evening. But I am pleased that I could help @1mum2boys, whoever and wherever she may be.

'I'm starving. Jinx, Mary Rose!' I laugh because we said it at the same time. I try to laugh and be warm with Mary Rose. She's a different girl since Tom left. I think the pressure gets to her sometimes. Of course, it's also her age; so hard to be a teenage girl. I wish she smiled more. If she smiled more maybe Carla would too.

I pour the wine, hoping that the Chardonnay will lighten Carla's mood a bit. The air around her is heavy tonight. She takes a sip, then sighs, 'C'mon, hand them over,' and she heaps the pasta on top of each plate that's passed to her. I jostle Susannah on my lap a bit so she won't fuss, praying she'll let me get through at least one meal today.

We could have used a vegetable tonight, I think to myself, but never mind. It's like I say to the mums online, it's all right to let go of the small stuff, as long as you're doing the big stuff, and loving your children is the biggest stuff of all. Anyway, it's nice of Carla to have me and Susie here. Carla has a big heart. Bigger than she knows. Dinner together will do us both some good. Connection – it's so important.

I top up my glass and say to Carla, 'What's happened, lovely? Tough day?'

'I've got to go into work tomorrow, and then three more night shifts in a row. So, Mary Rose, you're in charge,' Carla says, shovelling pasta in her mouth.

'I can always look in on them if you like, it's no trouble,' I offer, like I always do when she mentions her night shifts.

Carla grunts her assent, then addresses Mary Rose abruptly, 'Did you do your homework?'

'Carla . . .' I say, gently, to signal that she should lighten her tone, but Mary Rose interrupts me.

'It's not due until Monday, Mum. It's only Friday,' she says, irritated, exasperated with her mother, pushing the spaghetti round her plate.

To defuse the tension, I take a sip of wine and interject: 'Well, Mary Rose, this is lovely, really lovely, thank you,' pointing at my plate with a smile to deflect some positive attention on to her. She made tonight's dinner and I wish Carla would acknowledge her efforts. She's so tired, poor thing, I think she forgets the simple things sometimes. With a meaningful look, I encourage her to compliment Mary Rose, but she doesn't notice. I wish she would say, '*Thank you for dinner, darling*,' or '*How is drama club going?*' or anything at all. She just tells them when she's working and asks about homework, checking things off the list. They never laugh, her and the children.

I'm not judging her, of course. I don't judge any mother. I know she's doing all she can to keep everything going, like so many of us. She's so worried, trying to make ends meet with her stressful, underpaid job and inadequate support from Tom. Always scraping pennies together to make sure the children have what they need. But that leaves little room for fun, or conversation or relaxation, or just loving them. She's forgotten about the lovely part of loving children. If you love them just a little bit, they love you right back.

For a little while, only the sounds of cutlery on ceramic fill the silence until Carla says, 'Daniel, did you do your homework?' Poor boy, he's starving, he's had his whole helping and is looking for more. Mary Rose gives him half of hers. She's not eating much these days. I hope Carla has noticed. Perhaps I should have a word later.

'Yeah, I did because next match against Croydon is tomorrow. Coach says it's important. Can you take me? Can you stay and watch?' He asks hopefully although he knows the answer. He's very good at the footy. Very talented. He's in a proper club, the kind the big teams recruit from. I would go happily; if they asked, I would go. If I could.

'I'm working tomorrow, baby, I can't. Mary Rose will take you,' Carla says.

'But tomorrow's Saturday! Why can't he call Dad? Why's it always me? I've got my own life,' Mary Rose shouts.

Her plate clatters to the floor. Susannah, startled, jumps off my lap to the floor and dashes over to the little Moses basket by the sofa where she licks her paws to console herself and then curls up in the corner, tail flicking with irritation. I rush to help clear up, to mitigate the damage, but as I reach out my hand, it hits . . . well, of course, it hits the wall. The wall between our flats, dividing our two dinner tables. Me and Susannah on this side, Carla and the children on the other.

'Please, we've been through this. If it's not your dad's weekend, then I need your help. Mary Rose? Mary Rose!' Carla says, exhausted by the repetition of this conversation.

Mary Rose's chair scrapes against the floor as she pushes away from the table and rushes to her room, slamming her door. Carla's fork clangs on her plate as she drops it.

Someone should go after her. I wish I could go to her, console her, listen to her, poor girl. She has a point, doesn't she? Has Daniel called his father? So what if it's not Tom's weekend, why should she and Carla fill in for absolutely everything?

'Did you call Daddy?' Carla asks Daniel, knowing the answer to her question, but trying to find a solution to placate both children. She rubs her forehead as she says it. I turn to look at Daniel's face, the face I know is looking back at her on the other side of the wall.

'No, he'd only say no. He never answers his phone anyhow.'

'Okay, well, could you just try? Maybe he can this time . . .'

'It's just Sherry and the baby, he says she needs him. And anyway, it's not his weekend,' Daniel explains, disappointed, in a tone much older than his twelve years.

'Clear the table,' Carla says to him. 'Mary Rose? Where are you?' She gets up and I'm so relieved. She's going to Mary Rose after all, to let her know what a good girl she is. She

36

doesn't have the patience for adolescent dramatics, but this is why I know, despite everything, despite her surly manner, she's a good mother. She always digs down and finds a way, somehow, to love them more.

But then I hear, 'I don't have time for this shit, get back here and help clear the table . . .'

Oh, Carla.

'Daniel, let me help,' I say, as I get up to clear plates along with him. Fork and knife placed in parallel on my plate. Pasta bolognese only half eaten. I've lost my appetite, perhaps like Mary Rose.

Now is a good moment to speak to him, while we're alone. I press my face to the wall, the spot where I've found I can listen best and where voices carry further, because I think it must be on one of the seams of the plasterboard.

'Daniel?' I say as gently as possible, so as not to startle him. It's been some time since we've talked like this.

'Mum says not to talk to you any more through this wall, Miss.' He speaks to me as if to a child. But it's all ended too abruptly, tonight's dinner. I'm not ready for it to end. 'Sorry, Miss, it's just that I don't want you getting in trouble with Mum again.'

'Oh, yes, well, I just wanted to catch up with you. I'm just wondering how you are, you and your sister.'

'We're okay, Miss, but remember last time? Mum was well angry.'

'That she was,' I say through the wall. 'Yes, well, all right, dear. Have a lovely evening.'

'Okay, Miss.' I hear him shuffle away, then the juddering of a pipe when he turns on the tap to start the washing-up.

I sit on my sofa and Susannah jumps in my lap. 'I know. Don't look at me like that,' I say to her.

'This isn't a good time to call him, Susannah; it's dinner time, you know how hectic that is. He has to pick her up from nursery and get her home and feed her and Jamie will just say

37

it isn't a good time.' Susannah purrs, recovered from the earlier chaos.

'Well, Susie, nothing to do now but get back on top . . .' My voice trails off as I try to stand up from the sofa but find myself breathless, dizzy.

'Now, you see, that's the problem,' I say, closing my eyes to make the spinning stop. 'It's the routine, Susie, we went off routine . . . don't get snippy with me. Now, I'm not saying it's you who made me stop taking the pills, but you did have awful reflux last night and kept me up until the wee hours. And you know how I need sleep, Susie, my beautiful girl, especially if I've stopped taking the pills.'

I go to wrap my arms around her, bury my face in her lustrous fur, but she squirms out of my grasp, jumps off the sofa and shudders, as if my caresses have left a bad taste in her mouth.

When the dizziness stops I get up to clear up the plates from dinner but the mirror catches my eye. The antique one me and Jamie bought that time in one of those places on the side of the road in Bridport where we had gone for a romantic mini-break before we had Olivia. The mirror didn't fit in the boot so I wrapped it up in all of our clothes to protect it, and fit the seatbelt around it and sat with it in the backseat all the way back to London.

Jamie had said, 'What are you like, you silly moo?' and he laughed that kind of laugh that's not a laugh, that's more like a happy sigh that ends with a sideways grin and a loving shake of the head. The glass in the ornate, gold plaster oval frame has those black spots dotted about it, that sort of distress that old mirrors get.

'I know what will make us feel better, Susie. Let's have Girl Talk, shall we?'

I put her down gently. I take the mirror off the wall, lean it against the bed, and sit down on the floor cross-legged in front of it. Susie jumps into my lap.

'Now look at us, up there,' I say, pointing at our reflection. I hold her and smile for a few seconds, as if waiting for someone to take our picture.

'What? Oh, I know, can you believe it?!' I say to the mirror. 'No, really? Well, that's too good to be true,' I say to my reflection with a wide smile, making eye contact with myself. I try to show interest by tilting my head, the way you would do with any friend who was telling you a story.

I cock my head to the other side, and gesture with my arms, trying out different angles, crossing them in front of my chest, keeping one folded and using the other to gesture outwards. I try putting one hand on my chin, one across to show that I'm thinking about what's being said.

I say, 'I know, things are quite tough on Carla at the moment, she has so much on her plate. Single motherhood is very hard without the right support,' and I make a concerned face, one that would show my companion that I was listening, until I remember, and then I stop nodding.

I turn around and reach under the mattress behind me and pull out her letter. *Penny, please stop talking to my kids through the wall. Last time you really scared Daniel. It's inappropriate and you know that. I don't want to have to call the police. But you have to stop.*

I take a deep breath, and watch my chest rise and then fall in the reflection. I do it again and again until I feel calmer. I come back to myself. I look up at my reflection, whistle and do the hand gesture for cuckoo, spinning my finger next to my ear. 'What is she on about? Talk about paranoid. I would never be *inappropriate* with the children. There's a wall between us, for God's sake,' and I point to the wall dramatically in my reflection and give a half laugh at the ridiculousness of Carla's suggestion. 'A generation of overprotective parents, honestly,' I say, and shake my head.

Girl Talk over, I put the letter back under the mattress and ask Susannah, 'What shall we do next, kitty cat?' She doesn't answer.

I check the calendar to make sure it's Friday. If it's Friday, it's time to change the sheets and make cocoa and get to bed early so I can get into the reruns of *Britain's Got Talent*. I love watching the dreams of ordinary people come true.

But first, I must clear the table.

'We can't let standards slip, Susannah,' I say, and I move the bottle of wine to reach the plates and realise that it's empty. Well, no wonder I'm a little loopy!

'I drank a bottle of wine! Can you believe it? What am I like!' I giggle at Susannah, as if I'm tipsy, but I know it wasn't really wine. It's an old wine bottle that I refill with water whenever I have dinner with Carla and the children. I don't drink any more, of course, because of the pills, and now the withdrawal from the pills. And because I can't get wine bottles into the flat unless I open the door.

I change the sheets, get into bed, and Susannah nestles close to me. I sip my warm cocoa. I enjoy the audience gasping and laughing and crying and cheering.

Applause. Laughter. Applause.

'*That was amazing, I love you, that was brilliant.*'

Cue triumphant tear-jerking music. A woman's voice rises above the applause, it must be either Mel B or Amanda Holden. It's hard to tell, it's a bit muffled through the wall, although Carla's TV is on full blast. On Friday night when she's not working, she takes a shower and has dinner with the kids, which varies in its success, and then she finds marathon reruns of *Britain's Got Talent* or compilations on YouTube of past winners and Golden Buzzer moments, and drinks and watches it at full volume. I think Daniel sits with her sometimes, but it's usually her on her own, the applause and laughter making it sound like her flat is full of people.

I move my headboard aside as silently as I can – I detached it from the bed last year for just this reason – put my ear against the wall, and listen. My favourites are the singers, especially the little ones whom you least expect to be able to belt it out. I'm sure the magicians are good too but I can't see them, of course, to be able to judge. Carla likes the comedians. I hear her laugh out loud sometimes. I laugh to myself, very quietly, so she won't hear me.

There's a pause in the programme, a sudden silence. I pull myself away from the wall as quietly as I can to the very edge of my bed and hold my breath. I hear a *thunk* on the table next to the wall on her side, which I know is her bottle opener. She just got up for another beer, and I exhale with relief, not returning to my spot by the wall until I can hear the show is on again.

'All right, Susannah?' I say. She purrs and we listen together through the wall.

4

Saturday

Penny
Flat 1B

'What's it sound like, Mum? I'm at work. My back is fine . . .
Yes, the one with the broken lift . . . Who's going to tell Tesco,
you? You going to report me? Tell them I walked up a flight of
stairs? . . . It's extra money in my pocket, Mum . . . I'll pick up
your prescription on the way home . . . You already asked me
that . . . Okay, bye, bye . . .'

Darren puts his phone in his pocket and distractedly makes
his way towards the stairs with the hand truck of groceries,
nearly running over the tiny Asian girl sweeping the lobby and
the old Black lady with the lavender hat checking her post.
Darren, a big white guy from the East End, is not one for
noticing people, but even he spotted that the old lady was
wearing a church hat with her tracksuit. Another nutter. The
skinny Asian girl seems not to see him, so he says, ''Scuse me,
love,' loudly, and she starts. He gets a glimpse of her face and
for a moment he wonders what kind of Asian she is, like
Vietnamese or Thai or something, but then dismisses the
thought when cat food pouches begin falling off the top crate.

He says, 'Sorry, ladies,' as he picks them up, expecting no
response, and getting none. No matter, he had enough to deal
with without getting into conversations with weird Asian girls
and crazy old ladies.

Darren wheels the truck to the lift and presses the buttons
on the off-chance it might be working this time. It isn't. He
hauls the hand truck of groceries up the stairs, taking one at a

42

time, ignoring the twinge in his lower back each of the twelve times that the hand truck hits the next step.

'For fuck's sake,' he says under his breath as his phone vibrates again while he pushes the hand truck to Penny's door.

'What is it, Mum, I'm at work . . . No, I told you, after this shift I'll get your pills . . . remember? Yes . . . you'll have them, I promise . . . I'm ringin' off now, all right?'

She's getting worse. Darren doesn't like leaving her alone in the flat. What if she forgets to turn off the tap or the stove, or goes out and forgets to lock the door? Or forgets how to get home. Whole days go by when she forgets to eat. She's thin as a rail.

Darren knocks on the door of 1B and calls, 'You in there, Mrs Danford? It's Darren.' The rhythm of his Cockney accent echoes off the walls. He looks up and sighs at the fluorescent lights in the ceiling. Mental women everywhere he turns today. He's about to deal with one more.

The door to 1B opens but only as far as the chain will allow.

'Yes, hello, Darren, how are you?' Penny warbles at him, high-pitched and hoarse.

Half of her face is covered by the door. He sees one eye above the door chain, half a mouth below it. He remembers her as pretty once, that time he delivered to her and Jamie by chance, when they still lived together, and he got a look down her blouse as she bent over the crates of groceries. Shame she's a nutcase now. She had a nice rack.

'Fine, thanks. Now what should I do with all this, the usual? Or do you want to try to do this the easy way? Maybe opening the door today?'

'Same as usual, please, pass everything under the door chain if you don't mind. Oh, and here you are.' Penny hands him an envelope containing a twenty-pound tip and a shopping list through the narrow opening.

'Thanks,' Darren says, checking the envelope Penny passes to him before beginning their ritual. He takes all the bags out of the crates and lines them up.

43

'Chicken nuggets,' he says, and he pushes the bag of frozen nuggets through the opening under the chain.

Carla
Flat 1A

Carla holds the ice pack to her head, looks in the bathroom mirror, surveys the damage to her face.

'So, you went to see the lawyer about how to divorce me and keep your visa, is that it?' Tom spat through the phone at her earlier this morning.

'What? That's not why I went there, I swear. She just needed documents for the visa renewal—' she said, the hot flush of the lie crawling up her skin. Tom's voice carried through the phone, reached out to the air in front of her, so loud, like he was in the same room and not on the other side of London. She closed the bathroom door so the children wouldn't overhear them.

'The little bitch paralegal told me everything, Carla. I get the bills, remember? I saw the charge for a meeting, I called up, I asked what it was about, and the little slag told me all your plans. Tell me, darlin', what money were you going to use? Did you think you were going to pay the lawyer, and the thousands in Home Office fees, with what – the money I give you every month for the kids? I don't think so. And how were you going to pay for the divorce? Also with the money I give you? You listen to me. I find out you called her again, I'll stop paying the rent. I'll cancel your cards. And if you think you're so smart, you have so many plans, you can go apply for benefits. Oh . . . hang on a second . . . you can't apply for benefits, can you? Not allowed under your visa, is it?'

'No, Tom, that's not what I thought, that's not—' Carla stammered.

'You think you can stay here without me, Carla? You think you can do anything without me?'

'No, of course I don't . . . but you're not here, Tom, you're *not* with me,' she whimpered, losing her breath. 'I thought you might not want to be tied down to me anymore and maybe I could make it easier for you if I—'

'All I have to do is call immigration, yeah? One call. I'll say you left me, our marriage is over, and I'll say you're not letting me see the kids. I'll say you stole money from my business, I'll say you used me for my money and for a visa and it was all a sham. I'll say anything I like,' he said, quietly, in a harsh whisper. She heard Sherry cooing at their baby in the background.

'But I— But you left *me*. I didn't do—' Carla said weakly, unable, as always, to articulate herself with him.

'So, you're not going to dictate to me where I need to be and when to see my kids. *I* tell *you* when I'm going to see them—'

'I'm sorry, I just thought . . .' She couldn't get the words out. She trembled, thoughts jumbled, tears stifled.

She could hear that he'd moved to another room. No more baby noises.

'Before you complain about some Saturday morning football match, you best remember who holds your *fucking life* in his hands.' And before she could apologise, or plead, or explain, he rang off.

Still clutching her phone, she turned around to vomit, just making it to the toilet. That was not how that call was supposed to go. She called him this morning because last night he told Daniel that he would be free to take him to his match this morning, but of course he didn't arrive to pick him up. She called just to see if he was on his way, just to ask, just to—

'Mum?' Daniel called. 'Is Dad coming or not? I've got to go, I can't be late.'

'Um . . .' she said weakly, not knowing how to answer, her brain too scrambled to think.

'Get a grip,' she said to herself in the mirror, holding both sides of the sink, as her mind raced to find an exit that didn't exist. *If I leave and take the kids to New York, he'll get me for kidnapping.* She splashed water on her face, tried to slow her breathing with deep breaths, but couldn't find any air. *If I try to divorce him, he'll cut off the money.*

'Mum?' Daniel called outside the bathroom. 'Mum, c'mon? What do I do? Are you going to work? Is Mary Rose taking me?' *I won't make the rent and I can't go on benefits, so then he'll say I can't take care of the kids and he'll take them.*

'I'm not taking him, this is so *fucking* unfair,' she heard Mary Rose complain through the bathroom door. *If he takes the kids, I won't be able to do that other visa, to stay as their mom.*

'Mary Rosie, language,' Carla tried to admonish her, speaking to the mirror, trying to sound normal, like nothing was wrong, but she didn't have enough air to speak. *I can't ask the lawyer, he'll find out. I can't even pay the lawyer to ask a question. He'll just say I left him.*

'What are you doing?' Daniel persisted through the door.

'I'm *not* taking him, you *can't* make me,' Mary Rose proclaimed.

'Mum! Are you all right?' Daniel shouted, shaking the doorknob. 'Why won't you say anything?' *I didn't leave him. He left me. He left me? Didn't he?*

'Okay, just calm down, I'll . . .' Carla wheezed to her son, trying to sound calm and maternal behind the door. She reached for the doorknob, tripped over the bathmat, and that's when everything went black.

And now she's looking in the mirror, at the bruise, the cut, the wrinkles, the bags under her eyes. That's the third time she's fainted in as many months. The second bruise on her forehead. But not the first cut to her face. Those scars have faded, but she can still see them.

Penny
Flat 1B

'What next, bananas, eggs, cat food?' Darren asks, out of breath. He had just come back from rushing down to the street because he'd heard a chorus of car horns and a siren down on Bedford Road. He had been worried about his truck getting caught where it wasn't supposed to be because the stop here was not on his schedule.

'Shall we try the eggs, then?' Penny warbles at him, and he passes them through, one at a time. Then the tiny cartons of UHT milk, the kind meant for children's packed lunches. Pouches of Capri-Sun taken out of the box. Never loaves of bread. Only slim packets of thin-cut bagels or baps that are flattened on their way through but then recover their shape in Penny's flat. Right, he needs to tell her about that.

'I'm very sorry, Mrs Danford, but it looks like there was no rolls like you like and there was none of them bagels neither and also none of that muesli in the small bag.'

He pronounces muesli as *moose lee*, and for a moment Penny imagines a moose wearing kung-fu garb, a black belt, standing next to Darren, massive horns protruding from his head.

'No Alpen Swiss muesli?' she says, after a beat, and Darren can hear her rising panic.

Quickly, before Penny gets upset, he adds, 'No, but what I did was I went and found you the one you like, only it's in the big bag. But we can manage . . .'

'Yes, well, that's highly irregular, isn't it? I'm not sure . . .' Penny pauses, recovers composure. 'What I should say is how kind you are, Darren. How thoughtful. If you look after your mother even half as well as you look after me, then she is a very lucky woman. How is she, Darren?'

'She's all right, Mrs Danford, I'll tell her you asked after her,' he says, annoyed about her response to his muesli solution and slightly disturbed by her mention of his mother. He'd never spoken to Penny about her. Now he knows she eavesdrops on his phone conversations in the hall, and he wonders whether the extra money is worth this level of aggravation. After all, it's not like this woman is family. He's under no obligation to do what he's doing, breaking a bunch of bananas into its individual constituents to pass them through the gap under the door chain to this mentalist who couldn't leave her flat.

Darren is the cousin of a friend of a friend of Jamie's he used to see down at the pub. When Penny started ordering groceries online after they'd had Olivia, Darren happened to deliver to them once. After the Tube incident, Penny was released from hospital and her parents settled her into this studio flat. She'd been doing very well with a part-time job at the library. And Jamie had started visiting her.

But on the day she'd been let go from her job, a casualty of budget cuts, Penny had gone into Tesco when someone had walked out of an emergency exit door, triggering a loud alarm. Most shoppers paid it no mind, but the sudden, pulsing sound struck her in the heart, and she dropped her shopping basket, a container of yogurt exploding all over the floor. An old woman shook her cane at her and a shop employee began shouting. Penny tried to run away but she was disoriented and couldn't find the exit. That's when she saw the cage descending from the supermarket ceiling. That's when she screamed in the middle of the shop floor, 'I can't get out! I can't get out!' She stopped screaming only when the police arrived.

Since then, Penny had been too afraid to go back to Tesco. And she didn't want to order her groceries online because she was worried about the delivery men – strangers – knowing where she lived. She was sure she could get over it, she just needed a bit of time, a few sessions with her therapist. But in the meantime, she'd been eating only crisps and Mars bars, the closest things within reach of the door of the corner shop where she could just about manage a transaction as long as she remained very close to the exit. As long as she didn't have to go any further into the shop. Shops weren't safe.

When she told Jamie what happened on one of his evening visits, he called Darren and asked whether he would mind helping them out for an extra twenty pounds. It was meant to be temporary, to help Penny over that particular hump in her recovery, or what Jamie thought was recovery. Setbacks were bound to happen. Losing her job was a blow, as it would have been to anybody. But she couldn't exist on Walkers salt and vinegar crisps and chocolate bars forever.

Jamie didn't understand that her illness thrived on avoidance. That he was reinforcing the barbed wire around shops in her mind and paying for another step in her retreat from the world.

They agreed that Darren would do Penny's shopping and drop it off when he was delivering in her area. Jamie paid for the groceries plus twenty pounds for his trouble via bank transfer. Penny gave Darren a new list when she saw him and an extra twenty pounds. Memory was not a strength of Penny's. She tried to forget most things. She had forgotten, for example, that Jamie paid Darren to help her. But when Darren reminded her that he had already been paid, she insisted he take the extra money. She knew he bore the most risk in this arrangement, going off route and schedule to do this for her. She had so few ways to show her appreciation. It was one of the things she lost with her illness – the opportunity to be generous and to show gratitude. Giving Darren a big tip gave her just a tiny bit of control. The power to be thankful.

As Darren passes a single carrot through the door, breaking it in half because it's too long to go in at the proper angle, he notices Carla, in her doorway, ushering her kids out the door. She's wearing that little navy-blue thing, the satin robe that shows off her bosoms, her thighs. He's seen her in it before, on past deliveries, when they'd smiled at each other, but not

49

spoken. He's seen better breasts and legs on other women but there's something about Carla, her sad eyes, her wild ginger hair. Or maybe it was just her openness, her lack of shame or embarrassment, standing there, in that awful lighting, in that flimsy robe that didn't flatter her, which somehow made her that much more attractive. She seemed naked, even in her clothes.

He watches her send the children out, kissing the boy on the forehead as he says, 'You're sure you're all right, Mum?'

Darren pretends to be absorbed in Penny's carrots and not watching the family when he hears Carla say, 'Thanks, Mary Rosie.'

In the corner of his eye he sees the teen girl, in her crop top and leggings under her oversized puffer jacket. She says, 'Whatever, Mum, you owe me,' as she walks down the corridor.

Feeling that he'd more than earned his tip today, and with only a few carrots and the muesli left, the muesli Penny had not even appreciated, Darren says to Penny, 'Well, this is the last of it, Mrs Danford. I'm sure you can reach out and grab this other stuff out here, it's just a few bits and bobs, got to run to my next delivery, all right?' as he scrambles to get his hand truck and wheel it past Carla's door before she closes it.

'Darren?' Penny calls, but her voice is too weak to be heard, particularly by someone who doesn't want to hear it.

Penny watches Darren through the slice of a reflection she can see in the mirror that leans against the wall right next to her door. And then she understands. She sees him wheel to a tentative stop in front of Carla's door. She sees Carla clench the lapels of her robe together. Penny thinks for a moment that they would make a nice couple.

'He'd better be careful, though,' she mutters to herself.

5

Penny
Flat 1B

He'd better be careful, though. Darren doesn't know what's going on behind that door. At least she's had the decency to try to cover up on top. A good brassiere would do wonders for Carla, and everyone around her.

But never mind that now. We have a problem. He left my carrots in the hall. The bag of Alpen Swiss muesli. It's nothing I can't sort out but, 'Darren?'

He doesn't hear me. Or he doesn't want to.

I close the door. 'Think now, Susie, we can work this out,' I say, as she winds her way around my legs, back arched, meowing. I feel a tremble starting in my hands, a tightness in my chest, but so that Susannah won't worry, I start talking through it: 'A problem shared is a problem halved. In every problem lies an opportunity. How do you solve a problem like Maria?'

I bend down to give her a stroke, but she scampers off and settles herself in her Moses basket.

I must think fast now. I must sort this out, before anyone notices, before anyone sees. But first I must wait, wait for Darren to shove off, wait for Carla to close her door, wait for them to stop talking. I need the hallway clear. That's first.

I put my ear to my door and wait for silence.

'How's things?' the Tesco guy says, stopping at my door just before I'm about to close it.

'Not bad.' I smile, and try to cover up my chest, clutching at my robe. I look down, go to close the door, give a little wave, but he keeps talking.

'Kids out for the day?' he asks, and I see his face change in concern when he sees my forehead and the cut on my cheek.

'Yeah,' I say, wishing there was some polite way to tell him to go, to say *get out of here*, but he's not taking the hint and—

'Can I help you, mate?' Tom says, with his deep rasp, from over my shoulder, his hand creeping around my waist, pulling me into him. He's breathing hard, the congested breathing of having drunk too much the night before.

'Oh,' the delivery guy says. 'No, I was just going,' he says, surprised, seeing he got the situation wrong, thinking this is what it looks like. God, he has no idea.

I close the door.

'Who's that, then?' Tom says, making his way back to his breakfast at the table. It's the tone in his voice. That's where it starts.

'I don't know, he delivers groceries to the crazy lady next door. I don't even know his name,' I lie. It's Darren.

'Should I make more bacon?' I ask, trying to change the subject.

'He's got a thing for you then, does he?' Tom says, looking up from his toast, escalating, seething.

'No, I've never spoken to him before. More eggs? Coffee?' I say.

'Well, I guess a job like that's pretty boring, he probably talks to everyone,' Tom says, retreating, withdrawing. I'm relieved. We won't have to argue about the delivery guy. But if we don't argue then that means he has other plans for us.

'You sure I can't get you anything else?' I say, pretending not to know what's coming.

'No, thanks, love, why don't you put your feet up now, get some rest; you had a tough morning,' he says.

The sofa bed is still unfolded from last night, so he guides me over, covers me with the blanket. I try not to flinch. I try not to think too hard about what's next. Or that there's no choice.

When I passed out in the bathroom, Daniel called Tom, scared, not knowing what else to do. Tom rushed over, but I was up by the time he got here. He ordered the kids a car service and gave Mary Rose thirty pounds as a fee for taking Daniel to his match. That brightened her mood. It also got them out of the house. And left me alone with him.

He sits down on the edge of the bed beside me. 'I'm sorry about before, love. On the phone. I really am,' he says. I keep my eyes closed.

'That's okay,' I say. He inches closer.

'I've just . . . I've been under a lot of stress,' he says, brushing my hair behind my ear. He runs a finger along my chin, his callouses bumping along my jaw.

I don't say anything. I'm waiting to know which Tom this is.

'You know I love you. Do you know that? If anything ever happened to you, God, Carla, I don't know what I would do. My heart stopped when Daniel called and said you were out cold,' he says, as he runs the finger from my jaw, down my neck, to my collarbone. Along my collarbone, to the dip between my clavicles, where he lingers, where he rubs. I keep my eyes closed. I will his hand to move from there, from that notch where there is no bone, no muscle, to protect me.

'I know,' I say, with a jagged sigh. Because it's the truth, even if it's just the truth to him.

He leans in and kisses my cheek. I can smell last night's beer on him. His stubble scrapes my face like sandpaper. His

53

finger travels from my neck, down, down, down. And I know what he wants. And what I have to do.

Penny
Flat 1B

'It's all right, Susie, it's okay,' I say, panting. I don't want her to be concerned, but it's difficult work.

I struggle, forcing my broom out under the door chain through the opening to the hallway floor. I push and jab, trying to hook the bag of carrots and muesli in the corridor. The handle is too long and stiff to get it through the narrow gap, so I bend the plastic broomstick until it cracks in the middle and I stand on a chair to get the right angle to manoeuvre it out. But the blunt end gets no purchase on the slippery plastic bag of carrots and the slick bag of cereal. I'm sweating, panting, dizzy with the effort. Dizzy and breathless and terribly, terribly thirsty. It's the third day without the pills and I have landed in a desert this morning where there is never ever enough to drink.

'This won't do, Susannah, it just won't do,' I say, trying not to shriek at her, trying not to show in my voice how my concern is growing.

And then, 'Of course!' I shout.

I run to the closet, find a metal coat hanger – one of the ones from Jamie's shirts when he used to send them out to the cleaners – and I straighten it, tape the hook of the hanger to the end of the broom, and I reach and reach and reach for the carrots, hooking the bag then losing my grasp, then hooking it again until I pull it to the door. I hop off my chair and pull the carrots through the gap, the plastic bag tearing, inflicting wounds on some of the orange flesh, but otherwise, getting them into the flat not too badly scathed.

Next is the muesli. The bag is a slippery, harder plastic. But Darren had already made a small hole in it to let the air out so he could push it through, although he should have known – *he should have known* – that since he bought the big bag it wouldn't fit.

If I could just hook into that hole. My sweat and tears mix. I swipe at my face, then tug and pull, tug and pull, and – yes! yes! – the hook catches the hole in the plastic. I pull the bag towards the door, but – no! – the flakes spill out. The door presses into me as I push through the gap, my whole arm, my whole shoulder, I try to push myself through the gap, the wood pushing back at me, trapping me, not letting me out. I hook and I hook the bag again and again, the flakes spill, but I finally pull it to me, finally get it to the gap and then I stab, and stab and stab. And Stab. Stab, stab, stab. Stab again. And again. Until the Alpen Swiss muesli is pulverised. Until it is dust.

Carla
Flat 1A

This is how it begins.

'I didn't mean it, love, I'm sorry,' he breathes into my breastbone.

'I know,' I whisper in his ear.

'Forgive me?' He kisses my shoulder.

'Yes.' I exhale.

'Do you love me?' he asks the palm of my hand.

'Always,' I murmur into his neck, and wish it wasn't true, and wish there was another answer.

Penny
Flat 1B

'That was breakfast for two weeks, Susannah,' I say. She meows at me. Rubs against my leg. My breakfast is now a pile of dust outside the door. And they didn't have my rolls or my thin bagels, so there will be no bread.

55

I close the door and step over the groceries that litter the floor – loose carrots, a lone Wispa bar, foil pouches of Felix, Susannah pawing at one, wondering how to get the food out. I find the frozen chicken nuggets and put them in the freezer. They are the most important. Susannah meows at me.

'That's not the point, Susannah, I know I can take a pill.'

I regret being sharp with her as soon as I say it. She steps over the envelopes of chicken Cup-a-Soup and jumps in her bed, curling up with her back to me.

Then I hear them.

I lie down on my bed and listen. Or, I don't mean to listen, I just hear them, I can't help it, and I don't want to, but I do. Carla moans and Tom grunts, over and over, somewhere near the wall.

I cover my face with my hands, try to bury my head under the pillows. I have forgotten touch. It has been a long time since I've known it. I have not felt a brush of fingertips across the counter in the corner shop. Or a nurse's cold hand taking my blood pressure. Or the sleeve of my coat against the sleeve of a stranger's coat brushing past me in the opposite direction. Darren tries not to touch me when he passes each item to me through the door, as though I am contaminated, contagious. There is a second during which we will each hold one end of a carrot or one side of a pouch of Capri-Sun, but our fingers never meet.

Their sounds are guttural, primal. They make me writhe on the bed, curl my feet, tense my shoulders. Not from arousal, not titillation. The pills took that away from me long ago. It is hunger. Skin hunger. My nerve endings, unaccustomed to human touch, reach for it, like a million tiny plants under my skin bending all at once to find the light. Desperate for the light. I am starving. There has been no touch for so long.

I pull out the box from under the bed where I keep the winter-weight duvet and I put that on top of the one already on my bed and my grandmother's quilt on top of that and I pull all the blankets over my head. They are heavy all together, but the weight is consoling. I think of Jamie. Of nights with Jamie curled on one side, Olivia curled on the other, me pinned in between. The closeness, the warmth, the weight of them, he like a bear and she like a cat, curled around me, encasing me, heat radiating from her child's skin, his breath on my neck, his arm across my waist. I lay still and listened to the sounds of their sleeping.

It helps to wrap myself up like this, in a fabric tomb. It slows my heart, the dark sarcophagus of wool and down and memory. And regret. I put my hand up to my hair, to check Olivia's barrette is still there.

There is no bread and no muesli. There is no Jamie and no Olivia. No message on my phone, no plan to be anywhere, no job, no work that is due, no going out, no friend, no errands, no weekend walk in the park, no coffee in a take-away cup, no mums' night out, no little girl hair to brush and plait, no men's socks thrown in the corner to make me angry, no after-school activities to register for, no parent-teacher meetings, no lunch to pack, no appointment, nowhere for me to be, no one expecting me, no one waiting for me, no one missing me.

No one noticing that I am not there.

Finally, Carla and Tom stop. I uncover myself and lie for long moments on my bed staring at the ceiling, gasping, aching in my skin, wondering if they are wrapped in each other's arms or whether Tom has put distance between them the way men do even though he knows her arms long for him. Jamie never did that to me. Others, yes, but not him.

I am still for a long while before my mind turns to the mess of crushed muesli outside the door. How to fix it. How to fix it before someone sees it or before the man in 1C whose name I don't know complains. Susannah jumps on to the bed near my head.

'There you are, come here,' I say, reaching for her. But she walks across my pillow, steps on my forehead and jumps off the bed to sniff the blinking light of the vacuum charging in the corner.

Woman
Flat 2A–2B

Today I had good luck, Mother.

Today it was the day for cleaning the lobby and the corridors and the stairs. Every other day, I am sent to clean around the building before I do my other work. I think it is every other day, maybe it is every two; I try to count the days but sometimes I lose them. They used to wake me in the night to do the cleaning, so that I would not be seen. But after Baby came, his care occupied my nights. So now I clean the corridors every week in the daytime. They no longer watch me. They know I will not run.

Today I was sweeping the stairs and the halls and there is usually only dust and dirt, Mother. Not difficult to clean. Only one time was there blood. The morning after the Russian girl ran away, do you remember, I told you? Only that one time.

But today I had good luck, Mother. Today in the corridor on the first floor there was food, everywhere. All over the floor, the grains crushed into dust, but there were sweet raisins and nuts. And because I was alone, and because they do not watch me when I clean the corridors, I knelt down, and I ate it. Quickly before anyone could see.

The sweetness of a raisin, Mother. I picked out all the raisins first. Do you make the raisin cakes for Beauty? Do you tell her about me when they come out of the oven? And how I loved them when I was a girl like her?

The grain was like a dust but some of it was whole, and dry and hard to swallow, but when one is faced with luck like this, Mother, one does not walk away. What I could not eat I swept away into the dustpan. Such a shame to have to sweep the rest away, the bits too mangled or dirty to eat. I thought about it, about taking the flakes off the broom, closing my eyes, and swallowing, but even I am not so low down, Mother. Sometimes I must remind myself, with my long-ago voice, with the voice I had before I began Better Life, that I am not so low down.

Mother, today I had good luck. There were raisins. But also, Mother, a white paper, a receipt. I don't know the words except Tesco, and there is also a date. Whenever I find a receipt in the rubbish, or like this, on the floor when cleaning the corridor, or in the pockets of clothes when I do the washing at Laundrette, I keep it. I have not had a receipt for some time now. In Laundrette, Old Madame's till makes the receipts, but she never lets me near it. I never speak to the customers, never touch the receipts. This one says 18/01/20. 2020, Mother. The first receipt I found when I came here, the one I keep hidden behind the broken electrical outlet in My Lady's room, it says 2017. 11/03/17. Three years. That is how I know how long it has been. When I think that I have been here forever, when I start to think that I was always here and forget the life before this one, I have the receipt to remember.

There was a time before and there will be a time after. I cannot imagine it, Mother, but there will be a time after this one.

Carla
Flat 1A

And this is how it ends.

'I've got to be getting on,' he says, his back turned to me.

'Okay,' I say, pulling on my robe.

'This . . . what we just did, you know this doesn't mean . . . you know I'm with Sherry,' he says, pulling on his shirt.

'I know,' I say. 'Do you want to stay, have dinner with the kids?' I ask the wall.

'Not today. Work, the baby – I've got to get back. Tell them I love them,' he says, tying his shoes.

'Sure,' I say, staring at the floor.

'And no more calls to the lawyer, you hear?' he says, putting a hand through my hair, giving a sideways smile, before he pulls it back further, yanking my head back, doing it gently, pretending he's playing. Except he isn't.

'I'll take care of you,' he says.

And he will. One way or another.

Penny
Flat 1B

I have a plan. I will check the peephole first to make sure no one is there. Then I will open the door on the chain. I will then unchain the door and open it further. I will stand in the doorway and I will reach out with the broom and sweep all the cereal from the corridor into my flat and then hoover it up once it's in here, safe with me. I will barely need to take a step outside the door. If this were Tuesday, I could open the door and go out into the hall because going out is part of Tuesday's routine, but today is Saturday and it would be highly irregular.

I've protected myself. I'm wearing the woollen underwear from that ski holiday with Jamie that one time. The mechanic's boiler suit on top of that, the one splattered with paint from when we painted the flat before Olivia was born. Over this, the large men's trench coat, the one I found on eBay that I bought to make it easier to go outside, when I used to go outside on other days besides Tuesdays. Then my rubber kitchen gloves and the light-blue surgical face mask. Then Jamie's old Yankees cap, the one we bought in New York, and finally, my winter boots.

I bring the chair silently over to the door to stand on it so I can look out the peephole without anyone who may be outside the door noticing the shadows of my feet, like Mable does. And that is where I stay because, well – someone's there. The weight of all the clothing makes it hard to breathe and constricts my ribs, my chest, but I watch her. She is sweeping up the mess, sweeping away from my door, making a pile of dust in the middle of the floor, and first I think, the management, she will tell the property manager, he will knock on my door, I will have to speak to him, he will call Jamie, Jamie will tell the social worker, she will come round to the flat, she will know I stopped taking the pills, then she will call the doctor, it will all begin again, the calls, the visits, the doctors, the reports, the pills, the pills – but then she bends down, and kneels on the floor. She puts her hand in the mound of cereal, lifts it to her mouth – and eats it. I stay very still to make sure that she's real. She does it again.

Then the sound of metal scraping wood as I slip off the chair and it falls over, and I fall over with it. Susannah darts across the flat and meows, the rustle of the men's trench coat, the rubber sound of my gloves on the wood floor as I scramble to get up. It is a wall of sound and I am so thirsty, so thirsty. A trickle of sweat runs down my neck from under the cap, I feel the patch of sweat on my lower back where the old woollen undershirt rubs. I stand as still as I can once I get up, watching the clock. I stand still for eight minutes. I hear Carla's TV switch on. The slam of the door in the lobby downstairs.

I have a plan. I open the door on the chain and I look. She is gone. I unchain the door and open it further. The floor is clean now, except . . . except – I kneel down at the base of my doorway and just in the corner, just there in the corner of the door, under the hinges, where it meets the door sill when you close it, just there, are two raisins. She must not have seen them. I pick them up with my rubber gloves, pull down my face mask, and eat them.

THE STORY OF PENNY

2018

She's rounder now, softer, a layer like velvet under her skin, filling out the places where she was once sharp and angular, her clavicle no longer prominent. She was gaunt the last time he saw her, when they took her to hospital. He hadn't noticed how thin she had become until he watched the paramedics handle her, gently, like a sparrow whose wing had snapped. They touched her lightly, softly. Even though she swore at them. Even though she was psychotic.

She catches his green eyes, looking at her now, at the two buttons of her shirt dress pulling too tightly across her bust, the gaps between the buttons opening awkwardly when she sits down.

'You must think me quite pudgy now,' Penny says, blushing, turning away to undo the buttons discreetly, so they won't break, displaying a bit of lace at the top of her camisole underneath. Thank goodness she thought to wear it.

'It's the meds. They slow your metabolism, but they're working. I feel like myself again. Like the myself from even before the—' She doesn't finish the sentence.

'You look lovely. And that's good, about the meds, really good,' Jamie says, nursing his tea. Then there is silence. She notices the grey at his temples, the new salt and pepper in his stubble, the dark shadows against the pale skin under his eyes. She pets the cat.

'It's so nice of you to bring me Susannah. My therapist says that a pet will be very good for me,' she says, holding the cat in her lap, unsure whether this is the first or second time she has said this.

'It's fine, really, she only ever hissed and scratched at us all the time after—' he says, and sees her face and wishes he could take back the 'us'. 'Us', he knows, is like a knife stuck in Penny's spine, cutting off the feeling to her limbs.

He hurries to make up for it. 'Susannah was always yours anyway. She loved you best.' He sees her intake of breath. He waits.

'I'm not going to ask to see her. I've no right to ask that—' She clutches Susannah's fur forcefully. The cat meows and jumps off her lap.

'Pen—' he starts to say but doesn't know what to say after that.

Her flat is clean, she's wearing make-up. She smiles now. If you didn't know what she did, you'd never guess. He misses her. He loves her. He tried to act like she was dead, to accept that she was gone, but it was impossible. The letters she sent him. Her voice, her old voice, the Penny of Saturday night dinner dates and champagne picnics in the park and gauzy summer dresses, with a knack for eavesdropping on strangers' awkward first dates in small Italian restaurants – that Penny jumped through the purple ink. Lovely, funny, bubbly Penny. She sent the letters to his office address to show she knew she could be nowhere near Olivia, that not even paper she had touched could be near their daughter.

Her letters came from the hospital and then the group home. And then there were others, from her solicitor's office, to initiate the divorce and agree to Jamie's sole custody of Olivia. Her parents paid for it, put it all in motion, but it was her idea – or, rather, something her mother had said made her think it was her idea. A few months after she left Olivia on the Tube, when lucid thought had come back to her – not completely, but enough for her to understand what she had done – she thought the least she could do was the legal part so that Jamie wouldn't have to. She wanted to spare him the pain of having to ask.

The social workers said she didn't have to, that there could be limited contact, under supervision in a contact centre at first, and this could evolve over time, as she got better. But they had tried a visit under supervision, and it was disastrous. Penny, jittery and anxious, pale, with dark rings around her eyes, her hands trembling, was frightening to Olivia. Olivia would not go to her and they both cried uncontrollably in opposite corners of the room, each of them wondering where the real Penny had gone.

It was clear to Penny that Olivia knew not to trust her. And Penny thought she was right not to. But the social workers said she would get better, and she didn't have to give up being Olivia's mother; no one was asking her to do that. Everyone knew she did what she did because she wasn't well, not because she wanted to hurt her daughter.

But her mother had said, 'Supervised visitation? Really, Penny, don't be so selfish. What kind of mother sees their child once every two weeks in a contact centre? With strangers watching you? Is that what you want for her? Is that what you want her childhood memories to be? For God's sake, do at least one thing right.'

And Penny, who'd felt so helpless until then, finally understood there was something she could do to atone. Her final maternal decision could be one of protection for her little daughter. She could shield Olivia from the inconsistencies of her damaged mind. She could relieve Olivia of the burden of having her for a mother.

It was deeply painful, but, in that pain, Penny also found deep relief. Now she was no one's wife, no one's mother, no one's person to be relied upon. This way, if she was overtaken again by the agonies that inhabited her brain, there was no one to endanger, no one's trust to unintentionally betray with her madness. She was sad, of course. Desperately. But also, she was free. And so was her family.

For a long time, Jamie didn't answer her letters. He was shaken; stunned by his sudden single fatherhood and overwhelmed by the intricate logistics of child-rearing that Penny had always handled and that he had never appreciated or even thought about – the nit comb, calamine lotion, vaccination appointments, spare clothes for the nursery bag, hypoallergenic, perfume-free detergent, the portable potty seat. More than once he thought, *No wonder she went crazy*, when he navigated Tesco's crowded baby aisle, unable to discern the right size of night-time pull-ups, Olivia's fractious thrashing in the shopping trolley eliciting the tuts of strangers.

His life, with his beautiful wife and lovely daughter in their house not too far from the common, had disappeared one morning without warning, and the shock of it, rather than plunging him into emotion, had stripped him of feeling. He operated automatically. He made decisions for Penny's care in the beginning, as her husband, without anger or sadness, until her parents took it over. Two weeks after the Tube, after Penny's admittance to the psychiatric hospital, after the abrupt cancellation of the life he thought was his – theirs – he went back to work, did his job efficiently, ate lunch alone and spoke to no one.

Only Olivia could reach him, only she received a response. Every morning he searched her face for signs of psychological trauma, finding only smiles for him there. He slept on the floor of her room next to her cot and listened to her breathe at night. She stopped asking for Mama after about six months, when he thought she must have lost her memory of Penny or had finally learned, too early in her short life, that sometimes people just don't come back. He didn't show her pictures of Penny or talk about her. He thought it was better for Olivia if Penny just drifted away from her life, and if he closed the wound of losing her before Olivia could even remember it was there. It was only in the early hours of the morning as he stared, sleepless, at Olivia's bedroom ceiling, that he let himself feel, and shed quiet tears of mourning, a widower grieving for a wife who wasn't dead.

Penny's letters were not the letters of a stalker or maniac. Her handwriting was clear, her thoughts coherent. She did not plead with him or ask to come home. She never mentioned Olivia except at the end where she always wrote, 'I hope Olivia is well', understanding the boundary that she must never cross again. And over time, his heart could not help but give a little leap when he saw an envelope addressed to him in purple cursive sitting on his desk.

Finally, about two years after she left their baby on the train, he went to see her.

'Why on earth, Jamie, would you do such a thing?' his mother shrieked, appalled, disturbed.

'Because she's alone,' he said. 'And I love her and she's the mother of my child,' he didn't add, because he was the only one who still thought that meant something after what she had done.

The thing he saw in the CCTV footage that no one ever mentioned was that she was holding Bun Bun when she got off the train. Before Penny could explain it, he knew, without a doubt, that Olivia had thrown Bun Bun, her favourite stuffed bunny, on the floor of the train carriage. She often threw Bun Bun on impulse, as a stress response, at the most inconvenient and even dangerous times, like in the middle of crossing Tottenham Court Road, or when trying to get the buggy off the bus.

He saw his wife clutching Bun Bun and he knew exactly what had happened. The train was crowded, Penny was stressed, Olivia felt it, and she threw Bun Bun, and then she moaned repeatedly, a low-level dirge, 'Bun Bun . . . Bun Bun.' Penny tried to pick the bunny up, bending awkwardly, one hand on the buggy, trying not to fall. But the carriage was too crowded and too full of self-absorbed bastard Londoners who didn't see Bun Bun, or if they did, didn't care and didn't help her. He knew that Penny's final act before leaving their daughter forever was trying to save the toy she loved most in the world, the little bunny she couldn't sleep without.

But as Penny was saving the bunny, she noticed the carriage door was open, and so she pushed the buggy further into the car while she ran in the opposite direction because she had finally seen a way out. She left her baby on the train, but she had also rescued the child's bunny before she ran. Yes, she left her intentionally, yes, she could never be around Olivia again – yes, to all of these things – but did she love her baby girl? Yes. He knew she did. And he forgave her, but he kept that to himself, a chronic ache in his chest.

Her latest letter said: '*Mum and Dad have said that now that I'm doing much better, they are happy to pay for my rent and utilities for the lovely little flat we found. But I must never go see them or contact them by phone. That's the deal – that's what Dad called it, our deal. We can exchange letters, but Mum in particular can't handle much more from me. It makes me sad, of course, but I know they have done and are doing everything they can for me, and I think it is just the sight of me that is too much for them and I can understand that. Nate is in Manchester and he sent those lovely flowers when I was in hospital but I haven't heard from him since. Mum said that was because my sister-in-law is afraid of me and wants to protect their children. I can understand that too, and between you and me, it's a relief and a money-saver. Fewer presents to buy at Christmas! And the only thing those kids need protection from is their mother's pretences. She's grooming them for Made in Chelsea, that's the real crime – I mean, "Hermione" and "Orlando"? My God . . .*' She tried to make it sound funny, that her friends, parents, brother, husband, child – were all gone.

He went to her flat, and after the first time, he went back every Wednesday evening after work, just for a half hour, just so he could check on her, just so he could put his hand through her hair, just so he could sometimes hold her hand against his chest and breathe. Sometimes, for a few moments, it felt like it was just the two of them again, in their first little flat in Streatham, with the broken radiator and the candles stuck in wine bottles that she thought were romantic. She wasn't dead. She was alive, and his loneliness lifted every Wednesday evening; the emptiness of every part of his life that wasn't Olivia was filled up, for just that little while.

One evening, months after that first visit to her flat, he stands behind Penny, arms around her waist as she looks out the window, his face buried in her hair. Her hair still smells like coconut, even after everything. He is desperate to give her something, to do something that will fix her and bring her back. Maybe if she sees Olivia, maybe . . . but he doesn't finish the thought, doesn't think it through to its inevitable conclusion, before he says, 'Would you like me to bring Olivia to play over there, in that playground, so you can see her through the window?'

'Oh—' She is breathless at the thought. 'Oh,' is all she could say as he kisses away her happy tears and silences his paternal instincts.

It will be okay, he thinks. Surely nothing bad can happen, he will be there the entire time with Olivia, they'll be across the street, nowhere near her. It will be so good for Penny to see her; therapeutic, he reasons. It will be good for her and him too. Of course it will, he thinks, and breathes in her coconut hair.

6

Sunday Morning

Jamie
Bedford Road playground

'That's a good girl, that's it, just put your foot there and then step up to the next one . . . brilliant!' Jamie says to Olivia, as he steadies her foot on the large, dome-shaped climbing frame. It's the highest she's ever climbed, higher than the other parents seem to let their girls go, or their boys, but he lets her do it anyway. Olivia is dressed in dungarees with a hole in the left knee, her curls wild and untamed in the wind, a tangled mess upon her head. He knows the black Converse high-tops and the tiny black motorcycle jacket – with the little Led Zeppelin patch he put on himself – are a bit much. He tells people, when they inevitably comment, that she chooses her own clothes. He doesn't mention that he steers her towards them in the boys' section of the shop. That he is purposely training her to resist pink and princesses. That he has banned Elsa and Shopkins from the house.

He can't stand the way little girls arrive at the pitch on Saturday morning in tutus and sparkly sandals to play football, too precious to wear shorts and trainers. He hates the way their parents enable their addictions to unicorns and rainbows. He loves Olivia's boyishness, encourages it, and hides his pride when one of Olivia's kicks accidentally catches a little princess in the face and makes her cry. He knows too, deep down, that she craves a princess dress but she won't ask for one, because she knows that her wearing the black leather jacket pleases him. It doesn't occur to him that this – a girl

69

subsuming what she wants to please her father, the important man in her life – is an even more insidious shade of pink.

'Up you go, that's it,' he shouts, as he sees her reach the top of the climbing frame, leaving the rest of the children, girls and boys alike – several older and bigger and more able than her – many rungs below her. He wants her to be strong. And fearless. To make up for not having a mother she will need to be strong. Stronger than these other feeble, clingy, snotty children. And so he pushes her, ready or not, at every opportunity, to find her strength.

'You did it!' he shouts when she gets to the top.

'I did it, Daddy!' she yells from her perch, victorious. They both bask in that glory for a few seconds, the wind whipping her hair, until she realises, suddenly, that she is small, and very far from the ground, and that she doesn't know how to get down.

The shrieking begins.

'Daddy, Daddy, come get me!' she screams, loud enough for the mothers, who had previously raised an eyebrow at him when they saw how high he let her go, to hear. They now slowly walk towards the climbing frame to see how he handles this. But they pointedly do not look at him, and urgently usher their own children off the lower rungs, as if his irresponsible parenting might endanger their children as well.

'Now, look, you can do this,' Jamie says in a calm voice.

'I can't, Daddy, I can't!' Olivia screams, starting to cry, the terror almost palpable in her voice.

'Of course you can; just listen to me. Are you listening?' he shouts up to her with a deliberate tone of cheerful patience.

But she cannot listen. She can only grip the metal bars underneath her and scream. A hot flush rises up Jamie's neck as he thinks about what to do. He could go up there right now and grab her and the whole thing would be over in thirty seconds. But if he comes to her rescue, she won't know that she can save herself. And she'll never climb up there again. She

70

can do this. And she can prove to all the parents whose eyes are on him now that she is exceptionally strong, stronger than their little brats, and that he knows what he's doing.

He says, 'Now listen to me, Olivia. Move your right foot down just one step, can you do that?'

Through hyperventilating sobs, she screams, 'What's my right? What's my right?' and Jamie groans internally because he knows the other parents are now wondering why, on top of everything else, he has not taught his daughter her left from her right, speculating as to whether it's because she's thick.

'Not that one, Olivia, the other one,' he says.

'This one?' Olivia shouts and panics, holding up her left foot with a feeble effort, too frightened to move and too frightened not to.

'No, not that one, Olivia, the other one,' Jamie says, raising his voice, only just barely hiding his frustration.

And Olivia, attuned to the slightest change in his tone, is even more fearful now that she thinks that Jamie is upset with her. She tries moving her right foot, but it's pinned beneath her. She's stuck. And as she struggles to move, she slips through the rungs of the climbing frame dome, about to fall to the ground except that on instinct, and because she is, in fact, quite strong, she catches a metal rung with both hands. She dangles precariously from the middle of the dome. Tears streaming down her face so she can barely see, she knows she is high above the ground, far too high for a five-year-old to jump down safely. She screams.

Jamie, heart pounding, realising his mistake too late, awkwardly starts pushing himself through the climbing frame bars to get to her.

'Hold on, Olivia, I'm coming,' he shouts, and sees her left hand lose its grip on the bar as she shrieks, 'Daddy!', hanging now only by her right hand.

And just as he is about to pull the rest of his body through the rungs to get to her, he hears, 'It's all right, darling, I've got you,' and sees Olivia in the arms of a reproachful, ruddy-faced mother hen, the kind of woman who has always known what is best. For everyone. She, of course, got through to the centre of the climbing frame before Jamie. And she had, of course, pulled her own whiny, flabby child off the climbing frame moments before, when she saw what was unfolding. She believes that some people shouldn't be allowed to have children.

'Get your hands off my daughter,' Jamie shouts, struggling to pull himself back through the rungs of the metal dome.

The woman, still clutching Olivia, is, of course, already standing outside the dome. She says, 'Excuse me? I think you meant to say, "thank you".'

'She was fine, absolutely fine. I was trying to parent,' Jamie says, forcibly extricating Olivia from her meddling, judgemental arms.

'Oh, is that what you call it? Letting your terrified child fall from ten feet up – that's parenting, is it?' she retorts, crossing her arms. Jamie sees the other parents gathering behind her, their children clasped to their hips and legs.

He can feel it, that they all think he's inadequate, that he has no idea what the fuck he's doing, that his wife shouldn't let him be alone with the child. Except they don't know his wife is a lunatic, and that it's always him who's alone with the child because there is no one else. What the fuck do these arseholes know about him or his life or his kid.

He opens the arsenal.

'It's hardly ten feet up, and what about you? What do you call grabbing at little girls you don't know? What are you? Some sort of paedo?' Jamie shoots back before he can stop himself.

There's an audible gasp from the crowd of parents. He closes his eyes, buries his face in the crying Olivia's tangled blonde hair, and shakes his head, asking himself why he always takes it this far. Why he couldn't have just said 'Thank

72

you'. Why he couldn't have just smiled and been self-deprecating and said something charming like 'Parenting fail', or 'That's why God made women the mothers'. And why he couldn't have just grabbed Olivia when she cried in the first place.

'I'm sorry, I shouldn't have said that.' He tries to take it back.

'No, you shouldn't have. How dare you? I should call child services on you, I should call the police!' she shouts, red-faced, self-righteously indignant, but aware that something has shifted.

Because although she's in the right, although she's the hero who saved Olivia from a broken arm or a concussion, she's also now the paedo. Of course, she isn't, but these days, one can never be too sure. The word hanging in the air is enough to make everyone grab their children, shake their heads, and rush to the playground gates.

'Are you all right, darling girl?' Jamie says to Olivia, stroking her hair and rubbing her back, feeling dismal. Olivia, calmer now, lays her head on Jamie's shoulder, comfortable to rest there in his arms. The mousy-haired paedo gives him one more disparaging look as she leaves the playground pushing her buggy, holding her toddler by the hand. But he's over it now, he has other things to think about. For one, he hopes to God that Penny didn't see all that. He checks his watch. 9:47. Not yet ten, so hopefully she still hasn't opened her curtains.

Jamie turns around to look for Penny in the window above the laundrette in the building across the street from the playground. The window from which she watches Jamie and Olivia play every Sunday morning at ten. No one knows he does this, that he lets Penny see Olivia this way, at a distance, once a week. Olivia doesn't even know why they come here. She knows nothing about her mother.

They got here early today because it was the first morning of sun they'd had for weeks, and he was out of coffee, so he set off early to stop at Dirty Betty's for a takeaway cappuccino before the sun hid itself again, as was its usual habit in the skies over London.

He breathes a sigh of relief when he sees Penny's curtains are still closed.

'You're all right now, Olivia. Go play,' he says, putting her down and watching her scamper off, the last five minutes of terror shrugged off and forgotten when she sees a school friend on the seesaw and runs to join her.

He watches her play. He craves another coffee. He wishes he still smoked. He wonders if the mother of the school friend had witnessed the paedo scandal because she doesn't smile back when they make eye contact. At five past ten he looks at Penny's window, but the curtains remain drawn.

She is always early, Penny, but never late.

7

Woman
First Premier Dry Cleaner and Laundry

Today I am in Laundrette all day. Laundrette days are the hardest of all, Mother. There is today in Laundrette, then tomorrow I clean the corridors, then the next day is back in Laundrette. Usually I look after Baby, day and night. When Baby sleeps, I do my other work: the cooking and cleaning, the washing and sorting and tidying for the family – Sir and Madame, and their children, Master and My Lady. Also, Old Madame, Madame's mother. Round and round, all day and night, I keep the house and make the meals and tend to Baby. They run their business, Laundrette. Sir owns many across London. They have machines for washing clothes for customers but also there is other cleaning done by a machine that is not in the shop. For this a man comes with a van and takes piles of clothes away and then brings them back hanging in plastic and smelling of chemicals.

And sometimes, when the man comes, and I help him bring the clothes to the van, there will be a girl crouched in the corner on the floor, bags of clothes all around her, sweating in the back of the van where there is no air. That is her transport to Better Life. These girls, they never try to get out of the van. I never try to help them. It will only end badly for us both. They know that too, so all we do is look, Mother, look at each other and then look away.

Today I will iron men's shirts all day in the back room and the shirt press will burn my hands, and standing all day, with

75

my foot on the pedal of the press, will break my back. But I am stronger today. Last night I was permitted to forage and so I had food in the evening and breakfast this morning and it feels like a light has been turned on inside my head. I found a tea bag, still warm, and so I had tea last night and I was careful with it and so could have tea again this morning.

It is Old Madame, Madame's mother, who minds Laundrette usually. She is not kinder than Madame, but she ignores me and does not meddle with my work. She drinks her tea and reads her newspaper, only looking at me now and again to make sure I am pressing the shirts. She does not do what Madame does, yelling over her shoulder every few minutes to insult me, or, if she has had an argument with Sir, stopping me at my work to listen to her litany of complaints, and then smacking me across the face so that I will forget everything I heard.

Before Old Madame unlocks the front door to open for the day, it is my task to sweep and mop the floor. She sits at the counter, and I go to the front of the shop where I can look out the window as I clean. And on these mornings, I watch the little girl with her father. Every fifth or seventh day, I lose count, but they come to play across the road in the little park. She runs and he chases her. She sits on the swing and he pushes her. She falls down and he picks her up and dusts off her knees and she runs off. They laugh.

I think he is alone, without a woman. No woman ever comes with him. The girl's hair, all its tangled curls – no girl with a mother would be let out like that. He tries to tie it back but her hair resists. A mother would know how to tame it. Poor motherless girl. But how he loves her. The love I can see even from here, across the road.

Mother, I am losing her face. Every night her face is more shadow, less light. The sounds of my girl, Beauty, I lost them first. If I heard a child's cry now, I would not know if it was her. I would not know the sound of her cry, but I know too that she no longer cries for me.

Did you tell her my name? Does she ever ask for me, Mother? When? Was it a sunny day, the day she understood I was not there and was not coming back, and then did the sun never look the same to her again? Or did the truth of not knowing me pass through her in the pulse of a heartbeat, accepted and forgotten by the pulse of the next because she was too busy with her game, her doll, her imaginary world, to feel it? I hope so. I hope she has forgotten what I cannot.

You have shown her a picture of me, I am sure you have, but it has been years and children's memories are soft and now it is the picture that she remembers. It is the picture that is her mother.

I lost her picture, Mother. Did I tell you how I tried to save it? It happened when they took my shoes and gave me flimsy slippers – 'So you cannot run', is what Madame said. But I cut a groove in the foam in the heel of one slipper. And then I cut out only Beauty's face, cut away all the rest of the photo to make it as small as possible, and I took the tiny face, the size of a seed, and slid it inside the foam in my heel and still they found it. Madame flicked it away like a speck of dust with her long red fingernail and then hit me with the slipper.

Did I tell you, Mother, that later when I cleaned under Master's bed, I found the tiny face stuck to the bottom of his dirty sock? The tiny face tracked around this house, from foot to foot, foot to slipper to floor to sock under bed, and I found her again. So, I put her in my mouth, and swallowed her. Did I tell you that? How I peeled the tiny face from the dirty cotton, covered in hair and dust and crumbs, and how I swallowed the tiny face of Beauty so that they could not take her picture from me? She is inside of me now, but still, her face is fading when I look for her behind my eyes.

The little girl has climbed to the top of the climbing frame, too high, and her father is standing to the side and cannot reach her. But PC Grant is now crossing the road with his bag of laundry, and his uniform for me to wash and iron. He has no woman either.

I step away quickly from the window and rush behind the counter, to the shirt press, behind Old Madame, keep my head down, reach into the bag of shirts and lay one out on the machine. She hobbles to the door to unlock it when she sees him.

'Hello, good morning, Officer,' Old Madame says to him, in English, her smile warm and wide. She greets him like a son.

'How are we today then?' he says.

'Not too bad, not too bad, Officer,' she says. She goes on and they converse, but I don't know the other words. If I lean my head down and slightly to the left, I can still see the girl on top of the frame. I don't know if she's crying or laughing.

He says other words I don't know and then holding his clothes, he says, 'The usual?'

The usual. This I know means that I wash the uniform and iron it. I do not dare look up at him during their chat, only quick glances to the side to see if the girl has fallen. I keep my eyes on the board, press the next shirt, listen to the rising steam as I hold down the pedal. My hands tremble on the board, fingers shake so that I can't untangle the sleeves of the next shirt.

I glance again to the side, and the little girl is hanging now, by one arm, her father pushing his way through the metal bars to get to her. He will reach her, he is right under her, he will not let her fall, but a woman steps in front of him. She pulls the child's leg, hard, so that she falls and she grabs her. The woman is very cross with him. I touch the board without thinking, my hand catches in the press.

'Ahh,' I gasp, as quietly as I can.

'*Orada iyi misin?*' PC Grant says to me over Old Madame's shoulder. I do not know what he said, I do not know this language, and I do not look at him.

She says to me quickly, in the language we both know that he does not, 'He thinks you are a Turk.'

PC Grant speaks again to Old Madame, he says, 'No? She doesn't know?' And then other words and 'Turkish' and then 'Turkish' again. I do not know what he is saying to Old Madame but I know he is disappointed.

'No, not Turkish,' Old Madame says with a smile. I know enough English to know she said I am not Turkish, but she also did not name Home Country. She stands up before he can ask any more questions and blocks his view of me, and says in the language we both know, 'Go put water on that burn, you nasty whore.'

Then she says to the officer, 'I must help her, excuse me,' and PC Grant says other words that mean goodbye, and he whistles as he leaves the shop.

'You stupid girl!' she shouts at me when we are alone. 'Don't you try to get attention, you hear me? Do you know what police like him do with girls like you? Throw you in jail, give you to the Home Office, and deport you. Is that what you want? And when you get home, we'll come after you, you know this, yes? You will still owe us money, and we will get it, here or over there. So don't try any games with me. You hear?'

Spit flies from the corners of her wrinkled mouth as she shouts. Another look at me, then she looks over her shoulder to make sure no one is coming into the shop, and she pushes me and slaps me across the face with the back of her hand. She shuffles away in her house slippers, waddles back to her chair behind the counter and goes back to her newspaper, turning the page as though nothing has happened.

That is when I pick up the shirt press, Mother, with both hands, and throw it with all my force at the back of her head. The blow knocks her from her chair, and she slumps to the ground, the newspaper fluttering down to cover her, like a blanket. Then I step around her mountain of old flesh, careful not to touch the pool of blood forming around her head. I open the door and leave.

For a moment, I imagine what this would feel like.

For a moment, I imagine that I have done it.

I wrap my burnt hand with a face cloth from someone's bag of dirty laundry. I go back to the press, take out the next shirt, lay it flat, press my foot on the pedal. The steam hisses and rises.

Mother, when I speak to you like this, do you know it is me? Do your bones ache at night when they hear me? Does your spine crack in the wrong places trying to tell you that it's heard me? Mother, there is a pain in the groove of my hip. Is it you? Are you speaking to me too, Mother? Because our voices do not go far. Voices are weak. Pictures of faces do not last. Only bones are permanent. Bones remain when all the rest of us is gone. Mother, when your bones ache, it is me. Answer me.

If you can hear me, Mother, answer me.

8

Jamie
Flat 1B

At half past ten Penny's curtain is still drawn and she is not answering her phone. Jamie has no choice. He has to check on her. He's not sure what he'll do with Olivia – maybe the neighbour will watch her for a minute – but he has to make sure that Penny is . . . not dead. She's probably asleep, or mixed up her medication, or forgotten what day it was. There is probably a simple explanation for why she missed watching Olivia through the window this morning.

But also, Jamie thinks, she could be dead.

Mable
Bedford Road playground

Mable is on her way to the Kingdom Hall for Sunday service and crosses to the other side of Bedford Road. She stops to have a seat on the bench in the playground across from First Premier Dry Cleaner and Laundry. She is weak from fasting, a fast which began involuntarily because she had miscalculated her budget for the month, and after making her usual contribution to the maintenance of Jehovah's ministry throughout the world, she did not have enough for both the electricity bill and three meals a day this last week of the month.

She decides, however, to use this misfortune to fuel her faith, and she dedicates her hunger to Jehovah. Luckily, she has three stale crackers in her bag, and she has a nibble of these on the bench before she continues her journey to the Kingdom Hall. She notices, as she rests, through the window of the laundrette, the old, fat woman who runs it shuffle away from the counter towards the thin girl who works there. Mable has seen that girl in the building, cleaning the corridors. Mable could not say by looking at her where she might be from – some far-flung place where they might be trying to spread the Good Word, like Mauritius or the Philippines or some such island. Mable watches as the old woman looks round to make sure the shop is empty, and then sees her slap the girl across the face, hard with the back of her hand, knocking her against the wall.

Sensing an opportunity to reach a New One, Mable recites the words of Luke to herself: 'Keep on seeking and you will find; keep on knocking and it will be opened to you.'

Feeling stronger, Mable stands to resume her journey. She makes a mental note to stop by the laundrette. It is a place sorely in need of the Good News.

Jamie
Flat 1B

He enters the building using the spare key Penny had given him for emergencies. He knocks on Carla's door, Olivia gripping his hand more tightly the more reassuring he tries to make his voice. She doesn't trust his reassuring voice, which he uses only when something is wrong. There are raised voices behind 1A, and shuffling. A gruff woman's shout, a girl's mocking tone. They're arguing – '*I'm not scared of him . . . Yes, I know you have to respect the agreement . . .*' – and no one comes to the door.

'What do we do now, Olivia?' he asks rhetorically, not sure whether he should knock again and explain that it's an emergency. He's worried about saying that in front of his daughter and worried about what he'll find behind Penny's door with

Olivia next to him; what terrible thing the child may never be able to unsee. He paces the hall, thinking of who he can call, if any friend lives nearby. Can he just leave her in the corridor? How can he get to Penny without Olivia seeing her mother, who she doesn't know is her mother, sprawled out dead on the floor?

'Young man, are you lost?' Jamie turns around to find Mable staring up at him severely from under her lavender hat. After her stop at the bench, Mable thought it might be a good idea to use the facilities at home before she ventured on, in case it took her longer to get to the Kingdom Hall than she expected in her weakened state. But the lift that brought her downstairs this morning is now out of order and Mable has had to take the stairs and she thinks perhaps Jehovah is telling her that she needs to stay home today.

Jamie, surprised by Mable, falters, 'Good morning, no, I'm not – uh, madam – I just need to check on my, well—' The sentence he needs to say is that he has to check on his ex-wife because she didn't open her curtains this morning to watch their daughter play in the park so he has to make sure she isn't dead. But those are the wrong words to say in front of Olivia, the wrong words to get Mable to help him.

'Well, she's my, uh, friend in here, in this flat. I'm worried about her, but I don't want Olivia – this is my daughter – to come in with me, just in case, I—' he continues, self-consciously, knowing he is confusing his child, knowing this old woman thinks something unseemly is going on.

But Mable, knowing very well the anxiety of waiting outside a door for the person inside to open it, understands this young man immediately. Twice she has come upon the dead in her ministry. The first time, the door was partly open, and she just gave it a little push to find the man on the floor, just a few steps inside, the tangerines from his dropped food shop circling his head like a halo. She prayed to Jehovah to send help and, promptly, a neighbour arrived, and her prayer was answered.

The second time, there was a smell, faint but recognisable, and a hollowness when Mable felt the door. With Jehovah's guidance she called the police anonymously. She waited in a café across the road from the house and watched the front entrance until they came, leaving two hours later with the body. Then she stood and prayed aloud, with the café owner about to chastise her until he looked out the window, bowed his head, and let her continue.

'Well, it just happens that I have a load of magazines in here that need counting. Are you good at counting, child?' Mable says to Olivia, pointing at her tartan rolling cart.

'Don' worry, young man, she is safe,' she says to Jamie as Olivia cautiously follows her to the stairs.

Olivia, having experienced only Jamie's mother as a grandmother, who smells like talc and onions and won't let her play with her lipstick, had always hoped she would find one like Gran Gran on *JoJo & Gran Gran* from CBeebies, who danced and told stories and wore trousers. Mable looks much older than Gran Gran and not as much fun. And she's wearing a skirt. But Olivia, wanting very much to get away from the door where her father is standing, goes to the staircase where Mable sits down with a huff, and listens to the old woman tell the story of Jonah and the whale, which is interesting.

Jamie, uneasy about leaving Olivia with Mable but seeing no alternative, puts his key in Penny's lock, and turns it.

Carla
Flat 1A

'Because, Mary Rosie, I don't have that kind of money,' Carla says from the bathroom, using her even, practised, patient-mother tone, trying not to betray that she is horrified by the hair in her hand that has just come out in a clump from the root, at her scalp, when she started brushing it.

84

'Well, why can't you just ask Dad?' Mary Rose says, annoyed, from her seat on the sofa, not looking up from her phone.

'You can ask your father for extra money for concert tickets, but I won't do that, not for something that expensive,' Carla says, scraping her hair back into a ponytail, searching for bald patches at the back. The brush slips out of her hand and she bends down to pick it up off the bath mat, but when she stands up, the world spins and her heart races. She sits down on the edge of the bathtub to steady herself.

'Why not? Are you *scared* of him?' Mary Rose says, knowingly, disparagingly, pulling the phone charger out of her mother's phone and plugging it into hers so she can keep tapping away with her thumbs. Mary Rose has no problem letting her mother know how pathetic she finds her. She can't understand how her mother can think that she's managed to hide her dysfunctional marriage, the way her father uses her, from her and her brother. Like it isn't obvious. Like it hasn't always been obvious.

Carla, still waiting for the dizziness to ebb, doesn't answer her daughter. She knows Mary Rose understands what's going on. She knows what her children think of her.

She knows Daniel feels bad for her, but that Mary Rose feels only contempt, anger, and frustration that Carla isn't stronger. That Carla isn't the woman that Instagram and YouTube and Kylie Jenner and every ad of a tattooed, tube-top-clad, body-positive model keeps telling girls like Mary Rose that they will be one day – fearless, strong, empowered, wealthy, independent, dominant – and nothing like the over-worked, underpaid, body-shamed, self-loathing, misogyny-enabling mothers that birthed them. 'The Future is Female' reads the sticker on Mary Rose's phone case, but not the kind of female that her mother is.

Carla attempts to assert her parental authority. She just read about it this morning on a message board about dealing with teen girl attitude. First rule: don't cede control.

She says, 'I'm not *scared* of him. We have an agreement – a certain amount of money every month—'

'Yes, I know, and *you have to respect the agreement*,' Mary Rose says, mimicking her mother's flat American accent. 'You mean you didn't get a tip for your services yesterday when he came over?'

Carla looks at the back of her daughter's head, tilted towards her screen, tossing out her words like handfuls of confetti, not realising her last sentence was actually a grenade.

'What did you say?' Carla gasps, angry tears rising, unaware of how hard she is clutching the hairbrush in her hand. Mary Rose looks up from her phone and startles at her mother's sudden appearance, looming over her on the sofa, holding the brush raised above her. But Mary Rose knows her mother would never strike her.

Mary Rose knows that the mother standing over her – with her grey roots, her double chin quivering – is the mother who washes her school uniforms, who works overtime to afford her phone bill, who buys her chocolate when she has her period.

But she also knows this mother lets her father live with another woman and child without protest, and that she doesn't yell back, and that she's so weak, so defeated, that she won't even complain about the neighbour's whistling kettle that wakes her children at dawn, but just stares at the wall instead, drinking coffee in that tatty robe.

She is ashamed of Carla. But mostly, Mary Rose is ashamed of herself. Of how cruel she is to her mother and of how she can't control it. But rather than tell her mother that she is angry, and confused by what she sees between her parents, and unsure if she is a terrible person for still loving her father even though she knows he is a bully, and that she has gone too far with boys and it has left her feeling sick and afraid, and that she loves her mother but she can't trust her to protect her or show her how to act or what to say, because she can't even protect herself – instead of telling her mother all of this, instead of saying, 'I am

86

still a child, and I need you,' instead, she lashes out. It is what children do.

Mary Rose points her phone at Carla, poised above her with the hairbrush – jowls shaking, mouth twisted in anger – and taps the screen to take her picture. Carla hears the auto-mated camera sound that mimics what real cameras used to sound like, when she was young, like her daughter.

'Maybe Dad would like to see this one. Maybe when he sees what a hell you make my life, he'll find a way to make it up to me,' Mary Rose says.

Carla steps back from the sofa, lowers her arm, pulls at her T-shirt.

'I have to get ready for work,' she says, clearing her throat, pretending the awful moment hasn't happened, but wonder-ing when it was that she lost Mary Rose, when it was that Tom had taught their daughter so well.

Penny
Flat 1B

Jamie opens the door and does not see Penny at first. He casts his eyes quickly around the flat: groceries strewn across the floor, the cat asleep in the Moses basket.

'Pen—' he calls, but before he can even finish the last sylla-ble of her name, she flies out of the bathroom with a frying pan and a kitchen knife, attempting to scream, but the sound is weak and hoarse and muted by the surgical mask over her mouth. Without thinking, on impulse, he grabs both her wrists, almost picking her up off the ground, and she drops her weapons. The frying pan clangs loudly on the floor.

He lets her go, and she collapses on the floor in front of him.

'Thank God it's you, thank God it's you,' she says, over and over, in a breathless whisper.

All Jamie can manage to say is, 'Penny?' The smell of the overflowing litter box nearly knocks him over. He crouches down beside her on the floor, notices her mechanic's boiler suit, men's trench coat, rubber gloves, his old Yankees hat, the winter boots.

'Were you going somewhere?' he asks.

'Jamie, oh, it's awful. I have to tell you what happened. Darren couldn't get my usual muesli and he left it in the hall and the bag burst, and I couldn't reach it with the broom, so I got dressed so that I could go out and clean it up, but she got there first and I watched her through the peephole and she ate the raisins off the floor. And so I've been watching the door, and I've been armed, in case whoever is doing this to her made her come back here and show them where she got the food, in case she needed help, because then, later, at night, I looked out the window – here, this one, that looks at the tracks and the alley below where they keep the rubbish bins, it was very late – and there she was, she was going through the bins, a girl with black hair, an Arab sort of Indian girl, maybe? She had a plastic bag, and she was going through the bins and taking out food and putting it in her bag. She took half a sandwich from a bag of rubbish – it was still in the box, a ready-made one, which I bet was Carla's because of course you know what Carla's like – she took it and put it in her bag. And from my bag of rubbish – I knew it was mine because you know I reuse the Tesco bags – she took the crusts from the frozen pizza – because obviously I don't eat the crusts due to the extra calories, and all the weight I gained from the medication doesn't help – and dusted off whatever was on them and took them. A man watched her the whole time and then they went back into the building, so I got the pan in case he made her come up here to show him where she got her extra food.'

'Penny,' Jamie says, shaking his head, worrying about Olivia outside. He must have been in here for at least seven minutes by now; he has to get back to Olivia – he left her with a stranger, for fuck's sake – but Penny is ill. Really ill. He sees the Cup-a-Soup packets and cat food and single bananas disconnected from their bunch. He knows it means she's stopped opening the door to Darren again, that she makes him pass items through one at a time because she doesn't want to rebreathe his air or some other madness of hers.

'Penny,' he tries to stay calm, 'have you taken your pills? Did you skip your medication? Have you been drinking?' He gets up off the floor, leaving her where she is, and checks the medicine cabinet in her bathroom. The box of Olanzapine is full of blister packs, untouched.

'Have you stopped taking your pills? Why do you have so many in here?'

'Oh,' she answers from the floor, sweating under the weight of all her garments, 'oh no, of course I take them, of course. Those are the old ones, the old prescription; I have the new ones, remember?' And he checks her bedside table, where he finds Paroxetine, also nearly full, but for a few pills.

'I think she needs help, real help, Jamie. Something is wrong,' Penny says from the floor.

'I just . . . okay, listen, you're not very well, the flat is in a state; you need to see someone, you need help—' Jamie says.

Penny waits a beat, understands that Jamie is concerned, that he has the face that means he would be calling the social worker and the doctor and that she needs to sort this out, quickly.

'No, no, no help needed,' Penny says, shifting now, trying to get off the floor but finding it hard to move in all the clothes, weak and dehydrated from sweating in them for so many hours. 'I'm fine, you just scared me, that's all. I didn't know you were coming, I didn't know it was Wednesday already. I just lost track, lost track of the days.'

'It's Sunday morning. Olivia and I were in the park—'

'Olivia? Is she here? I have chicken nuggets. I'll just clean up this mess, won't be two ticks, I'll just pop those in the oven . . .'

Jamie watches as Penny makes her way to the stand-alone freezer in the corner that he bought for her last year so that she could order enough food for two weeks at a time since the flat only had a small under-counter fridge. He bought it after the episode at Tesco when he'd made the arrangement with Darren and he thought she would get better, that she would get over her thing about shops, that the agoraphobia was temporary, just a little setback, that she'd be fine when she found another part-time job. He bought it believing he could help her out of this.

'Just two ticks,' she says to him in a manically cheerful voice, holding a bag of chicken nuggets in her hand and turning on the oven. He watches her fumble with the knobs in her gloves and can see by the thickness and the stiffness of her hands that she is wearing more than one pair. She leaves the freezer door open and he goes to close it, but not before noticing that every drawer is full to bursting with bags of chicken nuggets.

'What is this?' he asks, gesturing to the freezer drawers.

'Oh, well, it's her favourite, isn't it? You told me, remember, that Olivia's favourite is chicken nuggets? And I thought, well, you never know, there might be a day when you brought her here and I wanted to be prepared. Or I thought maybe you might run out at some point and find yourself in a bind, so I thought you could always come over and take some of mine. And here we are. It always pays to be prepared. Where is she? Is she playing in the corridor? Mind, I wish you'd told me today was the day you were finally bringing her—' Penny's eyes are wide and expectant, smiling. Sparkling hostess eyes preparing to welcome a special guest.

He remembers. A year and a half ago, maybe, on a Wednesday evening visit. He met Penny at the door to the building. She was just getting home from her library job. She looked well and happy. She had a bag of groceries. They unpacked them in her tiny kitchen – fish fingers, string cheese, whole milk, potato waffles, carrot sticks, chicken nuggets, Petits Filous. Toddler food, not groceries for a grown woman. A faint alarm bell sounded in a back corner of his mind.

'Something wrong?' she asked him brightly as she put things away.

'No, nothing,' he said. 'I was just thinking that you're doing so well, getting to the shop each week, it's really good. These are Olivia's favourite too,' he said, handing her the chicken nuggets to put away.

There was a pause, a silence. They rarely spoke of Olivia, and never about the details of her life, her favourite food, her favourite TV show.

Before he left that evening he said he was proud of her. He kissed her on the forehead. She looked at him and he saw her there, his Penny. The bell fell silent. A false alarm. He kissed her cheek, very close to her lips. He could not help it.

Now he closes the door to the freezer that holds a year's worth of chicken nuggets. He watches Penny bustle around the tiny kitchen, so tiny the counter is just a sliver of wood wedged in between the small sink and the wall.

He should have cut her off. He should never have started coming to see her. He should never have believed that he could help her get better. She will not get better. Loving her will not make her better.

He says softly, 'Penny, darling' – because he does still love her, but he has to love their daughter more, enough for the both of them.

'Pen, I've got to go,' he says.

Mable
First floor corridor

When she hears the clang of the pan on the ground and then the young man's voice shouting 'Penny!' she feels Jehovah's tug on her sleeve that means it's time to move. Something is not right in 1B and the child shouldn't see it. Olivia is busy counting the steps between where Mable is seated and the landing above and then counting them backwards in case Mable is impressed by that.

'Child, do you like biscuits?' Mable asks. Olivia nods.

'What about milk?' Olivia knows she's not supposed to drink milk because of her dairy allergy, but she's not sure that this nice, but less fun, Gran Gran knows what allergies are, just like her real Nanna in Manchester who gives her milk every time she visits and calls her 'poor motherless mite'. Olivia nods again because old people really like milk and she doesn't want to disappoint Mable.

'Come with me, then; we'll go to mine until your daddy is ready, but let's be careful on the steps. Shall we count them as we go?' As Mable heaves herself off the steps and straightens her lavender ministry outfit, Mary Rose comes out of her family's flat to the stairwell.

'Morning, Mable,' she says, with faux sincerity. She notices the little girl. She remembers herself and Daniel, sitting on these stairs just a couple of years ago when he was still little. She'd quietly leave the flat with him and bring him here to wait for their parents to stop arguing. They could still hear the yelling, but she thought that if she kept him outside the flat, at least Daniel wouldn't have to see it.

Mable notices the tight, high-waisted jeans that cover her navel and the low-cut sports bra under her open jacket that covers little else. The face full of make-up.

Mary Rose says, 'Mum's had a tough morning, I think she could probably use a little chat.'

Mable catches her wrist, gently. 'Where you gon', child?' Mable says. 'You had another falling out?' she asks.

'You know what Mum's like, Mable. Anyhow, have a lovely day,' she says, and descends the stairs.

Mable shakes her head and makes a mental note to drop in on Carla later.

'Jehovah got me working today,' she says, as she reaches for the handrail and pulls her cart up behind her, getting a nod

92

from her Heavenly Father that it was all right that she had not made it to the Kingdom Hall this morning. He has given her more important things to do.

Penny
Flat 1B

Ignoring Jamie while she pulls out a baking tray for the nuggets, Penny says, in what she believes is a casual tone, 'So what do you think of that, then, Jamie, about the woman in the bins? I mean, do you think we can help? She must be starving if it's come to that, don't you think?'

'I've got to go,' Jamie repeats, spotting Susannah in the corner. Penny had found her, skinny and filthy, pawing around in the bins too, the ones outside their house. She brought her into breakfast that same morning, Olivia kicking in her high-chair and squealing at the sight.

She said, 'Look at the poor thing, I think she needs us, don't you?' and then she rubbed her face in the mangy, matted fur.

Jamie recoiled. 'Don't do that, darling – you don't know where it's been,' taking the disgusting cat from her, knowing already that Penny wasn't right, but blaming it on lack of sleep, on stress, on anything other than what it was.

'But what about the chicken nuggets? They'll be ready soon,' she falters.

'Perhaps your lady could use them, I don't know,' he says, pulling the door closed behind him, because what he says doesn't matter. Whether the lady in the bins is real or not doesn't matter. He has to think about his daughter now.

'Olivia?' he calls to the empty corridor.

'Olivia?!' he calls to the empty stairwell.

'Olivia!!' he shouts, dread rising in his throat when he realises his daughter is gone. When he realises that he hadn't even asked the old lady's name.

Woman
First Premier Dry Cleaner and Laundry

Old Madame goes to the toilet. This is a long process. First, she must carefully descend from her stool at the counter, sigh heavily, and pass wind. Then she must button up her cardigan. Next, she shuffles to the corner where she keeps her walking stick and says, in the language both she and Woman know, 'I have important matters to attend to. Do not get any ideas. You are being watched.' She motions with her stick to the car that is always parked outside Laundrette, always occupied by one or another of Sir's men, filling their time by nonchalantly scrolling through a phone or paging through the *Sun*. Then Old Madame shuffles to the toilet in the far back corner next to the large machine for washing duvets and pillows.

Woman continues to move the shirt press so that the steam hisses, and so that Old Madame will hear it, but she takes the moment to pull the pizza crusts from her apron pocket with her free hand. She eats them from the side that has no bite marks. She bites into them from the side of her mouth with her good teeth and she nibbles up to the bite marks on the other side, leaving a thin line of bitten-into crust. Even Woman can leave behind this little bit of bread. Even she is not so low down that she cannot leave her own crusts behind.

Mable
Flat 3B

'Child, do you know how to sing?' Mable asks Olivia, who nibbles a rich tea biscuit methodically, first eating completely around the scalloped edge. Mable was saving the last three biscuits for tonight, but never mind.

Olivia nods her head mid-nibble. 'I sing lots,' she says, crumbs on her face.

'That's good, singing is good for the heart,' Mable says as she opens the window next to the table, the one that faces the old railway tracks. The heating is always overzealous when it first comes on, no matter how low she sets the thermostat. As Olivia eats her biscuit and swings her legs and avoids her milk, Mable pulls out the two records she owns: Claudelle Clarke, *God is a Mountain*, and Aretha Franklin, *Amazing Grace*.

These were the only two things she kept from her worldly life before she began her relationship with Jehovah. Mable felt quite strongly that while Sister Claudelle and Sister Aretha were perhaps misguided in their faith in that they had not become Witnesses, surely some exception would be made for them to repent before Armageddon, given the wonderful contributions they would certainly make to Paradise. Mable did not play her records often, nor did she sing regularly, as only songs written and sung by the Witnesses were allowed by her faith.

But occasionally, Mable could not deny that she felt moved to sing. There was within her a need to raise her voice in jubilation, or sorrow, or worry, or thanks that prayer and study just did not satisfy. And in these moments, she would play Sister Claudelle's record or Sister Aretha's, and she could not believe that Jehovah heard anything but His own voice when those women sang. Today, with this beautiful child in need of her protection, Mable needs strength. She feels that extraordinary measures will be necessary, and that Jehovah will understand.

'I'm going to teach you a song now,' she leans forward conspiratorially to Olivia, 'but don' tell anyone it was me that taught you it. I'm not supposed to sing these any more, but this one, Sister Claudelle sings it, and it reminds me of home, and I've made a deal with Jehovah that I'm allowed this song here in my flat only – no one can know – but He says that's all right.'

Olivia nods gravely. She doesn't know who Hova is, and she doesn't understand why Mable's singing is a secret, but she takes secrets very seriously. And then she listens, as Mable begins to sing with the lady on the record: '*I saw the light, I saw the light, no more darkness, no more night . . .*'

Penny
Flat 1B

'Olivia! Where are you, sweetheart? Olivia?' Jamie darts up and down the corridor, calling his daughter's name. He pounds on Carla's door.

'Please, please help me!' he shouts and waits interminable seconds for Carla to open it, but she doesn't.

Then Penny opens her door, surgical mask replaced on her face.

'Jamie?' she calls from her doorway, careful not to step over the door jamb and into the hall. 'Jamie?' she calls, but her voice is too weak to carry, and he has already turned his back and frantically run down the stairs to search outside, thinking he should do that first because if the old lady has taken Olivia somewhere, she couldn't have got too far.

Realising Jamie is gone, Penny closes the door and picks up Susannah, who is winding her way around her ankles. She wants to ask him where Olivia is, why he's calling out and pounding on doors, but, of course, she knows he has it in hand. He would never lose Olivia, not like she had.

She feels for Olivia's barrette in her hair, under her cap.

'Shall we open the window, Susie girl? I'm feeling quite faint,' Penny says, a trickle of sweat rolling down her face.

The heating always comes on very powerfully, no matter how low she sets the thermostat. She opens her window wide, the one that overlooks the old Overground tracks and the small alley between the railway pillar and the building where the bins are kept. Where sometimes she sees the men dressed in black smoking cigarettes. Where she watched that woman forage for food.

She takes off her cap, the cold air feeling like a blast of ice on her sweat-soaked hair. She peels off her gloves, the trench coat, the boiler suit. She stands in front of the window in her damp woollen underwear, woozy from not eating or drinking for hours, dehydrated from sweating in all her layers and dizzy after not taking her pills for days – how many days now? She doesn't know. She drinks in the cold.

Being outside frightens her but not breathing the outside air. Penny loves windows and opens them whenever she can for three reasons. First, to make sure they still work so she can escape the flat in case of fire; second, to remind herself that the flat isn't an airtight box with walls that might cave in and crush her; and third, to know the weather. She likes to be able to say to anyone she might come across, like Darren, Mable or Carla, 'Lovely day we're having' or 'Dreadful outside, isn't it?' to sound normal. She wants to feel this one thing that everyone feels, because no one feels anything else that she does.

She hears singing. It's Mable, two floors above, singing her song about the light. She's heard her sing it before, when they've both had their windows open. Mable has a voice like a seagull, a deep, tuneless rasp, but she still belts out at full volume. Today Penny hears another voice, a little child's voice that takes the chorus, '*I saw the light*', when Mable finishes a verse. There's a little giggle when the song finishes, and Penny hears Mable and the child applaud.

'Susie, do you hear that, a lovely little voice, isn't it? I didn't know Mable had a grandchild. I must ask her next time she comes round,' Penny says to the cat as she turns away from the window to take the chicken nuggets out of the oven.

Olivia
Walking home from Bedford Road

On the walk home Jamie grips Olivia's hand tightly.

'Are we going home now?' she asks.

'Yes, I think we've had enough adventures for one day, don't you?' Jamie says with false cheerfulness.

Relief is still flooding his body, the adrenaline rush wearing off, leaving him feeling weak-kneed and exhausted. It took only moments to find Olivia. When he got outside, he saw a young girl with a duffel bag standing by the door, texting, and he asked her whether she had seen an old lady in a purple hat and a little girl.

'Yeah, that's Mable, she's in 3B,' Mary Rose said, not looking up from her phone. Jamie noticed the make-up, the tight jeans, the attitude, tried not to look at the sports bra, had a premonition of his baby girl as a teenager, and winced.

Jamie jetted back up the stairs as fast as he could to find Olivia at Mable's kitchen table, colouring a picture and covered in crumbs.

'She was good as gold, this one, you've done very well with her,' Mable said, and the diatribe that Jamie had planned to unleash on the old woman vanished from his head.

'I'm sorry we didn't stay in the stairwell, but it got very loud, and I didn't want Olivia to be scared,' Mable said. He thanked her over and over again, and Olivia hugged Mable's legs.

'Oh, don' forget to take this with you now, and you come visit me whenever you like,' Mable said as she gave Olivia the page she had coloured.

'Ah, one more thing,' and she pulled a peppermint hard candy from the bottom of her purse and leaned down to stuff it in Olivia's pocket. 'You take care of that for me now,' she said with a wink.

As they turn the corner of their road, Olivia gives him the page she's been holding and says, 'Hold this, Daddy,' and when he glances at it, he does a double take. It is a connect-the-dots picture of a soldier from biblical times holding a sleeping baby in one hand, the baby shape requiring the most dot-to-dot work. With the other, he's holding the tip of a large sword to the infant's back, ready to slice it in half. In the background the baby's mother screams, hands raised to her face in terror, alongside a stoic King Solomon.

'Olivia, what is this?' Jamie asks, trying not to sound alarmed.

'Miss Mable said this is a colouring from the Bible. I don't know what that is, but she said it's her favourite book. But see – I made all the bad guys pink.'

THE STORY OF MABLE

1982

Mable sits in her front room, sipping tea as the sun sets on her wallpaper. Clive put it up for her a few years back. They were the first on the street to have it and Mable was the envy of the other ladies. That was a good day. A happy day when they put it up and had their neighbours round to admire it. It is a photo mural of palm trees on a beach with a sun setting on the ocean in the distance, pink and orange hues illuminating the evening sky, creating haloes around the silhouettes of the palm fronds across the whole expanse of her front room wall. She no longer remembers seeing a sky like that herself. Every time she thinks of home, it is this picture that she sees. It has been so long that the wallpaper has become her memory. It's no longer in fashion, but she cannot part with it. Not now. Not when he put it up with his own hands.

She has just returned from work. She runs her feet, still encased in their white support stockings, back and forth on the grooves of the plastic runner that protects the carpet under her sofa, the feeling slow to return in her soles. She delivered two babies this shift, and she says a silent prayer for them now. For the one that is alive, safe in her mother's arms. And for the one that is dead, who died before his life had begun. It is part of being a midwife – the death as much as the life.

Yesterday she buried Clive. They had been married twenty-one years. He had lived for forty-two. But it took only minutes for him to die, seconds for the aneurysm, secretly lying in wait, to rupture, killing her husband and making her a widow. A title she was not expecting – at least, not so soon.

Yesterday she buried him and today she went to work. She sent the children to school. Her sister said it was cruel, too much too soon, but Mable is teaching them strength, because they will have to be strong without their father. They will have to live though he is dead and she knows no other way to teach them this lesson than to throw them back out to the world. It is painful, but it is quick. The sooner they learn that the world has no interest in them or their pain, that no one in the Mother Country especially could give a damn about them, except their own mother, the stronger they will be.

Mable would have liked to lie down next to Clive yesterday, truth be told, lie down and be covered up by the earth and sleep in its darkness with him. She would have liked to paper the inside of his casket with the palm tree mural and lie there with him and fall asleep under the pink and orange sky, listening to the sea lap at the shore.

If it were not for their sons, if it were not for her parents, dependent on the money she sent home, if it were not for the more than twenty years it took to build a life in the grey cold of England, she would have found a way to do that. She would have, if it were not also for her work. Her work of life and death.

Her friends said to take a week, a few days off, at least, but she went to work because if she had stayed in the house today – with his slippers under the bed and his shirts in the wardrobe and the teacup from his last breakfast in her kitchen still unwashed, where he left it, sitting on the table – she would not have survived. The enormity of what she must carry now, alone, would have crushed her.

'Muma?' Roy, her youngest, eight years old, says. He is holding hands with Devon, aged ten, both boys standing before her in their school uniforms, wondering why she is home. She is never home when they come back from school.

'Muma?' Roy asks again, but Devon knows better than to speak. Instead, he tucks his younger brother's shirt tails in, knowing how it irritates their mother when their clothes are in disarray.

'Nuh badda mi right now, boy,' she says to her wallpaper, sternly, unable to look at the two copies of Clive's face staring back at her.

When Marcus, her eldest, hears her as he comes through the front door, hears the departure in her speech from the perfect English she always demands in the home, he starts to usher his younger brothers out of the room. She rarely speaks this way to them. She kept the rhythms of island speech to herself. She hadn't wanted the children to learn them. She knew it would not serve them well in England.

Mable rises, silently, and they all stop moving. She feels the grooves of the carpet runner under her feet. Devon sees that one side of the collar of her uniform is tucked inwards, her cardigan askew, and it makes him uneasy. For a moment, the family stand in silence, the only sound the ticking of the wall clock. Then the boys make way, parting to each side of the plastic runner that leads to the kitchen. Like Moses and the Red Sea, Devon thinks.

'Muma?' Roy says again.

'Shh, leave Mummy be—' Marcus says to his smallest brother, but Mable raises her hand to silence him. She looks at the ground, at the bursts of teal and pink flowers in the carpet under the plastic, and she puts her hand on Roy's head. Then her boys exhale as she walks to her kitchen.

Mable makes dinner for her hungry boys, but she does not eat herself. She has been suspended for two weeks without pay and so she will have to ration their provisions carefully. Marcus, sixteen and already over six feet tall, eats more than most grown men. Of course, she will need to buy less as Clive is not here, but without his pay cheque, there is less to buy less with. And with her actions under review, there is the possibility that they will not reinstate her. She must prepare for this prospect.

After dinner, the children watch television, the three of them sitting on the floor at the foot of their father's armchair, but not in it. She does the washing-up and then sits at the kitchen table, alone, cradling her empty teacup, the tea long since drunk. Roy, after a few minutes standing in the doorway of the kitchen, observing his mother unnoticed, quietly slides himself between her and the table, leaving Mable no choice but to put down her cup and pull him on to her lap with a deep sigh.

'Muma?' he asks, but she can only respond 'Mmm', because she will cry if she says anything else. He prattles on about Daddy and heaven and his teacher and a game of tag they played today which made him forget his father was dead for a minute while he was running. But she does not listen. He does not notice her inattention, or that she has not put her arms around him. He is too young to feel that while he is touching her, she is not touching him. Being near her is enough.

She says only, 'Mm-hm', while he speaks and hears only the mother of the dead baby say over and over again, 'It was you! I said I didn't want you here and look what happened. It was you!'

Her trance is broken when Marcus comes in and sends his little brother upstairs to get ready for bed. Marcus sits next to her for a moment, putting a hand out to touch her shoulder but then thinking better of it. They look together, in silence, at the unwashed teacup in front of his father's seat.

'Leave it,' she says.

The next morning, as the children prepare for school, Mable puts on her uniform and leaves with them for the bus stop, as though it is a normal day. Devon, who has not spoken a word since the funeral, holds her hand as they walk. She can barely stand his touch, and when he feels her tense, he pulls his hand away.

She separates from her boys at the end of the road, and watches as Marcus shepherds his brothers across the street to the bus stop. She sees Clive in all the stages of his life walk away from her. They knew each other when they were children, she and Clive, back home, where the sun shone and the air was soft. Roy has the little boy roundness of eight-year-old Clive, and Devon has the sprint in his step of the ten-year-old Clive who never stopped running at that age, and Marcus has his father's height, his long legs, his strong shoulders that could, and would, carry anyone who asked.

She walks in the direction of the Tube and watches the bus carrying her sons drive past her, their faces in the window, but she does not wave to them. When the bus makes its right turn, it is safe for her to turn around and go back home.

In her bedroom, she does not turn on the light. She takes off her uniform. She leaves it crumpled on the bed, and then she thinks of the ironing. No point doing a job twice. She thinks of the uniform, what it meant when she first got it. With a heavy heart, she hangs it properly in the wardrobe. She pulls on her lavender dressing gown, the flowered one with the quilted collar that Clive bought her, and she leaves the bedroom, refusing to look at the empty slippers by the bed that await his return.

When she walks into the kitchen, she does not look at his teacup when she takes a chair from the table to stand on to reach the whiskey that he kept in the high cupboard above the refrigerator. He kept it where the boys couldn't see it or reach it, because that's the kind of father he was. She has always preferred rum, which they keep in the mirrored-glass drink trolley in the front room, but whiskey was Clive's drink. She reached for the bottle he thought she didn't know about.

She sits on the floor of the front room at the foot of his armchair. She watches the news at midday. *Today marks the one-year anniversary of the fire in a house at New Cross that took the lives of thirteen black youths . . .*

The voice drones on and they show photos of all the people who took to the streets last year and they talk about the "riot" more than they talk about the beautiful children who died. She switches off the telly. *Thirteen dead. Nothing said.*

It was not the first time that a white mother had asked for her to be removed from a room, or requested a white midwife instead of her, or said that she did not want her white baby held by her. It happened now and again. But it was the last time that Mable could pretend she did not hear it, or push it down, or take it, smiling, and get on with her job.

'It was you! I said I didn't want you to touch me!' the mother shouted from the bed when Mable brought in the flowers that had been delivered for her as she came to administer her medication.

'I am sorry for your loss,' Mable said.

She regrets only two things about what happened next. She regrets slamming the vase on the bedside table as she said it, not realising the force with which she did it, shattering it, water spilling everywhere, soaking the mother's hospital gown, and leaving Mable standing there, with a jagged piece of glass in one hand, a lily in the other.

There was blood. That was when the mother started screaming, when the senior sister was called, when the woman accused Mable of threatening to stab her with the glass, and when Mable stayed silent, because for a moment, with the broken glass in her hand, with the screaming, with the soaked bed, with the blood on the petals of the white lily, with the awful mother, with Clive in the ground, with three sons to raise on her own, with the poor, lost baby, Mable almost believed she was capable of it.

The blood was from a cut on Mable's own hand. She was the only one who was hurt by the broken glass. But this was considered to be beside the point.

'Of course I didn't threaten her,' Mable explained to the senior sister, consciously enunciating her t's and h's. And the senior sister believed this was the truth. She knew Mable, how reliable she was, how impeccable her service was. But this truth was not strong enough to erase the image of Mable, with blood on her apron, holding a jagged piece of glass over a crying, white mother. Even though the blood was Mable's own. Even though the claims of the mother were false, driven by grief. And hatred.

'We have to look into it, Mable, you know we do, you know how it looked,' her Irish supervisor said, and Mable remembered how they had both applied for the managing role as the lead midwife, and how Mable, though she had many more years of service, did not get it.

Mable passed two white midwives in the corridor as she left the ward. They looked at her sympathetically, as they respected Mable and felt sorry about the whole situation, but they did not know what to say. Then Pamela approached her at the lift, squeezed her hand discreetly, and also said nothing, because she knew there was too much to say. Mable was leaving Pam to carry it all alone now. The extra scrutiny, the intentional and unintentional judgement – the penalties they and all the Black midwives paid for their otherness. This is the second thing that Mable regrets.

On the eighth day of her suspension, as Mable pulls on her uniform tights, she stops at the knee of her left leg. It was more than a week since Clive was buried, almost two since the day he died. She cannot go on with the charade this morning. She pulls off the tights, puts on her flannel nightdress and her lavender dressing gown, and she tells her boys she is ill. She brings down the whiskey bottle as soon as they leave for school. It is almost empty now. She makes a coffee, pours the last drops of whiskey in, and sits across from Clive's teacup, still there, at the kitchen table.

When she finishes her coffee she knows what she needs to do. She pulls her overcoat on over her dressing gown, puts on her sunglasses and ties a scarf over her hair. At the corner shop she buys a Curly Wurly for Roy, a Marathon for Devon, and a Mars bar for Marcus, along with another bottle of Clive's whiskey.

Mable leaves the shop and, lost in thought, she walks closer, closer, ever closer to the kerb. She is startled by the honking horn of a bus that trundles past, the shock of it sending her tumbling to the ground after the wing mirror clips her ear. She drops the bag and the boys' chocolate bars fall around her, the whiskey bottle thudding to the pavement. Mable tilts her head up to a steel London sky, breathless. Stunned.

'You ought to be more careful, love,' a stout, freckled red-haired woman says, holding out her hand. 'You could've been run over.'

Mable takes her hand, and she and the stranger pick up her belongings. Mable reaches for the whiskey bottle and avoids the stranger's eyes as she's aware of the time of day and how it looks.

'Thank you very much, you're very kind,' Mable says, brushing down her clothes, noticing dried drips of coffee on the quilted collar of her dressing gown. She wonders, in horror, if they are from this morning, or the seven mornings before this one.

'I must be gettin' home now,' Mable says, and turns to leave when the woman stops her, gently putting a hand on her elbow. Mable flinches.

'Are you sure you're all right? Are you feeling steady? I could walk you home if you're nearby?' the woman says.

Mable is moved by the woman's kindness, but also instinctually does not trust it, in the automatic way that all city dwellers distrust humanity on the rare occasions it is demonstrated.

'No, really, you're too kind but . . .' Mable starts to say, but the woman persists.

She grabs Mable's wrist. Mable pulls it away, more forcefully this time.

'I'm sorry,' the red-haired woman says, 'it's just I believe He put you in my path today for a reason. Jehovah knows when His children need Him.'

'Oh Lord,' Mable thinks to herself, 'not one of these,' and asks her own God, the one she has worshipped every Sunday of her life, to get her out of this situation.

'You're very kind,' Mable says again, 'but I'll be all right.' She adds, 'God bless you', as an afterthought as she makes her way home, clutching the bag of chocolate bars for her sons.

She is shaken by the low she has reached. She is shocked by her transgressions – wearing her stained dressing gown in broad daylight, falling about on the street. She resolves that this will not do. There is no time for this. She has work to do.

'Mi head nuh good, Clive,' she says to her husband in her heart. 'Why yuh drop out, leff mi 'ere?' she says aloud, but quietly, as she throws his whiskey from the corner shop into the bin. 'An' the poor pickney dem, widout dem fada. It not right,' she says, and hears the tremble in her voice. She allows herself a few tears, under the cover of her sunglasses, but only until she reaches her front door. Once she reaches the house, this will stop, she tells herself, it must. She knows life and she knows death, and she knows which one she has been left with.

As Mable turns her key in the lock of her front door, she takes a deep breath, but she cannot stop the sobs.

The freckled red-haired woman, unnoticed across the street, jots down Mable's address. She writes next to it 'Black lady, dressing gown', as a reminder. She will be sure to call on her in a few days.

'I go only where You lead me, where You are needed most', she says in silent prayer to Jehovah, tucking her notebook in her handbag and making her way back to the bus stop.

9

Sunday Evening

Woman
Flat 2A–2B

Baby is asleep on my chest. He has finally stopped crying. He is not well tonight, Mother. But I rocked him and rocked him, and finally, he is asleep. My Lady sits at my feet. We sleep together, the three of us, in the nursery. Whenever Baby wakes, she wakes too, and sits with me or lays her head in my lap. My Lady has a pink princess bed with a canopy and Baby has a pretty wooden crib, but they both insist on sleeping with me on a mat on the floor that I roll up every morning and keep under My Lady's bed.

Madame does not rise for the day until mid-morning, sometimes not until the midday meal if she has worked late into the night as she often does, and Sir and Master have no interest in children, so none of the family ever come into the nursery. I'm sure I would be beaten if they saw how we sleep together on the mat, but the beating would be worse if I couldn't make Baby stop crying. The crying of Baby is the worse offence and keeping him next to me is the only way to calm him. As long as there is quiet Madame doesn't open the nursery door, Mother, so this is how I rest, the children of my masters clinging to me on the floor.

Baby is asleep on my chest so I say to My Lady, 'Shall we sleep now, come,' but she pulls something from the pocket of her nightdress.

'For you,' she says in the language we both know. It is a bar of chocolate. Mother, this is a great kindness because food is

My Lady's only friend, other than me. It keeps her company. It goes into her body and covers her in soft layers from the inside out.

Sir and Madame do not let her out; she is always here, like me, but they feed her, all day, anything she wants, to stop her from asking questions. I forage for my food in the refuse bins behind Laundrette but My Lady has a cupboard to herself in the kitchen. She wears the key for its lock around her neck. So, this chocolate is truly a gift. Because it is precious to her.

There is writing on the wrapper. I ask her what it says. 'Galaxy,' she tells me. I do not know this word. A beautiful word, I think.

I say, 'Thank you, My Lady. But my teeth, child, I cannot eat this beautiful thing. You are a kind girl,' and I stroke her long hair.

My teeth, Mother, two are broken. It was Master who broke them. He is My Lady's older brother. Almost a man but still a boy. A boy in a man's body, a man with muscles but a boy who cowers when his mother shouts. Did I tell you that Master broke one of my teeth because I forgot the two sugars for his tea? He broke my tooth with the force of his fist against my jaw, oval bruises at my chin. Really it was because I brought tea to his room when the door was not locked, and he was in self-communion with the family of dark-haired women. I think they are American. They are his constant companions on his phone and his television. There are pictures of them hidden in places where Madame does not look. Their voices come through his bedroom door at all times of day.

When he watches them on the television in the living room, they are almost life-size. The television screen is so big, like a cinema, and I wonder sometimes if they can see me through the screen with their dark American eyes. I thought Americans all had blue eyes, but these women are dark. I wonder if they are watching us, if they know that My Lady and I never leave. If they each have a woman like me that they keep. That is the story of the first tooth, Mother. The other rotted and fell out. And so, I cannot eat the Galaxy.

I gently put Baby down on a cushion of blankets next to my mat and as my eyes begin to close, My Lady nudges my shoulder where she has lain down on my other side.

'I have made it very small now. Try it,' she says.

She has opened the Galaxy and bitten off tiny pieces with her teeth for me to eat. She gives them to me with sticky fingers. They are sweet and silky.

'Thank you, lovely girl, sleep now,' I say.

I close my eyes and I can hear her eating the rest of the chocolate, crinkling the wrapper as quietly as she can. If I did not love her, I would tear it from her fat little hands, I would devour it in one bite. Hunger, just like My Lady, is my constant companion, Mother.

Hungry though I am, I let her eat it all now because I know that someday I will leave her too, Mother, her and Baby, just like I left Beauty. I let her eat now while I stroke her hair to make up for the pain that will come when I go. This is all that I can give her, memories of kindness. I am a leaver of children, Mother. It cannot be helped.

Penny
Flat 1B

'*Mary? Mary Rose!*'

That's the third time in twenty minutes Daniel has shouted for his sister. There's been a lot of shuffling around over there for the last half hour and it is now half past eight, and Susannah and I should be having our supper now – well, we *should* have had it between 6:00 and 7:00 – but this has been an unusual day. Jamie really shouldn't have come here. I wasn't prepared.

That's not true, I had plenty of nuggets. Plenty. I'd been preparing for a moment like this for well over a year. What he

III

did – coming here unannounced, on a Sunday, of all days, and not a Wednesday evening, like some sort of ambush – that's called setting a person up for failure, in my book.

Perhaps the flat wasn't tidy, but I could have dealt with that easily. The point was, I had the chicken nuggets that she liked. I was ready. But I got no credit for that. Only judgement.

'*Mary Rose?*'

There he goes again.

Woman
Flat 2A–2B

'The boy is shouting,' My Lady says to me. 'Who is Mary Rose?'

'I don't know, My Lady; don't listen, sleep now,' I whisper to her.

'I can't sleep. Why doesn't Mary Rose answer him?' she whispers back.

'She is busy, she has her own worries; sleep now,' I say with my eyes closed. Baby stirs beside me. Every night before I put the children to bed, Mother, I make supper for the family. But Madame insists that for family suppers she must add the finishing touches and present and serve the supper to Sir and Master herself. So, I make My Lady and Baby a meal in the kitchen and they eat there while I prepare the meal for the others. Then we three are banished to the children's bedroom and it is a relief. My only relief of the day.

'She is like Mummy, then. Is Mary Rose also very important? Mummy is very important. She does business,' My Lady says.

And then, 'Do you have a child? Is it a girl and does she miss you? Can you bring her here so I can play with her?'

'No, My Lady, I have no child,' I say, the same as I say whenever she asks. I do not want her to speak of Beauty to her parents in the accidental way of children's talk. I do not want her to remind them that Beauty waits for me, or for them to think I speak to My Lady about my family and use this as another reason to punish me. It is safer not to say her name.

'*Mary Rose!*' I hear the boy still calling through the floor, pounding on a door. He needs help, but I cannot help every child.

'I have only you and Baby to look after,' I say, my eyes so heavy I could cry, my heart so heavy I could die, when My Lady finally rests her head and sleeps.

Penny
Flat 1B

'*Mary Rose!*' Daniel calls, pounding on a door, the bedroom or the bathroom. I thought at first it was just another sibling argument, but the urgency in his voice, I can't pretend I don't hear it.

And so, for the past twenty minutes I have contemplated knocking on the wall and asking Daniel if everything is all right. I've been listening. Trying to judge the severity of the situation. But every action has a consequence. The stakes for my involvement are high. I must tread carefully.

Then, suddenly, close to my ear, 'Miss, are you there?'

Startled, I say, 'Yes, Daniel?'

'Miss, Mary Rose is locked in her bedroom. She was making weird sounds, she wouldn't answer, and then the sounds stopped. I don't know if she's ill or what. The flat is a tip; it looks like we were robbed. And the lights won't go on. There's all crazy lipstick drawing on the bathroom mirror. There's all sick on the floor. What should I do?' he asks.

'I'm sure it will be all right, darling. Where's your mother?' I ask.

'Mum's at work, and she won't pick up her phone,' he says.

I say nothing as I consider these facts, and then he says, 'I don't know how long she's been in there, I just got home from my friend's house, but something's wrong,' and I hear the tears in his voice. He tries so hard to be good, this boy.

'Call 999, darling, that's what you should do if you're scared, if you think she's in trouble,' I say, as calmly as I can.

'Could you do it, Miss? Only my phone is dead, and I don't know if Mum didn't pay the electric or what, but the lights won't go on and I can't charge it,' he says, his child's panic seeping into my flat through the plaster between us.

I have to think about this very carefully. Very, very carefully. I can't be sure there's an actual medical emergency and not just a girl asleep, and therefore I must consider how to communicate this to the paramedics if I call them. An additional consideration is that I will have to give them this address, and because I'm not in the room with Mary Rose, they will keep me on the line, and ask me questions, and they will do this long enough to register my phone number. They will arrive and ring my bell, and I will have to let them in, and they will knock on my door and ask for details and when they find that Daniel and Mary Rose are minors, they will demand to speak to me, and also then be forced to involve the police, and they will certainly make me open the door, and it is Sunday, and not Tuesday, and I am not prepared to do that, especially not if there are police. Never to the police. And certainly not after the day I've had.

'No, I'm sorry. I simply can't do that, dear.'

'Miss, please,' he cries. He's sobbing now. Poor darling.

That's what I say to him, 'Poor darling.' And I feel very helpless.

I feel his helplessness and my own. And Mary Rose's. All three of us, helpless, and then I can't stand it any longer, and I start to pull on my woollen underwear and the mechanic's boiler suit and my gloves so that I am dressed for opening the door to go and help him, but then – it occurs to me.

Of course! All he has to do is listen.

I say through the wall, 'Daniel, now pay attention. Go get a glass from the kitchen and put the open part on the bedroom door and put your ear to the bottom of it and listen. See if you can hear her in there, if you can hear her breathing. She may just be asleep, darling, with some headphones or something and she can't hear you.'

After a few moments, he comes back and says, 'She's snoring, Miss, like a man, she's snoring!' overjoyed and relieved.

'Well done, Daniel!' I say. 'Perhaps she just wasn't well and needed a nap, that's all. Your mother should be home soon. No need to worry. You've done very well. I must go now.'

'But wait, Miss, it's dark, and what do I do, that choking sound, if she does that again—'

He wants help, answers, reassurance. But I'm afraid I've had enough for one day. Quite enough.

Carla
Flat 1A

It all happens too fast. In a blur.

The way I lose my children.

The way he takes them from me.

As soon as I open the door to the flat, just home from my shift, I see the three of them in front of me, on the floor. My heart leaps into my mouth, and I drop to my knees.

'Mary Rosie!' I shout her name and try to go to her.

But Tom says, 'Stay back, Carla.'

And I don't understand. The flat is dark, lit only by the street lamps from outside. I try the lights. They won't go on.

'It would help if you had paid your bill,' he says, holding up the flashlight on his phone, blinding me with it.

'Daniel?' I say. 'What happened, why didn't you call me?' My voice shakes.

'I *did*, Mum, so many times, you didn't answer,' he says, sobbing on the floor.

'Tom? What's going on?' but he ignores me.

He speaks as though I'm not there and says, 'Daniel, go pack a bag for your sister and yourself. We'll go to A & E first, make sure she's all right, then you're coming to stay with me.'

He rises from the floor with Mary Rose crumpled in his arms, like a rag doll, crying quietly. I can't see her face in the dark. I smell the pool of vomit before I see it. I move towards them, and then I make out the empty fifth of vodka on the side table and now I understand.

'Oh, and she got a hold of those too,' Tom says, nodding towards a box of my Nytol on the table. 'She's a right mess, but I reckon she'll be okay, she's conscious. She threw a lot of it up, thank God.'

'But when, how? Mary Rosie?' I go to stroke her hair but Tom steps back from me so I can't reach her.

'I think it was probably after your argument this morning. She texted me the photo she took of you, Carla. I came over right away, and this is what I found. Look at this place. What's been going on here? She was so upset after whatever you said or did to her, look at the state she got herself into.'

I don't know what he's talking about, until suddenly I do.

'That photo? Tom, she did that on purpose, you know what she's been like lately. She said the most awful things, she asked if you tipped me—' I try to finish but he cuts me off.

'I don't care *what* she said, Carla. Nothing she can say deserves standing over her like that. Threatening to beat her with a hairbrush?' Tom says.

'I never threatened her – I didn't even know I had it in my hand—'

Daniel comes out of his room. I go to him. My work bag flies off my shoulder to the floor, spilling everything everywhere.

'Daniel?' I say, but he just shrugs my hand off his shoulder.

He says, 'I kept calling you. You wouldn't answer, it got dark, there's no lights. She wouldn't come out of her room, I didn't know what to do, I thought she was sleeping, I listened at her door, with a glass, like Miss next door told me to, then she was choking, I heard her choking. I thought she was dying, the puke on the floor, I was so scared, then Dad came . . .' he says all in one breath, and then gulps for air. He used to do that when he was little, when he had a nightmare and couldn't get the words out fast enough.

'Daniel, I— you mean Penny? Penny helped you?' I say, knocking the side of my dead phone against my hand. Then I remember. Mary Rose took it off the charger this morning to put hers on.

Tom says, 'It's all right, my boy, you don't have to say anything else.'

He is holding Mary Rose in his arms and so with his voice alone pulls our son to him, away from me.

I try to sound rational, calm, parental. 'Look, it's okay, I understand you got scared. It's okay if you want to stay with Dad for a while – both of you – that's fine, the important thing is getting Mary to the hospital, making sure she's all right, so let's do that first, c'mon—' I say, and stoop down to gather everything back into my work bag so that we can go, even though I know I'm not going anywhere.

'Just let me grab my keys—'

'I don't think so.' Tom stops me.

'What? Of course I'm coming to the hosp—'

'No, you're not,' he says. Daniel's eyes dart to his father, then to me.

With Mary Rose listless in his arms, Tom says, 'Think for a second, Carla. As soon as we get there, there'll be a thousand questions about how she got the alcohol, how she got the pills, why she wasn't supervised, and you're going to find yourself with a social worker. I'm their dad, and I'm not going to let that happen to my kids. They don't need that in their lives, on top of everything else. I'm going to say that you're at work, this was an adolescent experiment gone wrong. And then I'm going to keep them the hell away from you.'

'Please! You don't understand, she's not with you all the time, you don't know how angry she gets. She said such awful things to me, and I let her, I was so patient, she took that picture to be mean, and I didn't care, I know she's just a kid, I didn't even yell at her, all I said is I'm going to work—' and I can't control my tears now.

I am losing my children.

I knew someday he would try to take them.

I didn't know it would be today.

'Daniel?' I say. 'Look at me, listen to me, baby, I'm so sorry I wasn't here – my phone, it could've happened to anyone—' I know how I sound. So does he. He looks down at the ground.

'Look, I'll fix the lights, maybe we just blew a fuse, and then we can just get our heads together and calm down,' and, frantically, I go over to the fuse box, hands shaking, trying in the dark to figure out which one had blown, trembling, breathing hard, unable to remember how a fuse box works, knowing that it doesn't matter, because he's taking them.

I flip the switches, up down, up down, and that's when Tom turns around, and carries Mary Rose out of the flat.

That's when Daniel turns around and says, 'Bye, Mum,' a tear running down his face, and follows him. And they leave me standing here, in the dark.

THE STORY OF CARLA

2003

Carla is twenty-one years old. She sits across the highly polished, cherry wood, French colonial dining table from her parents, stares up at the crystal chandelier and tries not to cry.

She says, 'But can't you fix it? Can't you do something? I didn't *mean* for that to happen—'

'Carla, honey, we know, but we have to figure this out. That girl got hurt. "You didn't mean it" doesn't keep them from suing us.' Larry, Carla's father, says, as compassionately as he can, while privately wondering how long it will be before he'll be able to show his face at the golf club again.

Carla's mother, Diane, sips a vodka tonic, her second since they sat around the table twenty minutes ago. It is actually her fifth since four o'clock, but it hardly matters, given the circumstances. It's helping her to see her daughter clearly, for the first time.

'Can't we just deal with it when I get back?' Carla says, riffling through her Coach day tote and pulling out its matching make-up bag.

Looking at her daughter, Diane can see it now, all her own mistakes, right there in the stitches on Carla's forehead. In Carla, sitting there, reapplying her MAC Dare to Wear lipstick, while her life falls apart around her. Carla knows that, after she wears them down, Diane and Larry will handle her current catastrophe. So Carla can afford to turn her attention now to maintaining the perfect lip.

Diane understands suddenly and completely that it is Carla who will pay the price for Diane's expressions of unconditional love. Diane paid the bill, but it's Carla who will suffer the consequences of having a pink Hummer limo transport her friends to her lavish sweet sixteen. It's Carla who will know the true cost of Diane's determination that her pudgy, frizzy-haired, buck-toothed daughter would be counted among the pretty and popular girls, even if it required complex orthodontics and a standing appointment for a weekly blowout.

Every time she went that extra step, when her mother-in-law or her best friend or those bitches on the PTA inevitably commented on her excesses, Diane would say, 'Nothing but the best for my princess,' knowing in her heart that Carla would never fit anyone's vision of a princess, unless Diane made her into one. What seemed like indulgences to others, Diane believed were necessities for Carla, so that she would never feel inadequate, unattractive or worthless, the way girls who looked like her were always made to feel. The way Diane herself had felt her whole life. Until, of course, she married Larry, a plastic surgeon, and had a few discreet procedures.

In her vodka-soaked haze Diane suddenly feels hungry. She tries to remember the last time she has eaten anything besides a tiny can of undressed tuna on a bed of lettuce leaves with an ice-cream scoop of cottage cheese on the side for lunch. She has not bitten into a cookie for years. She only ever orders the house salad, entrée size, dressing on the side, when she has lunch at the country club with her friends. She didn't want that for Carla, the constant chafing of wearing a skin a size too small. She didn't want Carla to have to try so damn hard to be loved, or just liked.

But now it's clear that, despite her best efforts, Diane can't change her daughter's destiny. Carla made the mistake that every girl who is not the homecoming queen – or cheer squad captain, or comfortable in a bikini – eventually makes, and she followed a boy, in the desperate hope that he would notice her, realise she was not like all the other girls, and that she, even with her residual acne and muffin top, was what he really wanted.

Carla followed Robbie to a party, and then ruined her life.

Diane admonished herself. She should have told Carla that boys don't think beyond the tip of their penises until at least the age of thirty-five, and even then, it's a long shot for women like them, no matter how often they spray-tanned. Diane spins the cubes of ice in her crystal glass. Reflexively, she pinches at the roll of flesh that still bulges, ever so slightly, over her Donna Karan tailored trousers, under her silk Armani blouse.

She sighs, and vows to skip dinner, and then says, aloud, without realising it, 'What the hell's the point?'

'What?' Carla says, turning to her mother.

Diane, coming out of her trance, says, 'I mean, what the hell's the point of everything we did for you, Carla, everything, all these years?'

'Can't you see, Mom, that's what I'm trying to say. Just tell the lawyer that I'm going to London for a year. There's no use me being here waiting around to see what happens. Why should I put everything on hold? I worked so *hard* for this, *please*,' Carla says, trying to keep the frenzy of her delusions under the surface of her voice.

She was supposed to travel to London in a week's time to start her post-graduate master's programme at King's College, but her future was evaporating right under the chandelier.

'We can't do that, remember? The lawyer said that's not going to look good, not with Melissa still in the hospital. We don't know what her family's thinking yet. Or what they know—' Larry explains to his daughter, but Diane has heard this argument so many times today, she stops listening.

She closes her eyes, spins the ice in her glass, and focuses her hearing on the clink of the cubes against crystal. She remembers Carla, ten years old, winning the county spelling bee. When she stole the show as Yente in her high school's production of *Fiddler on the Roof*. A straight-A student through high school, then NYU. It wasn't the Ivy League (disappointing, really, after they had paid so much for the SAT tutor, and the application consultant, and Carla had put so much into getting elected treasurer of the student council) but still, she had done well.

And what happens now? Does that all disappear because she totalled the white Range Rover? Does none of that count because stupid Carla and that stupid Melissa in her Ford Focus listened to that stupid Robbie and raced to his house? After all Diane had done to build her up, Carla still thought so little of herself that when Robbie said to Melissa and Carla in front of the whole party, 'Whichever one of you gets to my house first gets to spend the night,' Carla didn't hesitate. She said, 'Bitch, you're going down,' to Melissa, and didn't think at all. Alcohol couldn't even be blamed for her lack of judgment because Carla hadn't been drinking. She was on Atkins.

Robbie – who Diane had always despised, who had always been the ringleader of Carla's group of high school friends and picked up that role when they all came home from their different colleges in the summer – drove off first in his convertible Beamer, his college graduation gift, and waited to see which one of these silly bitches would be the first in his driveway.

Diane doesn't know which is worse: that Carla was so desperate for the attention of that arrogant shit-fuck that she raced Melissa; or that Carla knew that Robbie never would sleep with her over her petite and pretty rival, even if she won. Which is why she did what she did. Or, rather, didn't do what she should have.

Carla told Diane and Larry, shaken and terrified in the hospital after the accident, about Billy and the Xanax he stole from his mom, and how he crushed it up, and slipped it to Melissa. Billy was going to ride in the Range Rover with Carla. While they waited out Robbie's ten-minute head start, with everyone at the party gathering to watch the girls rev their engines, Carla heard Billy say to Mike that he was just going to put it in Melissa's Diet Coke. It was just Xanax. It wouldn't kick in until she got to Robbie's, and then Billy could 'take care of her'. Carla heard Billy say this and watched him hand Melissa the can and tell her that she'd need the caffeine to counter the one beer she'd had. And Carla watched from the driver's seat as Melissa drank it in her Ford Focus, and thought about Robbie, and said nothing. It was just Xanax, she thought. It would take a while to kick in, Billy said.

They didn't tell the lawyers that. Billy won't say anything, of course. And they don't know for sure if they're blaming drugs for why Melissa crashed. They haven't heard about the test results yet.

But Carla is young. She made a stupid mistake in a youthful, selfish moment. So does everything that came before that night of awful decisions in Carla's life disappear?

Yes, Diane thinks. Yes, it does. Not just because it's embarrassing that it's in the local papers and Melissa's legs are broken and her Ford Focus is destroyed and her parents see Diane and Larry as dollar signs and want to sue to pay off Melissa's student loans. Diane and Larry have lawyers that can make all of that go away.

That's not what they're worried about. They're worried about Carla sitting at this table, not caring about the damage she caused, or Melissa's pain, or how low she brought herself for some boy. She's not thinking about a toxicology report that could implicate her in something criminal. Carla's only worrying about her trip to London, about a future she still thinks she deserves. And it's killing Diane – that this is how they raised her. That this is who she really is.

Diane listens to her husband try to reason with their daughter.

'You have to put it right, Carla, you won't be able to live with yourself—'

'But you don't know, Daddy! You don't know if that's why she crashed! She was always a crappy driver anyway—' Carla shrieks, hysterically.

'We're not saying to tell anyone what you did, but you jumping on a plane, flying away while Melissa is still in the hospital. It looks bad. It's going to make everything worse. They're going to start asking questions. Can't you see that, Carla? Don't you feel anything?'

Diane puts her glass down on the table. She gets up slowly. 'I'm going to bed.'

'But Mom—' Carla says, incredulous.

'I did everything I could, sweetie,' Diane says as she leaves the room, squeezing her daughter's shoulder as she goes towards the door. 'They just weren't the right things.'

She leaves them at the table and goes into her husband's study off the kitchen. She takes five hundred dollars out of the safe. She puts her credit card and the cash in the top drawer of the desk, and leaves it unlocked. She knows it's the first place Carla will look. She knows what her daughter will do. She sees no other way but to let her.

The next morning Diane goes to her accounting firm and Larry goes to his practice to do the work they have done for decades to earn the money for a life their daughter has taken for granted. When they're gone, Carla goes into the study. She finds the cash and credit card in the desk. She calls a car service and leaves for JFK. Her UK student visa was processed last week. It arrived the day after the accident. She can change her plane ticket at the airport and leave today. Easy.

After all, everything she worked for shouldn't be taken away for one mistake, one stupid night. It wasn't even her idea. It was Billy who did that to Melissa. And it was Robbie who said they should race. And Melissa would probably be fine. Eventually. Carla wasn't going to let this one dumb situation ruin her future. Her parents would just explain it to the lawyers. And anyway, it would all blow over by the time she got back.

'Oh my God, really?' Carla says to Tom, leaning forward on her stool, top buttons of her work blouse undone, a Martini in her left hand, right hand on his thigh under the bar. She is the part-time receptionist at his office. She is a student, or at least she tells people at work that she is. She finished her programme and her student visa ran out a few months ago, which means her right to work did as well, but she never told her boss and he never checked.

It doesn't matter. She's flying home next week. Turns out the blood test Melissa had just after the accident was thrown out by the lab, and by the time she had the second one, the evidence in her body, if there was any, was gone. But her parents still sued Carla, Robbie and Billy, and anyone else they could, for their part in that night. Just as Larry had predicted, they were especially bitter about Carla acting every inch the spoiled rich girl that she was, flying off to London, while Melissa went through months of gruelling physical therapy. They were convinced Carla knew more about Melissa's crash than they could prove. But just as Carla had predicted, Larry took things into his own surgeon's hands and capably, carefully fixed things with Melissa's father. They were ready to settle out of court, and Larry would make it all go away. But before he did that, he wanted Carla to come home. And Carla promised she would.

There is still a week before she leaves London, and until she has to go, there is Tom. Handsome and rich, dirty blonde, burly, the bluest eyes she's ever seen, the most attractive man she's ever met. Ever will meet. And he has chosen her as his companion tonight, and a few nights ago, and hopefully this weekend.

'Yeah, I did, I told him to fuck off, right there in the meeting, and he packed up his bag and he went,' Tom says, basking in the light of Carla's eyes.

'Oh my God, you're so, I don't know, like, brave—' she says, casting her eyes downwards. 'I never tell people what I really think.'

'C'mon then, let's practise. Let's work on your confidence. Tell me what you really think of me.' He smiles, he teases.

'Oh my God, I can't—' She giggles.

'Should I tell you what I really think of you?' he offers, his voice low.

She leans in. She looks up.

'I think you're gorgeous, Carla. I think you're smart. I think you don't give yourself enough credit. I think I'm taking you away this weekend.' He caresses her leg. He puts his hand through her hair. He kisses her and she thinks he is the first man who has ever seen her. She pulls away.

'Really?' she says.

'Of course,' he says.

He kisses her and she thinks she will remember this moment for the rest of her life.

'It's such a shame you have to leave,' he says. 'I could get used to this.'

He kisses her, and she thinks she loves him.

2005, three months later

'But how?' Carla says through her tears. 'He was healthy, wasn't he?' she cries on the phone to her mother.

'Men his age have heart attacks, Carla, the stress—' Diane doesn't finish. Her daughter doesn't deserve the full explanation. She redirects, angrily, 'Why did it take you three days to call me back?'

'My phone – I ran out of credit, I didn't get the message,' Carla says. Tom kept promising to top up her phone credit for her – the account was linked to his credit card – but then he kept forgetting. He was so busy with work.

'When's the funeral? I'll come home—' Carla chokes out the words, guilt crushing her chest.

Carla had not flown home as she'd promised her father she would. She went away for that weekend with Tom, and the weekend turned into a week. Champagne, bubble baths, and sunset walks by the sea. The best week of her life.

'Don't go back, Carla, don't leave me, we'll figure it out,' Tom said at the end of that week when she explained the flight to New York had already been booked. She had resigned from her job and her replacement had started. Her visa had expired. She couldn't get hired without a visa, she couldn't pay rent without a job, she just couldn't stay, not now.

'Then move in with me,' Tom said. 'I'll take care of you. I love you. Don't you love me?'

She looked at him. His startling blue eyes. His muscled chest. She saw the envy in other women whenever they were out together. She knew they wondered what a girl like her had done to get someone like him. She didn't know, but she didn't believe that she'd get a chance like this, a man like Tom, twice.

'Yes, I do,' she said, breathless, ecstatic. She was asleep in his arms in the bedroom they now shared when the flight to LaGuardia took off without her.

Larry came to London to bring her home himself a month later. He bought her a Louis Vuitton at Harrods and Sancerre with lunch at the Savoy.

'You're my good girl, Carla. You've just gotten a little off track, that's all. You'll be able to put it behind you now. But overstaying your visa for a boyfriend? That can't be a good plan. It's a boy who got you into all of this, isn't it?' Larry looks at his daughter.

'Me and your mother, we're so worried about you. Just come home with me, find a job. Make a fresh start. You're still so young,' he said.

'Come home, sweetheart, for me,' he said, holding her hand.

'Okay, Daddy,' she said.

Tom sat on the edge of the bed with his head in his hands while she packed, and said with a sad anger, 'I can't believe you're leaving now. This week of all weeks when I have this huge pitch? God. I thought you cared about me. It's the biggest week of my life, you know how hard I worked, and this is when you decide to turn our life upside down?'

'*Our life*—' she thought. His words held her, like his hands.

'Okay, Tom,' she said.

So Carla did not meet her father at Heathrow like she promised she would and today her father is dead. She pictures Larry, standing at the gate, listening to her voice-mail, his disappointment in her breaking his heart. She thinks of that Louis Vuitton, how she'd sold it to buy new dresses for going out with Tom, because he likes to see her in pretty things.

'No, you can't come home,' Diane says, snapping Carla back to attention.

'What? What do you mean?' Carla asks.

'You have to wait. You stayed over there with your boyfriend, so we didn't settle with Melissa's family. Your father was doing tough love on you. He wasn't going to pay them off until you came home. It was the only incentive we had to get you back here—'

'So? We'll do it when I get there, just pay them now—'

'God, Carla—' Diane gasps, incredulous. Her daughter can't be this selfish, this oblivious. 'It's not that easy. For once in your life, something's not going to be so goddamn easy. We've lost our chance. They got tired of us stalling. If you show up here, they're going to make a scene at the funeral. The father was wheeling her in the wheelchair in the parking lot at Target and he screamed at me – can you believe this – about how they're going to send the process server the second you land. I'll pay them, all they want is money, I'll get the lawyer to do it, but they know your father's an important man. There'll be hundreds of people at the funeral, these people are not afraid to ruin it. Carla, please, please don't do that to me—' Diane's voice breaks.

Neither woman speaks for a moment. Carla hears the ice cubes clink in her mother's glass.

'I'm sorry, Mom,' Carla whispers.

Diane feels a momentary flutter in her heart at the words. A brief memory surfaces of the weight of Carla's small child's hand in hers as they walked along the beach, long ago.

'I know you are, princess,' she says.

'What should I do?' Carla asks.

'Let me bury him,' Diane says. She tells her daughter that she will fix this. That in a couple of months, when everything calms down, Carla can come home.

'Okay, Mom,' Carla says, crying quietly, knowing that by then she'll be showing.

2006

It is one of their bad weeks.

Mary Rose cries desperately, but Carla is making Tom's dinner, and she has to get it right and the kitchen has to be clean before he gets home. He hates eating dinner when the kitchen is messy.

She turns the roast in the oven. She washes every utensil by hand because the dishwasher is already full and running. She opens the red wine. He likes the red wine to breathe for at least an hour before dinner is served. Mary Rose cries. Carla wipes down the counters and cupboards as she cooks. Mary Rose wails. Carla turns the roast again. She peels the potatoes. She pulls out the chopping board to cut them into even cubes, like Maribel, her mother's housekeeper, taught her when she was little.

The doorbell rings. Mary Rose screams. Carla doesn't answer the door. Tom doesn't like her answering the door if he isn't here.

Carla says to the baby monitor on the kitchen counter, 'Just a second, honey-pie,' and keeps chopping. She runs the blade through her index finger. Blood is everywhere. She wraps her hand, cleans up the blood, throws out the potatoes, finds another two to scrub, peel, chop.

Mary Rose, her cries unanswered, falls asleep. Carla cooks and cleans. Dinner is ready by seven. Mary Rose starts crying again. At half past seven Tom has not called and has not come home. Carla cradles Mary Rose, stirs the gravy, keeps the oven warming the roast. She puts the baby to bed.

Eight-thirty. No Tom. Carla falls asleep on the sofa.

At nine his key turns in the lock. Carla scrambles to her feet. Her heart thunders in her chest as she plates the food. She has managed to keep it warm. She serves dinner. She does not complain about his lateness or that he didn't call. She pretends that it's fine.

He tells her to sit with him. He takes down a glass to pour her some wine. That's a good sign. Then he stops short.

'What's this?' he says. He points to a red drop of dried blood on the countertop.

'Oh,' she says, 'sorry, I must have missed it. I cut my finger and—'

'That's disgusting, Carla. You cooked my dinner with bloody hands? I won't eat this. Throw it away,' Tom says, evenly, as he puts her empty wine glass back in the cupboard.

He watches her put the food in the bin. She cleans the spot of blood. She scrubs the pans, runs a mop over the kitchen floor for the third time today. He watches her clean, standing in the kitchen, sipping his wine slowly, saying nothing.

When she's finished, he says, with the same even voice, 'Order me a curry.'

Carla calls the curry house and places his order. She orders nothing for herself. She's trying to lose the baby weight.

The delivery arrives. While she's plating the tikka masala, Mary Rose cries.

'I'll get her, you clean this up,' Tom says, pointing at the delivery bag, the empty cartons.

She crumples the paper bag and tries to remember when it was different, if it was different. He doesn't raise his voice. He doesn't put his hands on her. But some days, he does this. Not every day, but enough days.

2006, six months later

'It's all gone?' Carla asks. She hasn't spoken to Diane in months.

'Almost. I'll have to sell the houses, the cars, most of my jewellery,' Diane says.

'Okay, but, you still have money like to live on, right, I mean that was just like, your extra retirement or whatever, you can still buy me a ticket, right?' Carla asks, palms sweating. She checks her watch. She has twelve minutes to finish this call at the payphone before she has to get back to the flat. Tom said he'd be out with Mary Rose at his brother's until three, and it was only a quarter to two, but to be safe she should be there by two, in case he calls and asks her to prove she's in the flat or in case he comes back early, and insists he said two when she knows she heard him say three.

'Your plane ticket is the last thing I can think about right now, Carla,' Diane says, hurt and angry, but mostly very, very tired.

'No, Mom, that's not – I mean I want to come home, to see you, to support you, I'll bring the baby—' Carla switches her weight from one foot to the other, worries the cuticle on her thumb.

'What home? We're losing them, both houses, don't you get it? That bastard lost everything we invested with him—'

'Yes, Mom, it's just, I want to, I can't do this—' Carla stammers. She remembers that time, when she was twelve, when Douggie Neubaum, from her class, swam out too far and drowned. And everyone could see him, including his mother, flailing, then going under, from the shore. They all learned then that it's a myth that the drowning yell for help. And they all thought that maybe that's the worst part, not having enough air to scream.

'You can't do this? Do you mean "can't" as in can't meet your father at the airport because your boyfriend's more important? Or "can't" as in can't even tell me when I became a grandmother—'

'Mom, not this again, that wasn't personal. Tom had a thing about not talking about the baby too soon, to *anyone*—'

'When are you going to tell Tom that I'm not anyone, Carla? I don't know you anymore. Are you calling me from the payphone again? I can hear the street behind you.'

'No – I went for a walk, I'm on my cell,' Carla lies. She doesn't use the cell to call her mother. Tom checks the bill.

'Fine. Well, if you're calling to ask me to buy you a plane ticket – God knows why you can't ask your boyfriend who I've never met, by the way – I don't have the money. I thought you might be calling to say you're sorry, or to see if I survived the blast from the bomb your father threw at our finances, but I guess that was too much to—'

The line goes dead. 'Mom?' Carla asks, but her international calling card has run out.

Carla takes the elevator up to the flat. She reaches her door at five after two. Tom is in the living room pulling Mary Rose out of the stroller. Carla is grateful she thought to take the extra five minutes to buy milk at the Tesco Express on the ground floor to make it look like she had a purpose for being out, in case he asked.

He looks at her. 'I told you I'd be back at two, where've you— Have you been crying?' he says, putting Mary Rose on the floor at his feet.

'Your mother again? Did she call here?' Tom moves towards her and she takes an imperceptibly small step back.

'Yes,' Carla lies. 'And I – had to go to the shop anyway so I thought I'd get some air—' Carla hiccups through her tears. 'I'm sorry,' she says, automatically.

'Oh love, come here,' Tom says, pulling her to him. 'I'm changing our number. I won't let her do this to you again,' he says. 'What did she want anyway?' he asks, resting his chin on top of her head, stroking her hair.

'I don't know,' Carla says. 'She's got money problems, it's bad, and I tried to talk to her but as soon as she said your name I hung up.'

'That's my good girl,' Tom says. 'Me and you, against the world.'

'Me and you,' she says, and thinks of waves crashing on the shore, of not having the air to scream.

2008

It is one of their good weeks.

'Well, we could get married?' Carla says, massaging Tom's shoulders. They're sitting in a bubble bath in an extra-large tub in a suite at Claridge's. They're eating chocolate-covered strawberries and drinking champagne. Earlier, he surprised her with a Bottega Veneta cocktail dress. It was a size fourteen even though he knows she wears a sixteen, but he said it was so lovely he just wanted her to have it.

'Of course I'll marry you, love, I told you after Mary Rose was born,' Tom says. They didn't marry then, though, because he said she should probably lose the baby weight first so that she wouldn't regret the wedding photos. And then they had Daniel.

Carla is twenty-six, Mary Rose is three, Daniel is eighteen months old. Carla isn't sure how she became a mother of two, how she missed her father's funeral, how it has been so long since she has spoken to her mother. How she came to London when she was so young but how she doesn't feel young anymore.

Last week, Tom told Carla she should go back to school and retrain. 'Do something with yourself instead of just sitting around at home all day,' he said. She remembers what a good student she was. She thinks, this could lead to a job, a way out. A way out of what? She pretends not to know the answer.

She inquired about classes at Birkbeck College, speaking hypothetically, and carefully dodging questions about her current immigration status. But the admissions counsellor made it clear that without a valid visa, she had no options for study.

''Cause if we got married, I could get a visa as your wife, and then things would be easier, you know? I could go to school, we could go to France or something, maybe, for a vacation . . . when the kids are older, I could work again—'

'Wait a second—' Tom says, pulling away from her hands. He speaks over his shoulder. She can see the creases in his face, the ones he gets around the eyes when he squeezes them shut because she's done something to make him angry.

'Your reason for wanting to get married is a visa? To go on holiday? Is that what you just said?'

'No, Tom, oh my God, no – I love you, you know that—'

'Everything I do for you and the kids, yeah, and this is what you've wanted all along?' he says, getting out of the bath, facing her, naked, letting the suds slip off his sculpted shoulders, his toned abdomen, making sure that she can see, as if she doesn't already know, how much more attractive he is than her, how much stronger, how much leaner, how in control he is of his body. Of everything.

'No, I love you, Tom. You're my life. We've talked about this before, I don't know why you're making it sound like that. I just can't travel, or take a class, or work – what are you doing? Where are you going?' she asks, stepping out of the bath, trying to cover up quickly so he won't see her naked, as he moves into the bedroom.

She stumbles into the room after him, and relief floods her, like she has just escaped a burning building. Like she has just been pushed out of the way of a speeding train.

'You should see your face, love,' Tom says, laughing, lying naked on the king-size bed, leaning on one arm, his bicep fully flexed.

'Gotcha!' he says, smiling a smile that she remembers from that long ago weekend that turned into a week.

'Oh.' She exhales the word, feeling the water drip off her hair down her back.

'Oh,' she says again, forcing herself to smile.

'Come here, you,' he says, and pulls her by the belt of her robe to the bed. He pulls it off of her, one shoulder at a time, slowly, exposing her under the light.

'Tom, the lights,' she says, conscious of her belly rolls, her sagging maternal breasts, crossing one arm over her chest, embarrassed, goose bumps rising on her skin. It had been months since they'd done this.

'But I want to look at you. Let me look,' he says, pulling her arm away. And he looks at her, and says she is beautiful, and talks to her the way he did when they first met.

'Let's get married,' he whispers, in her ear.

'Really?' she whispers back, hopeful, desperate, exhausted.

'Of course,' he says in her neck. 'You deserve it,' he says as he moves down her body.

And she almost believes that she does.

2011

Carla goes to the library after she drops the kids at nursery and school. She has to use the internet here because Tom will check her searches on the laptop at home.

She searches 'one parent taking children out of country'.

She searches 'parental rights without legal visa UK'.

She searches 'flights London to New York'.

She learns that leaving the UK with the children without Tom's permission is kidnapping. That the law would be on his side if he came after them. She learns that renewing her passport and getting ones for the kids would cost around £350. The cheapest flights to New York on Aer Lingus, with layovers, would still cost about £1200 for all three of them. Her allowance from Tom was barely enough for the groceries some weeks. She could never save enough.

She logs on to Facebook. Melissa had married Josh, who Carla knew in high school. Carla stopped posting after the accident, so Melissa and Josh never noticed that Carla remained on his list of hundreds of 'friends,' and he never deleted her. His posts are how Carla learns that Melissa eventually recovered and walks almost normally. Today Josh's post says that Melissa birthed their second baby, but the pregnancy caused deep-vein thrombosis in her bad leg, her right, which was more badly crushed than her left in the accident, and she almost died. Carla wonders if the thrombosis is her fault and if Melissa blames her for it.

She wonders if Melissa would be satisfied with the penalties Carla has paid these last seven years. Carla thinks Melissa definitely got the better deal. Even with the limp and almost dying. She'd like to tell Melissa that Tom didn't marry her, that he kept finding excuses – work, stress, the kids, her weight – until she finally understood that he was never going to. That her parents lost her inheritance in a high-profile investment scandal. That her mother stopped speaking to her because Tom told her to fuck off the last time she called, and she hasn't answered Carla's calls since. And surely, Melissa, all of that was worse than deep-vein thrombosis. Or, at least, it was equivalent.

She searches 'council house UK'.

She searches 'housing benefit'.

She searches 'child benefit'.

She learns she's not eligible for any of these because she doesn't have legal immigration status and so can't apply for any kind of welfare. Images of Mexicans in America – cleaning houses, mowing lawns, washing dishes in the backs of restaurants – come to mind. People she dismissed, never looked at, never said thank you to when they took her order or made her bed or delivered her burritos.

'Think, think,' she thinks.

She could take the kids and leave, get on a train and disappear into some small town, some village, in some damp, grey corner of England, like Manchester, or Wales. But they'd have nowhere to live, she couldn't afford it without support, she couldn't work legally, she couldn't apply for welfare. She couldn't even open a bank account.

She checks the time. She searches 'coq au vin' and writes down the recipe. It's what Tom texted that he wanted for dinner. And she always makes what he wants.

2014

Tom has not lived with Carla and the children for six months. He said he felt stifled, in need of a change. He said Carla didn't stimulate him. She never went out, she didn't work, she had no ambition, no hobbies or friends, she never had anything to talk about. He felt claustrophobic. It was too much pressure, her dependence, being the centre of her world.

Carla knows that the real reason he leaves her is Tamara. Beautiful, thin, young, professional HR manager Tamara. They met at work.

Tom tells Carla that he will, of course, always take care of her and the children.

'That's what real men do,' he says.

Tom deposits £1700 in their joint account every month. The rent for the crappy flat he moved them to is £1300. What's left over barely covers food and bills for her and two children in London.

He drops by to see the children rarely and unannounced. When he arrives, they are delighted. He takes them out for twelve hours when he says they're going for two. He keeps them overnight in the flat in the glass and steel high-rise where he now lives with Tamara and her kids. He doesn't tell Carla he's keeping them overnight and doesn't answer his phone until ten at night when she is frantic with worry.

She has a version of the same conversation with him, over and over:

'Next time, could you please tell me what your plans are so that I don't—'

'They're my kids, too, Carla. I have a right to see them when I want, and if you don't like it, you can tell it to a judge. Oh, wait a second, you can't. Because maybe that judge will put you in immigration detention. That's something to consider, isn't it? Remember who pays your bills, Carla . . .'

When the conversation is over, Carla shuts off her phone, relieved the children are safe, and drinks a bottle of wine, alone.

2015

Carla wakes up and she is thirty-three years old. After the school run, she celebrates with three screwdrivers and a family-size Cadbury Dairy Milk bar. At noon she heads to the chicken shop on the high street to start her shift behind the fryer.

Carla works at bars and cafés when she can. She'll get a job and then she'll put off questions about her visa and her passport and why she hasn't brought them in yet until the boss tells her not to come back. Then she moves to the next place. She waits for Tom's deposits. Sometimes they're on the fifteenth like he said they would be. Sometimes they're on the seventeenth or the twenty-fifth or the twenty-ninth, so she can't pay her phone bill and she gives the kids cereal for dinner.

She takes Mary Rose and Daniel to school; she feeds them, takes them to the doctor. She deals with haircuts and discount shoe shopping. She brings home the occasional takeaway pizza, if it's on the menu at her job, and reheats it for their dinner. She doesn't have the money or the energy for funfairs or the cinema. Tom does those things. He is the benefactor, the bestower of Harry Potter Lego sets and unicorn-themed bedding, patent leather Mary Janes and neon Nike football boots. But these things are kept at his flat. The kids aren't allowed to bring them to Carla's, where they still share a bed and the sheets were bought on special at Lidl.

'Mum,' Daniel asks one day on the way home from school, 'why are you poor?'

'We're not poor, honey,' she says, automatically.

'Because me and Mary Rose have two flats, and all our nice stuff at Daddy's,' he says. 'But why are you poor and not us?'

Her heart sinks into her heels.

'I'm not really poor, you know,' she says. 'I just make it look that way. I was born a princess, and my parents were the king and queen. We lived in a palace.'

'In America?' he asks, clutching her hand more tightly.

'Yep, I'm just in hiding here in England, so don't blow my cover, okay?'

'Okay,' he says, and Carla swings hands with him all the way home, and somehow gets herself to the end of the day.

2017

Tamara leaves Tom. Her sister and two brothers arrive at the flat in the steel and glass high-rise when Tom is at work. They pack Tamara's things. They never liked Tom, but were never able to say why. But then Tom told their mother to fuck off when she called Tamara, and then they knew. They escort Tamara and her children back to her brother's house.

Tom drives there later, turns off the car engine, almost gets out, then doesn't. She isn't worth fighting for, he says to himself. But the truth is that he's afraid – of being outnumbered, of being outmatched, of being revealed. When he's afraid he feels like his father, bleeding, cowering, whimpering in the corner of their living room after the bookie's heavies administered their penalty. That was Tom's last memory of him.

That's when his mother became how she was. Tyrannical, intimidating, dominating Tom and his brother because they were the only ones there. So, in the car, Tom feels afraid like his father and remembers the man's weakness. To shake it off, he tells himself Tamara isn't worth it. To shake it off, he thinks of his mother. And drives away.

At home he looks at Tamara's empty hangers in the closet, the bare bookcases in the children's bedroom. He pours a glass of red wine and calls Carla.

'I'm sorry, love, you can't imagine how sorry I am,' he apologises. He cries. He calls again the next day, and the next. He takes her out. He buys presents for the children. He tells her she's the only one. He wants them to be a family. She wants to believe him. She almost does, which is enough for her to take him back.

He moves them to a new build, a brand-new, three-bedroom flat with more space, on Bedford Road. He keeps the flat he owns in the steel and glass high-rise vacant but tells Carla that he's renting it.

One day he yells, 'Surprise!' as he pulls the car over in Soho, in front of the bar where they had their first date. He opens her door, gives her a bouquet of roses, and pulls a white dress from the boot.

She says, 'Oh my God, babe, it's gorgeous,' although she knows it's too small. He gives her a pair of white Jimmy Choos. He pops a magnum of champagne. He pours champagne for passers-by in plastic cups, he gets down on one knee on the pavement. He slides a ring on her finger.

He says, 'Will you marry me?'

She says, 'Yes,' and looks at the ring that won't slide past her knuckle. She drinks. She puts on the shoes, relieved they fit. She smiles. The strangers whistle and applaud. They go into the bar, Tom buys everyone a round, and she puts the ring on a chain she wears around her neck.

Tom goes out that evening, without her.

'It's business, babes, I'll make it up to you, I promise,' he says, and kisses her deeply, so deeply she arches her back. A movie kiss, she thinks. And she understands now, how actors do love scenes. How they make it look like love when it isn't.

She slides the ring on her chain up and down. She drinks a glass of wine alone. She considers the mistake she has made. One more can hardly matter now.

2017, four months later

But maybe it wasn't a mistake?

Maybe it had just been a few rough years. Tom was in his forties, and Carla read that men in their forties, especially fathers, can have emotional crises, and maybe that's all Tamara was. He had a demanding job, a family to support, his mother in a home, his brother who was always needing bailing out. There was a lot of pressure on Tom, and he just hadn't handled it well.

But he'd come back to her. He'd come back to her because she was loyal, because she stood by him, she was the mother of his children, she had proven herself. And this time, he is ready to get married. This time, he is serious.

He comes home when he says he will, and gives her money any time she needs it – not just her allowance – and he doesn't check the laptop any more, and he takes her out to dinner for date night once a week, and she's even lost a little weight, and he brings her tea in bed in the mornings. Well, he did that just the one time, and she doesn't like tea, but still, she is happy, she tells herself. Again, and again.

Tom makes an appointment with an immigration lawyer.

The lawyer says, 'You'll be granted leave to remain as a partner for an initial period of thirty months. After that, you'll apply for further leave to remain, and then again at five years, then seven and a half years, and then ten years of residence. At ten years, provided the relationship is still subsisting and the other requirements are met, you'll be eligible for indefinite leave to remain, which is permanent residence.'

'Ten years? I thought it was five, on the internet it says five?' Carla asks.

'She said ten years, love—' Tom says, squeezing her hand, but the lawyer answers Carla.

'You've had no legal status for a long time. The five-year route is for people with legal status at the time they apply or who are entering the UK as a spouse. You're on the ten-year route, and actually, the only reason we can do it this way is because the kids are British citizens,' she says, apologetically.

Tom says, 'Okay, sure, but what you're saying is we have to stay married that whole ten years, right?'

The lawyer knows what is really being asked. And she knows the answer she gives is not the one men like Tom want to hear.

She answers, 'In theory. In the event of divorce, Carla should get legal advice, but as she's the mother of two British children, she could submit an application based on being their parent, and then she wouldn't be dependent on a partner for her status.'

'Couldn't I just do that now?' Carla asks, before she can stop herself, seeing, suddenly, a tiny shaft of light.

'What? But we're getting married, love, what you always wanted,' Tom says. He shifts in his chair. He looks at the lawyer as he takes Carla's hand and holds it, and lightly kisses her knuckles. 'She's just nervous, that's all,' he says, with a smile.

'In the present circumstances, as you'll be married soon and you're co-parents, the partner route is the option that's open

142

to you,' the lawyer says to Carla, who stares down at the carpet, and says, 'Oh, okay. I mean, that's great.'

They discuss documents and forms. The lawyer takes out her business cards. She slides one across the desk to Tom, and one to Carla. She keeps her finger on the one she slides to Carla until it's in her hand.

'We don't need two,' Tom says.

'Just in case,' the lawyer says.

Carla reads it quickly to remember the name.

On the way to the car, Carla drops her bag and it spills on to the pavement. Tom bends down to pick it up, gathers her things, takes some candy wrappers and the business card and throws them in the bin right next to them.

'This thing is a mess, what are you like,' he says cheerfully, handing her the bag, kissing her lightly.

The wedding will be on a Wednesday. Carla asks to invite her only real friend, a mum she met at school, but Tom says it should be family only, intimate. His brother will be the witness.

Carla diets but the white dress still doesn't fit. She asks Tom if she can buy something else.

'If you can't zip up the back, just throw a jacket over the top, no one will know,' he says. Carla knows that she will know, but she also knows this doesn't matter.

When she asks him if she can buy a bouquet, Tom says, 'That's a waste of money.'

He says, 'It's not like this is a real wedding.'

'What? But I thought—' and the dread she had pushed down and pushed away, rises.

'Oh, grow up, Carla,' he says.

'I'm sorry,' she says, because it's always the right thing to say. She can't believe it's happened again. She thought it was over, she really did, she believed it this time, she thought it was different.

Her mind darts to the lawyer. She doesn't have to marry Tom, she could leave him, she could do the other application, the one based on the kids, the lawyer said, if they're not together. She doesn't have the business card. When can she get to the library to use the internet, how can she—?

And then he puts his arms around her waist. He slides his hands over her breasts, up to her face. 'I'm sorry, babe,' he says. 'I just meant I want to give you a proper wedding when this visa business is all over. Do it right, when you've had time to get in shape, get you looking gorgeous, get you a proper dress, anything you want, invite our friends, have a real knees-up. You'd like that, wouldn't you?'

'Oh,' she says, looking down at the carpet. 'Of course,' she says. 'I'm sorry.'

2019

Carla got legal status as Tom's wife last year. She gets a job at a hotel reception desk.

Then Tom meets Sherry at a party and has an affair with her. And a baby.

He tells Carla one morning as she sits at the table in her navy robe with the white lapels, drinking coffee.

'Are you leaving me?' she asks quietly, numbly.

'It's not like that, Carla; I'm just going to live there while the baby is still small. Sherry's in a bad way, she needs help,' he says.

'Are you going to divorce me?' she asks, bringing the hot coffee to her mouth, feeling it burn her tongue. She takes a second sip and lets it burn again.

'Why would I do that, Carla? I love you. I just made a mistake, but you know I love you, and it's not the baby's fault, is it?' he says.

Carla is crying silently. He thinks it's because he's leaving, and not because he won't let her go.

'Do you love her?' she asks, pushing her burnt tongue against her teeth.

He puts his hand on her face. 'Not like I love you, babe,' he says.

Lucky girl, Carla thinks, and her trembling hand loses its grip on her cup for a moment. The hot coffee drip, drip, drips on to her lapel, soaking through the satin to her skin, but she sits still, to feel the burn, and to not feel it at the same time.

He explains his plan. He doesn't want Carla to worry. It's just for a few months. He'll give her money for the children, keep his name on the bills and get his post sent there, keep all the evidence of their marriage so they have it when the time comes for her next application to extend her visa as his wife. He just needs some time with the new baby; surely Carla can understand that.

A few months becomes a few more. The cheaper, smaller two-bed flat across the hall next door to the lady who never leaves becomes available and Tom moves them in there. He's supporting two families, now, after all.

As the kids pack their bags to spend the weekend at Tom and Sherry's, she says, 'Are you ever coming back?' with her back to him as she rinses the dishes in the sink.

'Are you complaining?' he asks, knowing that she isn't, but deciding to call it that anyway.

'No, but if you're not, maybe we should talk about getting divorced—'

'And who's going to pay for that, lawyers and fees, Carla? You?' he says, suddenly behind her.

Carla stammers over her shoulder, hands still in the sink, 'I just thought – you could marry Sherry if that's what you want, that's all. I could do that other visa the lawyer said, as a parent—'

'Right, and you're going to pay for that with what? The money I give you for the kids? Did you think you'd pay for a divorce and a new visa and all the lawyers with the money I give you for the *children*?'

He moves her hair off her shoulder and rubs it between his fingers. She stops still. He whispers in her ear, 'Is that what you thought?' She shivers.

When Tom leaves with the children, Carla sits down on the sofa, sips a beer, turns on the TV, and plays with the ring on her chain. She pulls at it, hard, harder, until it snaps with a whip of pain on the back of her neck. They never did manage to get it resized. In the end.

Part Two

February 2020

10

Tuesday

Penny
Flat 1B

Olanzapine. Fluoxetine. Zolpidem. The package arrived today from TrustWorld Online Pharmacy by post, just as they said it would on the website, in a slim, plain, brown package that fitted in the letter box. You can order without a prescription, delivery is fast and discreet. On my debit card statement the transaction comes up only as Corner Shop, which is a relief as this does not arouse my parents' suspicions when they examine my account.

The timing is excellent as I have just learned that on Thursday, Alice Templeton of the Community Mental Health Team will be coming to see me. Again. Her third visit. She's going to ask about my meds. I have no intention of taking them, of course. Well, other than the Zolpidem for sleep, which I researched and sounds blissful. The other drugs are just for show, to demonstrate compliance. Compliance with authority is an important sign of mental stability. I bought them to show Alice that I have been dutifully taking my medication as prescribed. To show her that I am cooperative, tractable, no longer in need of supervision.

It's very convoluted, this part of things; I have to think two steps ahead of everyone. Jamie told my GP and social services that when he came to my flat he noticed my medication boxes were full and he assumed it was because I had stopped taking them. So, before Alice's first visit, I had to, of course, dispose of the majority of the pills so that I could say I *had* taken them, to show that I had started my medication regime again of my own accord. Alice, pleased with my initiative and obedience, told the doctor that I needed a new prescription, as I was running low, presenting me with a new problem. How to obtain the new pills to show that I complied and filled the prescription?

I cannot, at the moment, walk down the road to the pharmacy. I cannot walk through its sliding automatic doors, with which I am very uncomfortable, to the back of the shop, far from the exit, to stand and wait for my name to be called. One, no part of that excursion falls within my zone of safety, and two, I will not submit to having my name shouted aloud in public. Now, of course, I know the NHS has a prescription delivery service, but this too is unsuitable. Use of that service would involve a stranger knowing my name, coming to my home, possibly knowing my personal medical information, and that is an invasion of privacy to which I will not consent. So, how to obtain this medication to show everyone how amenable I am? The answer is TrustWorld Online Pharmacy.

However, in order for the drugs to be delivered discreetly and fit into the letter box, TrustWorld sends them as loose blister packs, without boxes. I have got around this as well. I simply put the new blister packs into my old prescription boxes and no one is the wiser. I push out the number of pills that I would have taken between Alice's last visit and today, to make it look like I've taken them. Now, of course, Alice might check the dates, and observe that they're incorrect on the boxes, and realise that they aren't new prescriptions after all. But I doubt she is that observant.

To be safe, if she asks to see them, I will keep my finger over the dates on the labels, open the box myself to show her the pills. She will see that the prescription has not only been filled but also consumed. I'll do it dramatically, flamboyantly, the way a crazy person would, but not a dangerously crazy person.

I'll do it in the manner of a benign eccentric, and after Thursday she will discharge me back to the GP, stop these visits, and leave me alone. Jamie did me no favours, bringing these people back into my life. None at all.

Jamie. He has stopped his Wednesday visits and his Sunday morning jaunts to the playground with Olivia but it is just as well. If he contacted me now I would not respond. He is no longer within the zone of safety. Of course, this has thrown a spanner in the works with regard to getting my rubbish to the bins. Jamie used to do that for me, every Wednesday. But not now; now getting to the bins has to be a part of Tuesday, taking out the rubbish on the way to the laundrette. It is an awful lot to manage, but, if I forgo recycling, then it is just one extra thing to think about on a Tuesday. And I am stronger now. I can do it.

The flat is clean, the litter box fresh. My kitchen cupboards are stocked, as is my fridge. The flat is very orderly. Last week I had a clear out of the closet and the drawers. I looked online to find out about organising small storage spaces with limited materials and I found this beautiful Japanese lady with the most lovely way about her, Marie, and she had the most brilliant advice about how to declutter. She has a special folding technique, but I'm afraid I didn't get all of it. I stopped watching when she started folding baby clothes.

Anyhow, I found my old running gear in the bottom drawer of my bureau, all of it too small, of course, all of it from a different life when I used to run. Imagine? Every morning, before work, before Olivia, running for miles along the Thames Path, in the early morning when London was still asleep.

Marie says to thank all of the things you can no longer use for the services they provided. I thanked them all. The tank tops, sports bras, the leggings and high-tech running socks. Relics of a daily ritual I no longer observe. I explained to the long-sleeve reflective tops and compression tights that there was simply no running in my future, given my present circumstances, as the hyperventilation associated with exercise brings on feelings that mimic panic attacks for many people – unfortunately, myself included – and, thereby, can inadvertently trigger one, thus best avoided for now. Nonetheless, I said thank you for our time together, and that I'll keep the memories of wind in my hair and the crunch of gravel underfoot. Then I tossed them all in the bin.

I must remember to wash my hair before Thursday. Proper hygiene is a sign of mental stability. Of course, I've been so busy lately, I haven't had the time.

I boil water for tea. I pet Susannah. I prepare to open the door. It is Tuesday, after all.

Carla
Flat 1A

I lift my face too quickly from the bare mattress and I feel like I've just ripped a layer of skin off my cheek.

'Ow,' I say. Oh shit. Why aren't there sheets on the bed?

'Ow!' I shout again, when I roll over and skin rips off the front of each thigh.

I stumble into the bathroom to put my contacts in. I look down. Underwear still on, bra, okay. No jeans, don't know where those went, but same shirt I had on last night, so, okay. When I try to put my contacts in, I realise I still have yesterday's contacts in my eyes.

'Ow,' I say, as I pluck the dry discs out. Fuck.

It hits me.

The bed sheet. He put it on, like a toga, because he's a big guy, because – shit, strip poker? Did we play strip poker?

'Carla? You up?' his deep voice bellows from the other room. Oh my God. What did I do, what did I do . . .

'Um, yeah, be there in a minute,' I say from the bathroom, trying to figure out if I'm going to hurl now or later.

I take my robe off the back of the bathroom door, throw it on, find my glasses in the pocket. How do I get him out of here? I sit on the lid of the toilet. It comes rushing back. The bar, the bet, the drinks, how many drinks?

Oh my God, so many drinks.

'I made breakfast, hope you don't mind—' he calls from the kitchen.

'Yeah, just looking for my glasses,' I call back. Are we, like, on breakfast terms?

'C'mon, you great tit, I've got a surprise for you,' he shouts. Tit? Did he see my boobs? Shit. Oh wait, no, he means the birds, nature, great tits, because it was Trivial Pursuit, not strip poker, oh my God, thank God.

Wait.

Strip Trivial Pursuit?

I can't go out there.

'Carla? Are you all right?'

Oh fuck.

Penny
Flat 1B

Honestly, the racket those two made made last night. And where did she find him? Of all the men in London, she finds Darren out and about on Monday evening, and brings him home? Cavorting about in there until all hours. Well, Susannah got some rest, but I am exhausted. They went on about birds – great tits, blue tits – into the night.

Tuesday is laundry day, usually, but ever since Tom took the children, Carla has been taking Tuesdays off. She works double shifts on the weekends now.

So, I've had to adjust to her new schedule. I used to wait for Carla and the children to leave in the morning. I'd lean out the window and see they'd gone into Justin's and then I'd know they were gone for the day and I could get on with what I

153

needed to do to leave the flat, go down the corridor and out to the laundrette without being watched or interrupted.

But now Carla is here all day sometimes. The fact that she might see me leaving with my laundry is a new layer of anxiety that I could really do without. But, Tuesday is laundry day, the day it is safe to leave the flat, and, well, sometimes there are things we just have to deal with, adversity we must face head-on.

I've prepared some answers ahead of time in case I happen to run into her. I practise in front of the mirror.

'*What are you doing? Washer broken?*' she might ask, pointing at my laundry basket.

'*Yes, it is,*' I'll say, calmly.

'*Did you call the landlord?*' Carla may say.

'*Yes, I did, but you know how difficult it can be to get these things sorted,*' will be my response.

I look at my reflection. My jawline has returned; there are new angles in my face, or angles I remember from years ago, before the medication. Before the Tube.

I continue, '*In fact, it broke two years ago and the management company called the repairman but I didn't feel it prudent at that time to let a strange man into my home. And while I was waiting to feel secure enough to allow a repairman to visit, I thought that it would be beneficial if I experimented with going to the laundrette. As Darren has no doubt told you, now that you are so well acquainted, I am not comfortable in shops, but the laundrette is a good middle ground, a place that resembles a shop, but does not exert the same transactional pressure. There are two tasks to complete there. Washing and drying. And, given the ubiquity of the home washing machine, laundrettes are nearly always free of customers on weekdays. Weekends, now that is an entirely different situation, Carla, but weekdays are calm and quiet. Now if you'll excuse me—*' I'll say and then walk off.

That will teach her to mind her own business.

Woman
Flat 2A–2B

'I am taking the children back to Kensington,' Madame announces to Sir, in the language we all know, as I take away the breakfast plates. Madame ate only toasted bread, but Sir requested Fullenglish today.

To make Fullenglish, Mother, requires two eggs, toasted bread, sausage, bacon, beans that are orange and from a tin, grilled tomatoes, and cooked mushrooms. On days when he has important business, Sir dresses in a dark suit with a waistcoat. He puts a handkerchief in the pocket of his suit jacket. He wears the heavy watch, the gold one he calls Rolex, the one usually locked in the safe with the passports. He is from Neighbouring Country, Mother, not Home Country. I do not know where exactly, but I suspect it is the east. I can see it where his cheekbone meets the hinge of his jaw. But on days like today he is Fullenglish.

'I told you the risk is still too great. It is better we stay here. They're watching Kensington,' I hear him say as I back out of the room.

Kensington is the first place they took me, Mother, after the plane. Kensington was the first year here, the flat that had the bathtub with golden feet of lions holding it up. Fine curtains. Deep carpets. In Kensington, Madame had me wear the black dress with the white collar and the white apron to serve tea to her friends. Her friends had long fingernails, Mother, painted many colours. If the weather was fine, they sat in the garden, with the roses. They were tended by the man Sir and Madame kept. He slept in the garden shed. The fine ladies didn't know this, Mother. I did. We never spoke, his was a different language, but I thought of him on winter nights.

'This is a hovel, it is disgusting, we are like cave dwellers here, and the children—' Madame says as I come back in, slowly this time, to gather the remains of breakfast.

Sir's voice flashes with anger. 'This is safe. It keeps them out of our business, how many times do I have to explain—'

'Then send us back to Home Country,' Madame says. 'I can no longer live this way—' she says with her face of a spoiled child.

'Are you stupid, Madame?' he says as though he is asking if she has had a nice morning, and he twists the ring on his finger, a habit of his when he is contemplating the infliction of pain. The argument begins, Mother, the one that starts like this, in hushed whispers, but ends always quite differently.

I back out of the room again, grateful that when we came here Sir enclosed this kitchen with an extra wall and swinging door to separate it from the living space. He also knocked out part of the wall between this flat and the one next door to it and installed a door. Old Madame's quarters are there, through the door, with a small kitchen and another bathroom. Sir and Madame have the large bedroom in this flat, Baby and My Lady have the other as a nursery, and Master has a large room in the flat across the hall. It is part of his obligation to the family to monitor the others who pass through that flat, the ones brought there to sleep on the floor for one or two nights on their way to Better Life. He does not complain. He is content wherever he is as long as his dark-haired Americans are accessible.

I scrape the plates in the kitchen. I hear Sir and Madame hissing at each other, and then My Lady comes tumbling in.

'Woman, shall I talk to Father today?' she says, rubbing her sleepy eyes. Her nightshirt is too small. It stretches across her belly. She looks for the key around her neck and reaches for the handle of her cupboard.

'My Lady, perhaps breakfast first, before sweets?' I say, and gently move her hand from the handle.

'No!' she shouts. And I do not press her because she loves me, but it is not my place. Even she, so young, knows my place.

I step away from her. 'Your parents are talking, better to wait,' I say.

I begin to wash the dishes. There is a machine for washing dishes, Mother, but Madame says every plate must be washed by hand because of the gold edging. Every knife and every fork also because they are silver. They are not silver, I know this by the weight and by the way the metal is wearing, the dull grey steel underneath coming through the lustre, but she insists. Also, the cut-crystal glasses. They are not crystal, only copies of crystal, Mother. I know because they do not ring. They are not heavy. I remember the two crystal glasses that belonged to Grandmother, the ones she was given by the British lady of the manor, from that fine house she cleaned for her, long ago, in Capital City.

'Shall I ask him now about school? Do you think he will let me go? Am I big enough?' My Lady asks me, holding a bar of chocolate in her hands.

'I don't know, My Lady,' I say, but I do know.

He will not let her go. It is his business or the people watching him. He doesn't want her to be seen. He doesn't want the family to be known. I am not allowed to leave the building, and so I cannot take her to school. And the rest of the family, Master and Madame and Old Madame, all have their jobs they do for the business. Old Madame runs Laundrette, Master drives the vans and monitors the flat across the hall, Madame assists Sir, speaking in whispers, often starting their work after midnight, laptops and ledgers spread across the table, all the lights off in the flat.

It is something about how we left Kensington, Mother. Moving house in the middle of the night. The man of the garden shed put our boxes in Laundrette vans and then he dropped the last box and ran. His feet were bare, his shoes in his hands. I learned this from the garden shed man, Mother, that when it is time to run, shoes are a hindrance.

'I will go ask him now, I'm sure he will say yes,' My Lady says, and before I can stop her she is at the table, interrupting her parents' conversation.

I open the kitchen door a crack to watch. Sir slaps her for her impertinence. Her chocolate bar flies out of her hand. Her eyes fill with tears, but she makes only small sobbing sounds as she holds her burning face.

I move to go to her, but suddenly Sir softens. He pulls her towards him. Sits her on his lap. He says, 'My Lady, I have told you many times, if you go to school, they will know we are here. They will find our hiding place. But we will not have to hide much longer. Just for now. Do you understand? You must tell no one, and you must not go out, and you must not go to school because it keeps us safe. Here,' he says, and he takes the remaining buttered toast from the side plate I have not yet cleared away and sprinkles a teaspoon of sugar from the sugar bowl over the top. He hands it to her.

'Now leave us be,' he says.

I step out of the kitchen to collect her, but before I comfort her I look to see where the chocolate landed. Where it landed will shape my day. If it landed on the wood floor, it will be easy to clean, and I am in luck. If it landed on the rug or the sofa arm – the white rug, the white sofa arm – well, My Lady will have brought trouble into my life today, Mother. And I do not have time for extra work. I am due downstairs in Laundrette. The shirts are waiting.

I put my arm around My Lady and take her to her room. I find a change of clothes for her. I return to the dining room, as quietly as I can, to clear up the chocolate. It has missed the white sofa, but not the white rug. It is on the floor on the far side of the room, behind Sir, and Madame does not notice me on my hands and knees. I pick up the chocolate, put it in the pocket of my apron and, with damp cloth in hand, I pray that there will be no mark left. No mark of chocolate and no water mark. It is the water mark that is more difficult to prevent, Mother.

'I am going to Kensington today. I am going to Harrods. I must go today because I left my coat there for alteration. They still have it, and the shoes I ordered; I've been waiting a month for them at least,' Madame says to Sir.

'What did you order? What name did you use?' Sir questions her, alarm in his voice. 'I told you never to do that, to take your things and go, pay cash. What alterations? Did you leave your name?' He is angry with her.

'Of course not. It is all paid for in cash. I gave a false mobile number, of course, as always. I am just going to pick up my things, and to have high tea with my friends . . .'

'You will go nowhere, you will do nothing,' Sir says, a low, cruel rumble in his voice.

'I am not My Lady, I am not a child. You cannot tell me what to do, where to go. I run this business too. It is my money as well. I will do what I like. I refuse to go down to that stinking laundrette and I refuse to keep living here in this awful place. I will move to Kensington myself, I will take Old Madame with me, I will—'

'You refuse nothing,' Sir says slowly, carefully, in an angry whisper through his teeth. He knows everything can be heard in this building so instead of shouting he pounds his fist on the table, so hard that his cup flies off its saucer and tumbles to the floor. Tea pools on the floor beneath his chair, slowly making progress towards the rug, a miniature tide crawling towards a white shore. I hold my breath. So does Madame. She has gone too far. There is a long quiet before I move, still on hands and knees, to catch the pool of tea. I am close to Sir's chair, close enough to hear him breathing. Close enough to see that Madame is frozen in her seat.

'Woman, leave,' Sir says, without looking at me. It seems today it is Madame's turn to be afraid. I leave as directed, eyes cast downward, knowing what is coming to her from her husband. He will take her across the corridor, to the flat where they keep the others for the night before they are moved on. To the one room where he has padded the walls, and doubled the carpeting to mute the sound, the room where no

159

one can hear the beatings for those who need to be taught their lessons. Silent Room. It does not happen often. If they are hurt too badly, they cannot work, and then what use are they to anyone, Mother.

He pulls Madame from her chair, and she knows better than to make a fuss. To make noise will only incur a worse punishment. Sir opens the door carefully, quietly, his twist on her arm guaranteeing her silence as they move across the hall. But it is, Mother, I am not sorry to say this, no less than she deserves.

I must go, Mother. Baby is crying. The shirts are waiting.

Carla
Flat 1A

'Voila!' he shouts, as I sit down at the table.

'Breakfast is served, my lady,' he says, smiling, putting a plate in front of me. 'The house speciality, madame, Dickanballs,' he says, and he can't hold in his laughter.

There are two fried eggs on my plate, each one lying on either side of a sausage with its end cut off, standing upright in the middle.

'Erectfast is served!' Darren says, doubled over at the sight of his own joke.

I can't speak. He's wearing the sheet from my bed like a sarong around his waist, with his Tesco uniform shirt on top, unbuttoned. He stops laughing abruptly, struck silent when he sees my face.

'Oh, sorry, I thought you'd find it funny,' he says, a hurt look in his hungover green eyes.

And it is funny. It's extremely funny.

'Darren,' I say, 'this is the funniest fucking thing I've ever seen in my life,' and I laugh. He laughs, and we laugh, and laugh, and laugh, until I can't breathe, until my laughs are so hard, they're silent, until I have to cough for air, until he laughs so hard he has to sit down and hold his head, until my stomach hurts, until I throw up, right there at the table. Right on to the sausage/penis.

We stop laughing. And that's when I start to cry.

Penny
Flat 1B

Quarter to ten. I'm already fifteen minutes behind schedule because of Carla and Darren and having to reconsider whether I should actually go ahead with the laundry today. They've been so raucous, I could barely string my thoughts together. But they've quieted down now, so I must forge ahead.

I put the boiler suit on over my bra and knickers. I learned the hard way that wearing woollen underwear to the laundrette is a recipe for heat stroke. So, the boiler suit, then the men's overcoat, rubber gloves, face mask, and Jamie's Yankees cap.

I check my bag of essentials. Coin purse, extra face mask, antibacterial hand gel, water bottle, Alpen Swiss muesli breakfast bar, phone, phone charger, flip-flops. The flip-flops are in case of explosion. It is well documented that in the aftermath of large explosions, the debris always contains a disproportionate number of women's shoes, primarily high heels, but other women's shoes as well, so many styles are impractical for running in emergencies. Flip-flops are, too, of course, but these are for afterwards. In case I lose my shoes, run barefoot, and then have to make my way home through the destruction.

I buy my detergent and fabric softener at the laundrette. I can't ask Darren to deliver detergent as the bottles will not fit through the space under the door chain. But this is one instance in which the ways I live my life are actually quite logical. If I buy detergent at the laundrette, I do not then have to carry heavy, unwieldy bottles downstairs along with the laundry. It is a practical solution, one anyone might consider.

Ten past ten. I have now been standing at the door with my laundry basket for ten minutes. *Open the door.*

All I need to do is turn the doorknob, open the door, and lock the door behind me. I put my hand on the doorknob.

Penny, open the door. Open the door, lock it behind you.

Carla
Flat 1A

I lock the bathroom door and run the hot water in the tub.

'Guess I'll head off now,' Darren says through the door.

'Okay. It was nice of you to cook; you didn't have to clean that up. I'm so sorry I ruined it,' I say, standing on the other side, mortified that he saw me crying into my own vomit.

'Nothing to be sorry for,' he says. 'Happens to the best of us. I probably should've checked how you was feeling before I put eggs in front of you.'

I lean my pounding head on the cold tiled wall. That's the nicest thing anyone has said to me in a long time.

'I'm sorry I was so drunk. I haven't done that for years. My life's really complicated right now . . . I'm trying to get my kids back, so I can't, I mean, last night—'

'No, I know. It was just a bit of fun. Don't worry, I won't be stalking you or nothing,' he says, 'unless you want me to.'

'Um, no,' I say. 'Sorry, I mean, you're great, I just—'

'It's all right. I'm no good at stalking anyway. Found my trousers and put the sheet back on your bed, so . . . hope you feel better soon,' he says and gives the door a little knock in goodbye.

I hear the door to the flat fall closed behind him. I sink into the hot water, and watch my skin turn red, and the quiet fills me up again. It's so quiet without them. I went out last night, just to hear people's voices, just to sit near someone, anyone.

To make sure I hadn't disappeared. Because my life is really small, and without the kids . . . at least when they hate me, I matter enough to be hated.

And that's why he took them. Because he knows I don't matter without them.

I've only seen them twice since they left. And I was talking to Daniel every day after school, but Tom started checking his bill, so, that's how that story goes.

I just have to wait him out. There's nothing else I can do.

I stay in the bath until it goes cold. Until I shiver. Until it hurts.

Penny
Flat 1B

At twenty-seven minutes past eleven, I turn the doorknob. One must keep trying. One must persevere, fail, and try again. That is the nature of this condition. Failure is constant. But every day, one more thing is taken from me. Checking the letter box in the lobby has become more challenging. I can only do it once a week now, on the way back from the laundrette. I used to order noodles from Justin's but I don't seem to be able to do that anymore. The anxiety of not knowing who might come to the door to deliver them, of having to open the door to a stranger, outweighs my love of noodles.

The door and I engage in this battle every Tuesday. I fear that the door may be winning. It is taking longer each time to leave. I could give up. It would be much easier to give up. But I've already given up so much: the shops, the library, the park, the bus, the noodles, the rain on my face, Jamie, the wind, the air, Oliv—

I must hold on to the door. It is the only way out.

Woman
First Premier Dry Cleaner and Laundry

I worry about the chocolate stains and the tea on the floor that I could not clean properly because Sir dismissed me to punish his wife. I must try to remember to get to those first when I go up to make the midday meal before Madame can notice. Or maybe the new girl will do it, if she's still there. If they have not moved her yet. They keep her in the flat across the hall. They are careful always with the new ones that we do not cross paths too often. They do things in the flat while I work in Laundrette. But they do not stay long. Only I stay, Mother.

Old Madame sits at the counter. She picks her teeth with a bent, gnarled finger. She smacks her lips. She sighs and passes wind and turns a page of her paper. She shifts in her seat.

'Tea,' she commands, without looking at me, and I put water in the electric kettle next to the shirt press to make her a cup. When it has boiled, I whistle loudly, and Old Madame turns around to look at me, but before she can chastise me for the noise, I throw the boiling water in her face. She screams in pain and falls off her stool and I step over her mountainous, writhing flesh, open the door and leave the shop. I imagine what this would feel like, Mother, as I pour the water over her tea bag.

I return to pressing shirts. PC Grant's clean uniform hangs on the clothing rack next to me. When I finish his shirts, I will put them all together in one hanging bundle. I keep pressing the shirts as Old Madame heaves herself up, sighs and farts and grunts and buttons her cardigan, picks up her walking stick and tells me about the important business she must now attend to before pointing to the car outside and warning me that I am being watched, like she does every day.

She shuffles off for her excretion ritual and I return to work, relieved to have a few minutes without the smells and sounds of Old Madame. So I am startled when the bells on the shop door ring. It is the old woman with the lavender hat. I smile but try not to show my teeth. She comes in sometimes to leave her magazines. Old Madame shouted at her the first time because she does not like Africans. But today she has appeared at just the moment that Old Madame has left the counter.

'Good morning,' she says. She keeps talking, but I only know these words, 'good morning'. I shrug and shake my head.

'Speak English?' she asks, in a kind voice.

'No, no English,' I say, and smile again, and look down quickly to the shirt I am pressing. She takes a step closer to the counter, and peers over. I feel the woman looking at my feet, Mother, noticing my socks, my flip-flops.

She says more words in English that I don't know, but I catch 'PC Grant' when she points at his uniform. Then more words. 'Good news,' she says, and these words I know. These words she says most often about her God. I look at her and nod. She must know PC Grant.

She waves her magazines in the air and asks a question which I think means she wants to leave them here. I recognise them, they are the ones she leaves under the door of the flat sometimes. I wish I had words to tell her how many times she has prayed with me through the door. That I am grateful for her prayers, whatever they might mean.

Then I think quickly. I have only a moment before Old Madame returns. I reach across the counter to the old woman and say, 'Good news? For help?'

She asks me a question, but I do not know the words she says. We hear Old Madame coming. She says more words, but I understand only 'help', 'child', and '3B'. I know this word, 'child', but I don't know which child she means, if there are other children, others who need help.

She takes my hand and squeezes. She wants to say something else but Old Madame is coming. She knows Old

Madame will shout and throw her magazines away. So, she hurries to the door, waves to me once, and leaves.

Penny
First Premier Dry Cleaner and Laundry

A quarter to twelve. Once I leave the flat, the stairs pose no issue because they require focus and concentration when one is holding a large laundry basket and distraction is an important technique for managing panic. It is at the bottom of the stairs, once I face the lobby and the front door, that I freeze.

Doors that one can push, like the front door, do not cause a problem for me. But automatic sliding doors I simply cannot abide. They create a situation in which one has no control, in which one's fate is left entirely to the whim of the sensor or the computer or the conductor, if they happen to be the doors of a train carriage. Doors with knobs and locks like the door to the flat make me uneasy, but I can just about handle them. I am always afraid that the mechanisms have the potential to jam or jar and then lock one in with no hope of escape, or lock one out with no hope of rescue. But doors that one can push, like the front door to the building and the door to the laundrette, these are a relief. In a world where so many doors require a leap of faith to cross their threshold, doors that I can simply push, that do not seek to imprison nor to permanently detain, are a pleasure. They afford me a small act of normalcy, a moment of not having to work so hard at being alive.

But the door is not why I freeze. It is Carla, on her way back from the corner shop. Her hands are full and she's fumbling about, her wallet in her mouth, trying to reach for the handle. She sees me. For a moment we each stand on either side of the glass door and look at each other, me with my laundry basket, her with her life in a shambles.

She shouts through the wallet in her teeth, 'Open the door!' as though it should be obvious to me that this is what I should do. I've forgotten momentarily that this is what people do in the world, open doors for others as a courtesy.

I put my laundry down, push the door open and say to Carla what I can remember of my speech, although I had not practised for this type of encounter.

I say, through my mask, 'Yes, I did, you know how long these things take to get sorted. It resembles a shop, but doesn't exert the same transactional pressures, washing and drying. Given the ubiquity of the home washing machine. Weekends, now that is an entirely different situation, Carla, but weekdays are calm and quiet.'

'Okay, whatever,' she says, and she brushes past me with her customary gruffness, not even the pretence of a 'thank you'. Her arm touches my coat sleeve. I flinch.

With her back to me, under her breath, she says, 'Fuckin' wackadoo.'

This is one of her favourite Americanisms. She uses it often. She seems to think that other people, and specifically we, the wackadoos, cannot hear her when she says it. I wonder who else inhabits this category other than myself and Mable.

I pick up my laundry basket and I finally find myself outside.

The laundrette is fifteen steps to my right. I have only to make a quarter turn, walk those steps, push open the door, and I am there. I breathe as deeply as my face mask will allow and begin the walk.

Mable
First Premier Dry Cleaner and Laundry

I waited until I saw that old woman go take her comfort break before I went into the laundrette because I have no interest in dealing with her mood today. I make sure the girl is alone before I approach. I only have a few minutes before the old lady comes back.

I say, 'Good morning.'

She looks up and she smiles, but she don' show her teeth.

I try, 'You ready for some Good News this morning?' but she don' reply.

I go up to the counter. 'You don' speak English?' I say, when I know she don'. But it seem polite to ask.

The girl says, 'No English,' and keeps ironing. She smiles but covers her mouth. I see now she has missing teeth. Piles and piles of shirts to iron. Her clothes are so thin, too thin for the cold weather. Her T-shirt has holes. Sometimes worldly people wear clothes with holes for fashion. The only way to know whether it is for fashion or due to poverty is to look at the shoes.

I get up on my toes to have a look at her feet. Socks only and thong sandals, like you wear for the beach. But this here, in the laundry, this is no holiday.

Behind her hangs a policeman's uniform.

'Oh,' I say, 'oh, look at that. That for PC Grant, is it? Lovely fellow, lives just round the corner here. I call on him sometimes, to share the Good News.'

She looks at me like she might know some of my words but not all. There's a light of recognition in her eye when I mention PC Grant. I don' know what to say next but I remember the Book of Revelation says: 'He had everlasting Good News to declare to those who dwell on the earth, to every nation and tribe and tongue and people' — and me and this girl, we don' share a tongue, but we have the universal language of Jehovah's love. She needs something, I know she does, so I must try.

'All right then, darlin', I'll leave some literature here for your customers to read about Jehovah's Kingdom while waiting for the wash. Is that all right?' and I show her my magazines.

I fix my hat so I can go, but then an angel intercedes from above and the girl grabs me by the hand and says, 'Good news, for help?'

I don' know this girl's trouble, or what evil surrounds her or what demon may want to take her down the path of the unrighteous, but I know when someone needs help. And I know who to ask to get it.

'You need help, child?' I say to her and look her in the eyes. 'If you need help, you come. Flat 3B.'

She don' use words. She don' need to. She tells me with her eyes she gon' to come when she needs me. And I will be ready. Me and Jehovah will bring her home.

I hear the old lady shuffling behind the partition, which means I must exit the premises. I squeeze the girl's hand one more time so she feels some love, and then I go, fast as I can.

Woman
First Premier Dry Cleaner and Laundry

I give Old Madame her second cup of tea and she says, in the language we both know, 'Crazy, foolish woman is coming. Watch her. Ridiculous idiot. Why they haven't locked her away, I do not know.'

I do not need to look up. I know who she means. I have time to press several shirts before she gets to the door.

Penny
First Premier Dry Cleaner and Laundry

I check my watch. Twelve. Fifteen minutes to get from one door to the next, but I am here. I was held up by the presence of a dog that had been tied to a post midway between the entrance to the flats and the entrance to the laundrette. I watched the owner tie up the dog and run into the newsagent. I do not, as a rule, cross the paths of animals. I waited for the owner to finish his business, which took an inordinate amount of time, and then he had the audacity to pop down to Justin's. Thank God he got a takeaway coffee and didn't decide to sit in. He then finally untied his dog and went on his way and I resumed mine.

I take up my position at the two machines nearest the door. Dark colours in one. Sheets and towels in another. Next week will be light colours. I alternate so that I don't have to carry too much or do more than two loads. I count out my change, put the coins in the machines and turn them on. Then finally, relieved, I can sit—

But—

My foot taps my laundry basket and I look down, and oh no, oh God, how did I—

How could I— I forgot to put in my bath towel.

It's lying there, in the basket. In all my haste, and dick and balls and Carla at the door, and then my speech and then the dog and its owner, and I finally got here, I finally got here, I tried so hard to get here, and now look, I've ruined it! Do I start another machine? For just one towel? I've never used three machines, and I don't have enough coins, do I? For three machines plus the drying? And if I can't dry everything, how will I get it home, it will be heavy if it's wet, and it takes so long to walk home, how will I do it?

'I've ruined it! I've ruined the laundry!' I shout, my breath caught in my throat. I am going to have to leave, how can I leave, leave all my clothes here? Leave all my bedding? What do I do?

I take out the phone and call Jamie with trembling hands. He doesn't answer. I leave a message. 'Jamie, my clothes, the laundry, please, I don't know what to do—'

Woman
First Premier Dry Cleaner and Laundry

'Go sort her out, the crazy, idiot bitch,' Old Madame says, turning a page of her newspaper. The woman in the mask and rubber gloves is in great distress.

Sometimes it takes her many minutes to walk by the shop windows before she can reach the door and come in. Most times she is calm and quiet, Mother, reading the old woman's God magazines until the wash is done. But now and then there is an explosion of emotion that she cannot contain. Once it was that the machine would not take her coins because it was full. Once another customer left behind a pair of underpants in the washer and this made her wild with distress.

Usually, Old Madame does not let me near the customers but she hates this woman and so she falls to me. Old Madame has reasoned that she poses no threat, Mother, so absorbed is she in accomplishing just the small task of washing clothes, barely able to open the door of Laundrette. She is a woman alone, of no consequence, invisible, damaged. She is like me, Mother, but also, she is not. I know I will not always live my life as I do today, Mother. But she, perhaps, always will.

I walk over to her slowly, gently. I say to her a phrase My Lady taught me: 'You are all right.'

She says words I don't know except for 'towel'. I see that she did not put the towel into the machine. I put my palm up and nod, to show her I can fix it. It has not been running long, so I stop the machine, punch the door handle twice, which unlocks the door even when the water has run, and pull it open. I put the towel in for her. I try to have friendly eyes, but I do not smile, Mother. I do not like to show my teeth.

'Thank you,' she says through her face mask, the kind that doctors wear, but also with her eyes which I can see above it. If I had such a mask, Mother, no one would see my teeth or the scar on the side of my chin. She has stopped crying. I see she has forgotten the washing powder as well, so I go to the counter and bring her back a packet. I try to tell her with my eyes to wait a moment and not to say anything and she seems to understand. I can tell by the shuffling sounds behind me that Old Madame is off to the toilet again.

'Finish what you are doing and go back to work, you whore,' she calls to me, as she makes her way to the bathroom. When she is gone, I take a dummy coin from my pocket and insert it into the coin slot. I press the button and the machine starts without the woman having to insert more of her own money. I nod at her and return to the waiting shirts.

Penny
First Premier Dry Cleaner and Laundry

It's so kind of her. She's so lovely. Dark eyes, long black hair. She is some kind of Russian, some kind of post-Soviet Eastern European. But she doesn't speak Russian to the old woman who hates me. It's a language I don't recognise.

I choke on the words when I say, 'Thank you.'

I put my hands on my knees and bend down to catch my breath, as if I just finished a long run. And when I look down, I see that she's wearing – she's wearing, she's wearing – my socks. She's wearing the old running socks that I threw away last week. She's wearing them with her flip-flops. Dark purple Under Armour technical running socks with a fluorescent orange stripe around the ankle. On her toes I can see the L and the R they put there for left and right, but she has them on the wrong way round. The thong of the flip-flops cuts into the socks, between her toes.

She walks back to the counter, but I keep my eyes on her feet. The water runs over the glass of the washing machine door. I said thank you to those socks and then I threw them in the bin.

She is the girl.

From the bins.

She walks behind the counter to press the shirts.

She is in trouble.

I touch Olivia's barrette in my hair and watch the clothes spin around in the machine. I watch the clothes spin and I try not to know what I know.

Carla
Flat 1A

'Yes, I understand . . . well, she's been staying with her dad, have you called him?' I ask the lady who calls from Mary Rose's school as I take the ibuprofen and Diet Coke out of the bag and swallow three of the pills. They've been trying Tom but can't get through. She didn't show up today and he hasn't reported her sick or whatever, so now it's a thing. Something about 'mandatory reporting' and 'unauthorised absence'.

I cram half a Snickers bar in my mouth while the lady says snooty things to me in her English accent, insinuating that I'm a terrible mother. Tell me something I don't know, lady.

'Okay, fine, we'll get back to you,' I say, mid-Snickers, before she can end the call herself.

And now, I panic. I want to call Tom, but he said don't call. Don't call him or them if I want to see them. But this is an emergency, right? Is she sick, did she run away? Wouldn't he tell me if something was wrong? Is she in trouble?

I don't call Tom. I call Lottie, her best friend's mom.

Lottie says, 'I'm afraid I don't know, Carla. To be honest, I don't want to get involved. I don't know what's happened between you and Tom, but he called me about Mary Rose as well and asked me not to speak to you. I'm sorry, but I can't get in the middle of this.'

'I'm worried that she's in trouble; school called and—'

'Carla, I hope she's all right, but I can't help,' she says and hangs up.

Well, fuck you too, Lottie.

The lump in my throat is so big I can't swallow or breathe and where is my kid? And when I stand up, everything spins, everything shifts, I can't find the ground. Nothing's where it's supposed to be.

Penny
First Premier Dry Cleaner and Laundry

There's a bench in front of the washing machine, moulded hard plastic and bolted to the floor. I sit down, carefully, keep my eyes on the washing machine doors, on the clothes spinning inside, on the suds and water running over the glass, because if I look up I will not be able to stop myself from looking at her, from trying to get a view of her over the old lady's shoulder.

There was an old man who used to lean on his walking stick in the playground and look at me from across the road.

The girl who ate raisins. The girl in the bins. The girl who is wearing my socks.

I would raise my blind and he would be standing there, leaning on his stick, looking at me. And I would look at him.

She's gone to the bins more than that one time. She found the socks I threw away.

I would lower my blind, and after five minutes I would check again, and he would be gone and that's how I knew it was half past eight.

It's winter. Her feet must be cold.

Sometimes I wish he'd come back, so that I'd know someone can still see me.

II

Thursday

Penny
Flat 1B

'Penny, you understand that your episodes last month were part of your withdrawal?' Alice asks.

Her NHS ID badge dangles from a lanyard around her neck and shakes furiously as she takes notes. It reads: Alice Templeton, Community Mental Health Team. The bottom edge of the plastic card scrapes her notebook page as she writes. Penny pulls her hand inside the sleeve of her jumper so she can dig her fingernails into her palm to help her tolerate the sound without Alice seeing.

Alice also cannot see that Penny is wearing shoes a size too small, which cause her pain. But the pain is helpful. It was a trick she learned at university to help her cope with big lecture halls. When she wore tight shoes, the discomfort would distract her from her anxiety. If she felt pain in her toes, at the backs of her heels, then she could concentrate on the pain and on the lecture, but not on looking for all the exits. The pain muted her fear.

Today, the pain is meant to diminish the distress and anguish that the presence of Alice in her flat is causing her – this stranger, in her home, asking personal questions, prying into her life, inspecting, prodding, judging. But Penny knows that it will only be a brief visit and that cooperation and compliance, above all, are signs of mental stability and she must – *must* – demonstrate them so that Alice's weekly intrusion will stop.

She pushes her foot hard against the front of her shoe. 'Yes, I do, I shouldn't have gone cold turkey like that,' Penny says, putting her other hand in her pocket so Alice doesn't notice her tremor, a symptom of withdrawal from her medication which she is pretending not to be experiencing because she is trying to convince Alice that she is back on her drug regime.

Her goal is to show Alice that she no longer needs home visits and can be discharged from community care back to her GP. The GP will only bother her once a year to schedule a health check, because patients on Olanzapine, a powerful antipsychotic, require a health screening yearly. But Penny will not need that in reality because she will no longer be taking it. Her greatest wish is for all of these people to just leave her alone.

'Panic attacks, sweating, dizziness, paranoia – if you don't wean yourself off these slowly, the withdrawal can hit you like a ton of bricks, especially given the length of time you've been on them,' Alice says as she writes without looking at Penny.

'Mm-hm,' Penny replies in agreement. Acquiescence and cooperation must be demonstrated, always.

'How does it feel to be back on the Olanzapine and the Fluoxetine? Are they helping?' Alice asks.

Penny is prepared for this question. She has rehearsed a combination of her recollections of the first time she went on these drugs with the many online reviews she's read from other patients to construct a plausible answer that would make it sound like taking them a second time has had a slightly different effect, adding a touch of realism to the charade.

'Well, you know the first two weeks, they're always hard. The panic gets much worse before it gets better. But I stuck with it and I'm calmer now, definitely. Fewer panic attacks. Quite sleepy though,' she says, putting a hand through her hair only to realise, to her horror, that she forgot to wash it. She quickly scrapes it back into a ponytail and hopes that Alice doesn't notice. So much had happened since Tuesday

– the laundry, the socks, the woman from the bins. It took her some time to recover and to plan her next step. She forgot about her hair.

'Any other side effects?' Alice asks.

Penny's side effects last time were a twenty-five-kilo weight gain, sleeping twelve hours a day, sometimes more, obliteration of her libido, brain fog and a loss of all emotion. She could still pretend and apply facsimiles of the feelings she knew were needed or expected in certain situations. Remembering to smile when someone smiled at her. Remembering to let Jamie hug her because not to would hurt him, even though his hands, that one time he kissed her near her lips – these ignited in her the echo of a feeling in the deepest cavern of her heart. Not even her heart, just her memory. When he said he'd bring Olivia to the playground that first time, she felt it, somewhere, but could not say where. Faded memories, old feelings echoing off the walls of her empty skull. Sensations are coming back to her now, emotions, thoughts, and while they are overwhelming sometimes, like a fireworks display in her brain that never ends, she is relieved that they are still there. That she is still able to feel.

'Craving for carbs, but I know that's normal. Overall, just a general quiet feeling, which is good, because I need it,' Penny lies.

'Yes, it's critical that if you ever want to come off these again, that you speak to a professional and get advice, because really, they do help you, Penny, and there shouldn't be a reason to come off—' Alice continues in a headmistress's tone.

'Of course, I understand, I had a wobble. It was a bad idea. And I know you're all concerned about me taking my meds, but here, I'll show you,' Penny says, and she gets up to open her bedside table, running a finger around the waistband of her skirt to feel a new pleasing looseness there.

She takes out the Olanzapine and Fluoxetine that she ordered from TrustWorld Online Pharmacy, careful not to open the drawer too far so that Alice doesn't see the Zolpidem for sleep. She hands the boxes to Alice, who gives them a cursory glance, just as Penny hoped she would.

'Right, so what are your plans for today then?' Alice asks pleasantly, with a smile, notebook down, leaning forward, arms crossed over her lap, a pose of intent listening, like a chat-show host.

Penny replaces the boxes and closes the drawer, smiles to show that she understands social cues, although she finds Alice's lean towards her to be aggressively positive. Even though it is Thursday and not Tuesday, for lack of a better answer Penny says, 'Laundry; I have so much to do.'

'Great, it's important to keep busy. And to keep a tidy flat. It looks really good in here,' Alice says.

'And why wouldn't it,' Penny says.

Penny wonders if Alice has ever had anyone come into her house and ask her about the last time she cleaned it. She wonders how clean Alice's oven is, if she could ask Alice when the last time was that she scrubbed the grout in her bathroom. When was Alice last congratulated for not living like an animal? They made so much of this always. The freedom to be messy is a privilege of the well.

'Maybe a hair wash today? That might be a nice activity for you, you'll feel great afterwards,' Alice says, not making eye contact with Penny and going back to her notes.

'Oh this? Oh dear, I must look a fright, this is a hair masque, you know, one of those new treatments you can do at home? I just didn't know what time to expect you and I put it in this morning, and don't you know but it's the sort you're supposed to leave on overnight, so I have to give it a couple of hours at least. That's the last time I buy this one! Such a faff!' Penny says, and with one hand on her waist she waves the other hand in the air the way she practised doing during Girl Talk.

She has surprised herself with the speediness with which she thought up this detailed story. There is a familiar swiftness to her thinking now that she has missed. A connection between synapses no longer dormant.

'I see,' Alice says, tilting her head at Penny, feeling that something is off. 'Which brand is it?' Alice asks, casually interested, as though she might like to try it herself.

'Uh, I can't remember—' Penny says.

'Then let's just have a look at the package, shall we? I love this kind of thing but I don't want to buy one if you wouldn't recommend it—' Alice says, and her interest is almost believable.

'Oh, well—' Penny wheezes out the syllables. 'I – it – I—' Her chest tightens because there is no package, and Alice has caught her in the lie. Penny looks down, focuses on the pain in her feet in the too tight shoes.

'Never mind, don't worry,' Alice says. 'Perhaps you can tell me when I come back next week. You'll let me know how it turned out.'

'Next week? But I thought I would be discharged back to the GP? Isn't that – didn't we—' Penny can't finish her sentence.

'No, Penny, there's no rush to discharge you. Not until we're sure that you're back on your feet,' Alice says.

Penny pushes her feet to the front of her shoes, pressing her toes hard into the floor, but she does this slowly, her ankles crossed and tucked under the chair, so Alice can't see.

'Back on my feet, yes, of course.'

Woman
Lobby

As she sweeps the lobby, Woman sees the girl staggering towards the door. She's the red-haired woman's daughter, from 1A.

She's not well. Woman can see that she's been drinking or taking drugs. Woman goes to open the door for her, but she does not reach it in time before the girl hits her head on the glass while fumbling for her keys. Woman holds the door open, and the girl stumbles in, goes to the corner of the lobby where Woman has just swept, and vomits. She slides against the wall of mailboxes and crumples to the floor.

Woman sighs, heavily. Another mess to clean up. And what does she do with this girl? Leave her? Wait with her? Knock on her mother's door? She cannot speak to the mother; she must remain invisible to the tenants. She cannot leave her here, Madame or Old Madame or Master will eventually see her and Woman will be punished for not doing something about her. The vomit must also be cleaned up before anyone sees it.

She kicks gently at the girl's shoe. Her head lolls on her shoulders. Woman opens the flap of the girl's school bag. A mobile phone lies at the top. Woman tucks it into her waistband. At least the girl has turned out to be worth the trouble she is causing.

Alice
First floor corridor

Alice closes the door to Penny's flat and lets out a deep breath. She holds two fingers to the bridge of her nose and closes her eyes. Because she'll bet anything that Penny will stare out of her peephole for several minutes to make sure Alice has left and is not returning, she moves down the corridor to the space between Penny's and Carla's flats, out of range of the peephole, before she leans against the wall and takes off her shoes for a minute. They've been killing her.

'Do I have to move up a size already?' she wonders, surprised, because she's barely three months pregnant. She hasn't even told her supervisor yet and her feet have already expanded.

''Scuse me, love,' a man's voice says, catching her off guard. He moves past her, down the corridor with a bag of groceries,

180

and opens the door to 1C. Alice wonders what he knows about Penny, what he's seen, or whether, like most people, he prefers not to look.

Penny is one of Alice's more challenging charges. She has a burning intellect behind the eyes, a vivid mind, awake and alert. A mind too aware of its dysfunction. So many people Alice saw were so lost in their illnesses, they didn't know that their lives could be any different than they were. Or they had been so ill for so long, they had forgotten any other way of being. Isolation and illness held hands, of course. Alice saw it every day; by now she'd met hundreds of Eleanor Rigbys, staring out of their windows at the grey city of millions, talking to cats that never talked back, eating, sleeping, dying – alone.

But Penny, Alice could see, the lucid part of her, her old self, was there and she was trapped, scratching at the walls, trying to escape. She was one of the ones that made Alice think that the line between sanity and psychic fracture was only the width of a thread; that but for some twists and turns of fate, whatever force it is that lets us walk every day on the path of mental wholeness, all it takes is a little tug, and any one of us could unravel.

Alice rubbed her left foot; that one was worse. Three more home visits today. She rummaged in her bag for her headphones, put them in, put on Sade. Her husband made fun of her love of Sade, but Sade always made her feel better when she'd had an especially hard appointment. She couldn't believe Penny tried that lie about the hair masque, and she gave herself a little pat on the back for playing Penny's game without embarrassing her too badly. Alice didn't want to humiliate her. But she did have to do her job.

Alice slides her flats back on. As she walks, she checks her bag for her wallet, keys, phone – another thing she always does after home visits because of that time a patient stole her Oyster card. Took it right out of her bag while she was taking notes and she didn't notice until she got to the Tube. Alice makes her way down the hall to the staircase, and takes each step slowly, still looking in her bag, changing the volume on her headphones, remembering her to-do list – pick up milk, send the meter reading, call Aunt Katie, order her niece's birthday present.

Because she is singing 'Smooth Operator' with Sade, lost in her thoughts, she forgets to scream when she trips over the body on the landing.

Penny
Flat 1B

When Alice finally leaves, Penny immediately takes off her shoes. The relief is a kind of anguish. The end of that pain begets another as her feet expand to regain their shape. She rolls her ankles in the air, one at a time, flexes and relaxes, notices the decrepit state of her toenails. But within seconds she remembers herself and checks the peephole to make sure that Alice has left.

Woman
Staircase landing ascending to the first floor

Woman picks up the barely conscious girl, throws her arm over her shoulders, and drags her to the stairs. She pulls her up, one step at a time, but then she hears it. The singing, the shuffling of feet, the plastic clatter of a lanyard with many badges and official-looking cards. She looks up for a moment as she lays the girl on the landing and she sees the pointed, flat shoes, hears how they clack on the tile of the corridor; she sees the crease in the trousers, the lanyard and its badges. She does not wait to see the person's face. She does not need to.

The wearer is official, important. Police, the stranger is some kind of police. Police in this country, Woman knows, important ones, do not wear uniforms, like in Home Country. They wear suits; they have necklaces of plastic cards. Police must not see her and also must not see the girl like this or she will call other police. Police always call other police in this country, especially for children.

Woman must let the red-haired mother know the girl is here. But Woman must also hide from police. She must clean up the vomit. She must get back to the shirts. She leaves the girl on the landing. She runs downstairs, silently, quietly, like the shadow of her shadow.

Alice
Staircase landing descending from the first floor

Alice doesn't fall, she only stumbles, but she feels a drop in her stomach, the kind that happens just before the plunge of the roller coaster, or when you're told news that you don't want to hear. She pulls out her headphones. A young girl in a torn school uniform, lying face down on the landing, wearing shoes with no tights or socks on this cold day, dark hair strewn over her shoulders.

Alice moves the girl's hair out of her eyes, and shouts, 'Hello? Can you hear me?' and puts two fingers to her pulse. She puts a hand under her nose, looks for the rising chest. The girl is breathing.

Her head rolls round and she slurs, 'Mum?'

Alice says, 'No, darling, I'm not your mum, do you live here?' as she scans the girl for bleeding, head injury, dislocated limbs.

'I live here,' the girl slurs, her eyes open now, but not focusing. Alice smells recent vomit on her breath.

'Where you do live, can you tell me?' Alice asks, but receiving no response, she checks the girl's pockets and her bag for a mobile, an ID, something to tell her who she is, and where her parents are.

Woman
Lobby

Unsure of what to do next, Woman's eyes fall on the vomit in the corner. She thinks of how to clean it up. She thinks of the pile of shirts waiting for her. The chocolate on the white rug and the water stain from cleaning it. She thinks of Old Madame. Of swallowing Beauty's picture. Of her teeth knocked out. She thinks of the ones that come in the night and sleep in the flat across the hall. She thinks of Sir's ring, that he twists round and round. Of My Lady's stretched nightgown. Of Madame serving the food that Woman cooks while Woman lies on the floor in the nursery, hungry, holding Madame's sleeping children. She thinks, and she thinks, and then she stands in a spot of the lobby where the echo is the loudest.

And she screams.

Alice
Staircase landing descending from the first floor

It is a Valkyrie shriek, a siren wail, an unearthly sound. Alice's mind flashes images of childbirth, of a train unable to stop, of her mother gripping her brother's coffin. She stands, grabs hold of the bannister, and she thinks that she cannot do this job anymore. She rushes down the stairs on her swollen feet, heart beating, hard, fast.

Carla
Flat 1A

'Hello?' Carla says to no one, drawn out of her dozing. She has only slept in snatches on the sofa. Tom texted her an hour after she spoke to Lottie yesterday:

I've dealt with the school.

He said nothing else. She assumes Mary Rose isn't in any major trouble. Maybe she'd just had stomach flu and he forgot to call the school. He was never good at the admin, she thinks. She doesn't press him, only texts, *Okay*. If she wants to see her daughter, she has to abide by his rules.

But something stirs inside her. A rustle in her instincts, a twist in her maternal gut that keeps her from sleeping, keeps her on guard, that's just heard something, that's pulling her to the door.

She goes out into the hallway.

'Hello?' she calls out. 'Is everything all right?' And when she reaches the stairs and sees her daughter on the landing, she knows the answer to her question.

Woman
Lobby

She steps into the broom cupboard under the stairs and wedges in with the buckets and mops. She listens. She hears the jangle of the badges on the policewoman's lanyard first.

'Hello?' the unfamiliar voice calls out. Woman can hear that the policewoman has opened the door to the building, to look out on to the street, to see if anyone's running away, if anyone's in trouble.

'What the fuck,' Alice says, like a sigh and half a prayer, as she comes back in. Woman repeats the words in her cupboard, silently, feeling their shape in her mouth, and waits.

Alice
Lobby

'What the fuck,' she says, as a question and a statement. She feels dizzy and puts a hand on the wall to steady herself. There's a strong smell of ammonia, as though the space has just been cleaned, and she notices that the floor in the corner by the mailboxes looks wet, newly mopped, but there's no sign of the cleaner. She doesn't want to be here anymore. She's tired and her feet are swollen and she doesn't want to be dragged into whatever's going on here. She's going to just check on that girl, take her to whatever flat she belongs in, grab her bag, put on Sade, cancel her remaining appointments, and go home.

But before she reaches the stairs, she hears, 'Hello? Is everything all right?'

'Oh God, what now,' Alice says aloud.

'Oh God, what now,' Woman mouths in the cupboard.

Carla
Staircase landing descending from the first floor

'Mary Rose?!' Carla shouts. She pushes and pulls at her, unable to shift the dead weight of her daughter's slight, limp body.

'Is this your daughter?' Alice asks, suddenly standing a few steps down from them. Carla notices the lanyard badges. A social worker. Fear, confusion, paranoia, crash in on Carla, setting her instincts ablaze, her brain exploding with the possibilities – the school sent this woman to check on them, or Tom did, he called social services and then dropped Mary Rose off here in this state to make her look like a bad mother in front of this woman who's going to take her away, or, wait, what did he say about social workers and the hospital and questions? He took her to the hospital, and now they're checking up on her, he gave them this address. Is she here to question her, was it the school? Was it Lottie?

Carla stammers, 'Um, what—?' covering for the wildfire in her mind.

'Do you need help?' Alice says slowly, registering the terror on Carla's face.

'I've got it,' Carla says, but yes, she does, God does she need help.

186

'Do you know what's wrong? Should I call an ambulance?' Alice says, calmly, reasonably, trying to catch Carla's darting eyes.

Just then, Carla's phone on the floor next to them vibrates. Alice sees the name on the screen. Tom.

'Hello?' Carla says. Alice hears the tremble in her voice. It's familiar. Her mother sounded like that too. Whenever she spoke to her father.

'She's here . . . okay . . . that's fine . . . I'll take care of her—' Carla says.

Penny
Flat 1B

Certain that Alice has left, Penny sits on her bed with Susannah in her lap, purring. She rubs her sweaty palms on the cat to dry them. She opens the drawer of the bedside table all the way so she can reach the sleeping pills at the back, pushed there where Alice wouldn't see them. She gets a glass of water from the sink. She takes one pill. Then another.

She hears a scream. A shrieking wail. A primordial yell. She hears Carla shouting. She hears voices and shuffling on the stairs.

She sits on the edge of her bed and thinks of her dirty hair. She thinks of pretty, blonde, smug Alice and how she behaves and dresses because she thinks she is hiding her pregnancy. She thinks of automatic sliding doors in supermarkets and pharmacies, how they are just like the doors of the train that pulled away with her baby. Of that girl in the laundrette, wearing her socks. Of eating raisins off the floor. She thinks of Jamie and the chicken nuggets she will never cook for her daughter. Of the reporter who followed her home that time, took a picture of her, buttons straining across her bust, eating a lamb kebab. Of the clickbait heading next to that picture in the online paper that read, 'Tube Horror Mum – pregnant

187

again?' That this is why she is afraid of strangers and hides in her flat. She thinks of her first from Cambridge and how her tight shoes got her there. Of where she is now.

Of how there are so many reasons to scream.

Alice
Staircase landing ascending to the first floor

'I really think you need an ambulance,' Alice says, when Carla puts the phone down.

'Who sent you? Did Tom send you? The school?' Carla says, her eyes leaping to Alice's face.

'No one sent me. I work for the borough. I was seeing a service user in this area,' Alice says, staying professional, protecting Penny's confidentiality.

'We're fine,' Carla says as she struggles up from the floor with Mary Rose clinging to her.

'Do you have a social worker?' Alice asks, because, well, just look at this woman.

'No,' Carla says, staggering to her feet, bracing herself with one arm against the wall, and hoisting Mary Rose up with the other.

'Mum, I'm ill,' Mary Rose groans.

'It's okay, sweetie, I've got you,' Carla says, with laboured breath.

'Do you know what she's taken? What she drank?' Alice asks, still controlled, still calm, although every internal alarm bell is ringing in her head. But she dare not touch the girl or her mother without consent.

'I'm ill,' Mary Rose slurs again.

'She didn't drink anything, she's fine, she just has . . . um, seizures . . . sometimes,' Carla pants, breathless, using the wall for stability, leaning Mary Rose's full weight on her other side as the girl moans and they take one stumbling step at a time.

188

Alice watches Carla struggle with her daughter to her flat. She notices the hem coming down on Carla's robe. She gets a glimpse of Carla's white men's briefs underneath.

The man from 1C opens his door, comes out and locks it, and when he sees the two women and the girl in the hallway, he shakes his head.

'She's too young to be running in the streets like she does,' he says to Carla, over his shoulder, as he passes them in the hall. He doesn't offer to help.

Alice hears him, has an impulse to kick him in the balls as he walks by her to the landing, but instead she asks, quietly, 'Has this happened before?'

He notices the ID badge on her lanyard.

'It's not the first time. Some people shouldn't be allowed to have children,' he says, making his way downstairs. The door to Carla's flat slams.

'Shhhhhit,' Alice says, under her breath, alone again in the hall. She takes off her shoes, leans against the wall, closes her eyes and initiates an internal review. As a social worker she has a safeguarding obligation to report anything she sees that may be harmful or potentially dangerous to a child. She really should knock on that door. At the very least she should call and make a referral, right now, to make sure children's services is aware of the family.

That girl was very drunk. Alice smelled vomit and alcohol on her. There was a scream, but it wasn't the girl, because Alice was standing over her when the scream started. The mum lied about the seizures. It's the middle of the day, that girl should be in school, and if she was sick, school would've called and Mum would've collected her. The mum was half dressed. The neighbour said this has happened before.

What if that wasn't the girl's mum? What if she wasn't her daughter? Who was Tom? The father? Was he abusive? Is that why her voice went like that? Or was he a pimp, a drug dealer?

What if the girl had been drugged because she's part of a teen prostitution ring? Or what if she's been trafficked? Or—

Alice stops. She shakes her head, pinches the bridge of her nose. It's an occupational hazard, her *Daily Mail* thinking, these spirals of horror she constructs. She asks herself, as she always does at moments like these, 'What are the facts, Alice?'

The girl said, 'I live here,' and asked for her mum. There was a scream, but there was no one downstairs. No one injured, in a struggle, or being attacked, no one asking for help.

The girl called the woman 'Mum' and Mum had looked distressed and worried. She was defensive, like a mother who loves her kid, and who's judged all the time, whose kid has done this before.

Alice recounts the other facts: she's light-headed, pregnant, exhausted, and so tired of the inner voice that's telling her to stay here and not let this go. She's so sick of the responsibility that comes with strong instincts. For ten years she's put other people first all day, every day. People who are awful to her, who are crazy, sometimes dangerous, and always sad. Her feet are huge, her heart is racing. And there's another voice, one that speaks rarely and softly, that says, '*You need to go, Alice.*'

She tries to think what a normal person would think, a person who hasn't seen the pain and degradation that she's witnessed, who doesn't know the utter depths of sadness that a human can reach. A normal person would say, 'The worst that's going to happen to that girl is a bad hangover,' and then they'd move on with their day, and not give her another thought. So, Alice picks up her bag, descends the steps and pops in her headphones, searching for Sade on her phone.

When she reaches the last step, she hears a phone ring over 'Smooth Operator'. The sound echoes through the lobby. She looks up, takes out one earbud, and traces the sound to the cupboard in the corner. It must be the acoustics, her high stress level, her imagination. The ringing stops.

Don't leave, she thinks.

'*You have to. The baby*,' the rare, quiet voice says.

'Hello . . . yeah,' a gruff male voice says behind her. A large man dressed in black that she didn't know was behind her on the stairs speaks into his phone. He holds the door open for her.

Her heart pounds in her ears. Her throat tightens. Her palms sweat.

'Thank you,' she says, as she leaves the building.

She rounds the corner of Bedford Road, turns off her music, and stops to make a call.

'Yes,' she says, to the emergency services operator, 'I need an ambulance.'

12

Friday

Penny
Flat 1B

'That can't be true, Mable, can it?' I say through the door.

'The signs are all around us, darlin'. They're everywhere. You hear about the locust, in Africa? You hear about the virus, the pestilence, in China? Coming this way? You hear about that madman over in America and his wall and how he friends with that Russian one and how he gon' to shoot that one in Korea, the fat one in the uniform? Now Jesus said, "Nation will rise against nation, and kingdom against kingdom. There will be great earthquakes, and in one place after another, food shortages and pestilences." It's there in black and white, in Luke, it says so, clear as day,' Mable says with great authority.

'Well, I had no idea, really, I didn't,' I say, intrigued. 'Locusts? I must say I haven't been keeping up on my current events. Things have rather – they've sort of – got away from me, but I'm going to have to go read up on all of this—'

'Sadly, not many do, darlin', they got their eyes closed to the truth, they keep their ears deaf to the Word. I'm getting ready, Penny, I'm preparing because the signs are there, and you must be right in your heart if you want to get through the other side of Armageddon to Paradise,' Mable says to me.

I stay silent for a moment and consider her words. Wouldn't it be extraordinary if it were true? It would be quite the coup for Mable, if Armageddon really did happen, if everyone who thought she was just a mad old woman all this time suddenly found themselves one day burning alive while she sauntered past, unscathed, to her Paradise that they refused to believe in. I'd be quite pleased, if I were her.

I'd love that kind of moment, an event to finally prove to all the Alices and Jamies and Carlas that I'm not crazy after all. That when you put it all together, how I live makes sense.

Mable told me once that in Paradise, after all the non-believers perish in the horrific fires, everyone who survives will be perfect, they'll never be sick again, or have disabilities, or anxiety, or any kind of illness. Their bodies will revert to their strongest and most beautiful form, and they will live forever.

I've tried to picture myself there, but I can't see it. I don't know who I would be if I were cured. The illness is all that I am. There is no me without it. I'd be a body with no bones in Mable's Paradise.

Mable is still talking. 'All right, dear? I'll leave it for you under the door, I brought you *Awake!* this time as well. Good issues this time round. The truth is clear, darlin', like crystal.'

She coughs, once, twice, and then she slides the magazines under my door.

'Thank you, Mable, look after yourself.'

She coughs again, quite forcefully. 'Are you sure you're all right?' I ask.

'I got Jehovah to look after me, darlin'; He'll look after you too, when you believe,' she says.

Mable leaves and I open my laptop. Her visit is a distraction and a relief, a sign of normalcy returning after all the drama and commotion of yesterday's ambulance, paramedics walking round here, knocking on doors, disturbing Susannah and interrupting my online correspondence. I have a lot of work to do now, as a result, and of course there's the news to catch up on, according to Mable. Events do seem to be unfolding as her literature suggests. I'm going to have to go through the back catalogue of the materials she's left me to substantiate her claims, because if the end of the world is indeed approaching, one should be prepared.

Carla
Flat 1A

Mary Rose is asleep in her room. It was a long night and she's dead to the world. I can't sleep, too much on my mind, and the flat's a mess. I do the dishes, clean out the fridge, scrub the grease off the cabinets. Sort the laundry. Mop the bathroom floor until it sparkles. I fill two garbage bags with beer cans and chocolate wrappers and pizza boxes, open the window to get some air in the place. I make a coffee and then I do the thing I've been avoiding all morning.

I knock on the wall.

'Penny—' I say, putting my ear to the wall. 'Are you there?'

Stupid question, she's always there. And even though that's weird and I think she's nuts and it freaked me out when she used to talk to the kids, I have to thank her. She doesn't answer, but I know she's listening.

'Anyway, just wanted to say thank you for helping us out yesterday. If the paramedics had barged in here, they would've called social services, because she was drunk, and you know, with me and Tom, it would've gotten really complicated. I don't know what he would say about me right now, probably something awful. So, thanks for the diversion,' I say, and wait for her to speak. Nothing.

'Okay, well, I owe you one—' and just then I can hear her, if I press my face to the wall.

'I don't believe that the state has the right to interfere in our personal lives. The state always thinks it knows the child better than the mother does and expects our mindless capitulation to its paternalistic wisdom,' she says.

'Um, sure,' I say. Shit, I've unleashed the wackadoo. But when the paramedics got here, she opened her door, which is a big deal for her, and started acting crazy and told them there was no drunk girl and said she was having a delusion. They checked her over and she acted calm then and there was no

194

obvious danger, so they left and told her not to do it again. She's loony, but she's smart. I mean, who says 'mindless capitulation' like that in conversation?

'Well, I'm gonna—' I start to say, but she cuts me off.

'She had no right, Alice, to call them,' she says. 'I heard her, talking to you in the corridor, asking if you need help instead of actually helping you. And then calling in the authorities when you asserted your independence. I'm sure it was her, how else would they have known to come to this floor,' she says, and I can tell she's getting wound up; there's an edge to her voice, or, as edgy as she can be. I need to end this before she goes off on one.

'Yeah, she was a total bitch. Anyway, that's my phone, gotta go—' I lie, and take heavy steps away from the wall so that she knows we're done talking.

'Carla?' her voice goes up. I shake my head. What now.

'Yeah?' I say. 'I'm just on a call—'

'You're an excellent mother,' she says.

Penny
Flat 1B

Highly anxious people are very good in emergencies. Because we're accustomed to living in a state of high alert, when there is actual danger present, we think quickly and act swiftly. So, while it was entirely out of routine for me to open the door, and to the paramedics, of all people, once I heard Alice questioning Carla and Mary Rose and then heard the sirens, I knew what had to be done. When they arrived, I was dressed in my boiler suit, face mask, boots and rubber gloves, so I was fully protected from their energy. After that, it wasn't difficult to behave in the manner which is expected of the mentally ill. People set quite a low bar for us. Of course, I was careful not to be too over the top, so they wouldn't feel they had to take me to hospital.

After all of the excitement of yesterday, I have decided to stay in bed today, with my laptop. Perhaps later I'll listen in on *Britain's Got Talent* if Carla turns it on. I check my usual motherhood websites to see what's been happening.

From: @aftergymprosecco
I'm canvassing for opinions. I agreed to a joint birthday party with another mother in DD's class who turns out to be vegan. I fully support everyone having their different beliefs, but now she's saying she doesn't want any animal products to be present at all for the birthday tea because she finds it offensive. I mean, chocolate cake, offensive? Is that reasonable? I said I didn't mind if we had two cakes, if she wanted to do something different for her child, but she said everything had to be vegan that was served. If I had known this ahead of time I wouldn't have agreed to the party. But now I feel like I'm in a real bind and going to have to either a) have an awkward conversation and pull out of the party or b) be forced to pay for someone else's lifestyle choices and deny my daughter what she wants for her own birthday. What do you think? Any thoughts appreciated x

'Any thoughts appreciated,' it says. I look around my flat. I watch Susannah stretch by the window. I wonder if she remembers going outside. If she remembers her life as an alley cat, scrapping around for food and sleeping under bushes or behind dumpsters, slipping under fences and hiding under parked cars. If she misses that life, before I found her. Or if she remembers living in the house with me and Jamie and Olivia, coming and going as she pleased, napping in the garden, hunting for birds, sleeping curled up at the foot of the bed.

I close my eyes and try to imagine, for a moment, a different kind of life, like the one lived by @aftergymprosecco. A life where, like her, I sit in a house after my child has gone to school, sipping a cappuccino made by a machine in my own kitchen, brow furrowed, reading and rereading my message about the dilemma of the vegan birthday cake. I look at my nails, admire my manicure, relish the clacking sound they make against the keys as I convey my distress and indignation to the world about the vegan bully, the one my friends and I gossip about when we walk our little dogs around the common after drop-off. Then I press send, pick up my bag, grab my keys, open the door, and walk to meet a friend for lunch after browsing in the shops.

How wonderful. How absurd.

I start typing.

To: @aftergymprosecco
Just to put my two pence in, for what they're worth, I'll share an anecdote which should assist you in gaining some perspective on your situation. Yesterday, my next-door neighbour found her teen daughter passed out on the landing, unable to get to her flat, because she had been drinking and, more than likely, TAKING DRUGS. Paramedics were called to the building. It's sadly no surprise that the child's gone off the rails, as the father left them to live with his girlfriend and baby, for the SECOND TIME, and refuses to divorce the mother in order to keep her dependent on him for her immigration status because she spent many years living here as an ILLEGAL ALIEN. And suddenly, he up and took the children, so recently she's been taking STRANGE MEN home to assuage her loneliness. One of whom, a Tesco delivery man, was STILL IN UNIFORM. Now, THAT is a problem.

What you have described is not a problem. Tell the vegan to find herself a beetroot and eat it. She's going to outlive you anyway, you know that. And judging from your screen name, you should probably think about your relationship with alcohol – do you really go to the gym

197

and then drink prosecco? I would love to go to the gym
but I've been housebound for two years due to agorapho-
bia brought on by post-traumatic stress. THAT is a prob-
lem. Do you know that a plague of locusts has overrun
Africa and that a deadly virus is about to kill us all?
THOSE are problems. Now, I suggest you put down the
prosecco, start baking that eggless carob cake, and thank
God that your life is so bloody wonderful.

I post it, because honestly, there are larger issues at hand
now; more pressing concerns upon us.

Carla
Flat 1A

'Try to eat, just a little,' I say to Mary Rose. I put the bowl of
soup on the coffee table in front of her, as Mary Rose sits
staring at the ladies on QVC who are talking about the cubic
zirconia deals of the hour. When she was little and she
couldn't sleep, this is what we used to do, watch them sell
synthetic gems, the hostess of the show running her beautiful hands with their acrylic nails over the sparkling pieces,
and we'd choose which ones we'd buy if we were as rich as
the queen.

'I didn't mean for Dad to take us away,' she says quietly. 'I
thought he'd just yell at you or scare you, like all the other
times.'

I watch as she closes her eyes, silent tears filling them up.
She puts the back of her hand to her mouth. Wipes a tear with
the cuff of her sweatshirt. Tom's old England Rugby sweatshirt that I used to wear to bed that she's adopted. It's so big
on her that she pulls her knees to her chest inside of it, pulls
the cuffs past her wrists, a little cocoon on the sofa.

'Oh,' I say, watching the blonde on TV tap a huge fake
diamond with her red plastic nail, wanting to reach out and

198

hold my girl but not sure if she'll let me. There was a time when my touch was all they needed. And wanted.

I look at my girl, so much prettier, thinner, smarter than I ever was. My girl who already knows that she is more than me.

All I can think to say is, 'How about a hot chocolate? Would you rather have that?'

'I was just so angry at everything,' she says, staring at the ceiling. 'And once I started, I didn't know how to stop – I mean with Daniel and Dad. I didn't mean to scare Daniel. I faked it, I drank egg whites and then water with baking soda. I looked it up on YouTube, for how to throw up. And I just poured half your vodka down the sink and messed up the flat and I really did feel sick, but also angry, but I didn't know Dad was going to take us away. I started acting like I felt better in the car, so he took us to the drive-thru at McDonald's and when he saw I could eat, he didn't take me to hospital. He said, though, if I ever got drunk in his house I wouldn't be allowed to stay. And he's horrible with Sherry too, Mum. He's just as mean to her. When we used to go there on the week-ends, they seemed fine, but when we were there every day – Mum, he's awful. She cries all the time. So yesterday me and Isabel cut school, and we went back to Dad's flat, and we drank all the wine and he came home because school called him to say I hadn't shown up again. And then he dropped me off here. He said he warned me, and you'd have to take care of me if I was going to be such a pain. I had to get out, Mum. So, I did it where he could find me and kick me out, but now look what I've done. Daniel's there with him alone, and we left you alone . . . I didn't mean to leave you alone, Mum—' and she cries and cries, first into the neck of the sweatshirt, then into her sleeve; big, heaving sobs.

She leans into me, but I take her shoulder, push her an arm's length away from me, hold her there, look at her face. She can't unknow it, I can't undo it for her, everything that's happened. I pull her into me, and she lets herself collapse in my arms. I kiss the top of her head and say the only thing I can think of.

'It's not your fault, princess. Don't worry. I'll fix it.'

Woman
Flat 2C

Mother, please, can you hear me? Mother?

They have put me in Silent Room in the flat across the hall. I have been here from when the sirens came until now. I think half the day and all the night, I don't know, many hours. There were others, three or four, a man and some women, already here, awaiting transport, but when Madame heard the sirens blazing, the police or the doctors – I am not sure which they were – at the door of the building, she tore Baby from my arms, and pushed My Lady into her room and locked it, and told Master to take me across the hall, to keep me by myself, in Silent Room. I do not know what they did with the others. If they are still here. Or if they are not.

Master had moved to take my arm as though by force, but really he only took my elbow gently, Mother. He shouted at me, but there was no need because I went without resistance. He wouldn't need to touch me at all and I would go.

They do not want to see police because they are criminals but I too do not want to see them. I too am afraid of what they will do, where they would send me, that they will arrest me, that they will deport me to Home Country. And once this happens, Mother, what will become of us? So, I did not resist, I went willingly wherever they wanted me to go until the police or the doctors were gone.

Perhaps the red-haired mother called them for the girl, or perhaps that woman police did, with her badges. Or maybe they came for the old woman, she has been coughing so. Or perhaps they came for the madwoman who washes her clothes at Laundrette.

'Stay here and do not move, do not make a sound,' was all Master said to me, before he locked the door and left me.

'Master—' I tried to say, to ask how long it would be, if he would remember I was here, what I should do – Baby, and My Lady, they needed their meals and their sleep – but he did not hear me.

Master was a boy of fourteen when I met him, before we came to UK. A boy on the edge of manhood. I know he remembers that when he was ill and came home from school in Dubai, I put cold cloths on his head, made him soup, brought him clean pyjamas. Not his mother but like his mother. Madame was revolted by his vomit and fever, his angry acne, his stooping shoulders, unaccustomed to their new height. She loved him only when he was clean, healthy, well presented, and even then she showed him no affection. When he brought home good marks to show her, she was not impressed. She did not embrace him. I would tell him, later, in the kitchen, in a whisper, that he was a smart boy, would be a smart man. I would make him his dinner and watch him eat what I was not allowed.

He is a man now, the youngest man that a man can be. The child I knew in him is gone. They have trained him in the business. He drives the vans, he lifts the bags of laundry to hide the girls. He takes me to the bins when I am permitted to forage. I know he remembers that I was kind to him and that is why he says cruel words that he must be heard to say and he does not touch me unless he must. It was only one time that he hurt me, that he broke my tooth. He remembers that I knew him when he was weak. When he was ill. When he sought love and was not given it.

How long will they keep me here, Mother? One day or seven? The last time something like this happened, when police came round because there had been a disturbance in the street outside the building, it was two days that I was locked away. Master came once to bring me water. I asked him how long it had been, how much longer it would be that I would have to hide and he said only, looking away from me, at the floor, 'If you do not want your family killed, you will ask no questions.' It was what they taught him to say. It was not without truth.

Perhaps you are already dead, Mother. They tell me all the time how close I am to killing you, how my recklessness will soon give them cause to contact Agent in Home Country, who will come and find you, and kill you because of my indiscretions, my questions, my bad behaviour. Maybe they killed you that time I angered Madame, when we moved here, and I asked if I could take My Lady to the playground across the road before I understood that they would never let her out. Maybe they killed you that time I hung Sir's shirts the wrong way round in the closet, the hooks of all the hangers facing out instead of in. Unless they killed you because of the time that Madame dropped a cup and broke it because she said I startled her when I came out of the bedroom and walked down the corridor. It was my presence that broke the cup in her hand. My being alive broke the cup and it was genuine bone china, Mother. Five hundred pounds added to my debt, Mother, and also, possibly, they killed you for it.

I have thought before, Mother, of telling PC Grant when he comes to get his uniform, of saying to him, 'Help,' and I have thought that if I said that word to him while I held his clean clothes in my hand, perhaps he would free me, perhaps he would arrest Madame and Sir. But I know that before he could even lock the handcuffs around their wrists and put them in the police car, within those minutes, Master would text Agent, Agent would send the command, and you and Beauty would be dead in Home Country before PC Grant even reached the police station.

I pull out the phone I took from the girl and turn it on. I have kept it tucked into a very tight top that I took from the bins the night I found clothes there. It is half of a top, I think it is for sport, for women here who I have seen out the window running, always running and running, in the morning, in the evening, running away from nothing, running to nowhere.

I asked My Lady to tell me the words on the front. 'Just do it,' she said. She tried to tell me in our language what this means. She said it means to do things. I wonder what kind of person needs this written reminder to do things on their underclothes. It is very tight and the phone is flat so I can keep it here on my chest and no one notices it under my shirt. I keep it turned off so it makes no sound.

Now I use the phone for its light to look around this room again although I know there is no point. The lock is on the outside of the door, so there is no lock to break. There is a vent behind one of the carpets that is hung on the walls. But it is too small, and where would it lead? Escaping this room is not possible. The phone still works; perhaps the girl has not noticed it is missing or does not want to tell her mother that she lost it.

I could call you, Mother, but you would have too many questions.

I text you instead: *All is well. Tell Beauty I love her every day. God be with you, Mother*. Perhaps it will reach you, perhaps it won't.

Then I turn off the phone, sit in the dark, and wait.

13

Saturday

Penny
Flat 1B

*Can't do the usual today. Too many orders. Had a delivery
around the corner so left two bags by your door on the
way. Won't be back any time soon. Sorry.*

Penny reads the text message from Darren again. And again.
She reads it so many times she is no longer sure if it is real or if
she has imagined it. She resolves not to look at the phone for
an hour and then to come back and see if it's still there. She
passes the hour by compiling an inventory of her supplies:
thirty face masks, three packs of antibacterial wipes, ten tiny
bottles of antibacterial hand gel, two pairs of goggles, one box
of disposable gloves, fifty-two bags of frozen chicken nuggets,
thirty-six pouches of cat food, one box of chicken Cup-a-Soup,
half of a bag of Alpen Swiss muesli, three lunch-box-size milk
cartons, two carrots, fifteen tea bags, one Warburton's thin
cinnamon raisin bagel. She counts how many months it has
been since she has had toast made from a piece of bread taken
from a loaf in a bag. Loaves of bread don't fit under the door
chain. She hasn't seen a loaf of bread in a long time.

She returns to the phone. Darren's text remains the same.
She opens her laptop and checks her favourite websites and
reads the posts about the surge in online grocery orders, deliveries booked now for weeks in advance, middle-class exclama-
tions of outrage at the dearth of Ocado slots. She feels the
approach of change, a shift in the air.

She hears the baby upstairs cry. The sound is faint, but distinct. She doesn't hear the child cry often. She's never seen it, doesn't know whose child it may be, or where it lives in the building. Sometimes she's not sure if it's a real baby, or just the one that cries for her. But the crying has been insistent today, frequent and urgent. Perhaps the baby also feels it, she thinks. The change.

She wonders what she will do when her bagel and her muesli and her carrots and Cup-a-Soup run out. She rushes to her peephole. She can see two white plastic bags of groceries just on the edge of her vision. She wonders how Darren got in without ringing her bell. Someone let him in. People in this building are so careless. He could have been anyone.

She feels tingling in the pit of her stomach, the beginning of panic, and she notices its urge to rise, but the urge is muted. There isn't enough space inside of her now for it to expand and take her over, not with her mind occupied by so many other things. She thinks about how lucky it is that she found the second pair of goggles. It is always good to have a backup.

Woman
Flat 2C

Master lets her out of the room and the light blinds her. He says, 'Baby won't stop crying, Mother said to let you out.'

'Master, may I have some water, please, son,' she says to him in the language they both know. She uses the affectionate diminutive for one's own little children. There is thought behind the word.

He surprised her when he came to the door last night with water and a piece of bread.

'Don't tell them that I did this,' he said to her. Their eyes met, and she could see that he was not made for what they were making him do. She could see that she was the closest person to him.

Penny
Flat 1B

Penny begins pacing the flat. Two bags of food. She hasn't even brought them inside yet, but they certainly will not be enough. Darren clearly can no longer be relied upon. External evidence suggests that he is facing severe pressure on the job. Or perhaps, after his dalliance with Carla and who knows what went on with them, he doesn't want to make his delivery for fear of running into her.

'That Darren!' Penny says, her fear and worry giving way to a rising anger as she paces. She stands in front of the mirror and shakes her head. She puts two fingers up to the bridge of her nose the way she has watched Alice do in their meetings and crosses her arms. She slaps her thigh in disbelief. She practises the angry gestures she will use for when she encounters him again, if she ever does.

'That Darren,' she says aloud, standing in front of her door, swept up in her own theatre of indignation.

'This is why the immigrants come take all the jobs. Because the British won't do them themselves,' she complains, throwing one hand in the air, so convinced by her own anger that she does not realise she has unchained the door to punctuate her outrage. She does not register that her hand is on the doorknob.

'That Darren and that Carla,' she huffs, aiming her words at the shared wall between their flats. And before she knows what she has done, Penny has turned the deadbolt one half turn to the right.

It is Saturday. She freezes.

She opened the door on Thursday. Twice. Once for Alice, once for the paramedics, but that was from necessity; she did that because she had to, to demonstrate compliance to Alice to stop her intrusions into her life and to protect Carla and Mary Rose from Alice's meddling, overreaching insertion into their lives. That was Thursday and today is Saturday. And her food, the only food she may have for weeks, is outside the door.

Penny looks at her hand on the doorknob.

Today is Saturday and she has almost opened the door again.

Almost.

Carla
Flat 1A

Carla, home from her shift, opens the door to her flat. She looks up. She nearly screams. She grips the handles of her shopping bags.

'What's the matter? Weren't expecting me?' Tom says from his seat at her table.

Carla says nothing.

'Thought I'd check my post while I waited for you,' he says. 'Checked some of yours too,' he says, pointing to a pile of letters and bills, all of them out of their envelopes and unfolded, flattened into a neat pile, the empty envelopes, ordered by size, in another neat pile.

'Looks like you've been falling behind again,' he says.

'Those letters had my name on them,' Carla starts to say, but changes course, and adds, apologetically, clicking automatically into submission, 'Sorry, I mean, I put yours and the joint ones on your pile. Mine were on my pile.'

'We're married, Carla. There's no "mine" and "yours",' he says, smiling.

'I'm sorry. I didn't want you to bother with them, that's all; it's not your fault I'm so disorganised,' she says. Seeing him has immediately flipped the switch inside of her to apology and self-deprecation, until, suddenly remembering her daughter, she calls, 'Mary Rose?' clearing her throat to keep down the dread.

Mary Rose comes out of her room, arms wrapped tightly around herself. 'I'm here, Mum,' she says, her eyes wide.

'Did you come to take her back?' Carla asks Tom, slowly stepping in front of their daughter, still gripping the grocery bags she hasn't yet put down.

He approaches them, extends his hand over Carla's shoulder to caress Mary Rose's cheek.

'This one? Nah. She can't carry on like that in my house, not like she does in yours. I won't stand for it. Didn't I tell you that, Mary Rose?'

The girl nods once, stares at the floor.

'Actually, I'm still waiting for my apology,' he says, looming over them both.

'Sorry, Dad,' Mary Rose whispers.

'That's better. Now go to your room so I can talk to your mother,' he says.

She turns to leave and then stops for a moment. 'Mum?' she says, looking at Carla, a question in her eyes.

'It's okay,' Carla says.

Tom, now sitting across the room, leans forward in his chair with his elbows on his knees. He is pleased with how the curve of his sculpted shoulders is accentuated by the pull of the fabric of his shirt.

'She's too much like you, I can't take it; the mouthiness, the attitude. Slamming doors and on the phone all the time. She's a handful. And this drinking thing, I can't have her in the house. I know it's just teenage stuff, but we've got a baby to look after; Sherry can't have all of that going on. She's got to learn there's consequences. If she's going to act like that, then she can live here, in this shithole. That'll teach her,' he says, leaning back now, brushing invisible lint from his impeccably ironed jeans. He looks up. 'You going to offer me a cup of tea? Seems everyone's lost their manners around here,' he says.

Carla, still in her coat, grocery bags at her sides, says, 'Sure,' and moves towards of his shirt the open kitchen across from him. He watches her every step. She takes off her coat. She makes the tea in silence. She sits down across from him. She wants her son. He knows she does.

'Did you put sugar in this?' he says, nearly spitting out what he sips from the mug she gives him.

'No, I know how you take it,' she says, from the edge of her chair, ready to stand up. And then, like an involuntary function, like breathing, she says, 'I'm sorry. Should I make you another one?'

'Forget the tea,' he says. She sits back.

'I forgot you can't make proper tea,' he says. She sits forward.

'Where's Daniel?' she says.

'I have an opportunity for you,' he says. She wraps her hands around the hot mug in front of her, and keeps them there, and lets her skin burn.

Madame
Flat 2A–2B

Finally released, Woman returns to the flat with Master. The light is disorienting. As soon as she sees her, My Lady runs to her, clings to her legs. Baby hears Woman's voice and he momentarily stops his crying. He reaches for her from Madame's arms, pushes his head into Woman's neck, grasps the fabric of her shirt as tightly as he can in his tiny fists, and begins a new round of wailing. The cry of relief that she has returned and of anger that she dared leave him the way she did.

Madame, annoyed at the children's rapturous reactions to Woman but also relieved that she is back to take them, says, 'I'm leaving this godforsaken cave. I'm going to the spa. Look after the children and clean the flat, it's disgusting. And when Old Madame wakes, you can leave the children with her to clean the corridors. You are behind on your work.'

Madame leaves the flat with My Lady and Baby clinging to Woman, giggling and happy. She is sickened by the display and desperate to leave the shrieking children and the cramped flat. She is so tired of the children, of Old Madame, of Sir's lack of respect and his constant dismissal of her ideas even though she is the one who understands the money.

She is tired, too, of the degradation they are forced to live in because of Sir's paranoia, his certainty that they are being watched by the police and by their rivals, his manic obsession with this building which he calls his Safe House, as though he is a big-time gangster who needs a safe house, and not just another anxious hustler in a city of hustlers, driving migrant women around in laundry vans, another cog in a machine that he does not realise is much larger than him and his petty operation.

On her way downstairs, Madame entertains her favourite fantasy: living alone in a luxury high-rise flat in Dubai, working as a highly paid accountant at a large international firm, with no children, no husband, no old mother to cart around. She would do the job she trained for in university, and wear Louboutins every day to the office, and drink cocktails in the evenings with handsome and charming European men who would find her both intelligent and irresistible. She would bed them, but never marry them.

She would keep hold of her money. She would keep hold of her passport. She would never let a man lock them both away in a safe, the location of which she does not know and for which she has no combination. Held there, with all the others, as though she is the same as one of these lost girls. No, she would never let a man do that again.

Woman
The building

Woman feeds the children, bathes and dresses them. She gives the flat a cursory clean, enough for now. She will do more later. Having done nothing but sleep between episodes of terror locked in Silent Room, Woman is both rested and exhausted, the adrenaline triggered by her captivity still not dissipated. She is so relieved at her release that the relief itself quells her hunger and thirst.

She must try and at least touch upon each of Madame's tasks before she returns. She leaves the children with Old Madame and goes to quickly sweep the stairs and corridors.

On the third floor she sweeps and mops and hears the muffled voices of the television and the old woman coughing. The old woman coughs and coughs, then stops, then coughs again. Woman waits until the coughing stops before she moves on.

On the second floor, to save time for her other tasks, she sweeps and mops just the middle of the steps and the hallways, bypassing, for now, the corners and edges.

On the first floor, she stops. She sees the two bags of groceries in front of Flat 1B. And Woman's delayed hunger from her confinement takes her over in a ravenous wave.

She knows it is the woman from Laundrette who lives here. She wonders what kind of illness causes her to gamble with her abundance in this way, to leave her food out in the hall, where anyone could take it. Woman sweeps and sweeps, she mops, carefully and precisely mopping around the two bags, the way a policeman would draw a chalk outline around a body. With each sweep she peeks into the tops of the bags, not touching them, squinting at the packages of food through the plastic, trying to discern what they are, if any are easy to take and put under her shirt, if there is anything she can eat with her damaged teeth.

When she hears the bolt in Penny's door turn with a loud click, Woman startles, and quickly moves to the landing.

Penny
Flat 1B

Penny turns the lock another half turn to the right and hears the bolt click, the turn pieces receding. She turns the lock again and watches the turn pieces click into place. She turns the lock one way – the brass bolts hide in the box, the door is free, it can be opened from either side, it no longer provides protection. She turns the lock the other way – the brass bolts slide into place, the door stays closed, no one can get to Penny, and Penny can get to no one. Turn one way, turn the other way, left, right, and back again. She studies the lock. She thinks about locusts. She thinks about Olivia. She thinks about Mary Rose. About Mable's forecast of the pestilence. About the woman in the laundrette. Turn one way, turn the other way.

Woman
Lobby

Woman quickly goes downstairs to the lobby to continue cleaning. She sweeps the floor in big wide strokes. Then she mops in wide arches, watching the wet mop draw dismal rainbows in shades of grey on the concrete. She draws one arch with her mop, then another, watching the wet floor darken. She jumps when the door to the building opens suddenly behind her. She stands aside as the three young white women from flat 3C bundle into the lobby, carrying their shopping in their hands because they forgot their reusable bags.

The one with blue streaks in her hair holds the door open for her flatmates as they laugh and joke. If Woman could read English, she would see that the one with pink streaks in her hair wears a sweatshirt that says, 'If You're Not Angry, You're Not Paying Attention'. They brush past Woman without a glance, giggling on their way to the stairs, trekking muddy boot prints through the freshly mopped floor.

Woman mops that section of the floor again and then continues to mop the rest. She paints an arch, takes one step back, paints another, a second step back, a third step, and the sharp corner of the steel handle of the door pushes into her spine. She stops. She drops the mop. She pushes the door open a crack and cold air whistles in. She pushes it further, feels the shock of her skin contracting in the cold through the thin fabric of her clothes.

She could run. She is alone, Madame is out, Sir is out, Master is watching the dark-haired Americans on his phone in Laundrette, Old Madame is with the children. She could run, right now. She puts one foot out the door. She has never used this door. She has always entered Laundrette on the ground floor through the entrance at the back. She has never set foot on this pavement of this street in front of this building where she has lived for three years.

In Dubai they locked her in the flat, but not here. They have never locked her in here because they know it is not necessary. She has no money, no passport, no English, no shoes. No friend, no food, no coat, nowhere to go. No idea where she is. No map, no way to get home. No kindness of strangers, no guardian angel, no police. They know the names of her family, of Mother, of Auntie. They know the last place she lived with her family in Capital City. She can run, but if she does, she cannot be sure that they will not hunt her family down, force them to pay her debt, or do worse.

Still, the cold air is something. She pushes the door. It opens a few more inches.

Penny
First floor corridor

Penny is unsteady on her feet. She swallows, hard. She is sweating, short of breath, hands shaking. She looks up at the fluorescent tube light in the ceiling. She takes one step. She takes another. She takes a third. She is emboldened. She is empowered. She is triumphant. She is normal, she is normal – she is normal! She could leave the building, she could go outside, to the shop, to the library, to the park, to her old house, where Jamie and Olivi—

And then the shouting starts behind Carla's door. Tom's voice, she knows. She must move, quickly, before they open that door and find her here like this. She hears 'divorce' and 'visa' and loud voices and then nothing. She must turn back. Pick up the grocery bags and turn back. She is panicking. She is frozen. She cannot move forward. She cannot move back.

Carla
Flat 1A

'I can't do illegal shit, Tom, you know that. If I get caught, arrested, wouldn't they deport me?' Carla says as evenly as she can.

'Can't, or won't, Carla?' Tom says, irritation just under the surface of his words, waiting for her to say the thing that will ignite it. She stays silent.

Tom shifts back in his seat, folds his arms. He likes the definition of his forearms when viewed in that position.

'Think of what I'm offering you, love. I'll let Daniel come back, I'll pay for the divorce, I'll pay for you to switch your visa to that other one based on the kids, I'll pay the fees and the lawyer, I'll pay for all of it so you won't have to worry. Your visa won't be tied to me, and we go our separate ways. All you have to do is collect some credit card numbers from the hotel, which you handle every day anyway. Right at your fingertips. Couldn't be simpler,' Tom says.

He stands and perches on the windowsill behind her. He reaches over her shoulder to get his mug of tea from the table. She feels his breath on the back of her neck where he lingers for a moment longer than necessary. He knows this is a favourite spot of hers. When he leans back on the window ledge, he enjoys the ripple of his abs under the tight cotton of his T-shirt. He knows she's turned on though she's trying to act like she isn't.

'What do you need them for?' she asks, swallowing hard, unsure of whether asking this will enrage him or make him laugh at her. It is always one or the other.

'It's a lucrative business opportunity, Carla; the less you know about it, the better,' Tom says, standing up to place his cup on the table, standing over her, his crotch hovering in her peripheral vision. He is so close to her she can taste his cologne. It's the one he's always worn. The one she loved when she loved him.

She stays very still and gives her answer to the tabletop. 'Okay, if what you want is a divorce so you can marry Sherry, then what if it was like a loan? What if I paid you back in instalments, over time? With interest,' she pleads. 'I won't ask for anything in the divorce, I won't go after you for child support, I'll take extra shifts, I'll get a second job to pay you back for the application fees and the lawyers and everything. Just please, let Daniel come home—'

He turns so that the zipper of his jeans brushes her arm and then he starts pacing in front of her, and he is in every corner of the flat at once. She thinks of that lion at feeding time, the one time she took the kids to London Zoo, when they had to walk two hours to get home, her carrying each child in shifts, because Tom promised to top up her Oyster Card but didn't, and when she tried to pay for Tube fare with her debit card, it didn't work because he'd closed the joint account that day.

And she didn't call him for help because she knew he wouldn't answer. But she was also afraid that he would.

'C'mon, Carla. You're barely hanging on to the job you have. And with what you earn, it'll take you years to pay me back that kind of money. It's a thousand pounds just for the application, never mind the lawyer and the rest of it—'

She looks for an exit and sees only closed doors.

'But if I get caught, I'll lose my job. I'll get arrested, no one will hire me again and what happens to the kids if I go to jail? Won't they send me back to America? Then they won't let me come back again, I read about it, in the papers. Tom, it's too much, too many risks—'

He stops pacing. He moves towards her, crouches down, and takes the ends of her frizzy hair in his fingers, grazing her breast. A chill runs up her spine, pleasure and fear. She cannot tell the difference when he is close to her. They have always felt the same.

He speaks in low, honey tones, tones that mean there's no way back. 'Would I ever do that to you, Carla? Would I ever put you in danger?'

He moves her chair, parts her legs, kneels between them, runs his hands up her thighs, puts his hands around her waist, looks up into her eyes. She tries to push away from him, but he pulls her closer.

'I know I hurt you, love. Let me make it up to you. Do this one thing and help me let you go.'

Woman
First floor corridor

Woman lets go of the door and lets it fall closed by itself. The urge to flee is gone. She needs only the image of Mother, murdered and slumped over her tea, of Beauty shrieking by her side, to drain the will to fight from her limbs. She feels a prolonged chill from her flirtation with the cold from outside.

She puts the mop and broom and bucket in the cupboard under the stairs. She will leave. But not that way. Not by running into the wind, wild, with no direction.

On her way upstairs, lost in her own sadness, Woman stops short when she sees Penny in the middle of the first floor corridor, hands in her pockets, her breastbone pulsing up and down in a ragged rhythm under the fluorescent light. Her eyes darting everywhere, Penny's top half looks like it's trying to curl into a ball, but her legs are rooted to the floor.

Woman approaches her slowly, cautiously, as though Penny is a wounded animal that she is trying not to frighten. She hears muted shouting, a man yelling at the red-haired woman in 1A. Woman steps closer, and Penny blows out some air. She does not look at Woman, but it's clear she knows she's there. When Woman is six feet away, she searches Penny's face until she gets her eyes to focus on her. She says the only English word she knows that seems to fit their circumstances.

'Help,' Woman says to Penny.

'Help,' Penny says to Woman.

THE STORY OF WOMAN

Woman is many women and she is one woman. She is not every woman. Many women know her life. Many do not.

Woman wakes at dawn. She uncurls Beauty's hands from her arm and covers her sleeping daughter with the blanket. She moves quietly in the room so that Mother, on the other mattress against the wall, is not disturbed. Woman puts on her house slippers and Father's old cardigan to guard against the morning chill.

Eyes still not fully open, she brushes her hand lightly across the photo of Father, pinned to the plaster wall just above the mattress. Inside herself she says to him, 'Watch over us.'

He is handsome in the photo, young, strong. His smile is mischievous. It is a photo from a time before he died in a street battle with Government soldiers/from pneumonia because there was no medicine/in an act of retribution for the death of the brother of the leader of Local Gang. Woman was only six years old. She is older now than he was when he passed. She remembers holding his hand, its strength and rough callouses. She does not remember his voice.

She boils water for herself and for Mother on the electric stove in a pan so that it will not wake anyone. It has four hobs, but only one works. Woman wakes at dawn so that she can make the morning tea alone and in silence in the kitchen they share with Auntie and her daughters, Lonely One and Young Pretty. Lonely One is with child, and Young Pretty is in her last year of school. The three share the other bedroom to save money to pay for Young Pretty's schooling and to help Lonely One, whose husband died in the mine/whose husband was killed in the raid on the underground gay club/whose husband was mistakenly killed by Police because they thought he was someone else, but she received no compensation and the police were not disciplined.

Woman needs her strength for the day ahead. Woman and Mother work very hard.

Woman and Mother work at Luxury Brand Clothing Factory sewing children's clothes. Lovely, bright, adorable shirts and trousers, jumpers and dresses, sometimes with American flags on the front, sometimes with the Union Jack. They have chronic coughs from breathing in the fibres for so many years.

Woman and Mother run a kiosk on the street in Tourist Area of Capital City selling colourful scarves and bracelets. Travellers, who have read about the inflated prices at Tourist Market, film each other on their phones haggling with Woman and Mother, feeling giddy when they pay three dollars for a bracelet instead of four. The dollar they have saved will make no difference to their lives although it will matter greatly to the lives of Woman, Mother, Auntie, Lonely One, Young Pretty and Beauty. But the travellers have had a Cultural Experience.

Woman and Mother pick coffee beans/collect tea leaves/harvest cocoa pods/peel shrimp/pick strawberries/harvest nuts/pluck olives. Their work is done for the day when their backs are broken and their hands are numb and their spirits are dead.

Woman and Mother are teachers in Local School. When and if they are paid on time, they make less than they would in the factory, or the kiosk, or the farm. But they believe in their community and their children and Home Country, and that their work is important, although it keeps them poor and it keeps them wanting.

As she waits for the water to boil, Woman taps the framed photo of herself and Man on their wedding day on the tiny shelf near the window. Inside herself she says, 'Good morning, my love. Watch over us.'

In the photo Woman wears a short white shirt dress with a tiny blue man on a horse embroidered on the front. Her friend brought it from the factory where she sewed, as it was one that had not passed inspection, the stitches crooked on the hem at the back.

Man wore a short-sleeved blue shirt which buttoned down the front. He found it when the delivery had come to Local School from Christian Church in America, which had gathered all of the clothing and shoes the congregants no longer wanted or needed – Christmas sweaters decorated with garish characters, free T-shirts from fun runs, old brassieres, men's dress shoes, silk ties, sequined crop tops, women's knee-high suede boots – and held a car wash to raise money to pay for the shipping.

Man's shirt has the word 'Gary' embroidered over the pocket. Woman remembers that the back, which you cannot see in the photo, said 'Holy Rollers' with a picture of a long-haired, bearded man holding a bowling ball. Luckily, 'holy roller' is not a known expression in Home Country, even among those who know English, and the man on the shirt is not recognisable here as Jesus. Otherwise, Man could not have worn the shirt because it would have triggered Religious Conflict with their neighbours. But the Church didn't think about that, or the impracticality of the knee-high suede boots, or the uselessness of the silk ties, or that the money raised in the car wash to pay for the shipment of the American Church cast-offs could have paid for food, or blankets, or medicine, or books and pencils for Local School.

Man died in the bombing/in the natural disaster/in jail, wrongfully convicted and poorly treated, two years after he and Woman were married. In Home Country, men die young and violently. Men die young and violently in America and

Europe also, at the hands of Government/at the hands of Gangs/at the hands of Terrorists/at the hands of Police. Reporters explain those killings as anomalies, aberrations, events that are against the values those countries stand for. Reporters come to Home Country too, but they explain the killings here as endemic, indelible, part of the character of Home Country and her people. But the young men die regardless of how it is reported.

Woman thinks sometimes that this is one of the many reasons it is easier to be a man. Their lives are short. They do not have to spend the energy of their youth and the strength of their middle age in the factories/farms/streets to feed the fatherless children. Woman is grateful that Beauty is a girl, that Woman will not be told when her daughter is fifteen that she has been murdered in a fight or act of retribution or become the collateral damage of political unrest. But Woman is sorry for her too, that she will not be released from the pain of life so quickly and easily; that Beauty will have to endure, long after her father and her future husband and sons have perished.

But, of course, there are the many abuses, often inflicted by the men, that cause the violent deaths of the women and girls, which are not reported as loudly or as often as the violent deaths of the men. And, of course, some women survive the abuses, and then try to but cannot forget them, as they work in the factory/farm/street, until, eventually, it is the memories that kill them.

Woman makes the tea, has a few sips on her own while staring at her wedding photo, then brings a cup to Mother, and sits on the edge of her mattress.

'Mother, it is morning,' she says. Mother wakes and Woman sips, and they do not speak for a long while but listen instead to the purring hum of Beauty's breathing.

Finally, Woman whispers, 'Today after work I will go, Mother, to see that woman from the market.'

'Yes,' Mother says, terrified of Woman's plans to work Abroad, but she understands that there is little choice. Mother knows the family needs her to do this. Lonely One will soon give birth; Auntie needs medicine for her diabetes; Beauty must go to school; and she, Mother, is getting too old to work so many hours. There were no men left in the family to earn money or to protect them. Woman could do both. She could give them Better Life. And so, Mother says nothing of her fear.

Woman puts on the white dress from her wedding photo. She pulls her hair back neatly. She kisses her daughter on the forehead, and inside herself she says, 'It will not always be like this.' Woman goes to see the woman at the market who knows about the jobs Abroad.

Woman is taken to a grand house in the wealthy part of Capital City. It has high walls around it, a uniformed guard at the gate. She is brought to an office where a rich woman dressed in fine clothes wearing many gold and diamond bracelets sits behind a large and highly polished wooden desk. When Woman sits down across from her, she notices that the desk is some kind of plastic made to look like wood and that the leather on her seat is not real. She looks again at the diamond bracelets.

'You may address me as Madame,' the rich woman says.

'Hello, Madame, my name is—'

'I know your name,' Madame says. 'We will not use your name when you are in my employ. You will learn that discretion is of the utmost importance when you work for a family of high esteem, like mine. Do you understand?'

'Yes, Madame,' Woman says, nodding, feeling she has already made a mistake and lost this opportunity.

'Now then, you will be responsible for looking after my son, who is thirteen, and my daughter, who is five. Do you know how to look after children?' Madame asks.

'Yes, my own daughter is three. I have helped to raise my

cousins, one who is sixteen, one who is twenty-two. I have a teaching qualification. I taught in secondary—'

'I thought you work in Luxury Brand Clothing Factory/in Tourist Market/in the fields?' Madame interrupts her.

'I do, but I taught before, when my husband was alive and still working,' Woman says.

'You have no husband now?' Madame asks.

'No.'

'Good,' Madame says to herself rather than to Woman.

'If you come work for me, then I will pay for your passport, visa, and transportation to the United Kingdom. We will apply for a domestic worker visa on your behalf. In addition to having all of your visas and transport paid for, you will be paid on a monthly basis, according to the terms of this contract,' Madame says, handing Woman an official-looking typed paper. Woman looks down and sees it is written in English.

'Madame, I am sorry, I do not read English,' Woman says, embarrassed.

'No matter, these are the documents we will need for the visa. All they say is that you will work forty hours per week and that you will be paid £1,250 per month. You will have a room to sleep in and your food will be provided. You will cook, clean and look after the children in return. These are our terms,' Madame replies, matter-of-factly, in the way that she has said many times before to many other women.

Woman's heart leaps in her chest. The wages for one month are worth half a year's work in Home Country. She thinks of Beauty and Mother, Auntie, Lonely One and her baby not yet born, Young Pretty, and how their lives could change. She thinks of the packages she will send to her daughter, full of books and toys and sweets. She thinks of medicine for Mother's cough and Auntie's diabetes. She thinks of the new home they could move to.

She does not ask about how long she will stay. She does not ask about her days off. She does not ask whether the cost of her visa and plane ticket and passport will be added to a debt that she will be reminded of every day, that will accrue interest that she will never be able to repay. She does not ask whether she will be allowed to leave of her own accord. She does not ask for the contract in front of her to be translated into her language, and so she will never know that the words 'Lease Assumption Agreement' were written across the top of the important-looking papers. Because what Madame showed her was the lease for her family's flat in a high-rise in Dubai, having nothing else to hand in that moment that looked official and written in English to show to desperate, destitute Woman. And so, Woman also will not learn, until she is already there, that Dubai will be their first stop and that she will see nothing of that country because she will be forbidden from leaving the flat for which she holds the lease in her hand, believing that this paper, written in English, is her contract for Better Life.

Woman returns home. In three days' time she will begin her training in Madame's house. Mother asks, 'Are you sure, Daughter, are you sure you will be all right Abroad? That Madame will look after you?'

'Mother, do not worry. All will be well,' Woman replies.

She is sure that if Madame is investing so much time and money in her visa and travel, if she is giving her training in her own home to show her how things will need to be done, then she is a very serious woman indeed and this is a proper and important position for a wealthy and respectable family. Woman will make herself indispensable. She will work as hard as she can, more than she agreed to, so that they feel that she has earned her keep and her wages. In one month's time, Woman will leave with Madame and her children for the UK. She will earn so much money. She will create Better Life, for herself, for Beauty, for all of them.

Woman works as housekeeper and nanny in Madame's house in Capital City. She looks after My Lady. She looks after Master. She cooks and cleans and washes and tends for ten hours a day. Madame is strict but not cruel. She does not smile easily, nor does she anger easily. She inspects Woman's work and tells her it is satisfactory.

One day, Madame says to Woman, 'You have exceeded my expectations. Perhaps when we reach the UK, we will find other work for you to do – help in my office, and you could earn a bit extra.' Woman feels expectation and pride. She works even harder to prove her worth.

But every evening when she returns to her family, her heart sinks with the anticipation of leaving them. As the day of her departure draws near, Woman pulls Beauty closer and closer. She holds her hands, her small face, she carries her every-where. On her day off, a week before she leaves, Woman takes Beauty to see the man with the camera in the market. He takes her photo with Beauty. Woman asks for two copies, one to keep with her, always, one to leave by the bed so her daughter does not forget her.

Beauty says, 'Can I go with Mama?'

Woman plaits her daughter's hair, a rock rolling round in her chest, and says, 'No, my Beauty, not this time, but I will call and speak to you every day, and we can sing songs to each other, and I will give you a kiss that you can take to sleep every night.'

And Beauty says, 'Mama gone a long time, Mama?'

'No,' Woman says, the rock growing larger inside her, 'No, Beauty girl, only six months. It will seem like no time at all. You will not even miss me. You will be too busy playing, and laughing, you will not even know that I am gone.'

'But take care of me, Mama?' Beauty says.

'Grandmother and Auntie and Lonely One and Young Pretty. And you will have to help and look after Lonely One's baby; you will be very busy. And me, I will still take care of you. Every morning when you wake up, you go to the photo of me and Papa and the photo of you and me, and you tap it and say, "Watch over me," and I will hear you across all the sea and all the land and I will watch over you all day,' Woman says.

She does not cry in front of Beauty then. She saves her tears for later, at night, when she is wrapped around her child as she sleeps the deep sleep of small children, when her tears can fall into the pillow, and disappear, Father staring out from his photo in the dark purple light of night, the only witness to her fear.

When dawn rises on the day she is to start the journey to Better Life, Woman holds her sleeping daughter as long as she can, inhales the softness of her perfect skin, and says inside herself, 'It will not always be like this.' She pulls on Father's cardigan for the last time, breathes in the smell of the wool, and then takes it off. She decides to leave it for Mother for the morning chill, to leave it for Beauty to sleep under tonight when Woman will already be hundreds of miles away.

She makes the tea on the electric stove, turns on the one working hob. She waits for the water to boil and holds her framed wedding portrait to her so close, it is as though she is pulling Man himself through the photo. She looks at it, memorises every detail of Man's face, sees her own faint reflection in the glass. She has grown older without him. She must love their daughter, work for their daughter, without him.

She makes the tea for herself and Mother. She sits on the edge of Mother's mattress. They sit together in silence, listening to the purring hum of Beauty's breathing.

Today, it is Mother who speaks first. 'Daughter, do you have everything?'

'Yes, Mother,' Woman says, barely able to say the words.

'It will not always be like this,' Mother says.

'I know,' Woman says. She places her cup on the floor and puts her framed wedding portrait in her sleeping daughter's bed. She kisses Beauty for the last time. She embraces Mother. Then she picks up her bag, and leaves.

Part Three

March 2020

14

Tuesday

Woman
Flat 2A–2B

Mother, she is gone. It has been some days – perhaps five, perhaps seven, I am not sure – but Madame has left. She has taken Old Madame with her. They have gone I do not know where, whether to Home Country or their home in Dubai. Old Sir, Madame's father, is ill and he is dying and they have gone to him. I pray they have not gone to Home Country, that they will not think to send Agent to you, to demand repayment of my debts.

Sir tried to stop Madame. They fought. She found the safe, Mother, where he kept her passport. She found it, broke it open, and found Old Madame's too. He kept them, just like he kept mine – that's what I heard her say, 'Who did you think I was, Sir – Woman? Any of your women?'

And he tried to pull at her, he tried to pull her across the corridor, but Master pushed him off, and Sir fell against the wall because his strength has left him, Mother. He coughed, and coughed, and coughed, and slowly moved down the wall to the floor where he could not find his breath. And she stepped over him and packed her bags.

She did not kiss the children. Only Old Madame stopped at the door before they left and said to My Lady, 'Keep your eye on Woman, child. Be sure she does as she is told.' My Lady did not understand, only wrapped herself around my leg.

Sir is ill, Mother, gravely ill, and he lies in the bedroom delirious with fever. It is just me and Master, My Lady and Baby. I must think quickly now, Mother.

Penny
First Premier Dry Cleaner and Laundry

I haven't seen her since the day she walked me back to my flat and brought the groceries in. And she's not here either. And neither is the old woman. Just the teenage boy. I put the change in the washing machine, check and double-check that I have done it correctly. I check and double-check the laundry basket as well, to make sure that I haven't left anything behind. I'm paying attention, much more focused than I used to be. Much more anxious as well, but such are the consequences of waking up.

The boy can't be older than seventeen. He's thin. His face seems permanently startled. The slightest bit of fuzz on his top lip. When I sense that he is looking down at his phone, I cast my eyes sideways, without turning my head. Earbuds in, he's absorbed in the screen. So he doesn't notice the eyes, watching him from behind the shirt press.

Sherry
Flat 29, the glass and steel luxury high-rise on the Thames

'You need to come get him,' I say, keeping my voice low, trying not to let her hear that I'm scared.

'Okay, but, did Tom say it was okay? Is something wrong?' Carla asks. 'Sherry?' She says my name because I'm not answering. Because she's not sure I'm there.

'Tom . . . he . . . Carla, I have to see my parents . . . my dad's sick, they're going to shut everything down, and I have to go now and Tom's at work, so . . . you have to get Daniel, before Tom gets home,' I say.

'Wait, you're leaving without Tom? Does he know you're going?' Carla asks, and I know what she's asking. But I can't say more. It's too risky. For both of us. All of us.

'Look, are you coming to get him, or should I tell him to take the bus or what?' I say.

'Are you leaving Tom? Or did he say I should get Daniel?' she asks.

This is why I'm going. So someday I'm not on the other end of a phone, asking a stranger if I have permission to come and get my own kid.

'Just come get him, now. No later than six. Six is too late,' I say.

'Sherry? Wait, are you—' Carla says, but I end the call.

'Daniel? Come here a minute,' I say, and he shuffles into the room, sad, pale, too thin. He's holding Amy. He's good with babies. He's a good boy.

'Your mum's on her way. Here's twenty-five quid. It's all I can spare but you keep it, okay? For you and your sister, for emergencies, or when your mum runs out, or if, you know, if you ever have to—'

'I know,' he says. 'Thanks.'

Penny
First Premier Dry Cleaner and Laundry

I watch the water wash over the glass of the door, again and again. I pretend to read the newspaper someone left behind on the bench. I let my eyes blur on the words because the news is all bad and I prefer to get my updates from Mable. She's very well informed.

Every few minutes I think of a reason to look at the counter – turn my head to put my hair behind my ear, cast my eyes on the clock above the cash register. But the boy doesn't move, doesn't even shift his weight on the stool, his mouth half-open, in his own enchanted world on the phone. The little eyes catch mine, for just a moment, then disappear under the press.

I take my time transferring the washing to the dryer. I fold the dry laundry when it is finished, and finally, the boy moves.

His phone rings. He answers in that language they all speak and walks to the back room of the laundrette, around the partition where I can't see him.

I take Olivia's barrette out of my hair, the glitter in the red heart still sparkling despite the chipped paint on the metal clip, and I leave it on the counter. I know my target audience. I used to work in marketing. I used to be a mother.

I get my laundry, put on my mask and gloves, and start the journey home.

Woman
Flat 2A–2B

There is so much work, Mother. There is no time to think. Sir sleeps; his breathing is heavy. The fever has him in its grasp and will not let go. I could stop leaving food, stop bringing him water, I could make him suffer, Mother; he is so unwell, so powerless. But everything must continue as it is until I am sure.

I clean the flat, take care of Baby, prepare the meals. In every spare moment, between every chore, I press the shirts. I can only use an iron here in the flat, it is not as easy as with the press, but I must get them done. Master said that I should watch the children and Sir and do the shirts and the uniforms here in the flat while he minded Laundrette. Madame said we must keep order, keep everything running until her return, and so we will, for now. For now, I obey Madame and Master, and think. And wait.

Penny
Flat 1B

'Susannah, stop it,' I say to the cat, as she winds her way around my hands and tries to sit on my keyboard. I take her on to my lap.

'You know that it's Therapy Tuesday, our new regime, now listen to this:

A fear hierarchy is a list of triggers which causes the patient to feel fearful or anxious. Ask the patient to write down a list of these triggers and then have her rank them in order from the least anxiety-provoking to the most. After creating the fear hierarchy, you can then tailor a programme of exposure therapy beginning with the least distressing trigger, gradually progressing to the most fear-inducing situation.

For example, a patient with a phobia of snakes may rank looking at a picture of a snake as her least fear-inducing scenario, while touching a real snake might be her most frightening. The therapist would therefore begin the programme of exposure therapy by looking at pictures of snakes with the patient until the patient no longer feels anxious during the exercise. When the patient has reached a level of comfort at the first trigger, it is time to move on to the next one in the fear hierarchy, repeating the exposure. Remember that exposure to any situation on the fear hierarchy must always take place in a safe space where the patient can be assured that no actual harm will come to her.

'So, all we have to do, Susie-Q, is make a list. And then we work on each thing one by one, and since it's Tuesday anyway, it will be easy to practise because I go out the door to do laundry on Tuesdays, which I already did today, so I can technically go out the door to do other things too, isn't that right?' I say to Susannah as I hold her up in the air over my head and she looks at me with that look that says she is merely tolerating the indignity of this act and graciously allowing herself to go limp for this display, but I shouldn't push my luck.

'It is imperative, actually, Susannah, that I start – that *we* start – because things are happening and we need to be ready,' I say as I bring her back down to my lap, hearing a crack in my voice that I didn't expect.

According to Mable and the internet, it seems that we are about to be thrust into the clutches of a great disaster with the virus closing in on us. I only allow myself a glance at a few headlines. I don't need to read much to understand. And should chaos erupt in this great calamity – rioting or looting or fires – and the need to evacuate arise, I have to be able to get Susannah out of here.

Mable said they are going to lock us all in. Prisoners in our homes. But that is why I must learn to get out. When I lock *myself* in, that is one thing. When someone else holds the keys, well, that occupies a different rank on the hierarchy of fear.

I open the cat food cupboard. We are down to the last few pouches. There is, as well, the issue of Darren not being able to deliver to me at all at the present moment. It is impossible to order any groceries online; there has been a mad rush in the shops, and Darren is working every God-given hour of the day and cannot continue with our arrangement. I have texted him to tell him I will pay more for his trouble, but there has been no response.

And Susannah and I find that we are swiftly running out of provisions. Most concerning is the cat food. I attempted chicken nuggets with Susannah, but her tastes are too discerning for that. And I know I always have the chicken nuggets to fall back on myself, but, somehow, despite my hunger, I can't bring myself to eat them. Not yet.

Jamie has called several times recently. There has been a break in our communications since his betrayal, and he leaves urgent messages asking if I am all right. I only respond with *Yes*, by text. He doesn't need to know more than that. He cannot be trusted with more information. Of course, he would love that, wouldn't he, riding in here to save the day, bringing me groceries, checking my medication, observing the 'tidiness' of the madwoman's flat. No thank you, Jamie.

Therefore, the exposure therapy is vital. I've been researching alternatives to medication for people who suffer with phobias and I think I might be on to something here. I open Susannah's pouch, put half of it in her bowl and stroke her as she eats.

'When one has a purpose, Susie, it is easier to fight one's compulsions. I must look after you when the time comes.' She purrs into her food, oblivious.

'Can you hear me, Susannah?' I ask, but she does not look up.

'I must look after you and we must find our friend, the laundrette woman. She's disappeared, Susie.'

I take advantage of Susannah's distraction to return to my work. As I understand it, each fear is broken down into several levels of exposure, each increasingly intense, until the fear is resolved. So, if one's fear is flying, the levels are: talk about flying, read about flying online, drive by the airport, sit in the airport lobby, et cetera, until one can get on a plane.

I, however, have several life scenarios which I find rather challenging, and so I decide to first write each of these out and rank them, so that I have a better idea of where to begin my exposure exercises, and start with those which are most pertinent to our present situation.

I type 'Exposure Therapy – Hierarchy of Fear – Preliminary Investigation' at the top of a blank document. Then I make a chart.

Rank	Fear
	Locks on doors for which the mechanisms are not visible, for which I do not have a key, or which are not familiar to me
	Sliding doors, particularly in supermarkets, large commercial centres, and on public transport
	Going outside on days that are not Tuesday

	Unfamiliar delivery men, repairmen, salesmen, or other such unknown persons who may come to my door seemingly for one purpose but in fact are doing so for a different purpose, that being that they are news reporters or paid informants for news reporters
	Big shops, libraries, theatres, cinemas, shopping malls, superstores, hospitals, GP surgeries, lecture halls, restaurants and other similar public spaces in which I cannot see or access the exits easily from every vantage point within their walls
	Public transportation vehicles underground and/or above ground which are controlled by a conductor whom I cannot see, and carriages from which it is not possible to exit unless the doors are released by said conductor
	Breathing other people's air that they have expelled either through exercise, coughing, exhalation of cigarette smoke and/or vapours from e-cigarettes, loud laughter, singing, etc.
	Panicking to the point of hyperventilation in public, requiring the assistance of well-meaning strangers who will involve police and/or medical professionals
	Drugs that make me fat and stupid
	The accidental death of Sus—
	Never seeing my daugh—

I stop. Apparently, the fear induced by the last two is too terrifying to even finish typing. Susannah jumps up on my lap.

'Shall we rank them then, Susie?' I ask her, looking at my chart, palms sweating, throat constricting, ears ringing. I get up, holding my cat, and slam the laptop shut.

'Perhaps you're right,' I say. 'Perhaps we'll leave that exercise for another day.'

15

Mali
Justin's Noodle Place

'No, the old lot is gone, they made it a big building,' Mali says to the old man as she serves his tea. She tries to explain that in a few days the café will be shut down and he will have to stay home, but it is hard to know how much he understands.

'But there was a lot, I remember it, I found a five-pound note there once,' the old man says.

'Yes, that was a while ago,' Mali responds. And then, 'Just a minute.'

She grabs Justin Jr, who is clearing the next table over, and says, in their language, 'Please, talk to him for a bit, I can't go in circles any more today.'

Justin Jr and Emma both came back early from uni. She put them to work in the kitchen. They didn't mind. It was working in the kitchen, the long hours, the heat, the sweat, that had given them the stamina and the work ethic to outshine all those flabby, spoiled, rich white British kids they had had to compete with to get to the top. It was the kitchen that had made them strong, that had paid for extra tutoring and music lessons; it was the place where they could still feel their father's presence when they missed him. Weekends spent in the café, working with their parents, doing their homework in the booths, was how the twins had been raised.

It broke both their hearts, leaving for university, knowing their mother would have to take the reins alone, without them or their father. But she wouldn't have it any other way. Mali didn't allow them to apply to universities in London. She wanted Oxford and Cambridge, and that's what her children gave her. But now the schools were closing and they left, before the chaos set it in, and she was happy and relieved to have her babies home.

Takeaway orders had been overwhelming the café for the past week. Mali needed a break. She had already put in fifteen hours today, with at least twelve of those hours spent worrying about what was coming and what it all meant. And how they were going to survive it.

'I take this one,' she says to Justin Jr, holding up Carla's order.

'Mum, I'll do it,' he says. He's so handsome, her son. Tall, like Justin. His complexion a blend of Mali's skin tone and Justin's parents' Kenyan roots, with dark green eyes. She can hear a change in his accent already from just a term spent at Oxford. Proper Englishman.

Justin Sr says to her, in her head, 'Bloody awful, love, look what they've turned 'im into. What do I say to Lord So-and-So now?'

'Nothing, you're dead,' she says to her husband with the same bluntness with which she had spoken to him in life.

'I need some air; it's just down the street, I'll be right back,' she says to her son.

Her own accent hasn't changed for thirty years. Although she misses out the occasional article or contraction, makes minor mistakes conjugating, she speaks English fluently. Yet she is often treated by GPs and bank tellers and shop assistants as though she doesn't. They change the words they use, they slow their speech when they address her. They ask her to repeat herself, when, if they just listened, they could understand her. How strange this country is, she thinks every time it happens, that being multilingual marks one out as other, inferior, less capable.

Mali picks up the order and leaves the café, grateful for the chill of the cold air after hours in the searing heat of the kitchen.

The moped drivers are waiting outside for other orders, but since Carla called hers in and she's a regular, Mali decides to hand-deliver it. Besides, she wants to have a snoop around the building again. She has secret hopes of getting a flat in there one day. She had been in once or twice before to deliver and had taken the opportunity to have a look around, to see if she could ascertain the layout of the flats in case one became available.

She crosses the road to walk on the side of the street with the playground. It is dark, with no one inside the gates, and Mali stops for a minute. She remembers her twins playing on the climbing frames and swings while she took quick cigarette breaks, before bringing them back into the café to sit in a booth and fold the takeaway cartons and wrap the silverware. Such good, helpful children.

'Do you remember, Justin?' she says to her husband.

'Course I do, love, course I do,' he answers, inside her.

Woman
Flat 2C

Sir is in a state of restless sleep. He sleeps most of the day and the night, but it is a disturbed, turbulent sleep, of coughing and sweating with fever. Woman makes sure that he takes water, but beyond this, she does nothing. He tries to speak to her when she comes in to change his water, but she tells him to save his energy, not to talk. He asks for medicine. She says she will send Master when he is finished in Laundrette. That is hours from now, but his suffering does not move her. Let his son take care of him. Or not.

Master is in Laundrette. Baby is napping in his cot. Sir is in bed. She must move quickly.

Woman says to My Lady, 'I will be right back, stay with Baby, do not disturb your father, I will be only a few minutes.' She leaves My Lady with two Galaxy bars and turns on the television for her.

Woman has taken the ring of keys from Sir's soiled trousers. She has only a few minutes. She leaves the flat, crosses the corridor to 2C, and tries to find the key that will unlock the door. She tries one, a second, a third, and then the fourth finally turns the lock. She enters each room, silently. She knows that they are often skittish, afraid, hungry, and they can react unpredictably if they are startled.

In a loud whisper, she calls out 'Hello?' in English.

'Hello?' she says in each room. She opens every cupboard, each closet. There is no one. She knocks lightly on the bathroom door.

'Hello?' she calls out, quietly. She tries the door. It gives. A young woman is trembling in the bathtub, half hidden by the shower doors.

'Do not be afraid; you can go. Sir is ill, Madame is gone. Go now, run,' Woman says in her language, but the girl is not from Home Country and she does not understand.

'Free,' Woman says, trying in English. 'Run,' she says, and a light turns on in the girl's eye.

'Go?' the terrified girl asks in English, not moving from the tub. She is thin, Woman sees. She is still wearing her clothes from Old Life – denim jeans, trainers, earrings in her ears. She still has on make-up. It is smeared across her face.

'Go, run,' Woman says to her.

The girl does not know if she should believe Woman. She does not know if this is another trap, another deception. She rises slowly, looking over Woman's shoulder, looking past her for others. Seeing no one else, she steps out of the tub. Woman motions for her to follow, then leads her through the dark, empty flat. The girl trips in the dark and grabs Woman's arm involuntarily to brace her fall. They both look down. A baby's pacifier lies under the girl's foot. Woman cannot think about who else has been in these rooms and who else has left them.

Woman opens the door for the girl and says, 'Run, go.'

The girl looks over her shoulder at Woman, and then she runs. Woman knows it will be dangerous for her in the streets, but it will be worse for her here when the police come. Then she would have no chance at all.

Penny
Flat 1B

'Right, if we're going to get some food, and be prepared, we have only a few days, Susannah. So, today, all we have to do is leave the flat, go down to the front door, touch it, and come back. We can do that. It is just a small challenge. Don't think about tomorrow, or Thursday, or Friday, and getting to the shop, that is too much to think about right now. Today, our focus is only on getting down to the front door, and then back up. All right?' Penny says to Susannah, stroking her back.

She has had to forgo the rubber gloves because Susannah is afraid of them and won't be held if Penny wears them. But she is wearing everything else: boiler suit, trench coat, winter boots, face mask, Yankees cap, emergency kit in her backpack. She has put Susannah into an old canvas shoulder bag with a flat cardboard bottom. This allows Penny to keep her arm tucked under the cat but provides a safety net should she lose her grip or Susannah try to make a sudden break.

Penny closes her eyes. She feels the warm, pulsing body of the cat under her hand. Susannah is nervous, her head alert and moving every which way, but she is purring, and sinking under the lip of the bag now and again, with just her eyes peeking over the top.

'*Yes, we can*, Susannah, come on now, remember the mantras,' Penny says to her faithful companion. Penny had read, during her extensive research into exposure therapy and other exercises that could help her with her phobias, that many people find it helpful to recite mantras, phrases or quotes, even single words, to help them get through situations they find difficult.

Penny and Susannah have chosen two. The first is 'Yes, we can.' Penny has always found President Obama to be a very calming presence. She likes to watch his speeches and clips of his press conferences on YouTube. It is his height, his posture, she thinks, and also, she feels, there is a tone in his voice that makes the listener feel that he definitely – certainly – would know the right thing to do in an emergency. 'Yes, we can' was also easy to remember in moments when one needed to act quickly.

'Yes, we can, yes, we can, yes, we can,' Penny says, breathing raggedly, turning the lock, one hand on her cat, the other on the doorknob.

'Yes, we can, yes, we can,' she says, stepping through the threshold, keys in her hand, prepared to lock the door behind her. She hears someone coming down the stairs at speed, running, skipping steps and it sounds like fear and she feels a wave of urgency from the runner, but she does not turn around until she hears they've gone. She cannot bear to have any witnesses. She inhales deeply.

'Yes, we can,' she says, as she faces the corridor.

Susannah meows. 'Yes, all right, all right, remember the next one, Susie,' Penny says, putting one trembling foot in front of the other, stroking the cat, trying to catch her breath. She feels a sudden wave of exhaustion. Not a physical tiredness, but a weariness of spirit, a devastating soul fatigue. She has a moment of realisation that her life is very hard, and it has been so hard for so long that she cannot remember when her life was not this hard. She cannot remember when she became like this. She is so ill. And she is so tired. So very tired.

When her shoulders start to shake involuntarily, Penny starts the second mantra: 'Victory at all costs, victory in spite of all terror, victory, however long and hard the road may be; for without victory, there is no survival.'

The shakes that often accompany her highest anxiety episodes have begun, but still, with her second mantra, the words of Churchill, she manages to move another step ahead. She likes the part about victory and survival. She likes to think of her grandmother as a young woman driving ambulances through London's burning, war-weary streets, lined with burnt-out, collapsed buildings. Penny tries to channel her grandmother's strength, her will as that young, fearless woman. But she can only feel what the burning buildings felt like, ready to fall. How they trembled and burned and smoked, how they knew they were too far gone to save. How they stood, exposed, ashamed that they no longer were of any use.

'Victory at all costs, victory in spite of all terror, victory, however long and hard the road may be; for without victory, there is no survival,' she is whispering now, because they are an awful lot of words to say while still breathing at the same time. Susannah meows and bites her hand. Penny is pushing down too hard on her in the bag. The quick pain brings back her focus.

'Victory at all costs, yes, we can, at all costs, yes, we can, without victory, there is no survival,' she says, mixing the mantras as she walks down the corridor.

'Victory at all costs,' she says, as she puts her foot on the first step of the staircase.

'Victory—' she says, her eyes closed, left hand gripping the bannister, and then—

'Do you have a kitten in your bag?' a small voice says behind Penny, forcing her to open her eyes.

Mali
Flat 1A

Outside on Bedford Road, a young girl walks past Mali at a furious pace, hands pushed down into the pockets of her cropped jacket. She is tall, underdressed for the weather. Mali can see her make-up is smeared and she keeps looking over her shoulder at the building. Mali looks after the girl and thinks to herself, 'Boyfriend trouble, so simple, the problems of youth,' and she waits for the automatic lock to open with the press of Carla's doorbell.

It clicks and she opens the door into the lobby. She takes her time walking through, looks at the lobby, the mailboxes, checks the skirting boards to see how clean they are, to get an idea of how well they looked after this place. She takes the stairs one by one, holding on to the bannister, looking at the lights, at the condition of the paint on the walls.

At the top of the stairs, she sees a woman wearing a trench coat and a face mask with a cat in a bag on her shoulder talking to a little girl in a princess dress sitting on the steps. She walks past them, pretending not to notice. She'll have to find out what floor this crazy woman lives on. She's not going to live next door to whatever was going on there with that one.

Mali knocks on Carla's door.

'Hi,' Carla answers.

'It's thirteen fifty,' Mali says, smiling, handing over the bag. 'How you are doing, you and kids? Haven't seen you lately,' she says to Carla.

'Oh, we're okay, I don't know, my schedule's been all over the place, that's why I haven't come by,' Carla says, because Tom taking the kids, and Mary Rose getting drunk to escape him, and her bizarre night with Darren that she still can't really remember, and Tom's constant phone calls and texts in the last few hours while he drives all over England hunting down Sherry and the baby, and harassing her about the credit card numbers – because of course he didn't forget about that – and waiting for the news at work any day now about what was going to happen to their jobs is too much to explain. Although she wants to. She wants to tell someone about how it has been. About how hard she's trying.

'How's the café?' Carla says.

'Busy, busy, busy,' Mali says. 'They going to close us down, I don't know what will happen. But my kids is home, so I'm happy,' she says, smiling.

Carla knows Mali's kids, the twins. Diligent, helpful, always polite and always there, helping their parents.

'You did really good with them, Mali, you really did,' Carla says, admiringly. There is a pause as she hands over the cash.

'Your family okay in Thailand?' she asks. 'This virus is all over the place over there, right?'

'Oh no, I'm not from Thailand,' Mali says, smiling, shaking her head.

'Wait, what? But I thought – I mean, the restaurant – you own a noodle restaurant?' Carla asks, confused.

'Oh yeah, that was Justin. He love the noodles. Made me learn to cook them, all kinds. Then he love it so much he buy the café. He wanted pub, but we got café instead,' Mali explains and shrugs.

'Really? So, what kind of name is Mali then?' Carla asks, surprised not to have known this about the woman she bought coffee from nearly every day for the past three years.

'Molly? It's English name. My English name I choose long ago. Because it easy to say.' The older woman chuckles as she puts the cash in her pocket and says goodbye to her customer.

On the way down the stairs, she shakes her head at this country, at how she is still a stranger here, after all this time.

Penny
Stairs between first and second floors

Penny looks up. My Lady is sitting on the steps above her, staring at her through the railing. She is wearing a princess dress, the back open because it is too tight on her to zip up. Her long black hair was plaited, but it has fallen out of the braid and is frizzing and tufting in all directions. At her temple, Penny sees, is Olivia's sparkly heart barrette, the metal clip worn and chipped.

'Oh, hello. This is Susannah,' Penny says to her, gasping for air behind her mask, trying to disguise her tremor. The girl and the barrette are a welcome distraction from her panic. This little one was in the laundrette, hiding earlier, the little eyes behind the press. But what does it mean? Penny is sweating, breathing heavily, but discovering that My Lady interrupts her cascading fear, the grip in her throat relaxes, just enough to let her speak. Speaking to children has never been one of her problems, not like speaking to adults.

'Why is she in your bag?' My Lady says, forcing Penny to think, to come up with a plausible answer.

'Because we're practising going out. She's an indoor cat. She hasn't been outside for a long time and she's afraid.'

'Oh,' My Lady says, accepting the information without question. Her eyes are wide and curious.

'Can I pet her?' she asks.

'Yes, of course you can,' Penny says, turning her shoulder bag towards My Lady.

Susannah pushes her head upwards, into the little girl's palm, eyes closed, relishing the contact, purring. Penny tries to think quickly. Now that she knows this little girl was in the laundrette, she tries not to lose the momentum of her discovery, although, she must admit, she doesn't know what she's looking for. Penny feels there is a connection here, something about this girl, and the woman, and the bins and the socks. She is on the brink of something.

'Do you live here?' Penny asks cautiously.

'My father says never to say where we live, and never to go to school, but he's sick now,' My Lady replies matter-of-factly, as though Penny knows what she's talking about.

'Oh, that's a shame,' Penny says, trying and failing to understand My Lady's child's logic.

A small woman brushes past her on the steps, looks over her shoulder at Penny and My Lady. There is a fragrant smell of food and Penny suddenly feels faint. Her stomach feels like it's turning in on itself, it has been empty for so many days.

'I must get out,' she thinks. 'Without victory, there is no survival.'

She notices that her heart has slowed, in these few moments with her cat and this child. She starts to feel a chill as her sweat dries and a draught blows in up the stairs and under her coat. Her fear recedes.

She hears Carla's deep rasp bouncing off the walls as she chats with the takeaway lady. She feels the space she is in. She has never sat on these steps, never walked on them in anything other than a state of terror, often hysteria, and she is surprised at how little she feels now. No panic, no fear. She is neutral. It is a new feeling, or rather, it is an absence of feeling, a vacancy usually occupied by panic and dread and catastrophe. She tries to think of something else to say to the little girl but then—

'And my mother has gone away to my grandfather because he's dying, so I'm looking for my nanny because I'm hungry, and my father is just in his bed,' My Lady says, stroking Susannah between the eyes.

'Your nanny? Does she work in the laundrette sometimes? Downstairs?' Penny asks. She is closer.

'When they let her out to work, she does. I've only been there a few times. Yesterday I found this barrette,' My Lady says, touching the heart at her temple.

'Yes, that's very pretty,' Penny says. 'What do you mean—'

'I'm going back home now,' My Lady says abruptly. 'Bye, Susannah Cat,' and she pushes up off her knees and starts up the stairs.

'Wait,' Penny says, rising from her seat with difficulty, trying to manage her coat and the cat in the bag and her back-pack. Before she knows she has done it, she is halfway up the next flight of stairs.

Woman
Lobby

She cannot find My Lady. She ran down to Laundrette after she let the girl go in 2C to put in some service washes, but when she returned to the flat Baby was asleep and My Lady was gone. Woman is frantic, checking the lobby, the cupboard under the stairs, opening the front door, putting the mop and bucket in the jamb so it won't lock behind her, stepping outside into the cold, trying to see if she had run into the play-ground. But no, she is not that adventurous a child. She would be too frightened to go outside after not having been for so long. She is somewhere in the building.

As Woman turns to come back inside, ready to run up the stairs with the bag of shirts she grabbed to iron in the flat, a person she has never seen before, yet knows very well, is coming down them.

'Hello,' Molly says to her in the language they both know, recognising Home Country immediately in Woman's face.

'Hello,' Woman answers, stunned, uncertain.

'Do you work here? I've never seen you before,' Molly says, quickly surveying Woman, noticing her socks and flip-flops, her thin clothes, the 'Just Do It' logo visible through her large, dingy T-shirt, her broken teeth.

Woman puts her hand up to her mouth out of habit. 'Yes, I work here,' she says, carefully.

'Do you clean?' Molly asks, taking a step closer.

'Yes, I do,' Woman says, taking a step back. She sees the high cheekbones of the people of the North, the wide eyes, the high forehead. She sees Molly's petite frame, her hands shaped by hard work, but not by Woman's work. Not in the way that Woman has worked.

'Do they treat you well?' Molly asks, cocking her head to the side. The woman before her is hollow. Molly sees her full lips, her arched eyebrows, her heart-shaped face of the people of the West. She hears the West in her speech.

'Yes, they do,' Woman says, desperate to say more, but remembering how Father died, and who did the killing, and who can be trusted by her people in Home Country and who cannot.

'Well, if you say so. But if you need help, if you need anything, I own the café at the end of the street. Come to the back door, you are always welcome. Any sister from Home Country is always welcome, especially once they lock everything down. You heard that is happening, yes?' Molly asks.

Woman nods, although she does not understand.

'If you don't want to stay here with them, now is the time to go,' Molly says, searching for Woman's eyes but not catching them.

'Thank you,' Woman says, and then adds, after a pause, 'Sister.'

She watches Molly leave through the front door, and shudders, telling herself it is just the draught of the cold, dark air of night.

Penny
Stairs ascending to the second floor

'Wait!' Penny calls as she struggles up the stairs.

Half of her brain is propelling her forward, urging her on, telling her that these are only stairs, this is only a building, the building she lives in, she is fine, she is fine, she is fine.

The other half screams at her, 'Danger!' It shouts at her, and tries to slow her steps, and constricts her chest, and tries to get her feet to turn and run in the opposite direction. But Penny clutches Susannah in the bag and takes one step at a time. It is difficult, after years of being sedentary and walking only to the laundrette and back. Penny is winded quickly, but she keeps going. And as she goes, heavily, one step at a time, pulling herself, willing herself up, she feels a rush behind her, a sprightly flash that throws her off balance.

Woman flies up the stairs, desperate to find My Lady, clutching the laundry bag of shirts in her hand. She shoves past Penny roughly, not meaning to, but she hardly knows what she is doing, she is so frantic about the girl.

At the top of the stairs, she gasps, drops to her knees when she sees My Lady, grabs her by both wrists, and whispers through her tears of relief, in the language they both know, 'Thank God, child, thank God.'

Penny recovers and looks up at the landing to see Woman kneeling at the feet of My Lady in her tight princess costume, gaping open at the back. Woman's shoulder is exposed by the wide neck of her T-shirt, a dingy fluorescent sports bra strap visible, the soles of her flip-flops pointing sideways, revealing the holes in the heels of her socks. A peasant crying at the feet of a royal child. A scene from the saddest fairy tale she could ever imagine.

The three are silent for a moment.

Penny – daring to speak first, knowing that if she does not speak now, she will lose her chance – says, 'Is this your nanny, little girl? Can you ask her what's wrong?'

My Lady kneels down to join Woman on the floor, holds her crying face in both her chubby hands and says, in the language they both know, 'Woman, don't cry, this lady has a cat, you see? In her bag. It is an inside cat. She says to ask you what's wrong with you?'

Woman looks at My Lady, then at Penny. 'Tell her that when I knock, I will need her to answer.'

My Lady, suddenly realising the importance of her position between the two adult women, lets go of Woman, straightens her dress, puts her hair behind her ears and faces Penny to say, 'When she knocks on your door, please answer. And can she please pet your cat.'

Penny nods at Woman and sits on the top step to be nearer to her. She puts Susannah in her lap.

'I'll answer, of course. What is her name? Does she need money? Clothes? Food?' Penny asks, while Susannah pads around between her and Woman, feeling concrete under her little feet for the first time in years.

My Lady turns to Woman and translates, 'She wants to know your name, but you know you cannot tell her that, that's what Father says. She says yes, she will come to the door. Do you want money or clothes or food or some sweets or chocolate maybe?'

Woman, stroking the cat's back to the end of her tail, nods at Penny, whose face mask is now draped around her chin, a trickle of sweat running down from the edge of her baseball cap.

'Tell her I want nothing. Just please when I knock, can she answer,' Woman says to My Lady.

My Lady says to Penny, 'She would like you to please answer the door when you hear her knock on it and also if you have sweets, please bring them. And the cat.'

'Of course,' Penny says. 'Of course.'

16

Tuesday, The Next Week

Woman
Flat 2A–2B

'Woman, what do we do?' Master says, leaving his father's room. 'He's not getting better.'

'Did you give him the medicine?' Woman asks.

'Yes,' he says, 'but it doesn't stop the coughing.'

'Call your mother, she will know what to do,' she says.

'I did. She said take him to hospital. Drive him in the laundry van and leave him outside, speak to no one, just leave him, with no wallet, no phone, no way to trace him. She said they'll treat him. He'll make his own way back.'

There is a long silence while she irons shirts. She knows he wants reassurance, instruction. She keeps silent. She keeps ironing. There are very few shirts this week, business has been slow, but there are never no shirts. There is never no work to be done.

'Woman,' he says finally, a tremble in his voice, 'Mother says she cannot come home for some time. She says that she and Grandmother are stranded, there are no flights, they do not know when there will be again. What should we do? And what do we do about that tall girl who ran away from the flat last week?'

We. She hears him say the word. She wonders if he has ever noticed that she calls him 'Master'.

'Do what your mother tells you,' she says, not taking her eyes off the ironing.

'But there are two new pickups. Father usually goes with me, but I don't know, I've never gone alone. Should I go alone? After I close Laundrette?' Master asks.

She thinks of how to answer him. She can say, 'Take your father to hospital, leave him there, drive away, and never look back. Never come back to this flat, never come back to your family. Leave before you are caught and forced to pay for your parents' crimes.'

She can tell him what she will do as soon as he leaves here, and if he is smart, he will not return. She can tell him to get his passport and his clothes, to take his father's money from the lockbox, to drop him at the hospital, to drive the van somewhere and abandon it and start a new life. His own Better Life.

But it was only once he brought her bread and water when they locked her in Silent Room. Only twice he brought her tea while she rummaged in the bins. He showed mercy, but rarely, and only the slightest mercy. Only the smallest.

Should she repay that mercy and help him leave?

Should she let him do as his mother says, and then return and discover what she's done?

She irons and irons and says nothing. She lays out a sleeve, flattens it, sprinkles with water, sprays with starch, then presses and presses, the iron always moving, until the crease in the sleeve is sharp enough to slice through flesh, hers or someone else's. Then a memory surfaces. Master's outgrown sweater that he left for her by her mat in the nursery.

She makes a decision.

'Master,' she says, spraying the starch, 'you must take your sick father to hospital. I will prepare the children but I want you to pack your things and—'

'Oh, right, the children, I forgot about them—' he says, and scratches his head. 'Should I lock them in Silent Room while we finish up in Laundrette? Or should I just take them and leave them at the hospital too, with Father? Then you can come with me for the pickups.'

She stops ironing. She looks at him.

He has told her the value of his mercies. It is not enough.

'Do what your mother said,' she says. 'Finish in Laundrette, do the pickups, take your father to hospital. I will look after the children and wait for your return.'

Master leaves the room.

'I am not his mother, Mother,' Woman says to her mother, as she keeps pressing the shirts.

Carla
Flat 1A

Daniel is still sleeping. Mary Rose is on the sofa, deep in texting with her friends. Daniel found her phone in the bottom of the bin one day a few weeks ago when he took out the rubbish. It was dead with its screen smashed and cover missing, but it still worked if she kept it plugged into the charger. They're both supposed to be doing remote school but she can't deal with that right now. Tom's going to call at some point today. Today was the deadline he gave her.

When Tom got home that day he saw right away that Sherry had gone. In his mad rush to find her, he didn't notice that Daniel's things were also missing, that Daniel wasn't home from school. He remembered his son suddenly, an hour later, when he stopped at a red light. He texted him, *Look after yourself, mate. I might be a while, there's some money on the table*. And Tom did not check for a response and did not realise that his son had also left him.

Carla received furious texts from Tom when he couldn't find Sherry at her parents' house in Bristol, or her brother's in Manchester, or her best friend's place in Birmingham. She got calls in the middle of the night from him in his car, where he'd been sleeping, talking about how much he loved Sherry, how terrified he was that she'd taken the baby and that he'd never see them again. He spoke to Carla as though she were not his wife, not the mother of his children, as though he was not blackmailing her, but as though she was his only friend in the world. And she knew that it was twisted, but also that it was true.

It wasn't until two days into his search that she got the text that said, *Guess you'd better go get Daniel, I need some time.* Tom assumed Daniel had stayed at his flat on his own, and Carla didn't correct him. She exhaled a breath she didn't know she'd been holding. She thought about Sherry. And Carla felt lucky. And afraid.

Though Carla had Daniel back, keeping their son hostage wasn't Tom's only weapon. He still had his favourite one.

'It's just one call, Carla, you know that,' he'd said a couple of days ago. 'I'll say it was all a sham. I'll say you lied on your application, that you fooled around on me, used me,' he said, and she could hear Sherry and the baby in the background. He'd found her after searching for five days, just in time for lockdown. 'I'll say you were planning to defraud your employer in a credit card scam. I have the evidence,' he said.

'What're you talking about?' she said.

'C'mon, Carla, I've got you recorded. You forget how much smarter I am than you. You forget there's different rules for you and me, that they'll take my word over yours, any day,' he said.

She doesn't know if any of it is true. She only knows he's going to call today. And that it's lucky she had the time to get the credit card numbers before she was laid off and the hotel closed. It's not so lucky that she's got no job now and no prospects of another one, with what's happening, and she really does need his money, and she really, really doesn't see another way out.

She sips vodka from a Diet Coke can, trying to calm her nerves, but the alcohol is having little effect on her. She can't blunt the edges, she can't blur the lines.

The paper with the numbers on it is folded into quarters. She spins the paper square on the table. Then she pushes the sharpest corner of the fold into each fingertip. She looks at her daughter, her beautiful slim daughter who looks like Diane, the grandmother she will never meet. Daniel shuffles into the room, eyes barely open, hoodie covering his bedhead, nestling down into the corner of the sofa, wordlessly making space by putting his sister's feet in his lap. He tilts his head back and closes his eyes in half sleep.

She wonders if he will grow up to be a shitty boyfriend. And if she will have to carry the guilt of his future girlfriends the way she carries Melissa.

She wonders if she will lose Mary Rose to some asshole who'll tell Carla to fuck off when she calls, and if she'll keep calling regardless because she'll know her baby girl is in trouble. Or if she'll stop calling because it'll be too hard.

Carla sips from her can. Her hair falls forward and she sees a grey strand. She follows it to her scalp with her fingers and pulls it from the root. Her eyes water at the sting.

She thinks about how Tom has all the money. How she cannot do this without the money. How she could call her mother. How that will be worse than calling Tom, worse than getting arrested for credit card fraud – what if she's arrested? If she goes to prison the kids can live with him and Sherry. And they'll have money and they'll be okay. If she goes to prison she won't have to worry about her bills. If she goes to prison maybe they'll deport her and there will be nothing she can do about it. And she might never see the kids again until they're grown.

If she goes to prison he won't be able to reach her any more.

Carla sips from her Diet Coke can. She picks up her phone. She finds the number. She makes the call.

Penny
Flat 1B

She was blinded by the fluorescent lights in the store windows, terrified by the traffic, stunned by the noise, disoriented by the people walking in different directions. But, holding firmly to

258

Susannah in the canvas bag on her shoulder, she remembered her purpose, the gravity of her mission. Susannah had no one else in the world, only her. She had no other choice.

Penny – sweating under the baseball cap, sweating around her face mask, hands sweating around the cat, sweating under her layers of wool underwear and boiler suit and trench coat and boots – made it to D and D's 24-Hour Food Express, opened the door of the shop, trudged through the few aisles, and managed to do the shopping.

And now, safely back in her flat, Penny says, 'Susannah, here you go,' and puts the cat food bowl down in front of the loudly meowing cat. She has not eaten proper cat food for several days and her protest meows – accusatory, enraged – finally quiet as she annihilates the food in the bowl.

Penny surveys her haul. Two bags of crisps, two boxes of Cup-a-Soup, three Pot Noodles, twelve pouches of cat food, a jar of pickles, a can of sardines, a jar of hot dogs which she now deeply, deeply regrets, a jar of Dolmio pasta sauce although she did not buy any pasta, a kitchen sponge, a roll of aluminium foil, a bottle of lemon juice, a package of Border ginger snaps, a box of matches, a bottle of toilet cleaner, a deck of playing cards, and a Bounty bar, a last-minute impulse purchase when she stood at the till.

Penny was so overwhelmed in the shop that she simply plucked things off the shelves, anything that came into view. She therefore did not buy tea, or tuna, or eggs, or bacon or cheese – which had all fallen below her eyeline. She did not buy oven pizzas, or oven chips, or spaghetti or orange juice, or tea biscuits, or hot cocoa, or milk, all of which had been within reach had she been able to turn her head.

But it doesn't matter whether Penny bought anything useful or edible, or whether it would last her more than a few days. What matters at this exact moment is that the cat is fed and that Penny has Pot Noodles to eat for dinner for at least three days and she has bought these things herself and brought them home. What matters is that she has done it. But in her state of elated exhaustion at her triumph, she suddenly remembers something.

'Oh Susannah, I wish you'd reminded me. A loaf of bread. Some toast would have been lovely.'

Woman
Flat 2A–2B

Master leaves the flat to finish the last hour at Laundrette before closing up, getting the pickups, and then taking his father to hospital. Woman made sure to instruct him to do things in this order, to give herself enough time.

Woman packs Baby's clean clothes and some nappies in a duffel bag with My Lady's three favourite outfits and her toothbrush. She packs Baby's plush toy dog with the torn-off ear and My Lady's special sparkly purse and her pink, stuffed unicorn. She asks the girl to unlock her cabinet and together they pack all of her Galaxy bars.

'Are we going somewhere?' My Lady asks, innocently, happily chomping through one of the Galaxies, which she could not help but open once she saw it.

'Your father is very ill, My Lady, and you cannot stay here,' Woman says, shoving Baby's ready-made formula and bottles into the side of the duffel, putting off the life-altering sentences she must say for just a few minutes more.

'Then where will we go?' the girl asks, still quite unaware that when she leaves this flat today, she will never see it again.

'My beautiful girl, you listen to me well,' Woman says, in the language they both know. She holds the child's round face in her hands and moves damp strands of hair off her forehead. Woman gets down on her knees so the girl can see her eyes, can remember her face if she remembers nothing else.

'It is time for us to be brave. Can you be brave?' she asks, and the little girl nods her head yes, and wraps her half-eaten chocolate bar back in its wrapper, to show she understands the importance of the moment. She is a clever girl. She understands from Woman's voice that something bigger is happening, something that will change her fate. Years from now, after she has survived Baby being adopted without her, when she is sixteen and leaves her last foster family for a room in the group home, her new roommate will offer her half a Galaxy bar and will not understand why it makes her cry.

'Are you leaving us?' My Lady asks the floor, too afraid of the answer to look in Woman's eyes.

'Yes, my lovely, I must go. And you must go too. You and Baby. Will you take care of Baby for me? Will you be a brave girl and look after him?' Woman says, pushing the child's hair behind her ear, close enough to smell the chocolate on her hot child's breath. The girl shakes her head.

Woman continues, 'Your father is very ill and must go to hospital and Master must take him there and look after him. And your mother is away, so I am going to take you to our friend, you remember, the lady with the cat?'

'With the cat, Susannah?' My Lady, her voice brightening slightly, not fully understanding that it is the first step of their permanent separation.

'Yes, you and Baby are going to visit with her and she is going to make sure you are safe. She will stay with you until a very kind policeman comes and they are going to make sure that no one locks you away anymore. And you will go to school, and play with other children, and go outside, and do all the things that you want to do. You and Baby. You will visit with the nice woman and the cat and then you will go away from here, from this building, to somewhere wonderful where you can do all the children's things you have missed.'

'Will there be parties? And cake? And animals? And games?' My Lady asks, lost for a moment in the fantasy painted in front of her. She weighs the attractive benefits against the difficult enormity of change in the easy way that children do, determining that the momentary pleasure of a cupcake is a fair price to pay for the loss of the only life she has ever known.

'Yes, all of those things. You will be happy. And safe,' Woman says.

'Is Mama coming back? I don't want to stay with Mama without you.'

'No, My Lady, I would never allow that. I will make her afraid to come back here. I will make it so that she is afraid of police and she will stay away,' Woman says.

'But will you come to see me and Baby?' My Lady asks, pushing the hair off Woman's forehead, the way Woman had done to her.

'Yes, in a few days, once you are safe in a new home,' Woman lies.

She does not want to lie, but she knows that the child needs hope more than she needs truth. Woman told Beauty the truth before she knew it was a lie. She told her daughter they would speak every day, and sing songs, and that she would come home in six months. Whether she lies or tells the truth, either way, Woman leaves and the children are motherless. But they can be safe. She can at least do that.

'All I want, my girl, is for you and Baby to go outside and go to school and grow up and be happy,' she says to My Lady.

'But I want to do that with you, I want to go outside with you—' The urgency in My Lady's voice rises.

'I know, you will, but for this little bit now, you must be brave, for me and for Baby. And I know you can be. I know how strong you are. And, My Lady, you must remember, tell no one about me. Tell no one that you know me. Even if other people say they know me, you must keep me secret. Do you understand?'

'Yes.'

'Tell me what I said.'

'Tell no one, you are secret. You are my secret Woman,' My Lady says.

'Good girl. Now let's go downstairs to see the cat. Would you like that?'

Woman tries to move the child along, to keep her from dwelling, to keep their momentum. She must make this as quick and brief as possible, before My Lady has time to question or panic or rebel.

Then the child stops.

'But what about Father? Should I say goodbye to Father?' My Lady asks.

Woman thinks. Is it better for her to say goodbye, or to leave, saying nothing? Is it better for her to have a final memory of the man, or to hope that she forgets him entirely one day – his tirades, his slaps, his locking her in – as her life moves on.

'Father is very ill, My Lady. Here, quickly, you can write him a note, slip it under his bedroom door. That will be enough.'

Carla
Flat 1A

'This is Gigi,' the lawyer answers, half listening, as she leans over her son's iPad and points at the two numbers he multiplied incorrectly. She ruffles his hair as she balances her four-year-old on her lap while he colours in a dinosaur.

When there is no answer, she says, 'Hello, can I help you?'

'I need Gigi Harrison. Is that you?' Carla blinks hard to concentrate.

'Yes, speaking—'

'It's Carla,' Carla says. She crushes the Diet Coke can in her hand. She wants to tell her what Tom's doing, what he's threatened, she wants to tell her—

'Oh, hi, what can I do for you, Carla?'

Carla is startled by the lawyer's friendly ease and she says, 'You remember me?'

'Of course,' is the lawyer's reply. She doesn't say she's waited for this call since the day Carla and Tom left her office.

Carla looks at the crushed can in her hand, at the strands of her hair on the table, at her children on the sofa. At the folded piece of paper, a tiny drop of blood on its edge from her sore fingertips. She remembers Mary Rose crying, long ago, in another room while she chopped potatoes with blood on her shaking hands.

'I need help,' Carla says.

Sir
Flat 2A–2B

Sir's sheets are damp with sweat and urine. The air is stale, thick with his diseased exhalations, air that he breathes and rebreathes again, that he coughs out, breath that he cannot catch. Half-drunk glasses of water line the windowsill. Untouched food festers on one plate, is dried stiff on another, the occasional fly darting at them. He sleeps almost continually.

Although Woman had meant only for her to push her note to her father under his bedroom door, My Lady decides to open his door very quietly and carefully, because she has never known someone who is very ill and she wonders if what she has imagined about what they look like is actually true.

She stands observing her father, the rapid and shallow movement of his chest under the covers. She notices the finger-nails on the hand that lies on top of the covers, how long they are, not having been clipped since he took to his bed. They are almost like her mother's but without the varnish. His gold ring looks loose now on his limp finger, although she remembers it being tight before, too tight, almost embedded in his skin. It was stuck, he had told her once, that's why he spun it round and never took it off.

Her attention is captured, for a moment, by the particles of dust she can see floating in the spotlight of the desk lamp on the bedside table, the only light in the room, and she imagines they are thousands of tiny fairies sent to the rooms of sick people, even not very nice sick people, like her father. She imagines that they are all singing the song from the show with Dr Ranj that she used to like to watch on CBeebies, and she joins them, in a hushed whisper: '*Be happy, be healthy, and get well soon. Be happy, be healthy, and get well soon. Get well soon.*'

It is all she can think of to say to her father. Woman has told her that it is wrong to lie, so she does not say 'I'll miss you' or 'I'm sorry I have to go', or any of the other things she's seen people say on the telly when they are leaving. Instead, My Lady places her note – hastily scratched out on the white billowing clouds of an illustration of Paradise from a *Watchtower* magazine – on his bedside table and waves quickly before she goes to the door and closes it behind her.

My Lady did not notice, because of the way that the light fell across the bed, that Sir's left eye was slightly open. She did not know that in the delirium of his fever he saw his daughter and he heard her song and in the space between consciousness and dreaming where he now spent all his time, he thought they were on the beach in Home Country, several years ago, when his daughter was very little and she held his two fingers tightly and screamed with delight when the waves touched her feet. When he knew what it was to love. When he did not know yet what he was capable of.

Woman
First floor corridor

Woman, with the duffel bag on her shoulder, carries Baby with her left arm. With her right hand, she grips My Lady's hand tightly, hoping that the child feels her love and not her fear. In the corridor the trio walk in silence, moving slowly, breathing fast. Even Baby is subdued and quiet, mesmerised by the fluorescent tube lights in the ceiling, the flickering of one and the fading of the other.

When they reach Penny's door, Woman puts down the bag, gives Baby to his sister, and kneels before the children.

'I know you can do it,' Woman says to My Lady, whose bottom lip is trembling, whose eyes are terrified.

'Yes, but when will you come back—'

'Soon. No tears now, you show me your brave face. Show me—' My Lady inhales, and straightens her back, and Woman brushes down the front of her princess dress. From the bag she pulls out My Lady's plastic tiara, and places it on her head.

'Remember that you are a queen. My warrior queen,' Woman says, and embraces the children for the last time. Baby puts his hand on her face, nuzzles into her cheek, and gurgles.

'Brave boy,' she whispers. 'Beautiful boy. It will not always be like this.'

Then she kisses My Lady's forehead briefly and rushes quietly down the corridor to watch from the shadow in the stairwell on the landing. She knows that Penny will not venture far enough out of the flat to see her. My Lady looks back at Woman as she knocks on Penny's door, adjusting her hold on Baby, and sees Woman nod at her for the last time, as she recedes into the dark.

It is this image of Woman's face that My Lady will remember, years from now, when she rocks her own newborn baby to sleep, and hums the lullaby Woman once sang to her on their mat on the floor, although she will not remember the words.

17

Penny
Flat 1B

Penny sits on the edge of her bed and looks at the two children whom she has only let past the threshold, closing the door behind them. For now, she cannot let them any further into the flat.

'What is your name?' Penny asks the little girl, realising she had never asked when they had last met in the corridor.

'Melody,' the girl says her English name and switches the baby to her other hip.

'Do you know what we're supposed to do next?' Penny asks her.

When Penny speaks to her she tries not to sound alarmed or confused, although she is both. And extremely uneasy. She watches as Melody puts the baby on the floor and sits next to him to play with Susannah. Penny thinks that as long as they stay there, by the door, and she stays on the edge of the bed, then she can manage it.

'We're supposed to wait here. A nice policeman is going to come,' Melody says. She is half-hearted in her playing. She is fake smiling and cooing for the baby, keeping him happy, like an adult would.

Her words cause a clenching in Penny's abdomen. Police just won't do. Not here.

'Policeman? What do you mean? Did your nanny call the police?' she says and clears her throat. Her chest tightens.

'Um, I don't have a nanny,' Melody says, remembering her promise to Woman, but also unsure how to keep it.

She looks at the floor and continues, 'But she said you are a very nice lady and there will be a nice policeman and you will keep us safe and make sure we get to the nice place where they will let me go to school and have birthday parties.'

'Yes, but did she call the police?' Penny tries not to raise her voice, but she's losing control of it.

Melody, sensing Penny's nervousness, continues, 'Because my brother has gone to do business like my mother told him to and she will not be back. She is away with my grandmother and they can't take any more planes because they are all shut down and the police are going to keep them away and my father is very sick. I left him a note.'

The only words Penny can hear in all the child's ramblings are police, police, police—

'But what do we do?' Penny asks, sitting on her hands, trying not to rock back and forth on the bed. She does not want to scare the child.

'I don't know,' Melody says. 'We're supposed to wait—'

'Yes, but for how long? And where?' Penny can't catch her breath. 'And how?' Penny asks the girl.

Penny suddenly realises that the woman from the bins doesn't know who she is. She doesn't know Penny is the Tube Horror Mum who left her baby on the train. And the woman left these children with her. She never would have left these children here if she had known.

Penny had said 'yes' when the laundrette woman, this girl's nanny, or whoever she really was, asked for help; Penny said she would open the door when she knocked and she would answer. And Penny wanted to help, she is trying to help, but now the baby starts to cry, Susannah darts under the bed, the room is hot, and Penny doesn't know what to do.

The girl picks up the baby, he screams, he cries, and all Penny can think is, '*The neighbours will hear, the neighbours know what I did, they'll think I kidnapped these children, oh God, oh God . . .*' Penny puts her hands over her ears to block the screaming, the crying, Olivia's small voice saying '*Bun Bun, Bun Bun,*' remembering how she said it over and over and over again until, until—

'Can you please take the top off this? If we put it in his bottle, he'll stop crying,' Melody says, standing just an inch away from Penny at the edge of the bed, handing her the formula. Her round, dark eyes look into Penny's, expectantly.

'I'm sorry, I can't—' she starts to say, trying to think of a way to get the children out of her flat, a way to find the woman from the laundrette, but then Melody says, 'Yes, you can, you just twist the top off—'

'No, I can't—' Penny is almost shouting now.

'Here, take the baby, I'll do it,' Melody says, and she holds out the screaming baby to Penny.

But just before Melody lets go of him, just before the baby reaches her, Penny jumps.

Mable
Flat 3B

Mable coughs once, twice, a third time. She is sitting at the table doing her budget for the month. She has received her pension and she has worked out that once she pays for her utilities and food, the rest will go towards her monthly contribution to the Brotherhood.

'Oh, wait,' Mable says. She remembers reading about a sister and her family in the Philippines, and she adds a few extra pounds to support the ministry in that faraway place. The elders should be pleased with that.

Of course, Mable could use a new tube of that cream for her arthritis, and it might be nice to make some jerk chicken with rice and peas for supper for a change, but it's nothing that her hot-water bottle and a tin of sardines can't solve. The money is needed for the salvation of others, and there is nothing more worthy of the pension she had worked her entire life for than that.

There is a knock at the door. She pulls her dressing gown around her close, and shuffles over in her slippers to look through the peephole. It's that woman, that foreign girl from the laundry.

'Yes, all right, I hear you, I know who she is,' Mable says to Jehovah, before she opens the door, ready to be the vessel of her God's will.

Carla
Flat 1A

For the past hour she's ignored the sound of the baby crying next door. She's trying to remember what the lawyer told her, what the lawyer said, but she can't think with all the noise. She assumes that Wackadoo is doing something weird, like watching birth videos over and over again on YouTube at full volume or pretending to cry herself to see how loud she could get. Or maybe it was her cat. Do cats make noises like that? Carla's sure she's heard cats do that. She's heard foxes do that, right? That high-pitched cry they do that sounds like a baby being tortured. Maybe she was watching fox videos, that crazy bitch.

Woman
Flat 3B

Woman watches Penny take the children into her flat. She knows it is hard for Penny to cross her doorway. She is sure that Penny will not leave her flat to look for her. Once Penny has closed her door, Woman runs up to the third floor. She knocks and Mable opens the door.

'Yes, darlin', can I help you?' Mable says. The old woman is not surprised to see her.

'Please, help,' Woman says.

'Yes, help,' Mable says, searching Woman's face.

'PC Grant, please. Children, 1B,' Woman says.

'What is your name, darlin'?' Mable asks, and takes hold of Woman's thin wrist.

'No. Children only,' Woman says.

Mable
Flat 3B

She doesn't understand why this troubled girl wants the officer, or who these children are, or why she wants the officer to go to Penny's flat, but Mable does not question it. She knows there is trouble, she sees the demons trying to impose their will, and so she will do what she is asked. She does not push for the girl's name if she does not want to give it. She can never know all the mysterious ways in which Jehovah works, she can only do His bidding, and so she nods at the girl. It is enough to know that she is running from evil and needs protection. And Mable and Jehovah will provide it. Mable looks at Woman's threadbare T-shirt and her thin cardigan with the holes in the sleeves.

'Wait,' Mable says, and gives the girl her wool winter coat hanging on the peg by the door. She gently puts a hand to Woman's face and says, 'Jehovah sent you to me, I will do what you ask. Know that He is watching over you. Go in His grace.'

The women hold hands tightly. And then let go.

PC Grant
At home, around the corner from Bedford Road

He has just got home from an eighteen-hour shift, dead on his feet. It's not like the stabbings and domestic incidents have stopped. Old people still call the cops on their neighbours for no reason and people still crash their cars and husbands still beat their wives. They do it more now, actually. If anything, the atmosphere is more electric than usual; the streets are empty but paved with silent panic.

When he gets home, he opens the door of his empty fridge, and wonders when he's going to get to the shop, and how he's going to see his dad.

He cracks open a beer, and the cold bitter bite of the first sip makes his shoulders drop for the first time that day. But then the doorbell rings.

'Fuck,' he says, but he's so tired he doesn't know if he said it out loud or in his head.

'Fuck,' he says again, under his breath, when he looks through the peephole and sees who it is.

He can pretend not to be here, but every time he's tried that she's waited him out. Last time he pretended he wasn't in when she knocked, forgot about her, and thirty minutes later he nearly jumped out of his skin when he was leaving for the pub and opened his front door to find her standing there, in his doorway, looking at him like she would a disobedient child. He has no choice. He opens the door.

'Evenin', Officer, sorry to bother you so late, but I've been asked to come and fetch you,' Mable says.

Penny
Flat 1B

Baby lands with a hard bounce on the mattress. It's a big bounce, he catches air, his neck braced for impact, his head whipping forward. But the shock of it makes him stop crying for a moment. The shock of it makes Penny stop crying too.

Melody, functioning calmly, as though she has not been left with a woman who has just dropped her baby brother, takes the bottle she's prepared and climbs up on to the bed. She props Baby in her lap, and he stops crying once the bottle is in his grasp.

She says to Penny, 'I'm hungry. May I have something to eat, please?'

Penny, leaning against the far wall of the flat, as far from the children as she can get, takes stock of the situation. She's quite capable, quite bright, this little girl. The baby seems all right, as long as he has milk and his sister.

Yes, we can, Penny says, internally, silently. *Yes, we can*.

She doesn't know how long they will be waiting or what exactly they are waiting for, but if she focuses on the present then she can get through this. *Yes, we can*. Something so awful was happening to that woman that she had to leave these children here. *Yes, we can*. And Penny feels a feeling like pride, like purpose, when she realises that she has been called upon to look after them. *Yes, we can*. Penny can do that, look after children. There was a time, not so long ago, when she knew how to do that.

Yes. We. Can.

Penny goes to her closet, finds the shoes that are a size too small and puts them on.

She clears her throat and says to Melody, 'Do you like chicken nuggets?'

PC Grant
Doorstep of his house

'It is urgent that you come, Officer. There are evildoers in our midst and there are children in need of protection. Please hurry,' Mable says.

PC Grant is about to say, 'What are you on about, Miss Mable?' and then something clicks.

The dry-cleaning ticket stapled on to the tag of his shirt a few weeks back. It had a dark red-brown drop on it, like a splatter mark. Like a dried drop of blood. It's his job to know what dried blood looks like. But he shrugged and pretended to himself that he didn't know what it was and he tore off the tag and threw it in the bin in the kitchen while he waited for the kettle to boil.

He had just wanted a quick cuppa before he left for his shift. He poured hot water over his PG Tips and thought about when he'd be able to get over to his dad's to help him clear the loft like he'd been asking for months, and he thought about how he'd have to avoid PC Rutherford after their kiss at the pub, and whether one kiss with a man meant he was gay. And he thought about how many years he had wanted a kiss like that, and how many years he had pretended not to. He thought about everything he could think about to avoid thinking about the little white ticket with its number, thirty-three, and the dark red-brown spot that nagged him from the bin.

They'd had training in this sort of thing. That Turkish girl in the laundrette – or Moroccan or whatever she was – she didn't look right, it didn't feel right, he knew it wasn't right. But for fuck's sake, he had enough on his plate. He didn't have the time or the energy to follow hunches about trafficking – based on no evidence, mind you – in the neighbourhood laundrette. He wasn't Columbo, goddammit.

'All right, Miss Mable, I'll be right with you,' he says, pulling on his coat and grabbing his badge and radio and keys and not thinking about the ticket stapled into his shirt.

Carla
Flat 1B

She hears the bleeps of the police radio and then pounding on the door and, oh shit, maybe Crazy really has lost it this time. Carla opens her door to see what's happening.

'What the hell's going on?' she asks, recognising the tall policeman, the one who always got his coffee at Justin's the same time she did in the mornings. Next to him was Mable, in her lavender church hat, her winter boots, and her fleece bath-robe, which Carla assumes she's wearing because she's also a loon.

'Do you know who lives here?' PC Grant asks Carla, recognising her from the neighbourhood and assessing, in the current circumstances, that she might be the sanest person here.

'Yeah, of course, it's Penny,' Carla says, and then, 'Mable, what happened?'

'I was asked to bring the officer. I have reason to believe that there are children in this flat in need of protection,' she says to Carla.

'Kids? What kids? She doesn't have kids,' Carla says.

'Then whose children are they?' PC Grant asks.

'I don't know, I thought she wasn't allowed around kids because of what she did that time on the— oh,' Carla stops herself.

'Oh, no', she says.

18

Woman
Bedford Road

I do not know which way the café is, Mother. But there are lights at the end of the road. I walk quickly, but I do not run so that I won't be noticed. Storefronts, people, cars. The ground shifts beneath my feet, Mother; with every step I push against the air. It requires all my strength. It is hard to see although light is everywhere. This city is so big, Mother. I have not even left the road on which the building stands and already everything is too big.

The woman from the North said her café was at the end of the road. I stand outside for a moment, to see if the people inside are from Home Country. A young man, very tall, sees me and comes to the door. He must recognise our people in my face and he says, without hesitation, 'Go down the alley, come to the back.' He says this in our language, Mother, but his accent is strange, it is not his mother tongue.

I do as he says. There is a small dark alley between the buildings. I walk through it to a doorway that is lit at the end, and the woman of the North stands there, her arms folded across her chest.

'What do you need, Sister?' she asks.

I hesitate, Mother. We cannot trust all of our compatriots here in Better Life. Perhaps she knows Sir and Madame. Perhaps she knows Agent. Perhaps she knows you, or she knew Father. I do not know if after I leave she will send someone after me, to retrieve me for Sir, or to keep me for herself. The risk is great, Mother.

I say, 'Passport.'

'British or Home Country?' she asks. I stay silent, not knowing the answer.

'British is riskier. Do you speak English?' she asks.

'No,' I say.

'Then you take the Home Country one, no one will ever believe you got a British passport and they care about their passports very much. They will send you to prison because they'll think you've stolen it.' I nod, afraid to say anything or question her.

'You have money?' she asks.

'How much is it?' I say.

'How much do you have?' she asks. I know better than to answer this.

'I will give you £200. Please, passport,' is all I say. Sir kept a lockbox on the top shelf of his closet. I knew this from hanging his shirts there. I took it down while he slept and found the key on his key ring. I tried every key until it opened and took £500, although there were stacks of money. I did not want to take too much knowing it could be added to my debt. That somehow, someday, they will find me, or they will find you, Mother, or they have already found you, and demand repayment.

'Emma!' she calls. 'Home Country!'

'Okay, Mum,' a young voice calls back, in English.

We wait for a few moments, Mother, and I say nothing.

'Do you want some shoes?' she says, looking down at my feet.

'No thank you,' I say, afraid this is a trap.

Finally, Mother, a young woman comes down. Emma. She is tall, like the young man. I give her mother the money. She hands me the passport. Inside, it is her picture with a Home Country name.

'So pretty,' I say. 'She looks nothing like me.'

'They will not notice, Sister. They think we all look alike.'

'Thank you,' I say, and turn to leave. A cold chill runs down my spine when she yells, 'Stop! Wait!'

I stand still, unsure if now I will die. If now, someone will finally kill me.

'Here.' Emma runs up to me. She hands me a pair of simple canvas trainers.

'I cannot pay for these,' I say.

'Free of charge,' she answers, awkwardly in our language. She smiles.

'Good luck,' she says, Mother.

Good luck.

Penny
Flat 1B

I hear Carla condemning me in the corridor. She explains who I am, and it takes only a few words for the officer to remember the story that was in all the papers and of course he will assume the worst about my present circumstances. He will assume that I have stolen them, hurt them, degraded them. It will never occur to him that I protected them. That I was called upon to shield them.

He knocks on the door again.

'Is that the nice policeman?' Melody asks. Inside.

'What's her name?' The officer says to someone. Outside.

'Mrs Penny Danford,' Mable answers. Outside.

'Should we open the door?' Melody says. Inside.

'How many kids in here, Miss Mable?' The officer. Outside.

'Are you going to answer it?' Melody. Inside.

'Do you want me to talk to her?' Carla. Outside.

Turn one way, turn the other way, left, right, and back again.

'Will they help us?' Melody asks.

The baby cries. Inside.

'No. They never do,' I say, and I put on my face mask and reach for my boiler suit.

Woman
Bedford Road

The sirens get closer, Mother. The police. The ambulance. They stop in front of the building. I see them when I round the corner past the café.

I hope I have done right.

I hope, and I will never know.

Penny
Flat 1B

The officer pounds on the door. He can holler all he likes, but we are not ready yet.

I put Melody in an old dress shirt of Jamie's, one with a frayed collar he could no longer wear to work which I had adopted as a nightshirt long ago. It reaches past her knees and is a sufficient substitute for a boiler suit. I give her a blue surgical mask to wear. And straighten her tiara.

For the baby I reach to the back of one of the drawers I cleared out, where I put the things to which I could never say goodbye, and I found Olivia's red hoodie. They found it in my bag when they took me to hospital, and though they gave Bun Bun back to Jamie, the hoodie was overlooked, and it was there in the plastic bag of my belongings that they handed back to me when I was released. It is too big for the baby, but will provide satisfactory protection for him. He won't abide the face mask, but he seems to like the hood, so that will have to do.

'I'm scared,' Melody says, after we dress her brother. The sounds outside the door are getting louder, the blue lights of the emergency vehicles on the street below flashing into the windows and casting intermittent shadows on the walls.

I pull down my mask and say, 'So am I, but that's why we're wearing all of this. It's like a force field, to protect us. I told her I would keep you safe, and I will.'

She sits on my bed and puts her hand in mine and with my other hand I knock on the wall.

'Daniel? Are you there?' I say, as loudly as I can over all the commotion I can hear through the door.

'Miss, are you okay?' He sounds alarmed. As he should be.

'Daniel, listen carefully. I expect that I am going to have to be away for some time. I would be most grateful, dear, if you would please look after Susannah in my absence. Can I trust you to do that for me?'

'Miss?'

'She is likely to be very upset this evening, and I find that in turbulent times she prefers salmon. It calms her nerves. Be sure to give her the salmon tonight. There's a good lad.'

Carla
First floor corridor

'Penny, if you don't open the door, they're going to break it down!' I yell as loud as I can. But she won't do it.

There's no other option. They have to do it. There's kids in there. Jesus, Penny, what are you thinking?

And just before the police are ready to break in, she opens it, and steps out, holding hands with a little girl wearing a man's shirt and a tiara, and, in her other arm, she's holding a baby, tear-stained and puffy-cheeked, rubbing his tired eyes with a pudgy fist, a surgical face mask hanging like a bib around his neck. She's wearing her going-out suit, the trench coat over the boiler suit, her baseball cap and surgical mask hiding most of her face. She leans down and says something to the little girl.

And then she straightens up and she says, 'I am Penny Danford. I abhor the intrusion of the state into the personal lives of its citizens—' and she keeps going, but it's hard to hear her once the cops grab her, and pin her to the ground.

Melody
First floor corridor

There are many people. I am looking for the nice policeman. I don't know which one he is. I squeeze the cat lady's hand and she leans down and says to me, 'Don't be afraid, look in the shirt pocket.'

I look and it is sparkling and gold inside the pocket, sprinkled with glitter. A magic pocket.

'Force field,' she says.

Mable
First floor corridor

When they cuff her, I say, 'Officer, is that necessary?' but they pay me no mind.

I say, louder, 'She's daft, but she's no criminal, she was helping that girl, that lost one; she asked for help, like she asked me.' I could see it right away, what that girl had sorted out. But who listens to old women.

Penny, she tries to explain herself, but who listens to sick women.

She says, 'She ate out of the bins, I saw her. She wore my clothes, my running socks, she asked me for help, to keep the children here. The little girl said a nice policeman would come, she asked me for help—'

But they have no interest in what she says.

She struggles on the ground. I do the only thing I can and turn to my Heavenly Father in prayer. He is the only one who listens. I ask Him to protect her. But I don' think He hears me

281

tonight, because, though she comes out her door with great dignity, Penny can't take a step no further and they have to drag her. And she starts to scream. And it takes four men to handle her, the fear in her is so strong.

And I don' understand. Because I heeded His call and I did what was asked. And He answers me, always.

But not now, not tonight.

19

Tuesday, The Following Week

Melody
Council Children's Home, South London

To the lady policeman, she says, 'No, she didn't hurt me, she's nice. She let me play with the cat. I had chicken nuggets.'

To the man policeman, she says, 'I don't know where Mother and Grandmother went but it was on a plane.'

When he asks again, she says, 'I don't know where. Brother said they can't come back because there are no more planes.'

To the social worker, she says, 'I was alone, just me and Father and Baby. Brother went to do business. There was no one else with us.'

When the lady policewoman asks her again, she says, 'I don't know where Brother went. He didn't come back.'

Melody says to everyone who asks her questions over and over again, 'I was alone with Baby, I was scared, Father was sick, I went to find the nice cat lady.'

She remembers not to tell their real names, like Mother said. She remembers not to tell them about Woman, like Woman said.

Penny
A large NHS hospital, Inpatient
Mental Health Services

'Is there anything else you can tell us about this woman, Mrs Danford?' the policeman asks. It is a different one to the one who was there that night. He is standing far away from her, not the way police usually stand, so close. She can't see his face properly because of his mask, but she knows it's someone different. Someone not in uniform.

'Where's my cat?' she asks. She sees the policeman look at the nurse.

The nurse says gently, 'She's with your neighbour, remember?'

'I think she was from a post-Soviet country, a very cold one, maybe Ukraine, maybe Belarus, some kind of Russian. Do you know if they gave her salmon? She had dark hair. She prefers salmon when she's distressed,' Penny says to the wall because she cannot look at the officer directly.

'Right. And you're sure you don't know her name?' he asks, although he knows it is futile.

'No. She ate from the bins. She wore my socks. She said answer if I knock, and I rarely have visitors, so when I heard the knock – it's quite important that she's fed regularly, routine is vital – I knew it was her and when I answered, she wasn't there, but there was the princess and the baby,' Penny says.

The policeman turns to the nurse and says to her, as though Penny cannot hear him, as though Penny is not there, 'Delusional, right?'

The nurse shakes her head discreetly.

But Penny does hear him. And she worries about Susannah and she worries about Woman. And she understands now that Woman chose her because Woman knows that no one would believe her. And Penny knows it too.

Mable
Flat 3B

'Can you describe her for us, Mrs Cartwright, the woman you said had asked you to find PC Grant?' the detective asks.

'Yes,' Mable says. 'She was surrounded by evil and hounded by demons.'

'Thank you, you've already told us that. Could you perhaps provide a physical description?' the detective says.

'Skinny, dark hair, so skinny. She was maybe from Mauritius or the Philippines – have you heard of that place? There is nowhere that Jehovah's hand does not reach,' Mable replies.

'And this woman, she asked you specifically to find PC Grant?' the detective asks.

'When Jehovah asks us to intercede in the prevention of wickedness, we must answer the call,' Mable says.

Later, when the detective confers with her colleague, she says, 'She's seventy-eight. I mean, she seems healthy, but she's not all there. She probably just got Grant because she knows him and she got a little muddled up. Maybe she ran into Penny earlier and got wound up about something.'

'How does Grant know her?' her colleague asks.

'She's known in the neighbourhood – Jehovah's Witness, she knocks on his door occasionally,' Sullivan says.

'Oh, well.' Her colleague shakes his head. 'Do we have anyone else, anyone not insane?'

Later, when Mable is in her flat having a cup of tea, she thinks about how the police spoke to her in condescending, gentle tones, as though she were a child. She thinks about how easy it was to throw them off their questions by talking about demons and wickedness. She knows they expect so little of the righteous. That the righteous are rarely believed. Mable knows that the laundry girl knew this too.

Carla
Flat 1A

'I never saw those kids before in my life,' Carla says to the female detective.

'And a thin, dark-haired woman, possibly East European, East Asian, South Asian, or Filipino? Did you see anyone fitting any such description on that night?' she asks.

'No. No one,' Carla says.

'Any woman fitting that description who is often in the building? A cleaner, perhaps?'

'No, sorry. I don't think we have a cleaner, do we?' Carla says.

The man across the hall in 1C gives similar answers. And the young couple in 3A. As do the three young women in 3C, although they do recall seeing a woman mopping the lobby once. But they are sure she was Black, although they do not remember her face.

PC Grant
Police Station

He sits at his desk, thinking about what he wrote in his report, what he told the detective, whether he left any holes, whether what he said matched what he wrote.

He reviews the scene again, as he has every day, multiple times, since that night.

He questions his actions. He pushes back from the desk, puts his head in his hands.

The safety of the children was the priority. He called child protective services.

Help for the mentally ill woman was the priority. He called the ambulance.

The girl's dead father in the flat on the second floor was the priority. He called the coroner.

He didn't know the dead man would be there. He only had a face mask, one he brought from a box he got at Homebase for when he was varnishing the floors last year, but it wasn't the right kind for finding dead bodies that pose a possible risk of infection in a pandemic. He didn't have gloves. And he is pretty sure he is fucked and going to get sick.

He went up to the flat the little girl said was her family's, 2A. The door was open. He found her father, dead, in the master bedroom. He saw some women's clothes, shoes, purses, but otherwise the bedroom closet was empty, as though a mum had gone on a trip.

There was a children's bedroom with a crib and princess bed. A thin blue mat on the ground. A kitchen with a sink full of dirty dishes. An ironing board in the living room, three crisp shirts on hangers, and a bag of wrinkled clothes waiting their turn to be pressed. He will not admit it, but he is relieved that none of the shirts on hangers are his. He shakes his head and says to himself that there is nothing unusual about an ironing board left out in someone's home.

There was no woman in the flat.

There were priorities. There were children, a mentally ill woman, a dead body. A lethal virus and he probably just caught it. There was no evidence of any other woman other than the statements of an elderly Jehovah's Witness and an incompetent agoraphobe who once left her baby on a train on purpose. And neither statement could be untangled into any kind of sensible explanation, unless demons and apparitions can be considered suspects.

There was no time for instincts about a girl he saw now and then in the laundrette. There was no time to dissect the stories of sick women and old women. There was nothing in the flat to suggest anything other than a mother who went on a trip and/or abandoned her kids, and a father who died in bed when lots of people were dying this way. Nothing to suggest anything other than another sad case of fucking awful people who shouldn't be allowed to fucking have children.

He feels hot. He unbuttons the top two buttons of his uniform shirt. *Did she iron this shirt?*

Let the social workers deal with the kids. Let the doctors deal with the sick woman. It was a brown spot on a laundry tag. It could have been from anything, from anywhere. His job was handling what was real.

The children are safe. The sick woman is in the hospital. The dead body was attended to.

He did everything right. He took care of the immediate needs. He helped everyone who was present and kept them out of danger. He needs to go home. He needs to check on his dad. He files his paperwork, gathers his things, leaves the station.

But deep in the place where he keeps his truths, he knows she was there.

And he hopes she got away.

Master
Men's bathroom, service station two hours outside of London

He quickly washes his face but realises that rushing isn't necessary. He won't be seen because there is no one here. The roadside service stop is almost entirely deserted. But he knows this also means that anything he does is instantly visible to the few people who are around. He skulks out of the bathroom and thinks about, but then does not attempt to purchase, anything at the KFC kiosk, the only one that has remained open with one masked employee, the shelf behind him nearly empty.

When he saw the police car and the ambulance in front of the building, he just kept driving. He didn't know why they were there, but he knew it couldn't be good and he knew he'd have to wait to go in and get his father. He had the pickups, two girls huddled in the back for warmth. He couldn't understand why these girls never brought the right kind of coat with them, why they thought England was going to be a warm country. He pulled over and called his mother. She didn't answer. So he did what he had been trained to do in these instances: he pulled away from the kerb and kept driving.

After he dropped the pickups and made the exchange later that night, he texted his mother to tell her what happened. He asked her, *Do you want me to go back for the kids?*

No, it's not worth the risk.

Are you sure?

They're not our children. They're no longer our concern.

It's been about a week now. His mother told him not to go back to the building under any circumstances and to wait for her instructions. She would make arrangements for him, find him a place to stay with their associates. So far, he has spent every night in the van. So far, he has not heard from her.

Part Four

January 2021

20

Angela
A flat in Epsom

She puts the baby boy down in the crib. She calls him Joseph, which the social worker said his sister said was the name the parents gave him, but he doesn't ever respond to it.

In soothing tones, she says, 'Joseph, now I'm just going to leave you for a minute, but I'm right here,' the way she's done many times before with younger babies, but as soon as she steps anywhere near the door, he cries hysterical, forlorn tears. She knows about separation anxiety and trauma in the under twos, she's had enough of them come through her home over the years. But never one with problems sleeping like this one.

When she can no longer bear the crying, she picks him up and takes him to the living room. He screams and then pushes hard against her, arching his back and kicking her with his fat little legs to get down. Angela watches him crawl as fast as he can to the blue yoga mat she had laid out in front of the TV. She had over-optimistically hoped she might do an online class tonight.

'Joseph?' she says, as she watches him put his head down, and she hears his tiny sigh of relief. Within seconds he falls asleep the way babies that age do, one cheek on the mat, head turned to the side, arms at his sides, knees tucked up under his tummy. A perfect child's pose.

'Guess you're a little yogi,' Angela says, lightly rubbing his back, as Baby sleeps on the mat and dreams of being held in loving arms that belong with a face he no longer remembers.

Baby's Mother
A flat above a nail salon, Soho

It still aches, where they cut her to take him out. She counts the months and knows he is more than a year and a half old now. When she worked in the nail salon near Soho it was so busy, so many customers, one after the other, all day long, she did not have time to think about him. She only thought of him at night, when she lay on her mattress on the floor of the room she shared with the other girls above the salon. Or when a customer would come in with her baby, a tiny, soft mound wrapped in tiny, soft clothes. Then she would look straight down at the customer's nails and not at the baby and she would think of her son and her scar would ache.

The nail salon closed. It is still closed. She and the girls do a different kind of work now. The clients are men who come to the room, not soft women with soft, tiny babies. Not many men. Many are scared off by the sickness now. But there are enough. Enough for her and the others to earn their food that the salon owner buys, but nothing else. No money to send home until the salon reopens.

She thinks now, as the next man comes in, that Madame was right. Her son was blessed and he also was a blessing. A blessing for her, because he cleared her family's debts, but also, in being given up by his mother, he was blessed. He would have Better Life. Madame promised his life would be better without her. She believes it is true.

'Hello,' she says to the man who has just come in.

She puts on her mask and gets back to work.

PC Grant
On his way home

He doesn't usually walk down Bedford Road, not since he started doing his own washing and ironing, but he fancied some noodles, so he thought he'd drop by Justin's for a takeaway.

'You managing this place all right, Mali?' he asks as he waits for his order.

'Just fine, we'll be okay, people still eat, you know?' Molly says, and hands him his order. 'On the house, front-line worker,' she says and winks above her mask.

On his way down the road he walks past the building. The sign for the laundrette has been taken down. The windows are boarded with cardboard signs announcing it as the future location of a Tesco Express. He thinks of the housebound lady who lives there, if she still lives there. He wonders if Miss Mable still lives there, or if she got sick. He hasn't seen her since that night. He thinks about the laundrette girl and wonders where she is, and then pushes back the thought.

When he gets home a few minutes later, he opens his door and finds a letter from Miss Mable in his post, declaring the Good News, and he smiles. He's glad she's okay.

His phone dings as he puts his noodles in a bowl. Rutherford. He can't get used to calling him John.

We still on for this weekend?

He texts back, *Have to check on Dad Saturday morning, but I'll text you after.*

Okay x

Okay, PC Grant texts back, his thumb hovering over the *x* for a moment, before he taps it and presses send.

Penny
Flat 1A

'Thank you, Daniel, that's so kind of you,' she says, as he puts the grocery bags down outside Penny's door. She tries to smile with her eyes while she gestures at her mask, reminding him to put his on.

'Oh right, sorry, Miss,' he says, pulling up his mask, accepting the hand sanitiser that she holds out with her gloved hands.

'How's Susannah?' he asks, looking over Penny's shoulder into the flat to see if he can see her. He's so tall now, she thinks.

'Not so well, but I'm keeping her comfortable. I'm afraid it won't be long now,' she says, as bravely as she can.

'I'm sure she'd like to see you, I'll bring her to the door,' she says.

'Oh, you don't have to—'

'No, it will do her good, it will raise her spirits to know you're here. Just a minute,' she says, and goes to fetch Susannah on the pillow she's adopted as her sickbed. Penny picks up the pillow, careful not to touch the fragile creature so she doesn't cause undue pain. She shouldn't move Susannah at all, but Daniel was such a help looking after her in the months that Penny was in hospital, she thought he should have a moment with her while Susannah was still in the earthly realm. She lays down the pillow in the doorway gently. The boy leans down to lightly stroke her head.

'Hey, Susie girl,' he whispers. 'Sorry you're poorly.' And then, to Penny, 'She's so skinny, Miss.'

'I know,' Penny says, holding back tears. Daniel stands up and says, 'I'm sorry, Miss. She's a good cat. I'd better get home. Mum said she'll call you later.'

'Tell her I'd like that,' Penny says.

She brings Susannah back into the flat, places cat and pillow on the bed, and puts away her groceries. She holds the loaf of Hovis Granary Medium for a moment. She feels its weight in her hands. There were years she didn't have a loaf of bread in this flat because it could not be slid through the gap under the chain. She still doesn't like going to the shops. If Daniel or Mary Rose are going for Carla, they always knock and ask if they can get her anything to save her the trip.

But she does manage, about once a fortnight, to get out and go herself. She finds it much easier now that most people wear masks and there are barriers between the cashiers and customers and hand sanitiser available. The new state of things has eased her anxiety. She sees the empty buses and knows she's not the only one who doesn't like being packed into a box full of strangers. She's not alone in thinking about breathing the air that others exhale. She doesn't feel so bad about the library, or the cinema, or any of the places that are not within her zone of safety, because no one else goes to those places now either. Her avoidance of these areas is no longer strange.

Penny feels, for the first time, like she belongs in the world she is living in. When catastrophe struck and the world around her panicked and scrambled to react and drew inwards, closing its doors, shuttering its windows, covering all of its faces, she was relieved. Everyone had finally joined her, learned the secret she had known all along.

Penny knows it will change. There will be a return to the venerated Before, and she will have to readjust. But she knows too that it will never be exactly like Before. There will be vestiges left inside of people of this time, that they will carry with them always. She will always have something in common with people, and a few of them, remembering their own fear, may even understand her.

Penny checks the time. She sits in front of her computer and props it up on a stack of books so that the camera catches her at a better angle. The new meds haven't caused as much weight gain as the old ones, but she still doesn't want to present a double chin. Double chins are not compliant.

'Hello, Penny, how are you today?' her new social worker, Tabitha, Alice's maternity cover, says from the screen.

'All right, I suppose,' Penny replies.

'That's good to hear. What have you been doing with yourself?' Tabitha chirps, trying to draw her into conversation.

'Oh, well, I've been watching my cat die, quite a slow and painful death. It is traumatic and agonising, but also very beautiful in its way, very poetic to watch the circle of life complete its final rotation in the small existence of Miss Susannah Caterson, elevating her inconsequential presence in our world, for just a moment, to that of a being in the next realm, which we Earth dwellers have no real knowledge of,' Penny says, smiling to herself internally.

She watches Tabitha try not to change her facial features as she scrambles for a response. Tabitha is far less experienced than Alice was, and so not as adept at maintaining a neutral facial expression. But that is quite all right, as Penny is more than willing to assist Tabitha in practising this important skill.

Melody
A house in Croydon

She sits looking out the window.

She looks at the dark street. Two of the houses across the road still have lights up, their colours dancing round the windows and bushes. They are for Christmastime. Christmas was not observed by her family, she only knew about it from the telly, but these nice people did a Christmas for her anyway. She received a chemistry set, a book about important women in history, and some new clothes, but none of them were pink. She thought this magic of Christmas they went on about all the time was not really so magical if these were the sort of gifts girls got.

But she does like the lights. Outside the windows of her old flat there was only the playground she had never played in. The nice people here have taken her to a playground. When she stood there, not moving, the man did not understand, at first, that she was waiting for instructions. She saw him look at the woman as the woman looked back at him. Then the man showed her what to do – how to go down the slide, how to sit on the swing. Later on, at bedtime, when Melody took the blanket off the too soft bed and lay down on the floor, she could hear the man and the woman talking in the next room. The woman said that they would need to take her out to play more. She said it would help her lose weight.

She remembers only a few things from that night. She remembers Woman, waiting by the stairs and watching, while she knocked on the cat lady's door. She remembers the cat. She remembers her tiara, the one that made her a warrior queen, and how she doesn't have it anymore because the mean girl – who was at the house she stayed in for a few nights before she went to the house that she lived in before this one – took it. She had to leave the house she was in before this one because the woman got sick and went to hospital and the man said he was very sorry but they only took her at a push in the first place, and they couldn't keep her now after all, because the woman died.

She remembers when the people who were not police, the social workers, told her that Father died. They asked her if she was upset. She wasn't. They wanted to know if she had any questions. She didn't.

She remembers the most important thing, that Baby lives with a woman in a place called Epsom. She does not know where that is, but when she is older, she will go there and find him. The nice social worker people said they will do everything they can to find a house that she and Baby can live in together, but for right now, they just don't have one. But they will try, they said.

Melody only knows that she must remember this word, Epsom, so she can find Baby one day, in case there is no home with room for them both.

Melody's Mother
The compound in Capital City

Sir and Madame have been gone many months and there has been no word of when they will return and so the house remains empty and she remains unpaid. When they are away, she is responsible for putting dust covers on the furniture and mopping the floors and washing the windows. She checks that the gardener is doing his work and the garden is not over-grown. But they usually send word and payment through their agent. She assumes they cannot travel now because of the virus. It is why the tourists have stopped visiting and why her sister and brother lost their good jobs at the big hotels. It is why they are all hungry now. They make sure her nieces and nephews eat first, for they are only children.

One of her nieces was born near the time of her own daughter's birth. She looks at this girl, her hair, her eyes, and wonders about her own girl, but does not speak of her. This painful emptiness where her daughter should be, but is not, is her fault, she knows. It is the consequence of having been so beautiful and young, enticing Sir the way she did, so that he could not stop himself from having her. From loving her. This is what he told her – that he could not control himself; she was irresistible. She had given him no other choice.

At least the child is with her father. At least she can see her whenever the family returns to Home Country, to this house. The child doesn't know who she is, of course. She calls Madame 'Mother'. It was their condition for keeping her job and continuing the pregnancy, that the child be raised as their daughter.

But when the family was last here, she heard the child say 'Mother', and so she turned her head. And then she worried, because she saw that Madame did not.

Carla
Flat 1A

Carla finishes making dinner for Daniel and Mary Rose. She makes up a plate of chicken and potatoes and broccoli and says, 'Mary Rose, go take this up to Mable.'

'Do I have to? She goes on for ages, Mum, isn't it Daniel's turn?' Mary Rose complains, without looking up from her phone.

'Just go, please,' Carla says, handing her the plate.

'I'm in the middle of something,' Mary Rose whines.

Carla says, 'Come on, if we're not careful, she'll get Jehovah to turn on us, so you'd better get up there and give her this 'cause we need to keep Him on our side.'

She tries to keep her hands busy. She pretends that making dinner is all-consuming. There is an email on her phone that she's too afraid to read.

Penny
Flat 1B

Penny taps her fingers audibly and sighs loudly, consulting her watch with an exaggerated swing of her arm as Tabitha consults her notes on screen, and says 'um' a few times as she looks for a follow-up question. Penny believes that she is more than justified in making inexperienced social workers feel uncomfortable. It is these tiny acts of retribution against the system that enable her to withstand the continued intrusion of the state through its medical ambassadors in the NHS. She finds it therapeutic, this disruption disguised as compliance. Her small rebellions masked as submission.

Tabitha finally says, 'Um, well, I'm sorry to hear that, how have you been coping with Susannah's illness? I know she's very spe—'

'What? What? Sorry, Tabby, can you hear me?' Penny says, moving her face in close to the camera and then moving it out, pretending to push buttons to fix the transmission. Tabitha told her at their first meeting that she would rather Penny not call her Tabby.

'Tabby? Tabby?' she calls out, and watches Tabitha move forward in her seat to adjust her computer.

Tabitha says, 'It doesn't look like anything's wrong with my connection, Penny. And it's funny how this does keep happening every time I—'

'Oh, I'm sorry, bad connection, bad connec—' Penny shakes her head and leaves the call and finishes the word, '—tion', out loud as she smiles and shuts her laptop.

Mable
Flat 3B

'Oh, thank you. You're too kind,' Mable says to Mary Rose, accepting the plate of hot food. Mable is suddenly ravenous, having not eaten anything except a few rich tea biscuits since morning.

'That's okay,' says Mary Rose, and she smiles and turns to leave as quickly as she can before Mable can rope her into an hour-long Good News session.

Mable calls to her back, 'Thank your mother for me—'

'Okay, fine,' Mary Rose says as she skips down the stairs.

Mable waits a moment at the door until she hears the girl reach the last step.

She is the only person Mable has seen today. Carla sends up a plate with one of the children every other day or so, but Mable prefers the boy. He always stays to chat for a while.

She closes the door, gets her cutlery, and sits down at her small table. She looks at the dinner Carla has made and calculates that she can have one third of the chicken and one potato. She will have one bite of the broccoli, because she really hates broccoli, but she will, of course, let nothing go to waste. She is able to make Carla's dinner plates stretch to cover at least two or three more meals every time, supplemented with crackers and tea. She reheats all of the vegetables that she hates, smothering them in a sauce she concocts with some Dunn's River Jerk Seasoning, the one condiment she allows herself to buy, and eats them for breakfast, to get them out of the way.

'Ah, forgot the tea,' Mable says to herself, and she goes back to the kitchen to put the kettle on. She moves slowly, more slowly than she used to. Her days feel very long now that she cannot take the Good News to the people. The Kingdom Hall stopped all in-person meetings and suspended all door-to-door ministry. It has been a time of loneliness and reflection, these past months when she has been alone all day in her flat, no one to share the Truth with, no one to study with, and no one to call on.

A sister or brother will call her on the telephone every so often, and they'll have a chat and read the Bible together. But to Mable's great irritation, every time they call, they try to convince her to get a computer or a smartphone so she could come to online meetings and stay connected to the Society.

'Don't you have a son or daughter, grandchildren, Sister Mable, that can come and help you?' the brother or sister will ask.

And Mable will repeat, 'No, it's just me,' remembering with a pain that grows deeper and wider the older she gets that her sister is sleeping under the ground, waiting to be reunited with her in Paradise. She never tells the caller that her children were disfellowshipped long ago, that they stopped believing, that as soon as they were each old enough to leave her home they also left the faith, leaving her alone with the Truth. And that there are grandchildren who have not been raised in Jehovah's light, and so she has never met them.

She never tells the brother or sister that when the fire struck her flat that terrible night, she was not able to rescue her sister but she was able to rescue the biscuit tin where she keeps the twenty-six Christmas cards her sons have sent her, twenty-seven if you count the one just passed, but that she answered none of them, because her commitment to Jehovah does not allow her to be in contact with those who have rejected the Fellowship.

Mable relies, instead, on the oldest technology there is, and puts pen to paper every morning, writing three letters a day declaring the Good News. Once a week, if it's not raining, she'll take a walk and stop along part of her old route, leaving her missives in letter boxes along with her surplus copies of *The Watchtower* No. 1 2020, the one she had in stock before the pestilence descended. No matter. The Truth, Mable knows, is timeless.

She hopes that the recipients will contact her at the address she provided. She thought about including her phone number too, and then decided against it. She didn't like the idea of strangers unexpectedly calling her at all hours and interrupting her day.

Once a month, after she receives her pension, Mable puts cash in an envelope and puts it through the letter box at the Kingdom Hall, sure that someone is there looking after the place and collecting donations so that the worldwide ministry can continue.

She had been hopeful, when everything started, that this was the beginning of Armageddon, that these were the Last Days, and that, very soon, Paradise would arrive on Earth at last. She was disappointed, however, when a brother informed her on the telephone that the Jehovah's Witness Governing Body had declared that this was not the start of the end. This pestilence, like AIDS and the Spanish Flu before it, was a sign, like all the others, that Jesus was on his way. In the meantime, they were all to adhere to government regulations, look after their health by practising good hygiene, and continue to pray and study. And of course, to donate whatever they could online at JW.org.

Mable sits before her dinner plate. She thinks of all the worldly people she used to engage with every day, and how much she liked them, even though she knew they were all destined for hellfire. They filled her days with colour and challenge. She knows, though, she would never share this with any brother or sister who called her, that there is goodness in some worldly people, there is love in them, and that perhaps they don't all deserve the torture that awaits them. She wishes there were degrees of hell for the non-believers, a place like Purgatory that those Catholics have.

Mable thinks of the worldly people she cares for most, and she bows her head over her plate and prays aloud: 'Jehovah, it is a bleak and weary time, it is a cold time, one in which we long for the warmth of the bright sun of Paradise more than ever. Please look kindly upon Carla for her generosity and thoughtfulness. Please look after the little girl, Olivia, and her father, who needs Your guidance, and her mother, who is fighting her demons within. And please, Father, wherever she might be, look down upon that young woman from the laundry and wrap her in Your grace, protect her from the evil that surrounds her, bring her to salvation in Your name, Amen.'

Penny
Flat 1B

She moves over to her bed and lies down next to her sleeping cat. Susannah's breaths are shallow and stuttering. Penny strokes her gently between the eyes, her favourite spot. They lie like this for a few hours, and when the time is right, and Penny can see the end, she says, huddling in close, face to face, holding her two front paws gently, 'It's all right, darling girl, you can go. You are the bravest, best, most beautiful, loving creature. You are the loveliest cat in the world. And you can go without me. We did it, Susannah, we did, and you don't have to stay here anymore. You go where it won't hurt you anymore. *Yes, we can*, Susannah. *Yes, we can*, and I'll never forget you, my darling girl.'

Mable
Flat 3B

Having finished her rationed supper, Mable rises to do the washing-up. She carefully wraps the leftovers and puts them in her fridge. She washes the single plate, the single knife and single fork, single teacup and single saucer.

She sits down to do her Bible study, but the words feel hollow as she reads aloud. She loses her place on the page. As she rises to make a cup of tea which she hopes will focus her mind, she thinks of the tin in which she keeps the Christmas cards. She fills the kettle and brews her tea and tries to quiet the thought of the tin. She tries to quiet the thought of the new plastic box which now rests next to the tin.

When the letters from Roy began arriving every week from the start of the pestilence, the lid of the tin would no longer close over them all. The plastic box she found next to Carla's bin out back, a discarded Carte D'Or ice cream container, was the perfect size, and waterproof, though she wished she'd found a metal tin, which would also protect against fire, as the last one had.

Mable brings her tea to the table. She closes her eyes and sips, but her restlessness will not abate. She will look at the latest letter only, she tells herself. It is too indulgent to do more than that.

She brings the plastic box to the table, opens it and, first, she looks at the photograph of her three sons, all of them now older than Clive was when he passed. She wonders if he too would have had the middle-aged paunch of Roy, or the receding hairline of Devon, or whether he would have stayed angular and taut like Marcus, his true age belied only by the look of weariness in his eyes from having seen too much.

She reads the first few lines several times. '*He is out of intensive care now. Understand, Mum, that not many people come out of there once they go in. Devon is lucky. We can only talk to him by phone. He says all he wants is to get back to work. You know what they say, doctors make the worst patients. We pray for him daily. I hope your God allows you to do the same.'*

Carla
Flat 1B

'Fine, whatever!' Mary Rose screams, as she slams the door to her room.

'It's not fair, Mum!' Daniel yells, as he slams the door to his room.

'Fuck,' Carla says, and she throws a pan at the floor because she has no door to slam.

They've just had dinner and their daily conversation about the thousand incomprehensible emails Carla has received from school about the work they should have done, didn't do, are going to do. Homeschooling two kids in secondary school with one ancient laptop isn't working out too well.

But really, she's picked a fight with them tonight because she's too afraid to read the email.

She grabs a family-size Cadbury Dairy Milk and begins ploughing through the first section. She eats the second, then the third. Then she calls Darren.

'All right, Carla?' he says when he picks up.

'It's here, finally, and I can't look at it.' She stumbles over her words.

'Well, I'm here, let's do it together,' Darren says.

She'd run into him about six months ago in Tesco. When he saw her shopping trolley – Alpen Swiss muesli, thin bagels, cat food – he said, 'How's she doing?'

They chatted for a bit about Penny, and then he leaned his elbow on the bread shelf and asked about her kids, and she leaned forward on her trolley and he told her about his mother,

307

who he was shopping for, until one of the workers said, 'Oi, you two, no loitering, two metres apart.'

At the till, Carla's cards were declined, a favourite new trick of Tom's, using the automated phone banking system to report her cards as stolen and getting them deactivated. She was grateful for the mask that covered half of her face, flaming red in embarrassment.

Darren said, 'Don't worry, I've got it, employee discount and everything.' He winked and paid for her groceries.

'Oh my God, I'm mortified, I'll pay you back, I promise,' she said once they got outside.

And instead of saying what he would usually say, which was not to worry about it, and insist it was his pleasure, he said, 'Okay, well, I can text you my number and you can let me know when you have the cash? No rush, of course,' and she smiled and blushed, though he couldn't see it, because she knew this was his way of getting her number. And he smiled and blushed too, though she couldn't see it, because he knew that she knew what he was doing, and he was glad.

They talk every day. When he's at his mum's in the evenings, after he puts her to bed, Carla sometimes asks him Trivial Pursuit questions, and he makes up dirty answers, and they laugh. They haven't gone out yet in person – they haven't been able to, he's had to be so careful about his mum – but they will.

'Okay,' she says now.

'Okay, you can do it,' he says.

She taps on the message, reads it, and starts to cry.

Mable
Flat 3B

She folds the letter she has written precisely in thirds, places it in an envelope, and writes Roy's address on the front. She opens the book of second-class stamps that she uses for her ministry letters and places the last one on the envelope.

She prays, 'I'm sorry, Jehovah, I don' mean to do what is not—' She stops when she cannot find the words, then tries again.

'Jehovah, I must ask You for—' but the prayer doesn't come. She wonders if He is turning away from her for the transgression she is committing. She knows what they teach, that it is against His will to contact family members who have renounced the faith. And she has followed this teaching, faithfully, for so many years. She wonders if she is brave enough to go against it now.

'It's too much,' she says out loud. She decides to go out. It has been several days since she was last outside and a trip up and down the stairs and some fresh air will help her clear her mind. She will go to the post box and wait for a sign from Him. She pulls on her fleece robe, not having had a chance to replace her winter coat since she gave it away to the laundry girl. She picks up Carla's plate to take with her, with the intention of returning it. She puts on the mask that one of the sisters sent her in the post. She puts on her lavender hat and adjusts the flowers at the back. If she's calling on people she needs to look presentable.

Finally, she puts her letter to Roy in the pocket of her robe. But she already knows what she will do. She doesn't need a sign. Jehovah is many things, but He is not a mother.

Carla
Flat 1A

'I got it, they gave it to me,' she says to Darren. 'It says indefinite leave to remain, it's permanent residence, I can stay, I don't need him anymore.' The relief flooding her makes it hard to speak.

When Carla told her lawyer about Tom's plan, his threat, his years of plans and threats, it became several conversations, over many hours.

'But it's not domestic violence, he never hit me,' Carla said, again and again. And the lawyer explained, again and again, that invisible violence is no less painful. That mental wounds leave scars as well. That the slow and creeping erosion of a person is as brutal as the breaking of her bones.

And then Carla finally understood what she had survived.

Carla is granted the right to stay permanently in the UK on the basis of domestic violence. It is a huge relief. But it will not solve all of her problems.

Tom will still be in her life. He is the father of their children. There will be the divorce, battles over child support and visitation schedules, and she knows he will make everything as difficult as he can. But they will both know that she won this battle, that she took this weapon from him. His favourite one.

'Oh my God,' she says to Darren, when she regains her speech. 'I've got to tell Penny, okay, I've got to go, I love you,' she says, without hearing it, or realising it, or knowing she was going to say it.

Darren says, stunned, 'What?'

'Shit, I mean . . . I didn't mean . . . fuck it, I do, okay? Deal with it. I gotta go,' Carla says as she hangs up to knock on the wall.

Penny
Flat 1A

'Penny! Penny!' Carla shouts as she knocks on the wall between their flats.

'Carla, is that you?' Penny says.

'Of course it's me, you wackadoo, you won't believe this . . .' Carla begins, but then stops. 'Wait, what's wrong?'

'Oh Carla,' Penny says tearfully. 'She's gone.'

Carla
Flat 1B

'I gotta help Penny!' Carla calls out to the children, who have headphones on in their rooms and can't hear her as she looks for her slippers and her mask. Penny is particular about masks.

On that night last year, as Carla watched the paramedics take Penny's vital signs, and strap her into a chair to carry her to the ambulance, what Carla saw was Melissa, strapped down on a stretcher after their cars collided. Melissa in shock, her leg at a bizarre, unnatural angle to her body. Her clothes gone. The paramedics cut her jeans off, but her top was also torn in half, almost exposing her completely, which happened when Carla pulled her out of the front seat of the Ford Focus and her shirt caught on the jagged, twisted metal. Because Carla did pull her out. She did call 911. She did hold her and tell her she wasn't alone until help got there.

As she was questioned by the police, Carla watched them lift Melissa – shivering from shock, half-naked in the hot Long Island August night – into the ambulance, and all Carla wanted to say was 'I'm so sorry.' Her guilt and sadness, the horror of what she had let happen, the shame of risking everything so a boy would like her, engulfed her. All she wanted from that moment on was to disappear. And to be punished. So, she ran away to London and met Tom, and found a way to do both.

As the paramedics loaded Penny into the ambulance, Carla asked, 'Can I go with her?'

'No, madam, COVID restrictions—'

And before she knew what she was saying, Carla said, 'But, she's family – she's my family—'

As Carla watched the ambulance pull away with Penny inside, she knew that her lie was the truth.

Carla called regularly for updates, and she and the children took care of Susannah, and when Penny was finally released from the mental health facility, it was Carla who came to pick her up.

When Penny got home and she ventured out to the shops for the first time, with some trepidation, she brought back a roll of aluminium foil, a light bulb, a bottle of Pepsi Max Cherry, a can of mackerel, and a small bag of salt and vinegar crisps, all of which she left in a bag as a thank-you gift at Carla's door. Penny still had trouble making decisions when she was in a shop. The lights and sounds, the walls, checking the exit, all continued to distract her as she tried to manage her breathing and panic. But Carla had been her friend. So, to repay her kindness, Penny put Susannah in her canvas bag, and went out, her gloves and face mask and baseball cap no longer so strange to anyone who saw her.

Now Carla knocks on Penny's door. Penny opens it and says, 'She's gone.'

'Fuck, I'm sorry,' Carla says. 'I'm going to hug you now, Pen, because that's what you need. I know it's not the rules and everything, but that's what people do at times like this, okay?'

As Carla approaches, Penny offers her hand sanitiser. And when they hug in her doorway, Penny can see, from the corner of her eye, the reflection of their illegal embrace in the mirror by the door, and she sighs.

Mable
First floor corridor

When she reaches the first floor, she adjusts her glasses and hat and stops to survey the scene. She finds Carla with her arm around a weeping Penny. She sees Daniel and Mary Rose, looking very solemn, from the eyes she can see over their masks. They each hold one side of a pillow on which a cat-shaped mound is covered by a tattered and claw-shredded pink baby blanket.

Penny, seeing Mable's eyes move to the blanket, says, 'It was her favourite. The pet cremation people are coming now, to take her.'

Mable steps closer, lays the plate she is holding at Carla's door with some effort, clears her throat and then lays her hand on Susannah's covered body.

There is silence until Carla says, 'Go ahead, Mable.'

Mable clears her throat again, nervous that the words will catch, that she will, as before, falter in her attempt to speak to Jehovah. She is about to try again, she starts to say, 'Heavenly Father . . .' when she stops.

She feels Carla's warmth, Penny's grief and her strength. She feels the children, their adolescent confusion and angst, but also, within them, flickers of hope. She feels the letter to her son in her pocket. She feels, more faintly, the laboured breathing of another son lying in a hospital bed.

Mable cannot deny that a spirit is moving her. Her words are failing her, but there is more than one way to reach her God.

She pulls down her mask, thinks of Sister Aretha, and begins to sing in her tuneless, hoarse, soulful voice. Penny cries. Carla cries. Mary Rose cries. Daniel pretends not to.

And Mable cries.

Then Mable closes her eyes and prays.

For all of them.

21

Woman
First Ending

Woman turns the corner of Bedford Road and walks all night until she has gone as far as her legs can take her from the building. She spends the day sleeping in an alley behind a dumpster. In the early evening, others come to forage for food there. A man in a van sees Woman and the others and tells them that there is work in the countryside, picking vegetables. Someone in the group who speaks the language of Home Country, among several others, translates for Woman. The man will take them there. Food and accommodation will be provided. They will be paid at the end of the month.

The man drives them to the north of England. They sleep on the floor of a windowless room. They are fed bread and water. They are not paid. They do not pick vegetables. They harvest cannabis.

Early one morning, police arrive and arrest Woman and the others. They are charged and sentenced to six months in prison. Woman serves three months. As she has no documents and possesses a false passport, she is released into the custody of Immigration Enforcement. She is sent to immigration detention for several months to await deportation to Home Country. Although the global pandemic has halted all international travel and everyone is ordered to stay at home, planes carrying deportees continue to fly around the world.

When she lands in Home Country, Woman stays in a district of Capital City far from her family. She is too ashamed to return to them without the money she promised to earn Abroad. She has nothing to show for her time away except her missing teeth and the dream of Better Life that she had promised but could not give them.

Woman
Second Ending

Woman turns the corner of Bedford Road and walks all night until she has gone as far as her legs can take her from the building. The next day, she comes across a queue of people receiving parcels of food at a church. A volunteer speaks to her in the language of Neighbouring Country. With effort, they understand each other. The volunteer explains there is help. She makes a call.

Woman is given shelter and food. Kind people listen to Woman. She is told they believe her. They suspect she is a victim of trafficking and slavery. She is told there is a government system for women like Woman. Woman is told it will take forty-five days for the government to decide whether they believe her story. She will be safe during this time and supported.

But it does not take forty-five days. It takes two years. During this time, Woman lives in emergency shelter, a bare room in an isolated, distant London suburb. She has no money. She is not allowed to work. There is no internet access. She cannot call her family. There is only day after day of waiting in her room, alone.

One day, the Home Office finally decides that yes, she is a victim of slavery and trafficking. It is good news. She may now apply for legal status. With it, she can work wherever she chooses, and she can send money home, and finally make Better Life.

But, for this application to be processed, she must also wait. Wait, and watch more time pass. And watch life pass. Alone in a room.

Woman
Third Ending

Woman turns the corner of Bedford Road and walks all night, but by the next night she returns to Molly's café. She is afraid, but if she does not take the risk, she will sleep on the street again. She will not survive.

Molly gives her a phone number and an address. Woman calls the number.

She moves into a one-bedroom flat with a group of six Women from Home Country and other places. None have documents. None have legal status. All have been let go from their domestic service positions because of the virus. Jobs are scarce for the Women.

But there are wealthy families in the smartest parts of London where the virus does not exist and the rules are not followed and dinner parties continue and groups of guests arrive at the beautiful old homes. Women work from 6 a.m. until 11 p.m., cleaning, cooking, looking after children, in and out of houses all day and into the night for anyone who will pay. They are paid in cash. They are not allowed to wear masks. If they get sick, they lose the job, and the next Woman comes in to take their place.

Woman cleans the houses. She goes in and out. She sends money home. She starts coughing. She lies on a mat on the floor of the flat until she is better. Then she goes back to the houses and works, and sends money home, and it is not Better Life, but it is something.

Woman
Fourth Ending

Woman turns the corner of Bedford Road and walks all night. One road leads to another, and another, year after year, until finally she reaches this road. She looks at its houses and its

316

people. She sees how it has changed. It is not as she remembers, and it is exactly as she remembers.

She stops and watches children play in a huge puddle in the middle of the road left by the rains of the night before. They laugh. They fill plastic bottles with water and chase each other round and round, pouring water on heads and down backs and flipping bottles in the air and watching the water fly out in streams as the bottles catch the light of the sun.

Woman stands in front of a house and watches her child, Beauty, laughing and playing in the street.

An old woman comes out of the house and begins sweeping the front step. She sees Woman. Woman turns to look at her.

'Is it you?' Mother says, holding Woman's shoulders with both of her shaking hands.

'Yes,' Woman says.

'Will she know me?' Woman asks.

Before Mother can answer, Beauty has run up to the house.

'Grandmother, I am—' but she stops speaking to look at Woman. Woman is familiar from the photo next to her bed. But she is different – older, tired and—

'Where are your teeth?' Beauty blurts out.

Woman shrugs. 'I lost them. Where are yours?'

'I lost mine too,' Beauty says, smiling a gap-toothed smile. 'But Grandmother promised they will grow back. Do not worry, so will yours,' she says and squeezes her mother's hand.

Woman kneels down to look into her daughter's face.

'It will not always be like this,' Beauty says.

And then she scampers away, to play in the sun.

Author's Note

I wrote *Little Prisons* during the lockdowns of 2020 and 2021. During that dark time of high anxiety and social isolation, Penny, Carla, Mable and Woman became very real to me. They lived with me, and I grew to care for them deeply. The issues they each confront and the lives they represent are difficult and complex, and they deserve our attention and our respect. But women who face similar issues in our real world seldom receive either.

My writing of these characters was informed, initially, by elements of my personal life. With regard to Penny's mental illness, I drew from my own struggle with anxiety, panic, and phobias which have affected me for the past twenty years. With regard to Carla, Mable and Woman, I have always been drawn to migration stories, such as those that these characters represent. I became an immigration lawyer partly because of my childhood as the daughter and granddaughter of Ukrainian refugees and growing up in an immigrant diaspora community where, as the first generation born in America, the idea of our success as the repayment for our families' sacrifices was a constant theme. Although my family's migration and my upbringing were very different to the paths travelled by Carla, Mable, and Woman, I empathise very much with the attainment of Better Life as a driving force within immigrant communities, and I witnessed great strength in many of my clients as they grappled with the challenges of its achievement.

However, my personal experience is just a sliver of the resources needed to write the stories of these women. It should be noted that I did not interview any survivors of domestic violence, trafficking or modern slavery. I did not want to use anyone's personal story as a template, and there are many secondary sources available from which insight can be gained without asking someone to retell their personal trauma.

To write Penny's story of anxiety, agoraphobia, and panic disorder, I found the memoirs *Wish I Could Be There*, by Allen Shawn, *Behind These Eyes*, by Ellen Isaksen and the novel *We Have Always Lived in the Castle,* by Shirley Jackson very helpful. In addition, the article 'The Life of the Skin-Hungry: Can You Go Crazy from Lack of Touch', by Sirin Kale, www.vice.com, November 2016, was helpful. Agoraphobia is not just a fear of going outside, as people think, but it is a fear of being in situations from which escape could be difficult or from which one cannot easily exit, and results in the person progressively avoiding situations that will cause them anxiety or trigger a panic attack, such as public transport, shopping centres, or crowds. Someone dealing with the condition may find that over time, their 'zone of safety', which are those places where they feel safe and where they do not think they will panic, may get smaller and smaller, as it does for Penny. I would like to thank Nkechi Iwegbu, consultant psychiatrist, Hannah Altendorff, social worker, and Fay Tomlinson, social worker, for their assistance with elements of Penny's story and the stories of Baby and My Lady.

When I practised immigration law, I handled applications for clients in Carla's position, for leave on the basis of domestic violence. The type of abuse perpetrated by Tom against Carla is known as coercive control which is included in the UK's legal definition of domestic violence under the Serious Crime Act 2015. The Crown Prosecution Service defines it as '*an act or a pattern of acts of assault, threats, humiliation, intimidation, or other abuse that is used to harm, punish, or frighten their victim . . . a range of acts designed to make a person subordinate and/or dependent by isolating them . . . exploiting their resources . . . depriving them of the means needed for independence, resistance and escape and regulating their everyday behaviour'*. Tom's continual reference to Carla's immigration status and his manipulation of legal information are common forms of coercive control that British partners use in abusive relationships with non-British citizens who are dependent on them for immigration status. However, it is important for non-British citizens to know that if they are experiencing abuse from a British partner, regardless of gender or sexuality, they are not required to stay in that relationship to stay in the UK legally, and they can obtain indefinite leave to remain on the basis of domestic violence. My sincere thanks to Barry O'Leary of Wesley Gryk Solicitors for advising me on the legal aspects of Carla's story.

The website freemovement.org.uk has a guide for applying for leave to remain on the basis of domestic violence. The National Domestic Abuse Helpline run by Refuge is 0808 2000 247. Their website is nationaldahelpline.org.uk.

I drew upon many resources for Mable's story. In 2018 the Windrush Scandal broke, revealing the UK government's devastating treatment, under Theresa May, of hundreds of Caribbean Commonwealth citizens who were suddenly and illegally detained and deported after decades of living in, working legally, and contributing to the UK. As an American mother of two British children, I realised then that I had little knowledge of who the Windrush Generation were and of Black British history in general. Like many British children, my kids were familiar with American Black history, but not with that of the UK, because that history is largely, and glaringly, absent from the curriculum. So, my sons and I began reading together about Black British history and reading British authors of colour to fill this gap in all of our educations. It was through this exploration that I learned that the NHS was built upon the labour of immigrants like Mable and of the inextricable link between immigration and the NHS which continues to the present. The contribution of Commonwealth migrants from around the world to the rebuilding of post-war Britain is something we should all know about.

When Mable watches the news, she references *Thirteen Dead, Nothing Said*. This was the slogan used by protesters angered by the inadequate police and government response to the New Cross Fire on 18 January 1981. Thirteen young Black people, aged fourteen to twenty-two, died in a horrific house fire at a birthday party. A fourteenth victim died by suicide two years later, aged 20. It was believed by the community that the fire was deliberately set as a racist attack. But no one was ever charged in the case and it remains unsolved to the present day. The National Black People's Day of Action took place on 2 March 1981 as a community response to the lack of police and government action in the case which deeply affected the Black community.

The following resources were helpful in the creation of Mable's character: the films *Black Nurses: The Women Who Saved the NHS* (2016, Maroon Productions, Paul Blake, producer, Victor Chimara, director); *Back in Time for Brixton* (2016, BBC, Emma Hindley, executive producer, Carl Callam, producer, Geoff Small, director); *Black and British: A Forgotten History*, episode 4, The Homecoming (2016, BBC, David Olusoga, creator and writer, James Van Der Pool, director and producer); *Blood Ah Go Run* (1982, Menelik Shabazz and Imruh Caesar, directors); film series *Small Axe* (2020, BBC, Steve McQueen, creator, writer, director, executive producer, Tracey Scoffield, David Tanner, Lucy Richer, Rose Garnett, executive producers, Anita Overland, Mike Elliot, producers). In addition, the books *Homecoming: Voices of the Windrush Generation*, by Colin Grant and the novel *Small Island*, by Andrea Levy were helpful. My sincere thanks to Professor Carol Baxter, CBE, David Godfrey, and Sarah Gregory for their insights, advice, and opinions.

All information about Jehovah's Witnesses and their beliefs was obtained from that organisation's website, JW.org. Special thanks to Ali Millar for her insights into Mable's faith.

Woman's identity and Home Country are never revealed. I did not give Woman an identity so that we can ask ourselves who we picture when we think of her and her captors, what nationality we ascribe to them, what skin colour we imagine them to have, and why we think what we do about them. I did not give PC Grant an ethnic or racial identity for the same reason. Not giving Woman an identity also emphasises the invisibility of survivors of trafficking and modern slavery. We come across people like Woman often as we go about our daily lives. We just don't see them. Or we think we don't.

In 2019, 10,000 people were referred to the UK authorities as victims of slavery. The real number is likely to be much higher. They work in plain sight as agricultural labourers, in nail bars, at car washes, as nannies and domestic workers. Some are forced into sex work.

People are trafficked into the UK for forced labour from countries including Albania, Vietnam and Nigeria. However, vulnerable British citizens, often children, are also targeted and groomed for drug trafficking.

Although there are many ways that traffickers bring people into the UK, Woman is brought legally with an Overseas Domestic Worker visa (ODW visa). This visa permits employers to bring their domestic staff with them to the UK for a period of up to six months to work in their private household. Many domestic workers brought to the UK on this visa have no control over their applications, have their passports taken by their employers, and do not know the terms of their visa or its expiry date. If an employer forces them to work without pay or creates difficult working conditions, they often have no way of leaving the situation safely, retrieving their passport, or obtaining payment. As of the time of writing, workers are not permitted to extend or renew their visas.*

Workers who manage to escape are afraid of detention and deportation and may have no choice but to work illegally as a means of survival or find themselves re-trafficked into another forced labour situation, as happens to Woman in her First and Second Endings.

In Woman's Third Ending, she is referred to the 'Government Programme' which is the National Referral Mechanism for identifying victims of trafficking (NRM). Survivors of trafficking and modern slavery may be referred to the NRM by designated 'First Responders'. These include police and certain charities. The NRM is meant to provide them with protection and support while the Home Office makes a decision about whether they have been trafficked or enslaved. As in the story, the Home Office is meant to make a decision about a survivor's status as a victim of trafficking after a 45-day period of recovery. However, as of the time of writing, these decisions usually take much longer, often two years or more. The survivor is not permitted to work during that time unless their visa is still valid and not expired at the time of their referral. But the many survivors whose visas have already expired at the time of referral are left in limbo with no way to support themselves while awaiting a Home Office decision. This makes entering the NRM an impossible choice for many.

As of the time of writing, if the Home Office concludes the survivor has been trafficked or forced into modern slavery, they

* The exception is domestic workers who are ODW visa holders who have been found through the UK's National Referral Mechanism (NRM) to have been trafficked. These workers can apply to extend their ODW visa to up to two years. It is important to note, however, that this does not provide any option to workers on the ODW visa to challenge their exploitation before their treatment equates to trafficking and can mean years in limbo while waiting for an NRM decision. See https://www.gov.uk/overseas-domestic-worker-visa/victim-slaveryhuman-trafficking.

then have a further wait without sufficient financial support or permission to work whilst their applications for asylum or leave to remain are considered. The NRM processes only a percentage of those who may be potential victims. Nearly 3,000 people identified as potential victims of trafficking since 2019 have been placed in immigration detention. The options for those in Woman's position are just not good enough.

The following resources were helpful in writing Woman's story: *Dignity, Not Destitution: The impact of differential rights of work for migrant domestic workers referred to the National Referral Mechanism*, Kalayaan, October 2019; *Supported or Deported: Understanding the deportation and detention data held on human trafficking and slavery*, After Exploitation, July 2019; *From One Hell to Another: The detention of Chinese women who have been trafficked to the UK*, Women for Refugee Women, July 2019; *Making a Slave*, (BBC Three); The Maid Slaves: How wealthy visitors to Britain trap servants in their homes, Sophie McBain, New Statesman, February 2016; The domestic workers trapped in homes with wealthy employers flouting lockdown rules, May Bulman, *The Independent*, February 2021. My deepest thanks to Kate Roberts, Avril Sharp, Lizzie Muir and Marissa Begonia for reviewing this manuscript.

If you are concerned about a situation you have witnessed, call the Modern Slavery and Exploitation Helpline 08000 121 700, 24 hours a day.

If you know of an individual who needs advice or if you would like to support the work of organisations who support domestic workers and survivors of trafficking and modern slavery, please contact the following organisations:

Anti-Slavery International

Anti-Slavery International works to end all forms of modern slavery across the world and bring freedom to the 40.3 million people living in slavery today.

Thomas Clarkson House, The Stableyard
Broomgrove Road, London, SW9 9TL
www.antislavery.org
Tel: +44 (0)20 7501 8920
Email: info@antislavery.org
Instagram: @antislaveryinternational
Twitter: @Anti_Slavery
Facebook: Anti-Slavery International

Kalayaan

Kalayaan works with migrant domestic workers in the UK to improve their rights and help them access them.

St Francis of Assisi Community Centre
13 Hippodrome Place, London, W11 4SFT
www.kalayaan.org.uk
Tel: 0207 243 2942
Email: info@kalayaan.org.uk
Twitter: @kalayaan

The Voice of Domestic Workers

The Voice of Domestic Workers is an education and support group calling for justice and rights for Britain's 16,000 migrant domestic workers.

www.thevoiceofdomesticworkers.com
Twitter: @thevoiceofdws
Instagram: @thevoiceofdomesticworkers

Acknowledgements

All my love and thanks to my husband Tim, and my sons, Leo and Rex. Thank you for making me laugh and for making me crazy. Thank you for every day we were locked down in the house together and I felt lucky and loved.

I am unendingly and sincerely grateful to my editor, Jocasta Hamilton. Thank you for your faith in this book and for believing in these four women.

My thanks to the entire team at Two Roads and John Murray Press. Thank you to Charlotte Robathan for taking care of my manuscript. Special thanks to Sharona Selby for her incredible eye and attention to detail.

A million and one thank yous to my agent, Alice Lutyens, for your support, optimism, encouragement, and energy.

Thank you to Sarah Gregory, Caro Fentiman, Ali Millar, Nicola Washington, and Penny Wincer. I could not have written this book, physically or mentally, without your feedback, insights, and support. Our monthly meetings in 2020 sustained not just my writing, but my sanity. I am grateful to the universe to have met you. I am in awe of each of your talents. It is an honour to work with you. It is a privilege to be your friend.

My love and thanks to my friends, Jessica Alexander, Diana Baxter, Lesley Bourns, Elaine Davenport, Alison Hunter, Jessica Jones, Barry O'Leary, and Mariah Pizzano for your time, your patience, your help and your feedback on my manuscript.

In the winter between 2020 and 2021, when things felt the most desperate in the pandemic, I would often not get outside for my allocated solitary exercise until the evening. I spent the days helping my sons navigate remote school with their dyslexia and ADHD, endlessly cooking and cleaning, and keeping everyone in my family from unravelling, as many caregivers – mostly women – did during that time. Frazzled and exhausted at the end of the day, I would go outside for a few minutes when my husband was finally done with work and could be with our frazzled and exhausted children. I would put in my headphones and walk the empty streets listening to Aretha Franklin sing, 'Precious Lord, Take My Hand' which she did as a medley with 'You've Got a Friend' on her gospel album, *Amazing Grace*. Like Mable, I have loved Aretha Franklin for most of my life, and her version of this very famous hymn is uplifting in a way that is hard to describe. I am not a religious or spiritual person. But at night, as I walked alone in the cold on my silent, lifeless street and listened to Ms Franklin's voice, I was moved to pray. I prayed for my family, for those who were dying, for those who were losing people they loved, for those who worked every day to protect us, for the uncertain world we live in. The power and strength of her voice in that dark time brought me the closest to God that I have ever been. Thank you, Aretha Franklin, rest in peace.